WE HAVE BURIED THE PAST

ABOUT THE AUTHOR

'ABD AL-KARIM GHALLAB was a Moroccan political journalist and novelist. He was the author of five novels and three collections of short stories. In 2004 he was awarded the Maghreb Culture Prize of Tunis. Ghallab's novels have been translated into many languages.

WE HAVE BURIED THE PAST

'ABD AL-KARIM GHALLAB

Translated by Roger Allen

Published in 2018 by
HAUS PUBLISHING LTD
4 Cinnamon Row
London SW11 3TW

A CIP catalogue record for this book is available from the British Library

ISBN: 978-1-910376-40-9
eISBN: 978-1-910376-41-6

Typeset in Garamond by MacGuru Ltd

Printed in Spain by Liberdúplex

1

In the city of Fez, the Makhfiyya Quarter was the residence of the Tihami family. The family was middle class and well off, one of those that enjoyed its own share of wealth and prestige, coupled with a total adherence to traditional values and the maintenance of respect, all within the confines of the society in which it existed – one that did not transcend the boundaries of the quarter where the family resided. Whatever wealth the family members had, however, was both modest and deep-rooted; they remained unspoiled by luxury and felt content and secure within their own environment.

Families like this did not hold themselves above poorer neighbours and workers who lived in the same quarter, nor did they aspire to quit the quarter in which they themselves had prospered. They were friendly with their neighbours and fully accustomed to being treated by them with all due respect. They made full use of the quarter's facilities – the mosque, of course; the baths; the baking oven; and the merchants who sold foodstuffs. All these different elements tied them firmly to the quarter and made it a society of its own, duly esteemed, respected, and venerated by everyone who lived there.

In the Makhfiyya Quarter the Tihami family had inherited a house with a huge, wide front door, where sheer neglect and a lack of attention had allowed time and decay to form a pact of their own. The crumbling high walls of the house gave evidence of both the extreme care that had gone into its construction and the total neglect that it had suffered ever since it had last had any contact with either builders or decorators.

Anyone standing in front of these lofty walls would have few doubts that behind them was the kind of residence with which Fez was familiar in the days when it was a city for the rich, well off, and privileged – times when people were eager to build huge mansions more like palaces than ordinary dwellings. They too would have large rooms, courtyards, fountains, and other amenities. When owners built them, their idea would be for the houses to serve as major sources of inheritance for children, grandchildren, and near and distant relatives who were less well off.

You would not be far off the mark if, in coming into contact with the Tihami family, you concluded that the house in which they lived had been their residence for generations. At certain times in the family's history, the house had been as busy as a beehive, filled with family members – fathers, uncles, children, and grandchildren, all of them living in a single social network. It was as though, within the Makhfiyya Quarter, they constituted a state in their own right, all of them orbiting around different tables three times a day for meals in the rooms or in the courtyard: one table for men, another for women, and a third for servants. Later on, the women would all gather – wives, unmarried daughters, and servants – inside the huge kitchen, while the men and boys would all go out to their workplaces and shops. The young boys and girls would either cluster together, yelling and screaming as they played, or else, in the case of the boys, go to the jurist's Qur'an school where they would learn how to read and write and memorise some suras from the holy book, and, in the case of the girls, to the lady's house to learn how to sew.

The exterior of the house hardly provided an accurate picture of the inside. Age and decay had not managed to do much damage to the spacious halls and wide rooms that the hands of skilled craftsmen had carefully decorated with mosaics, paintings, and other types of ornamentation. When the original owner had the house built, he was not planning a work of art but rather something that would show the extent of his wealth and luxurious lifestyle. In the house itself and its sheer size the women in the family – wives, daughters, and servants – all found a form of consolation from the highly restricted routine imposed on them by the life they had to live inside this extensive prison. The only time one of them might be prepared to leave the home was when she needed to go to the bathhouse or attend a wedding ceremony. For women and female servants, such opportunities arose only occasionally.

Eventually this mansion, with everything and everyone inside it, had come into the hands of Hajj Muhammad, doyen of the Tihami family. He was a portly man, with a pale complexion and curly beard. When it came to the hair on his head, the local barber gave no one the opportunity to find out whether it was white or black: he came to the house regularly every Friday morning to shave heads and trim the beards of those who had them. The only people who managed to escape his sharp razor were some of the family's playful children, who seized the opportunity of their grandparents and parents being shaved to take to their heels. That way they could avoid the rough hand that would otherwise clasp their young heads, douse them in soapy water using a decayed chunk of sponge, and then start on them with the razor, which by this time had lost its sharp edge.

Hajj Muhammad tended to his manner of dress with all the attention of an ambitious man. In summertime it would consist only of a single loose-fitting shirt, usually made of a fairly coarse fabric, although repeated washing had somewhat mitigated the roughness. His wife made a point of decorating it with a silken collar, from which a silk cord hung down to create a bow by which the two sides of the collar could be tied together on the left-hand side. This bow took the place of a button, and with it there was no need of a button in any case: the entire arrangement had no need of buttons nor of the civilisation that had introduced buttons into this society. Not only that, but Hajj Muhammad could make use of the dangling part to attach his heavy silver watch, with its cover that protected the glass from breaking. It also meant he did not need to wear a wrist-strap, as the younger folk did and which got in the way of them correctly performing the ritual ablution before prayer. Over this shirt he would normally wear a garment called the *mansuriyya*, which was really not much different in shape from the shirt itself, except that the fabric was less coarse, and the chest was decorated with a stripe of woven silk and silk ties of the kind made by Jewish women in the Mellah, which possessed a beauty of their own.

During winter, between the shirt and the *mansuriyya* Hajj Muhammad wore a woollen kaftan of similar dimensions, either red or pink in colour. It could also be blue or violet, so it could be shared whenever his wife needed to borrow it from her husband upon being unexpectedly invited to a reception of some kind.

Hajj Muhammad adorned his head with a turban that was tightly wrapped around a red fez. It was the very same barber who undertook the wrapping of this turban with tremendous skill and dexterity – it was something that only the most proficient barbers could do properly, being genuine specialists on everything to do with the head, even if it involved only measures to protect heads from extreme cold and heat. In addition to all this, there would be one or two jallabas, depending on the seasonal weather, topped by a burnous that in wintertime would be dark black – as protection against the severe cold for which Fez, and the Makhfiyya Quarter in particular, is well known among Moroccan cities. In summertime, when the temperatures were extremely hot, the top layer would be gleaming white. But, whatever the case, the appearance would always preserve a sense of nobility and convey an august demeanour. When it came to footwear, things would differ according to the season. In summer they would be white and light and thinly cushioned; in winter, by contrast, they would be yellow, heavy, and coarse, since they needed to be able to wade through the mud that covered the streets of Fez and to sink into the mire like duck's legs stuck in a stagnant pond.

Hajj Muhammad would hardly ever leave his residence until all the requirements of his august appearance and his mode of walking had been fully met. He would still criticise younger men who carelessly decided in summertime to drape their jallabas over their shoulders and tilt their fezzes to the sides of their heads. He would frown whenever he spotted them walking and rushing around, shouting and conversing too loudly – in his view, not showing their families in the best light.

'God have mercy on Hajj al-Tahir,' he would say. 'If he were to set eyes on his grandson Hamid, that young man who tears along the street with his fez in his hand, he would not hesitate to strike him with his cane and make him change his behaviour.'

This was the kind of thing Hajj Muhammad would yell to himself every time he spotted a young man who disliked wearing a fez on his head or pulled up his jallaba, ignoring tradition in the hope of shielding himself from the heat or hoping for a snatch of breeze on his legs.

2

It would be early morning when Hajj Muhammad left his house. Neither bitter cold nor pouring rain would deter him. Ever since he was a boy, he had grown used to observing the quarter as it woke up from the peace and quiet of slumber. As he rolled over in bed and gradually emerged from sleep, life with all its gentle quietude would begin to seep back into his limbs. One of his greatest delights was to wander through the Makhfiyya Quarter like an heir inspecting the properties of the two royal palaces. He would be delighted every time he walked around the quarter and noticed a new shop here or there, reopening in order to provide the quarter's inhabitants with their daily provisions. During the course of his inspection tour he would make a point of dropping in on the flour and sponge vendors so he could observe the boys at work, providing food for their families.

'All's well in the world, and there's a blessing for the early riser!'

That is precisely what Hajj Muhammad told himself whenever he relished the way the lowly quarter roused itself in the morning. Such early bustle meant that life was still flowing through the limbs of the quarter's inhabitants. That made him happy: life was still as vigorous and unruly as he had always known it.

The tour used to start in the morning when Hajj Muhammad left his 'mansion' after confirming that life had resumed its normal daily routine. There was movement all over the place, and the various shops – butchers', vegetable-sellers', grocers', and provision merchants' – were all full of fresh produce. At that point Hajj Muhammad would leave his house and, with his habitual calm demeanour and slow gait – these being traits that managed to earn him respect and provoke feelings of confidence and joy – would pass by all those vendors. He would extend a greeting to each one in turn, always accompanied by his traditional smiles, which gave expression to his essential kindness and probity. However often he bestowed such smiles, they never lost their genuine intent. The people in the quarter sensed that behind the smiles were feelings of respect and love that linked them to Hajj Muhammad. For that very reason they used to welcome him cheerfully and greet him with a smile too, lowering their heads out of respect and esteem.

When he went round the quarter, he would be fully dressed, with a burnous on top; he would never take it off in hot weather, nor would he wrap himself up in it for warmth when it was very cold. But, whatever the case, he could always manage to keep the basket hidden. Sometimes he would have to carry it himself, when he could not find one of his children to do it for him. His goal in using his children like this was to train them in the ways of the marketplace, to teach them how to tell good products from bad and haggle over prices. Most of the time, instead of one of his own children, he would use one of the many young maidservants who populated the various parts of the household.

Hajj Muhammad would leave the house at this time of day in order to purchase supplies for the family. He would be welcomed in every shop, not simply because he had been their customer for a very long time, but due to the great respect in which he was held in the quarter. Indeed, he could be said to be the Makhfiyya Quarter's mayor. For that reason he was always given genuine advice about purchases from the various vendors. He would be well treated, and the prices would be reasonable. Not only that, but more often than not the owner of the shop would advise him not to buy one product or another because the owner would know that the Hajj would not like it or would not feel comfortable about purchasing it. And he might well pause by the butcher's, but then quickly move on because he had not found anything there that took his fancy, or else because the price of meat had gone up a piastre or two.

In spite of the respect he had towards these vendors, he would never hesitate to quibble over prices, even though the vendor might swear an oath to the effect that he would lose at the price being discussed. Hajj Muhammad would regularly haggle with the butcher or vegetable-seller, something that had its own jocular side. He would never believe what they were telling him and would make every effort to win the battle by using his pleasant smile and swearing an oath (that he made sure never invoked the name of God, so as to avoid falling into sin). This haggling ritual occurred every single day, without causing the slightest anxiety or annoyance to the merchants from his constant arguing and attempts to get a lower price on things. In fact, they came to expect it from him; they may even have seen it as a token of pride and honour. Such was Hajj Muhammad's status in the quarter that they did not find his haggling as annoying as they did that of other customers.

No sooner did he return to the house than his purchases were subject to precise criticism. This piece of meat, for example, was unacceptable because it was not as good as the other one. This vegetable could not be used with the rest of them because it was of very poor quality. He would often weigh the meat on a small pair of scales that he kept in the house; he was totally unwilling to accept any meat or vegetables that were underweight, whether by a little or a lot. He would never hesitate for a moment to argue with the vendor in question; he would regularly return produce to the place where he had bought it if he detected the slightest problem in either weight or quality.

But, in spite of this ongoing quest for satisfaction, which almost amounted to stinginess, Hajj Muhammad was much loved by the quarter's shopkeepers and much respected in all the various sectors that had contact with him. He was highly regarded by all the generations of people who shared the life of the Makhfiyya Quarter.

He had lived his life with many people in the quarter and had become their friend; not only that, but he also managed to maintain such ties across successive generations. He would occasionally bump into such people and give them his usual smile: greetings would be exchanged, and he would chat with them and listen to what they had to say. He never rejected out of hand the many ideas and dreams with which younger heads were filled. But, as he listened to the aspirations of the gullible younger folk who had yet to experience life to the full and were only acquainted with those aspects of it that seemed bright and attractive, his responses were often laced with a certain harmless sarcasm, or a mocking laugh.

He used to like stopping by the shops of the tailor or the flour-seller, conversing about events in the quarter, the day's main news, and activities in the commercial sector, with prices going up or down. He enjoyed probing things in detail so that he would not lose his connection to the outside world. These conversations would provide him with information that would help him keep up with evening discussions and the comments of his friends. Most of these chats with shopkeepers would occur while they were waiting for prayer-time just before sunset, or else after the call to evening prayer.

As a result of all this, Hajj Muhammad became a personality within the quarter, one that its inhabitants and merchants could not do without. Everyone had a sense of his qualities as a kind of father or shepherd and his overall courtesy. Whenever he was absent – due to illness or travel – they would all miss him; and if he ever changed his routine when it came to touring the quarter in the morning or waiting in the evening for the call to prayer, they would all ask after him.

The thing that further enhanced the affection that the quarter's inhabitants and merchants felt for this beloved personality was his devoutness and close attention to preachers and spiritual guides. He would often attend homiletic gatherings and sessions of religious instruction which the shaykhs in the Qarawiyin Mosque or the Mawlay Idris shrine would regularly offer; there he would listen carefully to the commentaries on Muslim traditions and the biography of the Prophet. He heard so much of the Prophet's sayings (prayers and blessings be upon him!) and accounts of his life that he knew them by heart. His speech was always a melange of quotations from traditions and wisdom literature which he would regularly cite, even though not entirely accurately. Although he regularly listened to a good deal of sermonising and instruction, he was still unable to train his tongue or polish his language. Even so, he was quite prepared to make mistakes or explain what he had understood in his own colloquial dialect. In spite of everything he still felt that he was the quarter's legal expert and religious guide.

The lessons that he attended had a profound effect on him. They combined with his age and august temperament to make him a devout and conservative person, always concerned in case a slip of the tongue would cause offence or aggravate someone; or that his eye would trick him, and he would see part of a woman that the veil could not keep concealed – her eyes or hands, for instance; or that his heart or mind would let him down, and he would fail to offer counsel to people whom he believed he had the right to advise. He regarded it as an obligation to advise all the quarter's inhabitants, in accordance with the expectations of honour and religion.

3

Running the household alongside Hajj Muhammad's wife were five official maidservants. That number did not include the unofficial ones who were not allowed to be called 'maidservants'. The official ones were vestiges of the era of slavery. The eldest among them had come as part of the dowry of Sayyida Khaduj, the Hajj's wife. At the time of her arrival she was still a young girl, tall, well built, and with strong muscles. She lived with the family as an obedient servant, working in the kitchen and doing other household chores. She took care of the children, tending to their needs, raising them, and relieving their mother of such responsibilities. This continuous hard labour and a life of absolute deprivation had had their effect on this elderly spinster and her psychological make-up. Her posture had sagged, and she rarely did much by way of exercise. By now she much preferred a life of ease and some peace and quiet – whenever, that is, circumstances permitted.

The other female servants were younger than her and had more energy and drive. Each one of them had been acquired on some particular occasion. They were all Moroccan and had been brought from the far south when they were still young. They differed from one another in age and colouring, and they also varied in their degree of beauty. One of them had a dark brown complexion that was almost black, while another had white skin. The others had wheat-coloured complexions, that is, before the passage of time turned them a dull yellow.

Within the household of Hajj Muhammad these servant-women constituted a separate society of their own. They were a central part of family life and knew its secrets. As a result they could discuss the history of all its members, men, women, and children; they were especially adept when it came to talking about personal histories and the important events in the life of each member of the family. Even so, they operated on the fringes of the family and did not possess the same status and social position as the family's women-folk. Nothing could ever happen without these servant-women, and yet they would never be consulted about any matter concerning the family or about significant events in family life.

When they had some leisure time, they used to gather in a private room; because they had occupied it for so long, it had been dubbed 'the servants' room'. When they were not working, they would spend time chatting; sometimes there would be non-stop laughter as well, to accompany whispered comments. But that would only happen once they had made sure that the master was not at home and the mistress was not on edge but feeling quite relaxed. Their conversation usually revolved around the day's events in the kitchen and the house in general – and sometimes the street as well, if it so happened that one of them was given a special task to go outside and contact one of the family's female relatives. Street chatter was always a matter of shared gossip. Any number of men had no qualms about importuning female servants and shamelessly flirting with dark-skinned women within earshot of passers-by without finding the slightest degree of inappropriateness in their behaviour. Family traditions and the proper upbringing that these women had received may well have led them to show the necessary modesty and dignity as they went on their way. Even so, flirtatious expressions directed at them were bound to leave an echo in their ears that could only be expunged through an exchange of gossip and suppressed giggles that would emerge from the servants' room every so often when there was time to relax.

Memories were a frequent topic of the ongoing series of evening conversations among these servant-women. For each one of them, such memories sometimes acquired a patina of adventure, helped along perhaps by some basic but essentially human spirit of imagination. And they all enjoyed listening to the tales of kidnapping – that being the link that connected the two principal phases in their lives, the first of freedom, the second of slavery.

Many of these women, black and white alike, had only the vaguest memory of their original capture, leaving no trace in their lives of a period when they were free, had a family, and enjoyed a mother's love, a father's kindness, or a brother's affection. The only family they could recall was this new one in whose shadow they now lived, or the several families that had made use of them. They never remembered their original names, which their new ones had erased all trace of, even in the recesses of their minds.

But there was one of them who remembered it all, including her kidnapping. She could recall every detail of the event, even though she was young at the time. She could recall every feature of the person who had stolen her liberty; time had not managed to let her forget the first strange face she had ever seen in the small village where she grew up.

She had been a child of ten, living with her family in a small village in the south. She could still remember everything about life there, except for her own name – which had been Aisha. She used to go out with her brother and mother in search of water and firewood. Sometimes her mother would let her go with the shepherd or shepherdess to see where the best grazing places were, or to get her out of the house during household chores and to run off some energy, but only during the wonderful springtime when she was not worried about strong winds, extreme heat, or pouring rain. The sunshine would offer glimpses of the natural splendours to be found in the distant wilderness, far removed from the shade of houses, animal pens, tent tops, and bird nests.

One bright day the girl went out with the little lamb she used to play with; sometimes she would carry it, sometimes she would pull it along gently. She was looking for fresh green pasturage, running through the wide-open spaces, singing shepherdess's songs, and competing with them to tend the sheep, boasting that she was the owner of all the little lambs. Later in the morning she felt thirsty, so she headed for the stream to have a drink. There she went and never came back.

She could still recall that day long ago as though it were only yesterday; she could remember every single detail. She had described it so many times and its echoes bounced around her memory so much that it was firmly rooted in her consciousness.

Tripping lightly, she hurried to the stream, anxious to drink some cold water that would quench her thirst. When she reached the deserted stream, no peasants were to be seen and no shepherds were close by; the only sound in this refreshing scene was the twittering of birds. She felt completely safe, relishing the loneliness of the spot and actually enjoying the feeling of being on her own.

Jawhara – that being the name she was later called by when she became part of the distinguished household of Hajj Muhammad – approached the stream, delighted by both the purity and the coldness of the water that she bent down and scooped up in her small hands to quench her thirst and cool her face, which had been scorched by the sun and was turning red. On the surface of the clear, burbling water she noticed the figure of a horseman who had come so close to the spring that the horse's hooves were almost in the water. When she lifted her head, it was to see a strongly built man with a fine physique, bursting with youthful vigour. His face was red, his hair blonde, and his eyes blue; he was wearing a white turban, part of which hung down like a veil. Over his jallaba he was wearing a burnous, the two sides of which resembled the wings of a gigantic falcon. He was confidently holding the reins of a splendid horse with strong muscles, a wonderful gait, and delicate legs; it was nervous and was difficult to keep still – as though it were continuously ready to take off and jump.

Jawhara stared at the horseman in panic, but she soon felt calmer when he smiled at her. She smiled back, as though she had known him for some time.

She bent down over the stream again, feeling at ease, but she soon took notice when he asked her a question.

'What are you doing at this stream, little girl?'

'Having a drink, sir.'

'Is it cold, clean, and nice?'

'Very cold. Would you like a drink?'

'Yes, I would. But tell me, where are you from? Aren't you scared to be on your own in this deserted spot?'

'I'm not scared of anyone. I'm close to the pasture, and my small flock is waiting for me. I'll be going back to them in just a minute.'

'Wouldn't you rather come with me to my city far away? It's nice and a lot of fun.'

'No. My mother and father will be waiting for me when I bring the flock back in the evening. I don't like being away from the flock for too long.'

'Fill this jug of mine with some of your cold water. I'm thirsty!'

She took the jug from him, filled it up, and handed it back. No sooner had she done so than two powerful hands grabbed her, lifted her up, and put her at the front of the saddle. She hardly had time to realise what was happening before the horse was taking off with its rider and his captive, barely noticing the hills and valleys, high and low. One of the two falcon wings had enfolded her, and only her tiny face was exposed to any light. She found herself swaying in his arms, her body wedged between two powerful arms from which there was no possibility of escape. She tried calling for help, but her cries were lost in the infinite expanse. Looking behind her, she tried pleading with him, but found that his handsome face was buried in his head-covering; all she could see were his two blue eyes, rigid and determined. Outright panic robbed her of all strength, and she began to weep silently. Behind those tears the world was dancing, as were her own emotions, suppressed and paralysed with fear.

All she could remember about what happened next was that the horseman took good care of her. Her young mind was incapable of dealing with the horror of the disaster that this dreadful kidnapping had caused her. The man was kind and polite and tried his best to make her forget the bitter sorrow that she was bound to feel at being snatched away from her parents and flocks of lambs. He tried to remove her worries, particularly about her father, who would be furious at her for running away or simply disappearing – he had always insisted that she not be left alone with any man, whatever his status might be. This was what she came to realise for herself once she was in the house of Ibn Kiran, the slave trader, as she listened to her fellow victims talking about unmarried girls and widows and the price they would fetch in the slave market.

The horseman stayed with her for a while in a distant city, one that she heard was named Marrakesh. All she knew of it was a modest house in a shady part of the city that she entered and left at night. After that she was moved to Fez, the city where she was to spend the rest of her days. Once she had spent a few days in Ibn Kiran's house, she was moved to the house of her new master, Hajj Muhammad al-Tihami.

The horseman, whose smiling face she could still remember reflecting in the gently moving stream, had disappeared ever since he handed her over to Ibn Kiran. He had wished the trader well and urged him to take good care of her and demand a good price.

4

Jawhara could still recall that Ibn Kiran's house was modest and dark; it had a wooden door like that of an old bathhouse or a deserted garden in a village far removed from the city quarters. Its wooden lock only worked from the inside. The old door had a hole in it through which you inserted your hand to open the lock. Beyond the door was a long, dark corridor ending in a small, dimly lit hallway. In a corner directly opposite the doorway was a wooden bench with some old, threadbare pelts on it, upon which sat a human pile of flesh and fat, wrapped in a variety of jallabas that might be white or black, only distinguishable by a flushed face enveloped in old rags whose only purpose was to keep the bloated red face warm. This was Ibn Kiran, the slave dealer.

Over sixty years old, he was a short, podgy man with a white beard and a loud voice that could instil fear into the ears of his listeners whenever he chose to raise it. The unfortunate people who had fallen into his clutches could be made even more frightened when he became angry: his blood would start churning, his nostrils would flare, his eyes would bulge, and his face would turn scarlet. Then he would froth at the mouth, and spittle would fly from his wrinkled, toothless gums.

He may have been quick to anger, irritable, and given to much shouting, but he would soon calm down: his features would relax, and he would start smiling. This would particularly be the case when he spotted a new customer, or one of his many guests. The general view was that a ready temper was one of the requisites for a slave dealer; his aim was to teach the slave how to obey, accept orders, and show an awareness of their humiliation. His method involved raising his voice and yelling threats whenever one of the arrivals in the house of Ibn Kiran was about to do something that was not to the great slave dealer's liking.

Jawhara could still remember that day when the horseman handed her over to Ibn Kiran.

The door was opened in her face by means of a knotted rope held by a man sitting cross-legged on a wooden bench. This happened as soon as he heard the horseman banging on the ancient wooden door. After welcoming her, he pulled her towards him without even budging from his seat. The way he was sitting cross-legged made him look like he couldn't walk; either that, or else the sheer bulk of his body made movement impossible. He pulled her gently and then grabbed her head between his fingers, which still had enough power in them; it was as though he were handling a costly piece of goods. He turned her head towards him and looked at her face and features with the expert eye of someone assessing value. He then checked her entire body from head to toe, allowing his eyes to pause for a while on her breasts. Next he turned her round to inspect her posture from the back, pausing for a while to check her buttocks. Eventually he grabbed her by the shoulders, acknowledging that she was sound and healthy. Yelling for one of the women in this remarkable household, he gave her a gentle push and instructed the woman to look after her and see to her clothing and especially her hair. Saada – the woman's name – took her by the hand and led her to a room where she asked what her own name and family name was, and who had been her previous owner. It was clear that Jawhara did not understand the notion of a previous owner, so she did not respond to that part of the question, but Saada kept pestering her with questions that she could not understand.

'Why did he throw you out?' she asked. 'What led him to sell you?'

These were all words Jawhara was hearing for the very first time, and the way they kept battering her mind only made her feel more miserable and at a loss.

She could not understand this continuing stream of transfer from one place to another, nor was she aware of the secret of this strange household. She had not understood what the horseman and the fat man sitting cross-legged on the bench in the courtyard were talking about. The strange movements that the man had used in exploring her face, chest, and back seemed peculiar to her. The conversation with this woman only increased her confusion; she kept using the words 'master' and 'sale'. Saada did not wait for a detailed reply, but told her firmly to take off her clothes and handed her some thread-bare rags.

'Put these on for a bit while you're washing your clothes.'

Saada then turned her attention to the girl's hair and body. It all reminded Jawhara of the care and attention that her own mother gave her. Within this remarkable household she now opened her eyes to find an aggregation of women and girls of a variety of ages and complexions, from pink to black and white. They were all involved in household chores, shuddering in terror at the huge figure of the master who never left his place on the wooden bench. His eyes were always watching, and he kept up a non-stop stream of shouts, screams, and threats, upbraiding someone here and admonishing someone else there. Woe betided any woman who disobeyed him. The whip hanging on the wall behind his back could easily undertake the task of bringing her back to the straight and narrow path of obedience.

Jawhara tried to get closer to the group of women who used to gather for an evening of chatter in their communal space whenever the master chose to leave them alone. But she was so young that they all looked down on her and refused to let her sit with them. Even so, she was curious and attentive enough that scarcely a word uttered by one or another of the women escaped her notice.

The evening chatter usually involved discussion of the day's more trivial events, but the topic that most interested the women concerned the households of various masters, their treatment of servants, and the relationship of the mistress of their house to the servants. One of them spoke about the sheer uncouthness of the mistress and the jealousy that had churned her insides ever since the new maid had entered the household.

Another woman told them all about the fierce degree of supervision that her mistress had imposed upon her since she joined the household, to such an extent that she would almost never let her be alone with the master, even if it were to provide some service for him.

The third of them described how brutal the master was to her, punishing her for the most trivial mistake or the flimsiest rumour.

The fourth woman spoke in a whisper, cackling gleefully as she did so. Her eyes gleamed and her body shook as she told them what had happened, but unfortunately she was whispering so quietly that Jawhara could not make out what it was she was saying.

During these soirees Jawhara listened to many entertaining stories about the conflicts between masters and servants, hearing how servants would undertake to avenge themselves for their own honour and humanity. But eventually they would come back to the house of Ibn Kiran, from where they would be transferred into the hands of another master with whom (and with whose wife) they would play exactly the same role. It was always the same fate – one of them could count on her fingers the number of times she crossed the threshold of Ibn Kiran the slave dealer.

During these sessions the words 'love' and 'passion' would be uttered by some of the women, and the others would laugh happily. The younger ones would lean coquettishly over and hug each other gently in their arms. These gestures would have an emotional effect on the assembly, and everyone would then laugh so loud that it almost echoed. Sly comments, which were incomprehensible unless they were accompanied by eye gestures and raised eyebrows, would follow. This particular topic might arouse the anger of some of the more elderly women present; they would scold the younger ones, accuse them of immodesty, and threaten to tell Ibn Kiran about it.

From these conversations Jawhara learned a little about her own fate. The entire group occupied a single room, and the talk was all about masters and servants, buying and selling, the whip which would set on fire the back of any servant who was disobedient, and the revenge that would be wreaked on any servant-woman who tried to flirt with the master or whom the master himself found attractive.

It was a world of misery, trial, and degradation, one where slave trading became a means of solving problems.

Jawhara's dreams became nightmares as she listened to these women sharing their stories in these evening sessions.

From time to time she would hear a harsh yell from Ibn Kiran, as he summoned a servant-woman or maid. After putting herself to rights and maybe dressing herself in the best clothes she had, the woman would respond. The hearts and eyes of all the servant-women would now be focused on peeping through cracks in the door to find out what was going on. They would come back and whisper to each other about the new visitors. Jawhara would pick up bits of their conversation: 'he's a young man', 'he's good-looking', 'he's rich', 'if only I had your luck!', and so on. She was not able to look through the cracks in the door herself and did not dare imitate their behaviour, so she had no idea what was actually happening with Ibn Kiran. Frequently one of the women would disappear and then come back after a few days because, after a period of trial, she did not satisfy the new master or mistress. Or she might disappear for good, to be replaced by another, indeed many others. In the space of a couple of weeks droves of women and girls passed through this incredible house, but only a few would stay there for long, and most of these would be elderly.

One morning in the third week she heard a loud yell from the master.

'Aisha, Aisha!'

This was the name her father had given her before she was named Jawhara. She responded to the call in a panic and stood in front of the slave trader without noticing that there was another man sitting on the wooden bench beside him. The slave trader gave her an angry look as he told her to kiss the man's hand. Turning in his direction, she kissed his hand bashfully, then stood there panting nervously, her head lowered. She was still shuddering from the shock of Ibn Kiran's sudden summons, which had caught her unawares. She now turned and looked at the man who was examining her closely.

'What's your name, little girl?' he asked.

'Aisha, sir.'

'What's the name of your previous owner? Were you a servant in Fez, or somewhere else?'

She obviously did not understand what he meant.

'Yes,' she replied, unable to think of anything else to say. 'I worked at home with my mother and looked after the sheep too.'

The man laughed at her naivety, while Ibn Kiran explained, 'She's fresh. She was kidnapped from her village and brought to market. Believe me, Hajj, sir, she's precious goods. Under your care and in your hands she will grow and develop. Your wife will be delighted with her. Give it a try, for just a few days. You'll be helping me. She's a simple girl, completely unspoiled.'

Hajj Muhammad turned and examined her closely from the top of her head to the soles of her feet. Now he had an entirely different expression on his face. He kept smiling as he touched her face, shoulders, and hands, and looked at her chest, focusing with particular interest on her breasts. Grabbing hold of one of her hands, he turned her around roughly so he could look at her back and buttocks. All the while, Ibn Kiran was making comments and offering explanations, while Aisha had no idea of what was being said.

Ibn Kiran signalled to Aisha to go back to the room. The girls and women who had been watching everything through the peephole now bombarded her with questions, but she had no idea how to respond to them.

A few moments later she heard another summons from Ibn Kiran and stood in front of him again. He told her to get ready to depart immediately. Leaving this extraordinary place, she accompanied her new master to his house, the household of Hajj Muhammad al-Tihami.

5

Within the walls of the servants' room in Hajj Muhammad's house there were enjoyable sessions devoted to the topic of sex, and this was where the story of Yasmine was told for the first and last time.

Yasmine was one of Hajj Muhammad's slave-women whom he bought at the request of his wife, Khaduj. She had complained to him about the number of chores involved in running the household and the fact that Fatima – who had come as part of her dowry – was unable to do all that was required of her. Jawhara was too young to undertake such household needs, especially since such young children required a good deal of attention. Not only that, but the sheer size of the house demanded a larger number of servants.

In Ibn Kiran's household Hajj Muhammad discovered a young olive-skinned girl, youthful, pretty, and full of energy. She had been kidnapped in the Doukkala region, which is known for its wealth and fertility. He did not have to think about it for very long; indeed, he had no hesitation from the moment he saw her. The crafty slave trader was well aware of Yasmine's charms, so he raised her price very high. There was no use haggling, and Hajj Muhammad could not help himself. So he paid the price for her on the spot without consulting anyone or even demanding a trial period.

Yasmine could remember every detail of the day when she accompanied Hajj Muhammad back to his house. As she entered, she was dressed in her threadbare old wrap with a veil that revealed only her honey-coloured eyes. Once in the courtyard, he ordered her to go to the servants' quarters, while he went to see Khaduj, his face wreathed in smiles. He spoke to his wife for several minutes, then summoned Yasmine in order to present her to Khaduj.

'Here's the new servant,' he said.

Yasmine removed the veil from her face and bent over to kiss Khaduj's hand. Khaduj seized her hand somewhat haughtily and looked up at her with a frown. For several moments she stared fixedly at Yasmine's face.

'Why did your mistress sell you?' she asked arrogantly.

'It was fated, madam,' Yasmine replied. 'I couldn't bear to leave her and the children; they loved me just as much as they did their mother. She couldn't bear to part with me, but the devil... God curse him—'

'That's what you all say! I certainly don't want the devil who tempted you there to do the same thing here. What I want from you is loyalty, reliability, intelligence, and hard work.'

Yasmine then withdrew to the servants' room. Her wrap and veil were removed, and then she emerged with her svelte body and glowing features. Her olive complexion made her seem even lovelier and more radiant. Her jet-black hair, which she made every effort to hide beneath a scarf, refused to comply; such charms could not be hidden so easily.

She made her way immediately to the kitchen, where Fatima was busy preparing the meal. Yasmine went over to her, using a phrase well beloved of serving women.

'My sister!'

The feelings of women like these differed from those of their mistresses. They all treated each other like sisters, each having sisterly rights over the others – hence the use of this phrase when addressing each other.

Fatima gave the newcomer a genuine welcome. The hard chores which the household demanded were certainly in need of some more help, and now the master had obviously responded to the household's needs by purchasing a new maid.

However, the fact that Yasmine was so young and unusually

attractive for a servant or maid certainly aroused Fatima's interest, and maybe a bit of jealousy as well. But she also knew from experience that beauty in a maidservant was not necessarily important; energy and hard work were the gauge of success and the way to gain favour. Fatima herself had proof of this fact; there was no reason why Yasmine should be any different.

Having entered the kitchen, Yasmine was settled into her new world. She started working hard and diligently; from now on she would be following the well-marked road as an obedient working servant.

However, a significant incident interfered with this calm existence. In fact, Fatima was wrong in imagining that beauty was not an important factor when it came to maidservants. Without either intending or indeed wanting to do so, Yasmine managed to find particular favour with Hajj Muhammad. Whenever he summoned a servant-woman to perform a particular task, Yasmine's name was always the first; occasionally he would deliberately ask her to help him when he actually did not need any help.

Yasmine found herself favoured by Hajj Muhammad without Khaduj being aware that anything unusual was happening. She respected her husband and firmly believed in his probity and his love for her, which prevented her from ever questioning his behaviour.

Hajj Muhammad considered the issue from a different point of view. He was devout and religious, and addressed all his problems in the context of religion as he understood it. As he thought about the problem of Yasmine, he reached a conclusion of 'whatever your right hand possesses, God has declared lawful', echoing the Qur'an's statements on the subject.

'My right hand now owns Yasmine, who is intended for favour and pleasure, not just for service and hardship,' he assured himself. 'Concubinage was never something that our pious ancestors chose to avoid, nor did our forefathers reject it. It would be narrow-minded and excessively pietistic of me to deprive myself of what God has declared lawful.'

So here was Yasmine: a bounty from God, who had made taking her as a concubine entirely legal. Hajj Muhammad found himself yearning for her and was totally unable to resist the burning desire that surged inside him whenever she came to perform a service for him. He would feel her fire every time he summoned her to massage his body with her gentle hands; this would happen when he felt that particular 'enervation' after this gorgeous maidservant had taken possession of his mansion. He could recall one particular day when his nerves had been on edge and blood was surging through his veins, and she had given him a massage for the first time. It would have gone on longer if his wife had not been close by.

'Enough, that's enough!' Khaduj yelled at the girl to put an end to this scene. 'Go back to your quarters!'

Life was no longer normal. The Hajj preferred to respond to the calls of nature and religion, rather than remain in a state of deprivation disapproved by God.

'But what about your wife?' – the question kept preying on his conscience, but he came up with a swift response: 'She is my respected wife and mother of my children, someone with a particular place in my own heart and this household. She should be ready to accept a concubine if she does not wish to see another wife alongside her, someone who would challenge her status in the household, divide my heart and wealth between them, and split the running of the household and control of the family.'

And yet, how was he going to face her and persuade her to accept the situation without raising a storm of criticism or defiance, not to mention anger and annoyance in the entire household? He was well aware of how sensitive and jealous Khaduj could be, and at the same time he realised how readily she obeyed him and believed him to be the master who had to be obeyed. There was no need for her to confront him or oppose his wishes. She was a perfect model of obedience and compliance, avoiding any desire that would not please her husband, and going along with the slightest wish or whim that he might display.

So, he would lay the whole thing out to her just as it was. That was the method he had adopted in facing many of life's problems, and household issues in particular, and it was obviously the best way of dealing with the issue of facing his wife with the decision he had made about Yasmine.

Khaduj was currently away visiting her own family. They were all looking forward to a happy occasion, the marriage of her sister, Zaynab, which required that Khaduj be away from the house for two whole weeks; she would be seeing her husband and children only occasionally.

Yasmine was then the member of the household who was closest to Hajj Muhammad and most involved in his daily life. She would help him take off his jallaba and burnous and massage his body and feet as he lay spreadeagled on his spacious bed. She would prepare his bed and stay ready to serve his every need, until he dismissed her so he could be alone with his dreams.

But this time he did not dismiss her. She stayed by his side as he continued to give orders and instructions. It was obvious that everything about him – his behaviour, gestures, and conversation – pointed to a peculiar excitement that Yasmine was not used to in unnatural situations such as this particular night.

With a climactic mixture of excitement and agitation Hajj Muhammad told Yasmine to close the door. She seemed not to understand him, so he repeated the order firmly: she was to close the door and join him in his bedroom.

Yasmine was shocked. She moved back and slunk out carefully, hoping that it was not too provocative. Leaving the room, she headed for a distant part of this house with its maze of rooms.

He waited for Yasmine to come back, and waited some more, his heart full of passionate desire. As the minutes ticked slowly by, seeming to him like hours, he found himself prey to conflicting ideas: had she run away from him and refused to obey his specific orders that she share his bedroom? Or was it that she had disappeared to preserve herself for her own wedding night?

He stared at the light curtain covering the door, watching closely as it rustled quietly. It was moving... No, it was not. It was just that a slight breeze was toying with it on this spring night. How delightful and refreshingly peaceful it all felt!

He started hoping again. 'Wait, just a bit longer... She has only ever obeyed you.'

The curtain moved again, except that this time it almost completely uncovered the door behind it. It must be her! He lost all control and would certainly have leaped out of bed if he had not then heard the miaowing of a large cat that was familiar with the mansion and its occupants, and saw no reason not to sneak around at night and intrude into Hajj Muhammad's bedroom as it conducted its slow and methodical tour of the house.

Hajj Muhammad was on the point of unleashing his pent-up fury on the prowling cat, but he made an effort to calm down and regain control of his nerves. He tried now to rationalise his passion.

'Let's forget about it till a more suitable occasion... But Khaduj's absence gives me that suitable occasion. When will such an opportunity come again? The crafty little girl has realised what's afoot, so she wants to run away. Am I supposed to let her win? No, that way she'll learn how to be disobedient. I'll go looking for her and make her do as I say... But it's night-time. Where am I supposed to find her if I go looking in every nook and cranny? No, she's bound to come back. I'll wait...'

He pretended to be calm again and leaned over idly to grab his rosary, which he always kept beside his bed. His shaking hands began thumbing the beads, and a regular clacking sound reverberated in the quiet room, of which he was the sole occupant. The overall silence that shrouded the entire house after daily life had come to an end only served to increase the impact of the sound as the beads knocked against each other. His shaking fingers were unusually swift in the way they manipulated the rosary, but gradually they slowed down and eventually stopped. It was almost as though they were recording the aroused emotions of his heart without his even being aware of it. He put the rosary to one side so he could listen carefully.

'Footsteps outside the room. Yasmine, no doubt...'

He listened and waited, but in vain. Whatever it was that he had imagined to be footsteps vanished in the quiet of the night.

'Oh dear, she's run away.'

How could his sense of pride allow her to run away? Wasn't she just a maidservant, born to obey her master and not refuse his orders?

Finally he got out of bed in order to restore that sense of pride. He paused for a while before putting his feet on the floor. He looked for his slippers, but his anxious eyes let him down. He gave up the search and walked barefoot towards the door, pulled the curtain back angrily, and looked outside at the wide courtyard. He was suddenly scared. He could not see anything; the entire house was still and dark. He stared very hard in the hope of seeing a glimmer of light through cracks in a door or a window, but all he could see was darkness. The more he stared, the darker it looked. He looked up to the second floor in case he might glimpse a light in one of the rooms or corridors, but once again he was disappointed. He was alarmed and could not bring himself to leave the bedroom. So he went back in and stood by the side of his bed, befuddled and hesitant.

'Am I getting into a battle I'm bound to lose? No, that's not going to happen.'

When he went back to the door, he felt stronger, more agitated, and readier than ever. But as he pulled back the door-curtain again, the darkness seemed like a wild beast intent on crushing him. His new vigour sagged once more, his emotions intensified, and his steps hesitated. Even so, he begged the heavens above for help and looked up in the hope that the moonlight might help him find his footing and save him from this desolate atmosphere of darkness and silence. However, all he found in the sky above was a hue of dark blue and gleaming stars scattered here and there. He stood there in amazement, as though he had never before looked at stars enveloping the celestial dome.

All this had a more powerful effect on him than did the darkness. It was as though the stars were actually lamps to illuminate for the heavens the work of the earth's people, penetrating eyes to uncover the deeds of robbers, adventurers, and criminals that the darkness always tried to hide. He did not feel that he belonged to any of those groups, but everything around him made him feel that his situation was not natural.

Influenced by the effect that the sky's lamps had had on him, he retraced his steps, but he was still thinking to himself.

'This golden opportunity will slip through my fingers. I'm not going to retreat in the face of this obstinate little girl.'

The notion of 'opportunity' and 'defeat' preoccupied his mind as he thought about Yasmine's defiance. He forgot all about the night sky and stars, and started frantically yelling, 'Yasmine! Yasmine! Yasmine!'

His yells reverberated in every nook and cranny of the house. A tranquil beast was suddenly unleashed in the night, like cries of alarm or the howls of a wounded wolf. Every living being in the house heard it all.

Fatima leapt out of bed, and so did Abd al-Ghani, his eldest son, shocked and fearful. From the second-floor balcony an older woman of the family, whom the passage of time had left in Hajj Muhammad's household, looked down. His widowed sister rushed out of her quarters, shouting, 'My brother, my brother!' All through the house, lights went on. From everywhere anxious eyes looked down, and people in every part of the house held their breath. Fatima went over to him.

'Master,' she asked, 'is there anything I can do for you?'

'Where's Yasmine?' he asked. 'Send her to me at once and hurry up!'

His voice was tense and angry. Fatima withdrew, and his sister took herself away, although she had a fairly clear idea of what was going on in her brother's mind. The older woman upstairs felt as though she had committed a major crime by overlooking the master at a time when she did not have to show herself. Abd al-Ghani was furious that Yasmine had disappeared, his only thought being that she had not been around when her master had needed her.

Fatima went looking for Yasmine and eventually found her half asleep (or pretending to be), in shock and with her face covered; she was in a corner of the provisions room. No sooner had Fatima told her to go and talk to her master than Yasmine became alarmed and started crying. Even so, she could still not explain why she was so scared, indeed terrified.

Fatima understood everything; things like this were the subject of stories about servants. But it never occurred to her that a maid-servant might be unable to stand up to her master's will, so she forced Yasmine to respond to her master's call and dragged her to his room, as a sheep is dragged to the slaughterhouse.

Once again darkness fell on the now-quiet household, and the house's residents returned to their innocent dreams. The stars in the sky kept a watchful eye on the acts of human folly that darkness endeavoured to hide.

It was not long before another scream emerged from Hajj Muhammad's bedroom, one that echoed through the silence of the household. This time it was Yasmine who screamed.

6

When Khaduj came home after visiting her family, her husband looked happy and content as he welcomed her back. Actually, she noticed that his happiness was even more obvious than normal. He took every opportunity to make her feel content, and kept the evening chatter going for much longer than usual, and asked for more details about the wedding and other incidentals that normally did not interest him. He did his best to please her by talking about her family – her mother and father – and the trouble they had taken over the wedding celebrations, welcoming their guests and making them feel comfortable.

Whenever she had visited her family before and stayed away for an extended period, he had usually begun by complaining that she had stayed away too long. If he had agreed to her going, the griping might be moderate, even jovial, but it could also be more biting and serious if he had felt unhappy or anxious. In any case it would lead her to apologise for her absence and to ask for his forgiveness and forbearance. All this involved pleasure – and what pleasure it was! – as Hajj Muhammad was reacquainted with his beloved wife after a long absence.

But this time he deliberately avoided anything that might upset her or make her apologise and ask for forgiveness. He felt that he was the one who needed to apologise, to ask for forgiveness and gain her approval. At the same time he realised that the time would surely come; it would be better to delay things and come up with a plan to prepare the right atmosphere to resolve the issue and make his wife content with the new situation, now that Yasmine had become her rival as a bedmate.

Within the quiet framework of this family, it was not an issue that could be kept secret for very long, or erased by the course of events. Khaduj began to hear stories about the way her maidservant Yasmine had been recalcitrant; she had aroused Hajj Muhammad's anger and enraged him during the night when everyone had gone to sleep. The stories went on to tell how Hajj Muhammad had yelled so loudly that it had reverberated throughout the household; everyone had been frightened and had looked down to see what was happening. Khaduj then learned that Fatima had gone all around the house searching for the disobedient runaway girl. Once she had found her, she had grabbed her by the neck and forced her to go to Hajj Muhammad's room.

Khaduj now began to have her doubts about her husband. She now noticed that Yasmine was the person whom he preferred to respond to his wishes; that he had started to rely on her to help him every time he was on the point of leaving the house and every time he came back, needing help with taking off his clothes and with his baggage. Not only that, but she was the one he asked to give him a massage and provide relief for his exhausted body. Based on these vague notions, the doubts that Khaduj was nursing inside her now turned into things that were far more specific, thanks to the numerous rumours she kept hearing. Preference might imply both affection and desire, but conviction involved sympathy and love.

The jealousy that was eating away inside Khaduj severed all possibilities of doubt. She now decided to question Yasmine in detail. She began by asking how things had gone in the household during her absence and whether the servants had done their utmost to provide Hajj Muhammad with the life of ease that was his due. Yasmine found this line of questioning odd. It began in a friendly and innocuous fashion, but it never occurred to her that she was going to be asked about the infamous night when she had disobeyed him. No sooner had Khaduj asked about precisely that subject without the slightest degree of hesitation or reserve – indeed while seeming to be uninterested – than Yasmine faltered and was completely unable to hide her panic and distress. She tried to withdraw, but a violent reaction from Khaduj nailed her to the spot, quivering in fear and short of breath.

She now gave up all hope of keeping everything hidden or of concealing what Hajj Muhammad might well have already confessed to his wife. She remained silent, stubbornly silent, until, that is, her recalcitrance was shattered by a ringing shout from Khaduj.

'Confess, or else you've no place here after today!'

The threat rang in her ears and had a terrifying impact on her entire being. She fully understood what it implied, and her whole past now loomed before her eyes: the slave market at Ibn Kiran's house; men coming every morning to check on new arrivals; standing there to be examined and probed like a dumb animal; moving from one house to another to gain the necessary experience; the slave trader's voice announcing that she was clever and obedient, and above all a beautiful virgin girl. This last phrase had ingrained itself in her memory and continued to upset her. 'Virgin?' The question kept coming back, now answered in the negative.

Alas, she was no longer one of those girls for whom men would pay a very high price. Her own master could be the father of her child. And now yet another word repeated itself, as though to provide confirmation of a dreadful crime. 'Child?! No, no!'

Yasmine could not even entertain the idea of assuming all these burdens and being shunted around slave markets and households where she would be tested.

'I'll confess,' she told herself, 'and let what might happen happen.'

And so she responded falteringly to Khaduj's threat, utterly confused. 'I'm just an obedient servant,' she said, her eyes closed. 'I did my best to resist, but I had no choice but to obey.'

'Get out of my sight, you little trollop. I was a fool to have trusted you. You'll see how I deal with your betrayal and deceit!'

Deep down, Khaduj had not wanted to hear this honest confession. After living in an atmosphere of doubt, she now found herself in one involving facts. Sometimes doubt can be a lethal kind of torture, but more often than not it is kinder than destructive truths.

Now it was clear to her that she had a rival for her husband's affections. She was well aware from the actual cases she had compiled and identified that that particular night had not been some passing fancy but rather the implementation of a concerted plan on Hajj Muhammad's part, one aimed at making Yasmine his concubine and bedmate, and maybe the mother of children.

'The mother of children?!' Khaduj thought. 'What kind of utter disaster is threatening your own family, Hajj Muhammad? Here I am, a free and honourable woman and daughter of a respected family, and now my children are going to have siblings born to a servant-girl whom you bought from a slave market? All my hopes are dashed, and any confidence I had in your intelligence and respectability has been shattered.

'Shall I make it clear that I refuse to accept this situation and completely reject it? But what would be the point? He's obviously come to a decision, there's no doubt about that. Can I somehow break his resolve or bring him back to his senses, when he is so totally confident in his own personality, intelligence, and judgement? I'm threatened by disaster, and any resistance on my part will signal the start of that very disaster. No, I'm not going to object and resist. Instead, I'll declare war on this bedmate of my husband, until I can finish her off or get her thrown out of my house. But there'll be no actual battlefield; after all, she's surrendered and is happy enough. He's the one who's controlling everything. My war will be against him. He'll soon realise my intentions, but it'll be bad for me if he finds out that I'm at war with him.'

The possible strategies that she might adopt shrank in her eyes, and she burst into tears. She did her best to control her sobbing; it was not right for everyone in the household – the children, her husband's family, and the servants – to know that the lady of the house was in tears. No one should know why she was crying; that would inevitably indicate a weakness and lack of control, which would have a negative impact on her authority and influence.

She was still crying when Abd al-Ghani surprised her. She

managed to put on a false smile, but could not hide her tears or remove the grief-stricken look from her face. As she responded to his concern, she begged him to leave her to her own worries and concerns. Abd al-Ghani was disheartened as he left, realising from his mother's obvious unhappiness that there was some new disagreement of the kind that occasionally flared up between husbands and wives. Such situations usually returned to normal once tempers had cooled down and people were no longer so worked up.

The anticipated storm finally broke at noontime, when Hajj Muhammad came home exhausted by the heat and work he had been doing. What he wanted was a quiet place to relax, a nice cool atmosphere, and some delicious food to eat. But what greeted him instead was his wife's face, a tissue of sadness and distress. The smile from those dreamy eyes had disappeared, to be replaced by a bloated, teary visage. He did his best to ignore what he was seeing and busied himself taking off his outer garments. As usual, he called for Yasmine to help him do that and to relieve his exhaustion. But there was no response to his shouts. He turned to Khaduj and asked her to help him summon Yasmine. Furious, she looked away, unable to raise her reddened eyes to look at the man for whom she now felt a mixture of sensations – contempt and hatred on the one hand, and admiration, fear, and appreciation on the other. Her fear of his authority outweighed the love she felt for him, a love of the kind that was dictated by expediency and imposed by necessity. She admired him, but it was the kind of admiration inspired by power and strength. And yet, in spite of all that, she had never felt any contempt or hatred toward him until she had found out that he had taken a maidservant as a rival bedmate.

She did not respond to his request by summoning Yasmine. Instead, she ignored his request and turned her back on him. With that, she left the room, as though he were not even there. She had no idea how angry he felt at her ignoring him and then leaving – or perhaps she did know, but could not do anything else.

Nothing annoyed Hajj Muhammad so much as assaults on his

own honour. He had never felt so demeaned as he did now, and at the hands of a woman at that, someone over whom he had total authority and control. Never before had Khaduj deliberately shunned, despised, and disobeyed him as she had just done. When he made her angry about something, her response was always moderate. Her argument would be muted; she would protest meekly and show how upset she was in a conciliatory and humble fashion. This time, however, her display of anger was anything but gentle. She had gone far beyond any limit expected in their married life together.

Hajj Muhammad was all too aware of what was causing his wife's distress. Yasmine had disappeared at precisely the time when she knew he would need her help. He was also conscious of the fact that Khaduj's anger and furious reaction were due to a murderous feeling of jealousy or a resounding family scandal.

Inside him he could feel a combination of unsettling reactions to what had happened. Firstly there was the utter contempt he had been shown by his wife, who had always admired and respected him. The way she had looked at him harboured within it an accusation levelled at his honour and dignity. The liberty and power that he enjoyed in this household were now under threat. He loved his wife and gave her significant status in the household, but he could certainly not brook this kind of opposition to behaviour that he alone had the authority to choose and follow. He certainly would not be able to discuss with her the rightness of his actions or his absolute discretion in such matters, but it was clear that he must put an end to this recalcitrance. If he did not, then a curse would fall on the household, and forever.

Such was his fury that he leaped up and stood by the doorway. Every corner of the household then reverberated with a terrifying shout that shattered everyone's nerves and made Khaduj herself shudder, a shout that was nothing other than a call summoning Yasmine.

Yasmine herself was well aware that this whole matter was serious; this time she could not ignore her master's summons. Leaving the kitchen, she proceeded slowly towards the source of the yelling, with Khaduj watching and listening. Hardly had she entered the room before the curtains were lowered and the door locked.

Khaduj was now utterly shattered. Her features contracted, and she burst into tears, sobbing uncontrollably. She made her way to an isolated room where she could be alone with her tears and misery.

7

The advent of spring breezes brought with it the echoes of drums and cymbals, the magic of tales of jinn monarchs, the various whims of dwellers on earth, fascinating colours and smells, and the splendour of deep-red blood.

Each year in spring and summer a number of Gnawa celebrations were arranged here and there in the quarter where the ancient mansion nestled. Invitations would be addressed to maidservants, and the black-skinned ones in particular. Those Gnawa 'earth dwellers' who had in some way been touched by a group of jinn felt a very strong connection between themselves and the colour black, which made them believe that every black maidservant belonged to a jinn family, even though these people knew almost nothing about jinn apart from the kinds of legend that fed the minds of such women, black and white alike.

Hajj Muhammad's maidservants were in the vanguard of those who would be invited to the Gnawa celebrations, but he would not let them spend the whole night outside the house, even though he had no objections to them going to watch – he too actually had a deep-seated conviction that there was indeed a strong link between maidservants and jinn. So, each year, the women used to follow the news of the celebrations from a distance. They would talk about them as though they had actually been there and enjoyed playing the various roles, and go on to describe the roles that the main dancers had played in order to please the jinn and gain their affection.

But the occasion was not one that they were prepared to miss. Next to Hajj Muhammad's residence was a huge house where many brothers were living, men with large families. They all used to gather in this ancient house around an old mother whose husband had died when her children were young and even babies.

She served as the firm link that bound all these brothers, with their multiple lifestyles, to each other. She continued to gather them all around her as though they were still small children. She looked old, and her age confirmed it, and yet she still possessed a powerful will, a strong determination, and a dogged temperament. She was firm with her children and grandchildren and was quite prepared to start yelling angrily in the face of any of her children if she did not like something or it did not suit her temperament. If she became really angry, her yells would echo around and reach the neighbouring houses; everyone was quite used to it, and the yelling and screaming neither aroused their curiosity nor led them to investigate.

Like her children and grandchildren, everyone was convinced that her spirit was possessed by a group of jinn; that would have explained her behaviour. Her yelling was merely the jinn inside her body venting themselves. Rather than grumbling about it, the best idea was to placate them and do what they said, otherwise the jinn speaking through her might decide to take revenge. Rather than daring to complain, the best plan was to ask for forgiveness and seek reconciliation. Or you could recite the beautiful names of God, as something to throw in the face of the demon-jinn who clearly were in possession of her. By now her neighbours felt nothing but sympathy and compassion for her.

This woman's nerves were increasingly rough and on edge. Whenever springtime approached and the first signs of summer wafted their way past frozen souls, her yelling would become even more vicious and powerful. As far as she, her children, and her neighbours were concerned, this was simply a desire on the jinn's part to assert control over her spirit and to inhabit her body while the famous annual celebration was being organised. Animals would be slaughtered and offerings would be made in order to placate the lords of the jinn and ward off their desire for vengeance. Such opinions regarding her were well known by now. When her nerves were on edge and her arguments intensified, everyone knew that the time had come to hold the Gnawa festival.

For the maidservants in Hajj Muhammad's household this was good news. Their master always ignored the neighbours' celebration, but even though he did not allow them to attend it, he did not insist on keeping a close eye on them or tracking where they went. So they all made preparations, putting on their best new clothes and choosing colours that would most please the lord of the jinn's desires – dark black, bright yellow, or dark red. Among the leaders and lords of the jinn were those who adored those colours. Each woman was a prisoner of her own colour and could not rid herself of its sway. If she did not choose one, she would collapse in a heap until such time as she selected a kaftan that was either black, red, or yellow.

The festival night would begin in late afternoon. All the sisters who had been invited, all of them black or olive skinned, were welcomed; they all had a remarkable share in the jinn's world. They strutted around in their black, yellow, or red kaftans, all brought together as usual by these celebrations. Happy and laughing, they let out their ululations, as though they were celebrating a festival of peace between mankind and jinn, with no antipathies and no flare-up of hostilities that might spoil the Gnawa celebration.

The 'invitees' were actually not invited in the normal sense of the word. They all felt that they were members of the household, performing their duties as part of the celebration, sharing in the provision of services for the Gnawa troupe, and, through their movements in various parts of the house, enhancing the joy and liveliness of the celebration.

The so-called sisters in Hajj Muhammad's household were not allowed to leave the house in the afternoon; all they were allowed to do in those hours was to watch, and only after the official celebration had started. Even so, such was their eagerness to be involved that time after time they would head for the front door and peep through the opening or keyhole to see if the celebration had begun and to watch the preparations, if only from behind the doors.

The signal to start the celebration came in loud, stirring tones from the clashing cymbals of the troupe's leader, followed by a resounding thump from a huge drum. That was followed by other cymbal clashes in lively cascades of dance melody, interspersed with beats from a large drum, then a small one. The whole sound managed to have its own distinctive impact.

The troupe was arrayed in its wonderful musical pattern, with the leader in front. Behind him were the big cymbalists, drum-beaters, and medium- and small-sized cymbal-strikers. Hardly were they through the door before they started chanting songs in a mixture of Arabic and Gnawi – that is, a blend of African languages.

It was only now that the sisters in Hajj Muhammad's household would be allowed to slink their way somewhat sneakily toward the lucky house where the celebration was being held. Amid the lights coming from every part of the house and the number of people holding torches and lighted candles, the Gnawa troupe was clustered around its leader, organised and arranged according to the importance of the role that each member had to play – the repeated chants created a lively atmosphere to the accompaniment of cymbals and drums. In the bright light the sisters and the ladies whom the house was celebrating could make out the faces of the troupe's members. They were all usually familiar with those faces, but even so they began making remarks that went along with their suppressed instincts and the affection, awe, and respect that they all felt deep down toward members of the troupe.

For the sisters and the ladies who were the celebration's sponsors, every member of the troupe was a model of the jinni ideal. Here, for example, was Masoud, a tall young black man with bulging muscles, a strong build, prominent scarred cheeks, gleaming teeth, and reddened eyes, standing in the middle of the group, his head held high and nose in the air, beating his cymbal and fully confident that the sound it was making was louder than the others and would certainly reach the ears of all those women possessed by the jinn. He would thus be pleasing the jinn monarchs who were enlivening their night with such pleasure and delight.

The sisters believed that this Masoud had two distinct personalities. The first was the jinni ideal, which was merely the image of a young king, strong and muscular, well able to launch attacks and possess souls with force and resolution. The second was the human personality. His handsome manliness made him the focus of all kinds of sinful notions and the object of every woman's gaze, whether young or old.

And there was Fatih, who banged the big drum. By now he was approaching middle age, even though his dark, black complexion showed no signs of wrinkles. He still held the drum confidently, pounding it powerfully and keeping up a lively pace with the drumbeats. The turban on his head jumped around with all the élan of someone who is proud of his talents. Behind those drumbeats was the idea that he was giving all the jinni monarchs a good deal of pleasure. For them, drumbeats brought a special magic that even cymbal clashes could not rival, however many they might be and however separated the two sets of instruments.

This man Fatih had a particular place in the hearts of all the sisters. From the very first beat he would be the cynosure of all their eyes, arousing inside them all a tremendous admiration. He was someone blessed by fortune, with a special link to the jinn monarchs – one to which none of the other members of the troupe could aspire. In the women's minds he inspired a feeling of wonder. Even though he seemed well on his way towards middle age, he could still beat the drum with a power that spoke of virility and strength.

Then there was Amm Mubarak, well along his path to old age, whose cymbal clashes revealed a certain weakness and lack of vigour. He kept trying to raise his voice in song, but it could barely be heard alongside those of the younger members of the troupe. His voice did not come through because his lips had no teeth, or even roots of teeth, to rely on. Even so, Amm Mubarak was hardly lacking in qualities to admire. In him the women could recognise an old man (one of the monarchs on earth) who had devoted his entire life to the service of the spirits. He was indeed *mubarak* – blessed – someone in whose smiling visage you could sense a blessing and look for beneficence.

The first performance, or initial section of the celebration, was almost over. Members of the troupe now sat in front of the house, waiting to be served drinks that usually consisted of distilled red grapes and powdered-rice water. As a general din pervaded the house, the women running the celebration began preparing to offer these drinks to the troupe and the visitors, male and female alike. The female guests at the celebration would now begin making detailed comments on the performance.

One of them would start the discussion by saying something like, 'Masoud wasn't as lively and energetic as he usually is. You could barely hear his cymbals.'

'I've never seen him do as well as he has today,' another would respond with a cheery laugh. 'His voice stood out over all the others. I think you're annoyed because he avoided looking at you so much!'

'Tonight Saeed did his best to use the beats on his small drum to drown out Fatih's beats. Small chance! Fatih – well, he's Fatih!'

'The truth is that Fatih's beginning to look tired. Saeed's younger than him. Everyone at Hajja Aisha's celebration was shocked.'

'I saw him with my own two eyes. He was wearing a pink kaftan. He was the one who started the dancing, and no sooner had he started than a female demon took possession of him. His turns were so fast and light that you could hardly keep up with him.'

'He wasn't the one dancing; it was the spirit that had taken possession of him. It was his submission to those forces that was making the movement.'

The discussion continued amid waves of laughter, gestures, and repeated shouts. The talk was not actually artistic so much as emotional. The Gnawa celebration was an excellent opportunity for the group of sisters to rid themselves of the slavery imposed on them by their masters' households, one that controlled work, free conversation, and communication, as well as matters of emotion and any thought of sex.

Saeed the dancer was not Saeed the artist – in other words an authentic Gnawi. He was simply an attractive young man who had been possessed by an attractive young jinni. The hope for his intercession far outweighed any fear of his excessive zeal. The process of watching these celebrations and the yearning desire to attend them and dress up for them was not simply a matter of pleasing the jinni monarchs, but rather a way of relieving feelings of repression and an urge to escape to a world of freedom – freedom of feelings, emotions, and hopes.

Everything suddenly fell silent as the leader of the troupe raised his hand in the air and clashed his cymbal to announce the beginning of the second part of the celebration. The women, who were eager to hear more tales and comments, took the opportunity to cackle and whisper sarcastic comments in the ears of their neighbours about what would be happening once the cymbals started clashing again and the members of the troupe restarted their repetitive chanting; the second part would be even livelier and more energetic than the first, and the level of excitement would make its way into the deepest recesses of the souls of those women who were so eager for Gnawa celebrations.

The troupe opened the second part with a new melody, one that was both exciting and stimulating. No sooner had they started chanting than a young man in their midst sprang up like a demon-jinni, banging on his cymbal with powerful but delicate hand movements to an exciting and frenetic tune. His expression changed, his limbs tensed, and his eyes glistened as he began a deft performance of a pulsating dance, moving forward, then back, and pirouetting with feather-like leaps. He began a series of rapid, powerful turns on his toes, moving faster and faster, as the young men in the troupe usually did. The sounds emerging from his cymbal determined the process of this strenuous performance, one that acquired a good deal of its force from the thrilling chanting that emerged from a set of female throats exhausted by illness, misery, and deprivation. The troupe showed no mercy as they took possession of their audience's feelings. Everyone's nerves were on edge and their very souls were deeply affected. There was a sigh here and a shout there. One of the women stood up and started dancing, totally unconscious of what she was doing. Everyone looked at her, and several of her concerned sisters surrounded her, as shouts rang out:

'Leave her be! Leave her be! It's time for her to be set free.'

'Her personal demon has possessed her. You don't want to annoy her.'

'Poor woman! She's overcome with emotion. If she doesn't dance now, she'll go mad!'

The members of the troupe now took turns doing rhythmic dances to the harsh sounds of clashing cymbals and chanting. This went on until almost midnight. Then the troupe took a break, during which the guests, male and female, were fed amidst an atmosphere of frenzied shouting.

This break gave the troupe members, and their young men especially, an opportunity to put their main task behind them and chat with this woman or that. The younger sisters took the opportunity to give fulsome praise for the wonderful performance put on by the young man of their dreams.

'Your dancing was amazing,' one of them said, 'Are you just as good at other things?'

'Ha, ha, ha!' another one answered. 'He's a champion at everything, dear sister!'

'Your voice was different to what I'm used to,' another woman said.

'Did you find it more affectionate and delicate?' he asked. 'My voice does not express my own essence.'

Laughter could be heard everywhere, without anyone feeling either anxious or closely watched. Eventually the old woman who owned the house relaxed her features – perhaps for the only time in the year – and gathered around her the other old women who were enjoying the dancing and singing. They could remember the days of yore, with the sun setting in order to rise to a new morning overflowing with light and joy. As the lady of the house accepted her sisters' congratulations and prayers for her good health and security – that security of the soul to be found from the jinn's retribution – she did not forget to issue her instructions and to tease some of the invited women and even young and old members of the troupe.

The hostess for this occasion had broken her normal habits by wearing the very newest finery she owned; all sorts of colours and shapes rivalled each other for attention – dark reds, bright yellows, and gorgeous greens. Her clothing provoked all sorts of curious and sarcastic remarks, but on this particular night her goal was to please everyone, jinni monarchs and guests alike. She was smoking, and the cigarette dangling from her mouth looked ugly and out of place. She kept inhaling snuff as well, which made her eyes water and her nose look puffy, the whole mixing with the hairs of her moustache that dripped a foul liquid. Even so, none of this came as a shock to anyone; instead, they admired her, since as the hostess completely overcome by the frenzy of the occasion she was simply carrying out orders.

Once more the troupe resumed its dancing and singing, but this time it changed its routine and began making the rounds of the spacious house – all its rooms and hallways. At the head was the beater of the large drum, strutting along as he danced. He paused by each of the guests, male and female, and the members of the family, until each one gave him a 'gift'; if it were not enough, he would wait even longer. Behind him the troupe with their clashing cymbals would raise their voices in chant, as though to encourage people to give even more.

The tour of the house went on until the troupe had collected a large amount of money; it would be going into their own pockets, but at the same time it was an offering to the jinn monarchs and a protection against demons.

As people became more and more entranced, there seemed to be a strange tremor in the air. It felt like a moment of revelation when the jinn were released from their trammels. It was thus an ideal opportunity to please them and keep them entertained. What could please a jinni more than warm, dark blood coursing forth, and fresh milk poured into the earth's apertures as an indication of a desire for peace and the hoisting of the flag of safety and security?

Among the initial signs of this tremulous atmosphere was an unusual amount of energy from the troupe itself. The cymbals rumbled forth their sound as though they had not been doing so earlier. Their drums echoed in the night as though they were possessed. Their voices rose in repetitive chant, their ringing tones a sign of their ardour, and their hoarseness a clue to their quest for conciliation and surrender to outside forces. This sensation pervaded the entire atmosphere and infected the souls of the women present. With bated breath the members of the troupe hurried around with an anxious caution, as though they were scared of this critical moment. They were clearly affected by the rumours claiming that this crucial point was the time for evil devils to reveal themselves, the occasion for maximum damage and revenge. Their souls were totally influenced by the magic vibrations of the music, which had the power to exert control over anxious souls and fiery emotions.

Emotions were now at their peak. One of the members of the troupe clad in a waist-wrap leapt to his feet with a black billy goat in front of him, which was unsettled by all the noise and the sound of the relentless drumbeats. In his mouth he had a knife with a gleaming blade, which only enhanced the excitement. The other members of the troupe and their colleagues, with their snub noses and reddened eyes, clustered around him, scattering salt and pouring milk. A woman among them grabbed hold of a multicoloured turkey with feathers of seven or more different hues. The old woman had put herself to the test by searching for a seven-hued turkey that she could have ready for the moment of revelation – it was unacceptable for the hues to number less than seven. Another woman was clutching a gleaming white turkey, while others held black chickens. The women launched into ululations, but it was all lost in the mingled din of cymbals, drums, and chants.

The man now came forward and lifted the goat up high. As quick as lightning, the goat's legs flew up, but then he had it on its back. Grabbing it by the legs and stretching its neck towards the main drain of the house, he took the knife, and, as the grains of salt and drops of milk were added, applied the knife to the animal's jugular. As the dark blood flowed, the members of the troupe extended their arms, still shaking with their cymbals, towards the ground, then stood up and bent over as though to proclaim their obedience and submission. They kept chanting the song of peace, submitting themselves to the jinni monarchs and their armies. Every drain in the house received its share of turkey and chicken blood, those drains being the outlet to the world beyond feeling, the conduit whereby sacrifices are offered and through which flows the blood of seven-hued or gleaming white turkeys.

It seemed that the jinni monarchs were bestowing their favour on the troupe and those who were participating in the night's celebrations. After the moment of revelation the general atmosphere was calm, as the herald of dawn joined in the mood. People relaxed, and the harsh sounds of cymbals and drums diminished. The chanting was now more muted, and the members of the troupe performed their roles seated. Smiles were again to be seen on the lips of the women involved, and they all resumed their normal behaviour, laughing and sharing jokes. The assembly welcomed the advent of morning in an atmosphere replete with pleasure and tranquillity.

With the arrival of morning the maidservants from Hajj Muhammad's household slunk back to the house with all due caution, worried in case the master had already woken, looked for them all, and discovered that they had not yet returned. The master actually turned a blind eye to the fact that they were not there and was aware that they had only come back at dawn, but even so he held them to account. They swore they had come back early in the night, and the mistress of the household was willing to believe them. It was as though the entire household was reconciled to playing this game of subterfuge.

8

Yasmine was not happy about her position in Hajj Muhammad's household.

She was not a mere housemaid any longer, living a life of work and deprivation with all of them. Nor had she risen to the ranks of the ladies of the household, living a life of work and enjoyment, of complete control and entry to their private gatherings through wide-open doors. She was 'property owned by the right hand' (to cite the Qur'an), bought by Hajj Muhammad from Ibn Kiran's house.

The society in which she was currently living would not be one to forget that reality. Her master could not ignore what his hand had wrought, quite apart from the fact that she had borne Hajj Muhammad a son. She was still his concubine, someone for him to bed whenever the fancy took him. He had basically withdrawn from his wife, and habit and familiarity had both tamed her anger. As a result she no longer flared up every time Hajj Muhammad yearned for Yasmine.

Yasmine was in effect a wife, but neither a canonical nor an official one. For that reason she lived neither a wife's life nor a house-maid's; instead, it was that of a concubine. There was no finery such as wives wear, nor could she attend receptions as the head of the other women of the household. She had no authority like other female heads of household, and yet her status was higher than that of the other maidservants.

She never raised any objections to this position. The environment within which she was living had social conditions that were not drawn by the people living under them but had been for the most part inherited from past tradition. The master of the household – the only one with the authority to demand obedience – defined every single detail and particular.

She was unhappy, but not because of her social position inside the house or because of certain rights that she aspired to but was denied. No, she was unhappy as the mother of Mahmud.

She could tolerate the fine distinction between being a wife and at the same time not a wife. What she could not endure was when that distinction affected her son. He was Hajj Muhammad's son. The social situation inside the house would not allow Mahmud's father to lower him to some secondary rank among his sons, even though they were not all from the same mother, and in fact there was also a further distinction, namely in their skin colour (since Mahmud's edged a little toward olive).

When Mahmud was very young he received plenty of affection, mercy, and love, just like any of Hajj Muhammad's sons, including from Khaduj, the primary mistress of the household. She used to like watching him gurgle, then crawl, before he started tottering along. How she rejoiced when she heard him say his very first words, mispronouncing them in an endearing way. When he was little, she would lavish affection on him just as she would have done with any of her own children. She did not mind if he imitated her other children and called her 'Mama'. That is how it came to be that, as he grew up, he knew Khaduj as 'Mama' and called his real mother 'Dada', as if she were his nursemaid.

Yasmine felt free to enjoy this kind of equality, which she herself lacked in her own life. So she used her little son as a means of compensation.

Mahmud grew up and became a teenager. The first things that a child loses at that stage are natural love, affection, praise, and admiration. He no longer aroused Khaduj's love and sympathy; she started being annoyed by him in a way that she had not felt toward any of her own children. His movements around the house got on her nerves, and she would regularly yell at him and hit him. She complained about him to Hajj Muhammad and would be very happy when the boy's father punished him.

Mahmud started to feel discriminated against. His brothers hardly ever let him join in their games and activities, and his father hardly paid any attention to him, while he would regularly spoil his other children, giving them clothes, games, and other children's toys. Mahmud missed out on all of that. When he found himself among his brothers, he would raise a fuss whenever he thought he was being excluded, but Yasmine knew how to calm his temper and teach him how to put up with the hurt and exclusion, and all without making him feel humiliated or despicable.

Mahmud began hearing some new words from his brothers and sisters: 'black eyed' and 'maid's boy'. These words all fused into some disturbing ideas, but he was too young to understand them clearly. Even so, the words themselves suggested that they were linked to something shameful, although he had no idea what that was.

He was not black-skinned, though his colouring was somewhat different from that of his brothers, but almost none of them called him anything but 'black eyed', to such an extent that the word did not offend him any more. Once he tried to join a game that his brothers were playing, and Abd al-Rahman gave him a slap that really shocked him. He ran in tears to tell Khaduj.

'Mama, mama!'

Khaduj's nerves were on edge, and she was agitated. 'Get out of here!' she yelled at him. 'I'm not your mother. From now on, don't call me Mama. Your mother's that other woman... Yasmine.'

The young boy recoiled in shock. The way Khaduj had just yelled at him dispelled all thoughts of the slap he had received on his cheek from Abd al-Rahman. He did not cry, but his young mind started thinking, 'She said "I'm not your mother." But isn't she the mother of Abd al-Ghani, Abd al-Rahman, Abd al-Latif, and Aisha? "Your mother is Yasmine." Yasmine Dada. She's not my mother. How can brothers have a number of mothers?

'Black eyed, servant's boy... So, those words were actually true. "Servant"? What does that mean? All I know is my father, mother, brother, sister, and Dada. What does "servant" mean?'

Mahmud could not answer all the questions that his young mind was asking, but they still kept his tears dry and left him wandering in a kind of wilderness, in which he resorted to Yasmine.

As Yasmine clutched her son, she dried her own tears. She was feeling more affection for him than ever before; she gave him the kind of hug a mother gives when she has dearly missed her only child for most of his life. This marked the return of Yasmine's feelings for her son, now that Khaduj had rejected him. She would give him just as much as he gave her; what he gave her was the love of a son, and she in return was giving him mothering, with all the love, affection, and sympathy she could convey. Mahmud recognised her love and affection, but he was not fully aware of the real extent of the feelings that Yasmine was having for the first time; he assumed that she was just trying to make up for his real mother's angry confrontation with him.

Yasmine strove to put an end to the mental and emotional turmoil that had Mahmud swirling in its clutches. She did her best to remain strong, but her tears let her down. With tears pouring down her cheeks, she gave Mahmud an affectionate look and spoke to him in a barely audible voice.

'My darling, you're a big boy now, and you need to understand.'

'Understand? Understand what, Dada? Abd al-Rahman hit me on the face. You can still see the marks on my cheek!'

'Don't worry about that; it's over. You'll make it up with each other.'

'I will if he doesn't do it again!'

Yasmine tried to bring Mahmud back to the main subject. Drying her tears, she put on a serious expression.

'Mahmud,' she said, 'you can understand now, and you have to know the truth.'

Saying 'Not a word!' she cut off any attempt on Mahmud's part to ask for an explanation.

'You're not one of Lalla Khaduj's sons,' she went on.

'Lalla Khaduj? You mean my mother.'

'It's true: you're not one of her sons. You're my son. I'm your mother.'

'But you're Dada!'

'I'm not your dada; I'm your mother.'

'My mother? So are you the mother of Abd al-Ghani, Abd al-Rahman, Abd al-Latif, and Aisha as well?'

'My dear boy, you must understand. I'm your mother, only yours. The others have Khaduj as their mother. She's the one they call "Mother". From now on, don't call her that.'

'What should I call her?'

'Call her... call her... "Aunt", "Auntie", whatever you like, but—'

'I'll call her "Lalla", as you and Dada Fatima do.'

Yasmine let out a sob that surprised Mahmud.

'He's going to call her "Lalla",' she thought to herself, 'as though he were a mere slave like his mother and Fatima. Is that going to be his fate now that his father has started ignoring him and Khaduj is fed up hearing him call her "Mother"?'

She talked to Mahmud again. 'Don't call her "Lalla". It's enough to say...'

She almost said 'Father's Wife', but then she thought, 'That might offend Khaduj and make her yell at him again. Her pride is such that she'll never lower herself so far as to acknowledge that her husband has a child by another woman; not only that, she'll never accept hearing the shocking truth whenever the words "Father's Wife" are used.'

'It's enough just to say "Auntie",' she went on.

'But Dada, I mean Mama, why isn't she my mother when she's mother to all the other children in the house?'

Yasmine became annoyed. 'Because I'm your mother,' she said impatiently. 'I'm your mother! Aren't you happy too that I'm your mother?'

Mahmud could not understand why she was so angry, so he

decided not to argue about it. 'Yes, you're my mother. I understand that now. It's just that—'

'You're still being stubborn. Forget about "it's just that"!'

'Explain to me, Mama. Is my father my father?'

Faced with this invocation of doubt on Mahmud's part, Yasmine's mind was a blur when it came to the truth. She decided to erase any shadow of doubt in Mahmud's mind.

'Listen, my son. Your father is your father – Hajj Muhammad.'

'So, he's my father,' Mahmud mumbled, not understanding, 'and he's Abd al-Rahman's father too. But Abd al-Rahman's mother is not mine?'

Now Aisha surprised them both while they were talking. Mahmud went over to her, hoping to get her to help him understand what Yasmine had been telling him.

'Aren't I your brother, Aisha?' he asked her.

'You? Yes, you're my brother. But you're the one who attacked Abd al-Rahman.'

'He hit me without me even going after him. But never mind. God is forgiving.'

'My mother has forbidden us to play with you again, otherwise—'

'I'll play with Abd al-Latif then,' Mahmud replied.

'He won't play with you either, because our mother has forbidden it.'

'So even you believe that she isn't my mother?'

'You're the servant's boy.'

Here was another blow to rock Mahmud's existence. Yasmine turned away so her tears would not give her away. However, Mahmud was curious, so he questioned Aisha.

'Servant's boy? What do you mean by "servant's boy"?'

'I don't know. But all my brothers say that you're the servant's boy.'

By now Yasmine had dried her tears. 'Don't keep saying those words,' she interrupted. 'Mahmud's your brother. That's enough.'

'But he's not our mother's son.'

'Who told you that, young lady?'

'My mother. And my brother Abd al-Ghani told Abd al-Rahman.'

'Mahmud's my son,' Yasmine yelled as though to defend her own motherhood. 'My son!'

'But you're a dada, and Dada Fatima doesn't have any children.'

'But Dada Yasmine does have children. This is my son. Does that make you happy?'

'So Mahmud is not the servant's son?'

'That's right, I'm not the servant's son,' Mahmud interrupted, directing his words at Aisha. 'My father is your father.'

'That's what Dada says...'

Yasmine grew tired of this conversation, every word of which opened festering wounds in her heart.

'That's enough of this chatter. Can't the two of you find something else to talk about?'

'But Dada, how can Mahmud be our brother when he isn't Mama's son?'

Yasmine lost her temper and decided to clarify the lesson they were not understanding.

'Listen, you two! A man of a certain age, like my master, can have two, three, or even four wives. He can have children with any of them. They're all brothers and sisters through their father, but each one may have a different mother. Do you understand?'

The two of them clearly did not understand. They dropped the whole issue, although Mahmud's young mind was still swirling as he thought about the problem.

9

'Why were you so late yesterday?'

'I've told you a thousand times: don't meddle in my business.'

Thus began a fierce argument between Abd al-Ghani and his brother Abd al-Rahman.

'If you're that late again, I'll complain to your father. Then you'll see how he'll punish you.'

'Sneaking and complaining is all you're good at! Isn't there something else you could be doing?'

'Your tongue needs cutting out. You've started defying even those who are older than you.'

'If you're older than me,' Abd al-Rahman answered angrily, 'then you should have more respect for yourself and stop harassing me.'

'I'm older than you, and it's my job to keep you in line.'

'You're always giving yourself responsibilities that aren't yours. You're my brother, not my father.'

'Your elder brother is like your father. You should do what he says.'

'Do what he says?'

Abd al-Rahman's guffaw was both sarcastic and defiant. Abd al-Ghani could not stand his younger brother's insolence; he saw himself as the eldest brother and the most sensible, thus regarding himself as his father's deputy with regard to all his responsibilities.

Abd al-Rahman made a threatening gesture, and his brother raised both hands as he confronted him. Abd al-Latif, their younger brother, who was watching the squabble with a certain amount of curiosity and sympathy, let out a loud laugh. Whenever one of them threatened the other, he was delighted by the thought that he could be about to witness a major or minor fight. What made him even happier was the idea that Abd al-Rahman was able to demolish the superiority that his eldest brother was claiming for himself, something that he tried to exploit to lord it over his younger brothers.

Abd al-Ghani had inherited his father's domineering personality. Ever since he had been aware, his entire mental outlook had been focused on Hajj Muhammad. Since his early teenage years his father's august demeanour, remarkable piety, and infinite influence had dazzled him, and he looked up in awe at the face of a hero who managed to combine heroism, audacity, and manliness.

That explains why he decided to exert the paternal role in those areas where his own authority might be effective. However, in doing so, he clashed with a stubborn brother, someone who was delighted to pose a challenge.

Abd al-Ghani felt that his sense of honour had been insulted by Abd al-Rahman's scorn, not to mention the obvious malicious pleasure that Abd al-Latif had shown. He was anxious now to re-establish his status and dignity.

'You've turned into a vagrant!' he yelled at Abd al-Rahman. 'I'm going to see how to put an end to this behaviour.'

'You've turned into an old man,' Abd al-Rahman scoffed. 'We're going to see how to bring you back to your youth!'

Abd al-Ghani started yelling even louder, and this attracted Khaduj's attention. She was worried and wanted to know what the argument was about. Bitter experience had taught her that it was yet another disagreement between Abd al-Ghani and Abd al-Rahman.

'Again!' she shouted, totally out of patience. 'You're having another fight, as though you were enemies!'

Abd al-Rahman was keen to dispel any accusation of enmity. 'He's been hounding me again, spying on me, and threatening to betray my secrets.'

'You need to know the reason,' said Abd al-Ghani. 'He was out late last night—'

'I was out with my old friends in Makhfiyya Square.'

'And who gave you permission to mingle with those types?'

While they were arguing like this, Khaduj looked from one to the other.

'I don't need your permission. I'll tell you yet again that you're not my father.'

'And I've told you that I'm just like your father.'

At this point their mother ran out of patience, like a judge when confronted with two opposing parties.

'You're the one causing all the problems!' she yelled at Abd al-Ghani. 'Why do you have to harass him with this police inquiry?'

'That's exactly what I've been saying,' said Abd al-Rahman, interrupting them both. 'He's behaving just like a policeman: "Where have you been? Where have you come from?"'

Khaduj now turned to him, and Abd al-Ghani got the impression that his mother was giving him the opportunity to defend himself.

'I'm not going to leave this reprobate alone,' he yelled.

'Say "reprobate" again,' Abd al-Rahman interrupted, 'and I'll bust your teeth for you!'

Khaduj now realised that there was no end to this argument. She did her best to use her maternal authority to bring the dispute to an end. She ordered them to stop arguing and to stay away from each other.

She decided not to take Abd al-Rahman's side so as not to inflame things even further. Even so, she was extremely unhappy about the kind of personality that Abd al-Ghani was showing; the attitude he was adopting disturbed her greatly.

'He's just a young man,' she told herself. 'Not only that, he's just like his father in the way he dresses, his posture, his gestures, and his interests. As day follows day, his speech sounds more and more like Hajj Muhammad's; the same topics, the same mode of argument, and the same issuing of instructions; and the same nosiness about everything involving personal behaviour, the household, food, and servants. His voice has even started to sound like his father's, as though their vocal cords come from a single nerve.'

Khaduj now turned in order to leave the field of battle.

'Listen, you!' Abd al-Ghani shocked her by saying, 'O she who is leaving—'

This made Khaduj furious. 'Don't I have a name?' she yelled at him as though scorched by a hot coal. 'Aren't I your mother? What's this "you" and "she" all about? Don't you know how to say "Mother"?'

This shocked him, and he said nothing. The only thing on his mind was that his mother was supporting Abd al-Rahman.

He had not realised yet that he was imitating the way his father addressed his mother. He had started saying 'you' and calling her 'she', and hardly ever used 'Mother' or called her by name because Hajj Muhammad did not do so. Like all husbands, he never called his wife by her name; it was not socially acceptable or appropriate, just as it was also wrong for a wife to call her husband by his name. To do so would arouse the amazement and disgust of the entire community. 'You', 'he', and 'she' implied husband and wife whenever he was talking about her or she about him.

Abd al-Ghani had no intention of insulting his mother or degrading her status. He was simply using Hajj Muhammad's mindset, talking like him, and adopting the same internal logic. For that reason his mother's remarks surprised him. He tried to rescue the situation by saying, 'My father says "you" when addressing you and calls you "she" when talking about you. Why don't you get mad with him too?'

Abd al-Ghani's stubborn attitude made Khaduj even more furious. 'So here's a little boy,' she went on, 'whose clothes, stride, and mode of talking now turns him into a man of his father's age!'

Abd al-Rahman and Abd al-Latif both had to suppress their giggles, but a dagger-look from Khaduj had them both raising their hands to their mouths to throttle the laughter in its cradle.

'Wake up,' she told Abd al-Ghani, to conclude what she wanted to say. 'Try to imitate your colleagues and take a look at young men like yourself. I refuse to hear you say "you" or "she" to me ever again. You call me "Mother", and you should be proud of it!'

Khaduj now withdrew, but she had managed to open a window

for Abd al-Ghani on to a different world. He had been following in his father's footsteps unconsciously, but now he had clashed with his mother, whom he loved just as much as he did his father. He had thought that she approved of his behaviour, but now she had opened his mind to new vistas with regard to his peers – new thoughts about the way he walked, dressed, and talked, and the kind of things that he thought about and that interested him.

'My father never talks to me about such things,' he told himself, 'when he takes me to the mosque, or to the homilies in the Qarawiyin complex and Mawlay Idris.'

In his mind's eye he saw Abd al-Ghaffar and Mawlay Abd al-Tawwab as they repeated the homiletic lessons at the shrine of Mawlay Idris and the Qarawiyin Mosque. The words of the homilist rang in his ears, aspiring to heaven and avoiding hellfire.

'My mother's an ignorant woman,' he told himself. 'If she saw Sidi Abd al-Ghaffar and Mawlay Abd al-Tawwab, she would not be so disapproving of my clothes, my walk, and my mode of talking.'

Hajj Muhammad had been thinking about his sons' futures. Because Abd al-Ghani was the eldest, Hajj Muhammad had been planning a future for him that closely mirrored his own ideas. It simply involved a clothing shop that would guarantee the continuity of a profession that the Tihami family had inherited for generations, from grandfather to father to son.

Until it was time for the first stage on this long road, Abd al-Ghani had had no job, since he had grown too old to stay with the other children at the Qur'an school run by the jurist from the south. This was why he was always so keen to fill his time by following all the activities of the household, the family, and his brothers. But now the day had come when he had clashed with his own mother. She had opened his eyes to the fact that he was now a young man, like other boys his age. Her very words kept toying with his feelings. They were knocking on the door of a closed soul, one that had never launched itself into the welcoming world whose adventures his mother had now shaken him into exploring.

10

Abd al-Rahman had found himself in Makhfiyya Square without knowing how he got there, or how it was that he had acquired this group of companions that formed one of the many circles in the wide space. The feeling he had, however, was that in this square he was discovering his own heart and mind. After returning from the Qur'an school he would spend some time in the square; for him it would be the happiest time and the one with the most physical and mental activity. No such consolations could be found inside the house, because any activity involving the children disturbed the adults. Life in the house was subject to very strict regulations; the children had no choice but to go along with them. The absolute authority with which Hajj Muhammad imposed these rules brooked no opposition or contravention of his instructions.

Abd al-Rahman found no consolation at the Qur'an school either, because the jurist from the south functioned by terrorising the children. No sooner did one of them even make an attempt to sniff freedom on the breeze than he would be ordered to raise his legs high in the air to receive the bastinado on his feet with a quince cane. The miscreant would then return to the reality of his terrified fellow students.

For Abd al-Rahman and his colleagues and friends, Makhfiyya Square represented a world of freedom; they could talk unobserved and raise their voices in such a way that the echo coming back would not take the form of a threat or a warning. They could laugh out loud and not simply smile, and the walls around the square would echo their laughter without the inevitable 'Shut up. Don't be so shameless!'

When Abd al-Rahman was with his group in the square, he would only ever see Abd al-Ghani walking by in the distance. News of his elder brother's presence would come in the form of a warning, which would make him hide in a doorway or the bend of an alleyway until Abd al-Ghani had disappeared. Then Abd al-Rahman would reappear and join his friends' circle once again.

They would talk about everything their senses encountered: each person's experiences were a subject of intense debate. The Qur'an school was a rich topic for tales, stories, discussions, and analysis of the personalities of the jurists and the pupils. Then there were things like fights with brothers, fear of fathers and mothers (this being a topic where the child's genius and various tricks would emerge), anecdotes about shopkeepers and their customers, and people living in the quarter, each of whom had his own spot when it came to chatting with the group of children from outside the quarter whenever they happened to pass by.

Many members of the group were particularly good at withering criticism, subjecting the Qur'an-school teacher to their analysis and harsh opinions, which prompted sarcasm and admiration at the same time. The best of them was Muhammad Two-Heads, who always felt inferior because his head was so big and elongated, though his inferiority was not reflected in any sense of frustration, fear of society, or psychological withdrawal. To the contrary, he made use of its scope for provocation and acclaim. His head was a site for experiment, exploiting the powerful feelings that distinguished him. Every day he would make up stories and fables about his enormous head, stories that made them laugh but at the same time admire him, endearing himself to his friends and turning his huge head into an object of pride, not inferiority.

Muhammad's head was the key that opened up discussions about other people. No sooner had he finished one of his Two-Heads tales than he would move on to subject passers-by, male and female – people from the quarter whom he did not know – to description, analysis, and sarcastic comment. Once finished with them, he would then talk about the quarter's grandees, people who had earned the respect of everyone in the quarter. Hajj Muhammad al-Tihami was not exempt from this: his name would invoke a storm of laughter when there was talk about his piety, severity, seriousness – which scared the quarter's children – and the traditional smiles he would bestow on the shopkeepers and local grandees whom he met during his comings and goings.

Whenever Abd al-Rahman joined this group, he too laughed heartily at Two-Heads when he imitated the Qur'an-school teacher yelling at the children in the school, or when he poked fun at the halva-seller by the arcade. He would pay with a *mawzuna* coin, and the man would think it was a sou, worth more; Abd al-Rahman would then take an extra portion. He would laugh as well when Two-Heads dealt with Si Abdallah, the mosque imam, or Hajj Muhammad al-Tihami, Abd al-Rahman's father.

He laughed out loud when his companions looked to see how this sarcasm aimed at his own father was affecting him, and he could not stop himself laughing, so his companions got the impression that it did not bother him. But as soon as the group broke up and he turned to go home, he realised how serious the things that Two-Heads had been saying were.

'How bad am I for not objecting to Two-Heads' comments about my father?' he asked himself. 'He's a cheeky boy, there's no doubt about that. He talks about the schoolteacher, the mosque imam, and my father the same way he talks about the halva-seller who falls for his tricks. He's self-deprecating about himself and his big head, so there's nothing wrong if he rattles on about this person or that. But what about my own father? Is it right for him to be so critical? He goes too far. My father's not like other people!'

This train of thought came to an end when he reached the house and encountered Abd al-Ghani's vicious glances, which no longer bothered him. What really mattered was that Hajj Muhammad had not yet returned to the house; all that worried him now was his father's punishments and his mother's anger.

In the Makhfiyya Quarter Abd al-Rahman had come to hear about the experiences of Abd al-Qadir al-Rahmuni, whose father had transferred him from the Qur'an school to the secular academy.

'Secular academy?' was the unified cry from all the children.

'That's right, the secular academy.'

'What does that mean, "secular academy"?'

'Is the teacher in charge like the one at the Qur'an school?'

'Are the pupils' slates bigger than the ones we have?'

'Does the teacher beat you with a whip or a cane?'

'Are the pupils children or adolescents?'

'Do you have to sit on mats like us?'

The questions flew from all directions. Abd al-Qadir realised that he was now a recognised entity among his comrades. The fact that he was different gave him some power over them.

He gave himself free rein as he told them about the secular academy. The good things that he described opened their young minds to a new realm. As Abd al-Qadir told them about the school, he used unfamiliar words: teacher, class, blackboard, notebook. He pronounced French words that aroused both admiration and shock. But above all he filled these children's imaginations with a strange new world.

'By "teacher" you mean the jurist, right?' Abd al-Rahman shouted.

'No, no! Are we still talking about Qur'an school?'

'So what does "teacher" mean?'

'The teacher's a young Christian. He's clean-shaven and wears nothing on his head. He has a nice suit and shiny shoes. He stands up and teaches us all the time. He asks us questions, and we answer. He talks to us about new things, things we've never heard about before.'

'Does this Christian teacher instruct you on the Qur'an and its suras?'

Abd al-Qadir was clearly fed up with answering these questions. 'You don't understand,' he yelled at Abd al-Rahman haughtily. 'If you're so keen to find out, go and ask your father to transfer you to the secular academy.'

Abd al-Rahman's mind wandered away from the rest of the group. 'Ask my father to transfer me to the secular academy?!' he thought. 'If the southern jurist at our Qur'an school heard that, he'd bash me on the head or cuff me on the neck. And what if my father heard it? Or even worse, Abd al-Ghani. This school that Abd al-Qadir describes sounds really great! But a Christian teacher?! No, no! I can't recite to a Christian teacher. What can the Christian teach me? My father would certainly not exchange the jurist for a Christian. That's out of the question.'

Abd al-Rahman's attention now went back to the children surrounding Abd al-Qadir, and he found himself listening to a question being asked by another child who seemed very interested. 'Is there a Qur'anic jurist at the school?'

'The jurist comes once the teacher's lessons are over,' Abd al-Qadir replied, 'and in the early morning too. But he only recites for a short while, then leaves.'

'What about beatings and the bastinado?'

'There's none of that, but we're still scared of the Christian.'

That gave Two-Heads his cue. 'The jurist himself is scared of the Christian!'

This provoked a gale of laughter. Everyone looked at him to hear the rest of the story.

'Last Tuesday the jurist arrived late. The Christian subjected his feet to the bastinado!'

There was another gale of laughter, which bothered another group of young and older men in another corner of the small square. 'Watch yourselves!' came the warning from one of them.

The children now turned back to Abd al-Qadir, asking for more information.

But just then Abd al-Rahman realised someone was shaking his shoulder firmly, and a friend was whispering in his ear, 'Watch out! Take care! Hajj Muhammad's on his way here! Run, and fast!'

Abd al-Rahman took off, not stopping until he reached the house, with Abd al-Qadir's words still ringing in his ears. 'Ask your father to transfer you to the secular academy, ask your father to transfer you to the secular academy...'

11

Springtime in Fez was no ordinary season to be welcomed by the city like all the other seasons. The inhabitants of Fez celebrated the arrival of spring like no other season of the year. Winter would force them to keep themselves warm, and they would need to stock up on provisions for the weeks or even months during which the entire city would be beset by mud and pouring rain; they would hole up inside their homes. Spring on the other hand invited them all to let loose and liberate themselves from the material and psychological siege that winter had imposed.

The first breezes of spring would start to blow, and with them would blow freedom and a desire for liberty. As you walked along the city's narrow alleys, you could sense the scent of freedom radiating from its sleeves. It was not simply that you could feel its perfume filling your nose; you could actually see it in people's unfrowning expressions, in eyes bursting with joy, and in tempers that now reflected a sense of satisfaction. Now people were in a better mood and so did not lose their temper for the most trifling reason, nor did the alleys fill with disputes and arguments which would bounce off the high walls and involve anyone who happened to pass by.

You would feel it too in the sunshine which would slink with its soft, brilliant, and illuminating light into the city's alleyways and narrow streets, and give the decaying walls a pearly light. It would make its way through the cracks in closed windows and into apertures that would project light into salons and corner rooms. This fresh glow was the gift of heaven's freedom to an earth in chains – spring's great victory over a bitter winter that had finally disappeared in defeat.

The advent of spring in the alleys and streets of Fez was capped by the arrival of crowds of villagers and Bedouin, who would bring with them the season's harbingers: pitchers of milk with curds of fresh cream floating in them. They would arrive on their donkeys and mules, which had themselves regained their energy after the bitter cold of winter; they would re-establish ties that had been almost severed by the long winter months, ties linking them with landowners, sharecroppers, and herders. The rural visitors would invite the city landowners to come out and visit their properties and rejoice in the first signs of the barley, wheat, and corn crops. The landowners might spend days or weeks strolling around, relaxing and enjoying themselves; at the same time it gave children, women, and servants the opportunity to spend their annual vacations in the open air, once a year leaving behind the walls of their houses and the lofty boundaries of the city.

The month of April witnessed preparations for families to move out to their country estates. Such preparations were always visible in the more prosperous neighbourhoods of Fez. Mules and donkeys would leave the city for the desert regions loaded down with lighter items of household furniture, tents, cooking utensils, tea, and food. Should an overloaded donkey or mule come to an alley that it could not pass through, the only way anyone could pass would be by adopting a posture close to full prostration and crawling between the animal's legs; either that, or else bending down and making their way under the bags on either side, making sure not to unbalance things or bump their head into the pans and cooking utensils packed inside.

In springtime Makhfiyya was one of the most active prosperous quarters. Most of its inhabitants were connected to the land and owned fields and small or large estates outside the city. So, when spring arrived each year, the quarter would bustle with desert people moving to and fro, while in summer and winter mules and donkeys would be seen carrying wheat, barley, and olives – the products of their fields – back to the city.

Hajj Muhammad al-Tihami owned a large estate in Awlad Jamia, most of which he had inherited and to which he had added a number of hectares purchased from local inhabitants. They would ask to borrow money from him. He would make the loan, even when it totally swallowed up the value of the parcel of land he had used as part of a debt-repayment deal. They would agree to the plan, despite being reluctant and far from happy about it. Even so, they would continue to stay at the estate, ploughing the land as sharecroppers for Hajj Muhammad's benefit. He was happy with these labourers, since they continued working hard as though the land still belonged to them, while they were content with the way he treated them with a degree of generosity, as though he were still their neighbour.

As Hajj Muhammad moved out to the estate, he was eager to see the first positive signs of the annual harvest in the form of the ripening green stalks that covered the extensive spread of fields. Ewes, lambs, and cows wandered hither and thither, they too being delighted by the advent of spring. Hajj Muhammad brought the entire family with him; it was their right to relax and enjoy themselves, to leave behind the high walls of the Fez house once a year, and to be able to ride mules and donkeys as they set off for hills and valleys bursting with greenery and fresh air. They would spend days in the arms of nature, burying life's boredoms in the fields and compensating for the strictly limited horizons of the Fez mansion with a limitless world of freedom, air, sun, and light.

Hajj Muhammad would enjoy morning tours organised by the chief farmers on the estate. He would ride on a saddled mule; every morning he would visit a different segment of his vast kingdom. The area in question would never be all that far from the estate buildings, but he still preferred to ride and to be surrounded by the farming supervisors, the majority of them either former landowners or their sons. They would cluster protectively around his mule, walking either in front or behind as though he were some Persian or Byzantine sovereign. The farmers were very happy to provide this kind of entourage for Hajj Muhammad, since he only visited them once a year. It was obviously better for them if he went back to the city feeling content with their work, relaxed, satisfied, and confident in their honesty. It pleased him too to see them behaving like obedient servants and submissive beneficiaries in the presence of their benefactor, but he never displayed any imperious authority or arrogance; he simply did the rounds with them, riding a mule while they walked on foot. He talked to them as friends and asked them questions about farming, the nature of the soil, and future production – delighting in their positive responses. Even though he knew the answers already, he would question them about the borders of his property. Once he was sure of their answers, he would put on a fake air of curiosity in order to hear one or other farmer state in no uncertain terms that in this region his own property had no equal among all the wealthy inhabitants of Fez. He liked to argue with them about it.

'Does Hajj Abd al-Wafi own more than I do?'

'Certainly not, Hajj! Your land is bigger, more fertile, and richer.'

'Don't you know that he's bought a new estate from Muhammad ibn al-Hajj?'

'The estate that Hajj Abd al-Wafi has bought,' came the sarcastic response, accompanied by some laughter, 'was offered to you dirt cheap. We refused to buy it!'

'You're the one who owns the real gold, Hajj!'

'How can we compare land that's fertile, productive, and blessed with land that's stony and gets flooded and dried out?'

Hajj Muhammad beamed as he realised the extent to which the farmers were doing their best to please him, to the point of playing fast and loose with reality – he preferred it that way, so that he could reassure himself of reality as he wished it to be rather than confronting some other reality that was actually the case. They in turn were happy to see how satisfied he was, and their leader went even further. By now, the group had reached the edge of the property, and he could feel a sense of pride in the midst of this flourishing field.

'This land has a great future, sir,' the head farmer said. 'Wheat will be wheat, and barley barley.'

This made Hajj Muhammad feel proud; he was delighted by what he was hearing. The farmers were sitting all around him, staring at the face of their benefactor. But his response revealed some of his hidden concerns.

'Only if you can be loyal to me. The blessings disappear if there's no more than a minimal level of honesty.'

Hajj Muhammad's implicit accusation did not come as a surprise; they were used to hearing it, and he was equally used to hearing their defence. The link between accusation and defence was shrouded in a certain obscurity, the exact nature of which none of them dared to probe. The chief farmer's frigid response came with something close to insouciance.

'Your food would betray us as well, sir, if we were behaving that way to you.'

'If we weren't to be trusted,' another man burst in, 'the land would not have produced the kind of harvest that it did last year.'

'Decent folk don't renege on the blessings they receive!'

Hajj Muhammad allowed himself a smile. He told himself that he did not believe these claims of loyalty and trustworthiness. He did not trust them completely, believing that if they did not steal from him they would not be able to survive. Even so, he realised that he could not keep his land working without these men. Even if they stole things, they were still reliable.

'Everything I own,' he told himself, 'is part of their work; ownership of land has moved from them to me, from their ancestors to mine. They continue to serve it with the same feelings as they had when they were the owners.'

Hajj Muhammad laughed at them. 'Well, Qadur,' he said to their chief, 'so you've married again. Isn't that because of the profit you made off the land this past year?'

Qadur's mouth broadened into a huge smile, which gave an extra brush of masculine beauty to his tawny face, full of youthful vigour. 'How can we do better than you yourself, sir?' he responded with complete self-confidence.

'But why did you marry again, when Fatina is the mother of your children and has gone through a great deal in life with you, both hardships and good times?'

Qadur's shrewd, gleaming eyes now assumed a somewhat bashful expression. 'We're Bedouin, Hajj, sir,' he said, turning away. 'We suffer a lot, and Fatina...'

He paused for a moment, but Hajj Muhammad gave him a friendly smile to encourage him to finish his thought.

'Fatina takes care of the tent and the children. She collects water and firewood and sometimes works in the fields as well. Morning and evening she milks the cows—'

'And so,' Hajj Muhammad finished the sentence for him with a laugh, 'you've brought in Rahma to help her!'

The farmers surrounding the Hajj laughed gently. They all looked happily at Qadur, who was in fact delighted by Hajj Muhammad's interest and concern, which had made him the primary topic of this session with their landowner.

As noon arrived the sun became hotter, reminding Hajj Muhammad that he needed to go back to the house, situated in the middle of this fortunate estate.

12

Hajj Muhammad went back to find Qadur's womenfolk gathered in the shade of a huge vine, along with the wives and daughters of the other farmers. They were eating yoghurt and listening eagerly to stories from the Bedouin women.

When they spotted Hajj Muhammad approaching alone on his saddled mule the women jumped up in horror; Qadur and his colleagues had taken a different way to go back to their tents, which were pitched far from the old house, so that they would not be able to set eyes on any women of the household.

As the women leapt to their feet, they disturbed the recently hatched chicks all around, which were constantly chirping in sheer delight at the advent of spring, pecking at seeds, pulling up grass, and busily running hither and thither.

Hajj Muhammad made no effort to be especially sociable; he merely stopped for a while by the gathering under the heavily laden, leafy vine. The women and girls were so shy that it almost amounted to fear. They started kissing his hand, touching his saddle with their fingertips, raising them bashfully to their mouths as a sign of blessing. Hajj Muhammad did not miss the opportunity to throw questions at Fatina, Qadur's wife; he asked about her companions' names and their jobs, and she duly responded with all necessary modesty.

Fatina was not only the wife of the estate's supervisor, she herself was also the supervisor of part of it: she had her responsibilities, just as her husband, Qadur, bore the responsibility for the major portion of the farming work. Fatina was in charge of the sheep, cows, mules, and domestic animals – matters of shepherding, pasturage, production, and milking. This occasion gave Hajj Muhammad the opportunity to ask her about the cattle and other animals he owned, just as he had asked her husband about his landholdings and their produce.

Fatina was able to respond to his questions in a knowledgeable fashion, in line with her experience and responsibilities. His questions involved a certain amount of normal enquiry, but also scepticism and outright doubt. He did not believe the information that Fatina was giving him about his cattle, just as he had not believed what Qadur had been telling him about the land and crop production. His tone of voice made no attempt to conceal his concerns, and so Fatina opened her responses with oaths such as 'may God let my burnous-clad master make me crawl' or 'may God deprive me of my children'. This kind of oath may not have made Hajj Muhammad feel any more confident, but it did make him feel proud as he listened to a detailed estimate of one aspect of his possessions from the mouth of a farming woman who was responsible for part of his property.

As he listened to Fatina swearing her oaths, Hajj Muhammad realised that there was no way of disbelieving her or calling her to account. He knew that he had property, and a lot of it. Time and the stewardship of the farmers would suffice to expand his properties, the only way to increase both land and cattle production. Even so, he was happy and satisfied; he had no fears, since his ownership of land guaranteed him considerable wealth. He had no desire for anything more, because his concept of riches had its own boundaries, ones that he might already have reached.

As Hajj Muhammad talked to Fatina, encircled as he was by subservient Bedouin women, he kept comparing her with his wife, Khaduj. He could not avoid facing up to an idea that kept occurring to him. Here was Fatina, a useful and capable woman who could look after his land and produce, while being the wife of a farmer and mother of his children; Khaduj on the other hand was mother of his children, mistress of the household, and that was it.

These Bedouin women, modest and timid as they stood there

submissively, stimulated the man with the bearing of a hunter in the forest as he bestrode his splendid mule. While he listened to Fatina's answers, he was distracted and kept staring at one Bedouin girl or another. Their fresh appearance and beautiful bronze complexion was a source of delight, as was the blooming good health that showed in their rosy cheeks, black eyes, and bushy eyebrows. What he especially admired about them was their freedom from excessive dress and the constraints of wearing head-coverings and veils.

'How would it be,' he thought to himself as he avidly surveyed them, 'if I had one of these women as a wife to rejuvenate me and share her sprightly vigour, her rosy complexion, and her energy with me? City women simply don't have this youthful health and energy. Their pale faces freeze your body and make you want to be sick… But these women are all Bedouin! What would people say about me if I married a Bedouin woman and made her a co-wife of Khaduj? My standing certainly wouldn't allow such a thing; society doesn't condone it. They would boast about being my in-laws. What would these farmers who tend my lands think if I asked to marry one of their women? Yes, they would boast about being my in-laws, and I would become a farmer with a farmer's wife. They might impinge upon my status; my land might be at risk. Marrying a Bedouin woman would make me a Bedouin myself. Assaults on my lands and cattle would become that much easier, because these Bedouin have been doing it already. The respect they feel for me is safe and sound as long as I maintain a distance from them. And then there's Yasmine. No, no! Yasmine's not a wife, she's a concubine. Having a Bedouin woman as a concubine is allowed, but people won't allow her to be a wife; society won't accept it.'

While these contradictory thoughts were swirling in his head, Hajj Muhammad's imagination took flight, but it was the commanding voice of Khaduj that finally brought him back to earth. She had been following his conversation with Fatina and had a good idea as to what his imagination was telling him as he looked at the Bedouin women.

'Get off the mule,' she told him. 'Dismount, so it can feed.'

As he prepared to do so, Bedouin girls raced each other to grab hold of one of the stirrups so the saddle's balance would not be disrupted when he lowered his bulky frame to the ground. As he bent over to get down, his face almost touched that of the young girl who had won the race to grab the stirrup. The smell of her filled his nostrils, and he could almost hear her heartbeats pounding from the effort she was making to hold the stirrup; it had almost got away from her, since Hajj Muhammad had put all his weight on the other one. At the crucial moment he remembered that Khaduj was watching him like a hawk, so he dismounted and turned his face towards the house as though completely unaware of everything around him.

Khaduj hurried after him to tell him about her plans for dinner, but he was in no mood to listen to any talk about food or household matters. She brought him back to reality by telling him about the gifts that the Bedouin women had brought.

'Muhammad Tawil's wife brought us two chickens,' she told him. 'They're small but plump. Yumna, Ali's wife, brought us some milk—'

'With the cream on top?'

'I'm not sure, but it looks like it. Al-Burnousiyya brought us a bagful of eggs.'

Khaduj was now alone with her husband. The scene she had witnessed when he was chatting with the Bedouin women made her prefer to be alone with him. By now she was more familiar with his personality than he was himself, and knew best how to handle his whims. Even so, she felt laden down by a piece of news that she felt she had to convey to Hajj Muhammad. It made her anxious for her husband and herself, and for the time that the family was spending on holiday in the countryside. Would she have to tell him this thing that was weighing her down and making her miserable? As she talked to him about things of trifling importance, she told herself he would blow up, go into a towering rage, and punish the offender.

'If that's the case,' she wondered, 'can I still keep it all a secret? He's just a young boy, of an age when silly mistakes can be forgiven.'

As she sat there in Hajj Muhammad's presence, she lived a dreadful moment as she rehearsed in her mind the scene she had witnessed. In a derelict and deserted part of the house she had surprised Abd al-Ghani in the act of hugging Tamu, Qadur's daughter, as she struggled to escape his clutches. If the shock was bad enough for Abd al-Ghani, it was much worse and more damaging for the young girl, who had no idea how to resist the strength of the son of the estate's owner and master of its inhabitants. The expression on her face showed the true extent of the disaster that had now befallen her as soon as Abd al-Ghani had enticed her to this deserted spot, but the scandal of her discovery in Abd al-Ghani's arms was a mercy, since it had rescued her from an even more disastrous calamity.

The young girl had lowered her head in shame and departed, bearing on her young shoulders the heavy burden of a dangerous crime in which she had played no part. Abd al-Ghani also departed, but Khaduj did not allow him to escape her curses, rebukes, and threats. The whole thing weighed heavily on her, and she thought seriously about unloading it on to Hajj Muhammad. But what scared her was the idea that a relatively trivial event might turn into a major problem, or even a full-scale disaster.

Hajj Muhammad noticed how distraught and unhappy she was looking, and only one idea came to him. Pulling her toward him, he proceeded to exploit the fact that they were alone together. This made Khaduj forget all about Abd al-Ghani's escapade with Tamu.

13

The sun was beginning to go down as Qadur returned to his family from work. His life was one of routine in the meadow, in the middle of which his tent was pitched alongside the flocks of ewes, lambs, and cows. They would return to the meadow after spending a cold winter's day, or hot summer's day, being tended by children and young men who devoted their lives to grazing animals and managed to derive some pleasure from their miserable existence among the livestock and the dogs. They formed friendships with other young people, and they all tended the animals with affection, sharing the duties through the scorching heat, bitter cold, pouring rain, and blistering sun – a life of isolation amid the lush grassland.

Qadur was always anxious to be in the paddock when the animals returned. He had full confidence in Fatina and knew she was quite able to welcome the sheep and cows back, prepare their fodder for them, and milk those cows that needed it. Even so, he preferred being there, particularly during springtime, to welcome a new arrival or to make sure that the animals were all safe and sound after their daily trek. He also wanted to hear reports from shepherds about the day's events – trivial things most of the time, to be sure, but that was life for the shepherds and for some of the farmers as well.

When Qadur pulled back the tent flap, it was to find Fatina sitting in her usual place, with a bowl between her thighs in which she was rolling the couscous to serve for their dinner with Hajj Muhammad's family members. She was an expert at the operation and did it quickly and perfectly; she was well aware of the value of fresh couscous when it is offered for a family dinner. Urban folk are particularly fond of it when it is made and cooked by Bedouin.

As Qadur waited for the flocks to return, he sat there discussing the day's events with Fatina. The only fresh thing to talk about was the life of their guest family, in their house and in the fields – their short trips into the fields and visits to the spring, the ladies riding donkeys and mules, the children admiring the chickens and lambs, the women in particular all wanting to eat yoghurt and crusty bread spread with fresh butter.

The family from Fez found the Bedouin a source of both entertainment and a good deal of unfamiliarity – something that made them not only curious but also often mocking and even scornful. When the Fez family was at the estate, the normal routine of the Bedouin was disrupted, and things became more serious and unusual. The situation provided Qadur and Fatina with unusual topics for conversation, which took them away from the usual subjects of fields, cows, and markets.

At first the ideas of the city folk, men and women alike, seemed naive, trivial, and ignorant. To a man of over fifty like Hajj Muhammad and a woman approaching forty like Khaduj, everything was peculiar. The people from the city seemed scared of everything, things that the Bedouin could not imagine frightening anyone. What made Fatina laugh more than anything was that everyone in the Fez family was scared of the dark, imagining that a fierce wild beast would pounce on whomever it set eyes on. Whenever the wind blew out a candle in a room, there would be a loud scream as though the entire family were in imminent danger. Fatina was amazed that members of the family, both young and old, were incapable of walking anywhere in the dark, as though nature had only ever created light. She talked about the way that Khaduj and even Yasmine – who had first smiled in such fields – and all the children were so amazed that the farmers would sit in the dark and have wonderful evening gatherings in the open air, with no light save the twinkling stars in the heavenly vault. It was topics like these that formed the bulk of conversation in the Bedouin family circle, often provoking its own level of mockery and scorn.

But on this particular occasion Qadur had another topic to talk about, something that had emerged from his discussion with Hajj Muhammad.

'What do you think,' he asked Fatina, 'of a man who's intent on lowering our share of wheat production this year?'

As Qadur uttered these words, he was staring off into the distance, at the fields of wheat stretching endlessly away.

Fatina stopped kneading the couscous and gave her husband a curious, disapproving look. 'He's doing it to us again, again?! It's your fault! Every time you show him how reliable you are and how much trouble you take in tending the fields and the animals, it only makes him even more eager to stint us.'

'He's just like a little babe. Every time the subject of land production comes up, he assumes we're all thieves stealing his money and grabbing his harvest for ourselves.'

'How much would this land produce if it weren't for you, Muhammad al-Tawil, and Isa ibn al-Hajj's son?' She guffawed. 'So let him plough it for himself! Suggest to the Hajj that he take care of his own land so we won't steal it all. He can tend his flocks of sheep and cattle too, then we won't be drinking their milk or selling off their young, as he imagines.'

Her mention of 'his own land' stirred up a secret anger in Qadur's mind; he frowned as though avoiding burning embers. He had been resting his head on his arms, but now he sat up straight. '"His own land"!' he yelled. '"His own land"! I can barely say the words. I know full well whose land it really is...'

Fatina was busy with the couscous grains, turning them with her hands on a plate made from doum leaves. 'Whose land is it?' she asked, knowing the answer full well. She went on to ask another question that was bound to provoke a response from Qadur, 'You mean Hajj Muhammad's land left to him by his parents and ancestors?'

Qadur gave a grunt of total denial. 'God have mercy on my father and uncle!' he sighed. 'They both told us about the land and how they'd lost it.'

'You mean they sold it?' she asked, again knowing the right answer.

'Yes, the way a slave's sold to his master.'

'The way a slave's sold to his master!' Fatina commented with a laugh, making Qadur even angrier. 'The master can perfectly well sell that same slave. He's a slave. What the master owns is his property.'

She had achieved her goal, since Qadur was now furious. 'Master and slave!' he yelled. 'The curse that's been afflicting city folk has now started affecting us in the countryside.'

'Don't we have servants and slaves here, just like Fez?'

'You don't even realise. You may be a servant, and I may be a slave. Neither of us has to change our colour!'

'You mean you can be sold in the market, just like my uncle, Fatih?'

'Certainly, and there's no need of a market either.'

Fatina turned toward Qadur as she tipped the tray and scraped off the residual couscous. 'You sound crazy today,' she said. 'I don't understand what you're talking about.'

Qadur scoffed loudly. 'Just imagine,' he said, 'that you borrowed money from Aisha, Ali's daughter, so you could buy some lambs. Then they all died. How would you settle your debts?'

'But why would I go into debt only for all the lambs to die?'

'Just imagine it. Use your imagination.'

'How would I settle the debts, you ask? I'd give you all my brace-lets and necklaces, and entrust the whole thing to God.'

'Well, that's exactly what happened to my father and uncle.'

'Did they have bracelets and necklaces?'

'No, no. What they had was land. They borrowed from Hajj Muhammad's father, and it seems that he gave them a very generous loan. But then, they fell into so much debt that, when the amount they owed was equivalent to the value of their land, the only thing they could do was to hand it all over bit by bit till it was all Hajj Muhammad's property.'

This sequence of events came as a shock to Fatina; she had never expected to hear it all explained in such logical and simple terms. She stopped her work and stared off anxiously across the lands that stretched into the far distance. The sad expression on her face was her only reaction.

She turned toward Qadur again, in time to hear him say, 'With all that in mind, can Hajj Muhammad really say "my lands"?' When she did not comment, he went on. 'These lands – my father's and grandfather's lands, Muhammad al-Tawil's father's and grandfather's lands, Isa ibn al-Hajj's son's, and Ali al-Tahira's son's as well. Those people,' – he pointed towards the house occupied by Hajj Muhammad – 'they're interlopers! They stole our lands!' He was yelling, becoming even more upset. 'They used small change, which the more gullible among us thought was a lot of money, but actually it was money forbidden by our religion, since the wind simply blew it all away just as it blows away bits of straw.'

Fatina felt sorry for him and did not argue. She simply let him vent his own grievances.

'Just before he died,' Qadur added, 'my late father made me promise never to go into debt.'

'Too late?'

'Yes, too late. But I'm never going to go into debt. And I'm going to get it all back, so I don't have to stay a slave to be bartered over in the slave market.'

Now Fatina tried to calm him down. 'Don't say things like that,' she replied sympathetically. 'You're still working on your own land.'

'My own land! Oh yes, it's my own land! But Hajj Muhammad can throw us off it – me, you, and our children. He can lower my wages and my share in the profits.'

'No, no, don't go on like that.'

He ignored her warning. 'And he can accuse me of theft, and make insinuating remarks about my reliability and incorruptibility.'

'But the wind blows away that kind of remark.'

'Maybe so, but it comes from a deeply flawed heart. If Hajj Muhammad could do it, he wouldn't leave any of us on his land – "*his* land"! When this land is liberated and returned to us,' he added with a sneer, 'we'll have a big celebration!'

Fatina followed Qadur's remarks by saying, 'Now the Christians are treating them the same way they dealt with your father and your livelihood.'

'The Christians! Oh, good grief! He'll take all the land for himself. He may even throw us off it as though we were the ones who originally stole it!'

'Don't panic! The way you keep raving about this will only bring us bad luck. It's the kind of talk that you don't want Muhammad al-Tawil to hear. If any of them heard it, it would be in Hajj Muhammad's ear before we even knew it. The status you enjoy with him makes them all jealous. Any one of them could easily become your boss!'

From far off the sound of sheep bleating could be heard with the sheepdogs running happily around, all of which announced the return of the flocks. Qadur could also hear the young shepherds yelling eagerly at the sheep as they herded them towards their pens.

As the procession made its way back, Qadur's features relaxed, and he set off running along the track that the flocks would be taking, forgetting his discussion with Fatina, while she carried her bowl over to the stove.

14

Summer beset the city of Fez; the narrow, damp alleys felt its full impact. The city was besieged by heat and folded in on itself. In summer the people of Fez shunned their dark, heavy jallabas, their kaftans weighted down with silk threads, their fibre or wool burnouses, and their head-covers wrapped in hefty turbans. Instead, they wore lightweight jallabas and burnouses in bright colours. But there was no escape from the intense heat. Most of them knew only the city in which they had been born or had spent most of their lives. Their only hope was to die inside its walls. Most of them were acquainted only with the parts of the city inside its walls; indeed, they knew only the quarter where their family had resided for decades. It was as if they had taken root in that very quarter along with its dilapidated walls, its lofty entryways, and its low roofs from which flimsy spiderwebs hung down, musty and dark.

This is why most inhabitants of the ancient city could not break out of the vicious siege that summer imposed on them. There was no way to get out of the city in the steaming-hot summer; even people who owned lands in the countryside hunkered down and avoided the heat in the shade of the crumbling old city.

Children felt the summer restrictions more than adults, forced as they were to spend the long, hot days crammed inside the walls of the Qur'an school, all squeezed in like lambs in a tiny pen – although, unlike lambs, they could not even express their frustration and resistance by bleating. The Qur'an school was a prison in which both prisoners and guards had to suffer. The Qur'an teacher could not allow a refreshing breeze of freedom and relaxation to blow its way into the school, nor could he let them all go at noon when it was hottest. He was to serve as the ever-faithful custodian of the children in the narrow school space crowded with pupils, where the intense heat got on their nerves, made them all perspire, and turned their young minds both lazy and apathetic. They would nod off and nap. Their tiny heads would fall over the heavy writing-slates, but a vicious blow from the teacher's cane, on the head, face, or back, would wake them up with a start. In such a dangerous situation they would all be permanently on edge, torn between the urgent need to sleep and terror at the thought of the long, punishing cane which could reach any of them wherever they were sitting and however hard they might try to hide behind another pupil's back.

Of course, the merciless heat that affected them all did not exempt the jurist either. However hard he tried to resist, it wore him down too; he would do his best to avoid falling asleep by shouting at the children, 'Read your slates!' or 'You, recite...!'

He continued shouting out these instructions even though the children had no idea what they were chanting; was it genuine recitation, or merely a facsimile of it? When he felt himself dropping off to sleep, the jurist would resort to a mechanical gesture to ward it off by lashing out at one of the children with his cane. This would create a noise throughout the schoolroom which he believed would immediately wake them all up with a jolt. But no sooner was he back in his own corner than a listless feeling would slink from mind to body, and all that could be seen would be young bodies making mechanical movements like a clock pendulum swinging unconsciously. That same feeling affected the jurist as well. He would doze off with his eyes wide open, but as soon as he realised it was happening he would pounce on the pupils to rid himself of the drowsy feeling.

Abd al-Rahman had to endure the trials of summer, the Qur'an school, and its master during those scorching hot days, but eventually night brought with it some relief from the searing heat. He would then meet up with his friends from the Makhfiyya Quarter in its long, branching alleyways, where cooler breezes freshened the air and let the people who gathered there feel that they were alive and breathing normally. The oppressive atmosphere in the Qur'an school was a primary topic of their conversation, but Abd al-Qadir al-Rahmuni would guffaw as he told his companions how much he was enjoying the opportunity to relax, sleep, and enjoy himself during the long school vacation that lasted for three months.

'Three whole months?!' the children yelled back at him in an amazement akin to sheer envy.

'The secular academy's closed, and all my schoolmates are on vacation because heat like this doesn't help you study.'

'You lucky dog! Our master doesn't even know the word "relax". We're reciting stuff from dawn till sunset!'

'Ha-ha-ha!' Abd al-Qadir's mocking laughter made the children angry; they all felt even more jealous.

Abd al-Rahman now recalled what it was that Abd al-Qadir had whispered in his ear the first time he talked about the secular academy: 'Ask your father to enrol you.'

'Should I?' he wondered. 'Who could approach my father with such a request? My mother? Abd al-Ghani? If my father hears talk about this school that dismisses its students for three whole months, he'll encourage the Qur'an teacher to punish me... Even so, I have to try. I must take the risk. Qur'an school? I can't stand that merciless prison any more! The secular academy... no beatings, no canes, no summer classes. That's paradise, not a school.'

The very thought of this school occupied Abd al-Rahman's mind, senses, and emotions. Whenever he spoke to his brothers and his mother he constantly mentioned it. However, he avoided talking to Abd al-Ghani about it, in case he blew up and opposed the idea before there was even a chance to approach his father with the request.

As the summer months began to fade, Abd al-Qadir started talking to his friends in the Makhfiyya Quarter about the upcoming semester and how he was about to purchase books, notepads, pencils, and a schoolbag. Abd al-Rahman's resolve began to reassert itself, and he finally decided to let his father know that he wanted to join the secular academy.

His mother was the best conduit for approaching his father. He was not used to asking his father for anything, nor was Hajj Muhammad accustomed to allowing his sons to make requests of him. And it was the mother who could be persuasive in a way that the sons could not. When it came to the secular academy, it was very doubtful that even his mother could manage it, but, whatever the case, she could certainly avoid the furious reaction if Hajj Muhammad thought the request sufficiently outrageous to demand reprimand or punishment.

Khaduj listened patiently to the lengthy and tempting explanation that Abd al-Rahman offered as he tried to persuade his mother of his desire to transfer to the secular academy, but she could not summon enough courage to promise him that his father would accept the idea. When Abd al-Rahman pressed her, she insisted that she could not undertake such a tricky task, but when he kept up his pressure, she agreed to try – if a favourable opportunity presented itself when Hajj Muhammad would be willing to listen and respond.

As the days rolled by, October was almost upon them, and Abd al-Qadir was talking a lot about his school. Abd al-Rahman now tried even harder with his mother, complaining that he could no longer stand attending the Qur'an school and having to stare at the teacher's face there. He could no longer memorise his tablet or recite a sura by heart.

One dark September morning when heat and clouds combined, Abd al-Rahman was surprised to hear a fierce command from Hajj Muhammad: 'Abd al-Rahman, wait! Don't leave for school yet. Wait for me.'

Hajj Muhammad's tone of voice sounded anything but happy. Even when he was actually feeling content, his voice could still sound serious and even harsh. Without actually looking at the expression on his face there was no way of telling whether he was content or annoyed. So, on this occasion Abd al-Rahman could not tell from the voice at a distance what mood his father was in.

Abd al-Rahman waited to leave the house with his father. He did not dare ask his father what he thought; instead, he kept sneaking glances to see if it was possible to discern Hajj Muhammad's mood and determine why he was accompanying him to the Qur'an school.

He soon gathered that Hajj Muhammad was not happy at all; from his total silence he deduced that his father had something in mind and was formulating a plan. But he could not work out exactly what that involved. All he could do was to trail behind his father, with no idea what the goal and purpose might be. When they reached the Qur'an school, Hajj Muhammad let Abd al-Rahman go first and enter the schoolroom ahead of him. As he went through the doorway, he took another look at his father's expression and saw that it was even more rigid and angry than before. Now he realised.

He went over to the jurist's bench and kissed the proffered hand in all due humility. He did not notice that, meanwhile, with a simple gesture, an exchange had taken place between his father and the jurist. He only realised what had occurred when the jurist grabbed him by the scruff of the neck. He turned to the door only to see his father turning his back on him and leaving the schoolroom.

His feet were now lifted to receive fifty lashes of the cane – that being the content of Hajj Muhammad's gesture to the jurist. A savage punishment, no doubt, but it did not extinguish Abd al-Rahman's determination to fight, and fight again, until he became a pupil at the secular academy for children of the elite.

15

Abd al-Rahman was an inquisitive student. It was not just that, unlike the majority of his new schoolmates, he had not learned French or studied Arabic grammar. He was curious about many other things too, things that may well have also aroused the curiosity of the other students – but his curiosity was on an entirely different level to theirs.

They all noticed the obvious differences between the teachers al-Yazighi and Monsieur François. The explanations of the former were most of the time utterly incomprehensible, while those of the latter were understandable, even though spoken in a foreign language. The former delivered his lessons with an entirely false aplomb, without even bothering to look at the students he was addressing. The latter, on the other hand, would spring out of the corner and stand in the middle of the classroom; their young minds would spring with him, attentive and understanding, without the need for commands or arrogance. Al-Yazighi's classes inspired respect, awe, and a reverence for learning, but they were tedious, while François's classes may have suggested simplicity but were, in fact, a confirmation of life itself.

Al-Yazighi would stand in front of the students, ranting and raving so much that they felt compelled to be even more defiant in order to provoke his tirades further. Monsieur François did not give al-Yazighi any kind of sanctuary. He would stand in the middle of the classroom adjudicating between the students and their other teacher, often coming down on the students' side of things, not hesitating to announce his decision in front of their foe. The aged al-Yazighi would be forced to submit humbly to the decision.

Monsieur François did not rant and rave, because there was no reason for him do so. Those students who misbehaved or failed to understand something were punished in a straightforward way, and they accepted it with an open heart. He wore tailored clothes and shoes with laces. He did not wear a skullcap, a fez, or a turban, and his long hair protected him from winter cold, summer heat, and gusts of wind. To the students, al-Yazighi – with his corpulent body, pale complexion, and thick spectacles on a rusty frame – appeared more like an old, traditional tribal shaykh, who might live in a ramshackle tent.

François gave the impression of being open minded; he moved freely and swung about like a young man. His speech was carefully regulated, and his gestures controlled. So he seemed more like one of the students, though enjoying the additional liberty of being their teacher. Al-Yazighi on the other hand looked weighed down, firstly by an ageing body growing ever heavier as time went by, and secondly by the learning and the residue of wisdom in his mind that he was supposed to be imparting to and embodying for his pupils.

François was fulfilling a mission of mind and life, always eager to get the message across, with a responsibility to do so. If one of the children did not understand, he would see the fault in himself and try a different way of communicating the idea. Al-Yazighi felt the same weight of responsibility, but he showed it only in the way he would recite things from memory in a stentorian tone, using mechanical gestures that completely failed to connect with the children, merely bringing his hands together in a meaningless movement to create an irrelevant clapping sound.

The students discussed these differences during their breaks, and in lessons too, but none of it was either specific or profound. They simply talked about some of the more obvious aspects with a good deal of withering sarcasm and a fair amount of mockery. One of them would stand in the middle of the schoolyard during break and do imitations of al-Yazighi. The other students would burst into laughter. It was a moment of freedom, so none of them felt any constraints. They also competed to imitate François as much as they did al-Yazighi, but in his case it was a matter of admiration rather than the mockery that was reserved for his colleague.

The main square in Makhfiyya also witnessed performances of this kind. But now it was not just the quarter's inhabitants – the flour vendor, the mint and halva merchant perched on the sidewalk, and Hajj Muhammad al-Tihami – who were the objects of these charades. A whole new element was now added, one that was rich in images, gestures, new words, and great ironies. Sometimes one would encounter al-Yazighi, dressed in his jallaba, turban, burnous, and spectacles, reciting his lesson in the square with his habitual pomposity and his repertoire of gestures, reactions, and pretension. There would also be Monsieur François, deft and lively, rushing around among the students to illustrate a word on the blackboard or spelling out a foreign word in syllables in a way that sounded both funny and strange.

Two-Heads was not the only theatrical star in the square, nor was Abd al-Qadir al-Rahmuni any longer the only hero when it came to talking about the secular academy, the teachers, and the science and French classes. The stage spawned other talented actors among the students attending this elite school, among them Abd al-Rahman.

To his peers, Abd al-Rahman was a talented actor. But whereas Two-Heads only poked fun at the personality he was portraying and used raunchy language to raise a laugh, Abd al-Rahman went deep into the genuine differences between the Qur'an school and the secular academy, and between al-Yazighi and Monsieur François. For this reason he was rarely either funny or dismissive; rather he was most effective at influencing the children's minds. He was the one who managed best to arouse their curiosity, stimulate their aspirations for the future, and nourish hope for a better life in their young minds.

But Abd al-Rahman no longer found a sufficient outlet for his ideas in Makhfiyya Square. The new things he was learning stimulated in him a strong desire to know what goals one might have, what kind of future might open up before the school's students.

When it came to the conspicuous differences between al-Yazighi and Monsieur François – amusing sometimes, and never less than remarkable – Abd al-Rahman never regarded either the acts or the appearances of the two men as just something to laugh and scoff at. He always emerged from his amused contempt with one overriding question: why?

Why was it that al-Yazighi, the august teacher and perfect model of rectitude in the country, could provoke such mockery and scorn? François, to the contrary, was a perfectly ordinary person without pretence or airs; he never made use of his person, clothes, or manner of working to gain the kind of respect that invoked admiration and encouraged imitation.

Why was al-Yazighi so incapable of dealing with his pupils, who were all young and naturally timid and shy? Why did he have to go to François to ask for help? François was younger than al-Yazighi, so why did he possess such an amazing, magical power that al-Yazighi did not have?

Why was it that everyone else respected al-Yazighi, kissing his hand and shoulder on the street, and yet, as soon as he was inside the classroom with his pupils, he turned into someone else – not the kind of person who inspires respect, whose shoulder one kisses, or to whom one lowers one's head as a sign of reverence?

A whole series of illustrations came together in Abd al-Rahman's mind: his father Hajj Muhammad; Mawlay Abd al-Ghafur, whose night-time classes his father attended at the Mawlay Idris shrine and the Qarawiyin Mosque; his brother Abd al-Ghani, still a young man but already emulating al-Yazighi's behaviour, though no venerable scholar himself. He could come up with any number of examples from among people he knew, people he saw, and people who talked to him about al-Yazighi. In every case the story about al-Yazighi was the same, with no variations.

So yet again the insistent question posed itself: why? But his young mind could not come up with an answer, so the issue faded away, to be replaced by a new kind of enquiry: 'Are all the people in whose bosom we live – at home and on the street, in city and village, in shop, mosque, Qur'an school, and secular academy – are they all models of al-Yazighi, Mawlay Abd al-Ghafur, Abd al-Ghani, and the flour and halva seller?'

The question sank from the surface to the very depths, to be replaced by another more brutal and insistent enquiry: 'François isn't a fellow countryman of ours, but he offers us a different model, one that's marked by movement and life. Is it smarter, stronger, richer, cleverer?'

And yet these questions, which were forcing themselves on him with such insistence, also gradually sank into the recesses of his mind, leaving behind them a new question: 'What about me? Am I going to be François or al-Yazighi?'

Setting out for school, and every day at school, and in every class, his mind encountered two possible models of behaviour, and he found himself having to decide which one to pursue in order to avoid losing his way.

One used a particular strategy with the young pupils, but he would find himself needing to seek help from the other to protect himself from their dirty tricks.

The other got the things he talked about into the pupils' minds.

One tried to reach their minds while sitting in his seat.

The other leapt around with fresh opinions, ideas, and words, stimulating the children's minds through his sheer activity.

One brought his hands out from under his jallaba to yank out a victim.

The other used chalk, pencils, paper, and books as part of his work.

'So,' Abd al-Rahman wondered, 'which one of them shall I be? Al-Yazighi or Monsieur François?' Once more the question settled at the back of his mind, leaving him in a confrontation with a test, a dilemma, a labyrinth.

16

Abd al-Rahman's new life at the academy proceeded, as did those of the other students who were embarking on a journey in a new world. He no longer paused to think of how he was rid of the jurist in the mosque school and free of his summer and winter prison. His new world had made him forget all about the old one with its positive aspects and idiosyncrasies. Hajj Muhammad had no role to play in this life; he had handed his son over to a school in which he knew from the start that he could not be involved. He could not talk to the new school's director the way he could to the Qur'an-school teacher, or make suggestions. If he were to propose something, the reaction would not be complete agreement as was the case with the jurist. So he had left Abd al-Rahman to his own fate, without questioning him about his studies, following his progress at the school, or inserting himself into his life outside the house.

However, through his elder brother, Abd al-Ghani, Abd al-Rahman was not completely divorced from his former world. Abd al-Ghani assumed that his authority over his younger brother would never be terminated; he was older, more sensible, and more upright in his behaviour. By now Abd al-Ghani was involved in commerce. Hajj Muhammad had set him up in a little shop in the Qaysariyya Market and given him some capital, not for the purpose of making a profit, but rather to train his son and familiarise him with business matters.

Abd al-Ghani's transfer from Qur'an school to commerce had convinced him that he was exceptional and reinforced the idea that within the household he could play the role of second fiddle to his father. His primary point of experiment was Abd al-Rahman. After his younger brother had transferred schools, something he himself had been against, Abd al-Ghani tried even harder to be domineering, and to take over the role that Hajj Muhammad had now relinquished because he had discovered that he could no longer fulfil it.

Sitting around in the evening, Abd al-Rahman was reading a French book, while Abd al-Ghani amused himself by chewing gum, doing his best to overcome his boredom by unconsciously using his mouth as a rapid chewing device; occasional popping noises would be heard, as though he were trying to use it to compensate for his sense of absolute isolation. Abd al-Latif was sitting beside the two of them, as was Yasmine's son, Mahmud, who kept looking curiously at his two elder brothers as though from their personalities he could glean the best example for himself: Abd al-Ghani, all about money and commerce, a miniature version of Hajj Muhammad, and someone Mahmud feared because of his meanness to him and his beatings; Abd al-Rahman, the high-performing student who earned respect for the number of books he brought home which no one else in the house could understand – the new model, he was unlike anyone else in the house. Their sister, Aisha, was beside them all; by now she was no longer a child, but had become a young woman hastening toward her own future.

Abd al-Ghani found the silence enveloping the room utterly aggravating; even his own popping noises did nothing to relieve the atmosphere. He longed to have someone ask him about his new life in the shop, his commercial profits, and his customers, with whom he would haggle as they tried to get a lower price, and about his neighbours and the various aspects of their lives. But Hajj Muhammad would not fulfil his desire, because he actually disdained the commercial activity in which Abd al-Ghani was now engaged. Even though he was not about to give up on a future career for Abd al-Ghani in business ventures, he still considered his son to be in training, and that it would require a good deal of time for him to become a successful merchant. Nor did his mother, Khaduj, satisfy his longing; she was only concerned about household matters and never bothered to ask Hajj Muhammad any questions about his work in either commerce or agriculture, and so Abd al-Ghani was not concerned about whether his mother spoke to him or let him talk to her about his little enterprise, his daily experiences, his haggling with customers, and his secret struggles with neighbouring shopkeepers in the market.

Thus he was hoping that Abd al-Rahman would feel like arguing with him, so he could have an opportunity to show off how rich he was and how much money was in his shop's cash register. But Abd al-Rahman disappointed him; he was busy with his book and the exercises he had to do, things that were a complete mystery to Abd al-Ghani whenever he heard him repeating words and numbers out loud.

Finally he could take no more of the oppressive silence. 'Haven't you had enough of that heretical nonsense during the day?' he asked from where he was sitting. 'Do you really have to spend the night at it as well?'

Abd al-Rahman gave his brother a contemptuous glance, but he did not hold it for long; he needed to get back to the problem he was dealing with as soon as possible. He left Abd al-Ghani's remark hanging like a question mark in the silent void.

Abd al-Ghani now started chewing his gum furiously. What really infuriated him was that Abd al-Rahman was ignoring him in a way that showed his defiance and contempt, which had begun to show themselves since his transfer to the secular academy.

'Hey, you! I'm talking to you! Can't you spare us all this heretical gibberish?'

Abd al-Rahman looked up again, with increasing reluctance. Abd al-Ghani repeated his question, and this time Abd al-Rahman decided to respond. 'And can't you spare us that chewing noise? You're making as much noise as women do!'

His cutting comment made Abd al-Ghani even more annoyed.

'That academy's beguiled you,' he said with obvious menace. 'If I were your father, I wouldn't have let you go to that place for heretics!'

Abd al-Rahman let out a huge guffaw and made no effort to suppress it; indeed, he wanted it to reverberate in Abd al-Ghani's ears and heart. 'You know absolutely nothing about heresy or belief,' he said. 'You're as angry about my being in the academy as you're happy about being in your shop. You'd be better off not talking about the academy. You know absolutely nothing about it. You've never even been through its doorway.'

Abd al-Ghani frowned. One of the things that really upset him was that Abd al-Rahman, who was younger than him, now had a status beyond his own reach. Even so, he could not argue with his brother's logic.

'You'll see!' he threatened angrily. 'You'll see if you're going to stay at that academy!'

The threat was enough to provoke a defiant response. 'Oh yes,' he responded, 'I'm going to stay at the academy. Not only that, but Aisha, Mahmud, and Abd al-Latif will be going there too. We're going to give you a free hand in your shop so you can carry on measuring clothes with a tape measure.'

'Aisha, Abd al-Latif, and Mahmud? Are you out of your mind? Aisha's going to the girls' Qur'an school, and Abd al-Latif is going to the Qarawiyin. Mahmud's success at the Qur'an school won't be repeated at the academy.'

Aisha, Abd al-Latif, and Mahmud, who were all sitting there, looked curiously at the angry faces of their two elder brothers, unaware that this fierce argument was actually about them.

Aisha's imagination had never gone so far as to contemplate the possibility of going to the academy; she had never even heard of daughters of elite families going to any kind of school. She had heard mention of the female teacher's Qur'an school where young girls would go to memorise parts of the sacred text and prayers. But it was not intended for daughters of wealthy people; she had heard its name mentioned, but conservative families would not agree to send their daughters to that school, where girls would also learn how to sew and help the female teacher in household chores. Now, for the first time, she was hearing the word 'academy' from the lips of a furious Abd al-Rahman. She did not take the matter seriously, but concluded that it was only the heat of the argument that had led her brother to defy Abd al-Ghani and threaten to enrol her in the academy.

Even so, Abd al-Rahman's very mention of that word aroused strange sentiments in Aisha's mind, without her even getting involved in the argument itself. 'Academy?' she thought to herself. 'Could it be my luck to go to the academy every morning and come home every evening with books, notepads, and pencils as Abd al-Rahman does now? What would my mother have to say? And my father too? What would the reaction of all my female cousins be?'

Her imagination fired, and she now started dreaming about the street outside bursting with movement, about the academy full of girl students, and the teacher, yes, the male teacher. 'Male teacher? Do girls sit in the teacher's classroom too? Do they learn along with the boys?'

That question kept nagging at her. These issues would have led her to ask her brother, but looking over at Abd al-Ghani was more than enough to stop her. His fury was reflected in his eyes, like two burning coals. His expression of raw anger connected with her dreamy look, and the entire vision dissolved in the face of such fury. She said nothing, leaving her ideas and questions to retreat deep inside her.

'Get up, you!' Abd al-Ghani yelled at Mahmud, having spotted glimmerings of hope in the young boy's happy smile. 'Get up and go to your mother!'

Abd al-Ghani had no desire to see Mahmud – a maidservant's child, after all – aspire to attend the academy, since that was exactly what had encouraged Abd al-Rahman to challenge his authority and given him a sense of superiority.

As Mahmud stood up, he could barely suppress his smile. Abd

al-Rahman's words had restored his sense of his own worth. As he left his brothers' company, Mahmud no longer felt cheated. For him too, Abd al-Rahman's statement that he would be attending the academy had stirred some happy dreams.

Abd al-Ghani felt defeated. Looking over at Abd al-Rahman in fury, he found his brother still buried in his book, reading and memorising. Getting up angrily, Abd al-Ghani stormed out of the room, still chewing on his gum.

17

Hajj Muhammad had no idea about the things people were talking about and the rumours flying around. He knew nothing about the alarming tales rocking the city, their echoes reverberating in every quarter. Tongues kept wagging, but it was all very obscure. Hajj Muhammad paid no attention to the initial stories; he always tried to remain aloof from people's gossip and assumed that this supposed convulsion was much the same kind of thing – just the sort of flap they created once in a while in order to inject some life into things and preoccupy their minds when the city was otherwise in a somnolent mood, with both trade and industry in a lull. However, the rumours kept impinging upon his consciousness, and public chatter increased to the point where every person, however oblivious, knew about it.

'What's this people keep saying about the Berbers?' Hajj Muhammad wondered. 'About the victory they've won?'

The question buzzed around inside his vacant mind, but he could not come up with an answer.

He expected that Sayyid Abd al-Ghafur's class at the Mawlay Idris shrine would have something by way of answer to this question, which continued to lurk and hover over Hajj Muhammad's limited horizons. However, the shaykh knew no more about what people were discussing than he did; the only interest his classes had, as far as most people were concerned, was in designating things as being either permitted or forbidden and in regurgitating quotations from the texts of Ibn Ashir or the commentary of Mayyara. What was certain was that neither Ibn Ashir nor Mayyara had anything to say about the Berbers or the possibility of their victory.

So, Hajj Muhammad ignored all the fuss. News about the Berbers and some victory was of no interest to him – although, in truth, the very word 'Berber' still made him a little nervous. Whenever the name came up, he would recall the time when he was young, when the Berbers had taken up arms and posed a threat to Christian colonialists present in the country. People had felt safe only in the cities of Morocco while the Christians put an end to the resistance in the mountains. Now that people were using the same words again, Hajj Muhammad recalled bitter memories that lingered from the past.

When he returned to his house at lunchtime, the heat was at its height. The city's streets and narrow alleys were scorched by the relentless sun, and the ground was steaming, giving off a smell which combined the stench of animal dung and the refuse of the Bu-Khararib River. Hajj Muhammad was surprised to see Amm Muhammad al-Dallal hurrying in his direction; he looked downcast, as though carrying the world's burdens on his shoulders.

'Hajj, Hajj!' he called breathlessly, the way a fighter gasps for air, 'Have you heard the news?'

Hajj Muhammad did not pay him much attention, being inured to the kind of psychological crises regularly suffered by people like Hajj al-Dallal. Even so, he raised his weary eyes to look him straight in the face, as though to ask, 'So, what's the news?'

'They're reciting the Latif, the prayer for mercy, in the Qarawiyin!'

'The Latif?!'

'Yes, the Latif. Something really terrible must have happened.'

Hajj Muhammad now looked a little more concerned, but he was anxious to preserve his august demeanour and to appear to everyone as a man who could not be disturbed by events. 'This year's crop production was low,' he commented with apparent disinterest. 'That's probably why people are reciting the Latif.'

This did not convince Muhammad al-Dallal, yet he lowered his head out of respect for Hajj Muhammad's comment. 'May God have mercy on us and be gentle with us,' he muttered. 'There's nothing good left in the world.'

With that he continued on his way, carrying the burden of a still-obscure tragedy on his shoulders.

That evening Hajj Muhammad shut himself up inside the house; he did not wish to hear any more alarming news from people. It was his habit to cloister himself inside his own house without really meaning to do so, finding a refuge there that would spare him from hearing things he did not wish to know about.

However, the news kept banging on people's doors. Hajj Muhammad may have felt safe inside his house, but Abd al-Ghani managed to bring in the news, even though it was no more than what al-Dallal had talked about earlier: he reported that a huge crowd had assembled in the Qarawiyin Mosque, recited the Latif, and then left.

Hajj Muhammad was of the opinion – as was Abd al-Ghani – that that had been the end of things. The sunset hour had driven people to do something unusual, and the Qarawiyin had provided a stage for it. All that it had involved was people reciting the name of God the Gentle and Kind in the Qarawiyin Mosque.

Next morning, Makhfiyya Square was thronged with people talking about the recitation of the Latif in the Qarawiyin Mosque; Hajj Muhammad could not avoid bumping into the news with every step he took. He was, of course, used to people gossiping, but he was amazed at this level of concern.

Every other word people spoke or heard was about the recitation of the Latif in the Qarawiyin Mosque, and about the Berbers and their victory. Once again the news perplexed Hajj Muhammad; he could not come up with an explanation or figure out how the words 'Latif', 'Berber', and 'victory' could be linked in any kind of logical fashion. He had no desire to ask questions, to appear to people as somehow lacking information, or to enquire of someone who might want to ask him the very same questions. He kept repeating a phrase from the fifth sura of the Qur'an: 'Do not ask about things that, if revealed to you, would annoy you.' He did not like prying, in case the resulting information would upset him.

But once again the news invaded his fortress. Abd al-Rahman

returned from his school with the truth about the situation that had led to the recitation of the Latif, the news that had led people to repeat it in a frenzy throughout the city.

'The French are trying to forcibly convert the Berbers to Christianity... They're trying to impose a new legal code on them that is not derived from Islamic law. They've started encircling the Berber regions to cut them off from the Arab regions. Islam is in danger...'

As Hajj Muhammad listened to this he was utterly amazed, but showed no emotion and asked no questions. He was anxious to hear more, so he made no attempt to stop Abd al-Rahman talking – as he usually did when his son spoke of things he knew nothing about. Instead, he simply let him go on talking. He was all ears.

'The French are now taking the second step in their attempt to rip Moroccan unity apart. If they carry out their plan, an entire region of Morocco will become Christian and speak French. Morocco's religion, language, and unity are all under threat...'

Hajj Muhammad was not affected by everything that Abd al-Rahman had said, but the phrase 'Islam is in danger' carried him into a strange new universe. His devout soul was now beset by a fear over the fate of Islam itself.

He was usually an optimist, with no worries about a faith with a God who always protected him – as he would always reassure himself. Yet now the heavy impact of the logical words that Abd al-Rahman had spoken worried him greatly, and he, like other people, felt compelled to call on al-Latif, God the Gentle, to remove from his faithful community the grave danger that was threatening Islam.

Hajj Muhammad had no idea how he managed to drag himself the next day to the Qarawiyin Mosque carrying his skullcap and rosary. He joined everyone else in reciting the Latif prayer and found himself caught up in an unusual atmosphere of faith that he had never experienced before in his ritual prayers and the intercessions that he would regularly pronounce after them. This profound communal cry for help was an expression of a deadly despair, one that filled his very soul with a sense of panic, fear, and a striving toward God. Forgetting everything else, Hajj Muhammad joined the huge assembly in its recitation, embodying the grave danger being faced by Islam. Every corner of the mosque reverberated to the sound of a powerful and effective voice that once again intoned, 'Gentle God, your protection!' Voices in every direction echoed the words, as though an electric charge had been emitted that carried with it a sense of the profound disaster they were confronting. As Hajj Muhammad continued his fervent intonation of the words along with the crowd, his voice blended with the sound of his rosary beads clashing against each other in his fingers. So emotional was the situation that the sound of the voices in unison brought tears to his eyes.

After that, Hajj Muhammad went regularly to the Qarawiyin to pray the Latif prayer; he felt that it was as much of a religious obligation as performing the Friday prayers with the congregation. He even called in Abd al-Ghani, someone with whom he rarely shared any secrets.

'From today on,' he told his son, 'make sure you go to the Qarawiyin to recite the Latif.'

As time went by, increasing familiarity with the Latif recitation in the Qarawiyin did nothing to erase the profound psychological and religious burdens that people were feeling. In fact, those burdens only renewed and intensified when another sentence was added to the words of the Latif itself: 'O God, O Kind and Gentle One, we ask for Your kindness in the face of what fate has dealt us; do not cause a rift between us and our Berber brethren.'

Hajj Muhammad had the sense that he was beginning to understand things; he could feel the danger threatening Islam. But he still refused to consider the implications of the new phrase 'do not cause a rift between us and our Berber brethren' until Abd al-Rahman specifically elaborated on it.

'The true value of the Islamic community is its unity,' Abd al-Rahman told him. 'We're the Moroccan people, but we won't be if the French divide us up into Arabs and Berbers. The nation is ours as long as we are a single community. Once those foreign interlopers separate us, we'll turn into a cluster of nations, some Muslims, others adhering to the invaders' faith; some will speak Arabic, others the invaders' tongue. Dividing people by religion, language, and law is the invaders' way of obliterating this community's solidarity.'

This was a new language that Abd al-Rahman was using: community, nation, unity, interlopers, invaders. Once again Hajj Muhammad found himself feeling dizzy, but he resorted to the basic understanding whose obligations he had undertaken along with everyone else, reciting the Latif. For him, the basic understanding that he had picked up along with all the others at the Qarawiyin was enough: an imminent danger was threatening Islam, so it was necessary to seek refuge with God so that He could ward off the danger being faced. Hajj Muhammad had the feeling that the fancy words Abd al-Rahman was using, words he had heard at that school of his, may have been serious – but they did not resound with him as did the shouts of the worshippers in the Qarawiyin.

Days went by, but they could not continue in a straight line forever. One steaming-hot morning, people awoke to something they had never encountered before. The city was buzzing with news of boys and men having been snatched from their homes and flogged in the so-called House of Ibn al-Baghdadi. These were the ones who had motivated everyone to gather in the Qarawiyin, recite the Latif, and beseech God not to 'separate us from our Berber brethren'. The word went round the city that guards had been placed by the entrances to the Qarawiyin, threatening anyone who pronounced the Latif with the same treatment that the young men had endured in the House of Ibn al-Baghdadi.

To express their anger, the people made the city grind to a halt; there were strikes, and shops closed their doors in protest at how things had gone so far that the sons of the city were being flogged and believers were not allowed to say the Latif prayer.

Now Hajj Muhammad was really worried. He had never imagined that the perfectly respectable religious activity in which people were engaged at the mosque could provoke the authorities to such a level of anger that they would flog young men and close the mosque.

He left the house for the Makhfiyya Square, wanting to see the strike, something he had not witnessed since his childhood, when merchants had closed their doors for fear of being hit by bullets during the clashes between Muslims and Christians. He discovered that the shops had indeed closed up now. He was still taking a long and careful look at things when he was surprised by a loud voice making an announcement through a megaphone.

'Open your shops! Open them now, or you'll only have yourselves to blame...'

Hajj Muhammad observed the anxious expressions on people's faces. The young men all looked defiant, but the sound of those words resonated in his ears and mind, and blended with the words of the Latif. Looking at the closed shops, he realised that his own status in the quarter would not allow him to take a negative stance. The echoes of the megaphone's words overwhelmed his ears, his heart, and his senses. They rang out loud and clear in front of the shopkeepers.

'Open your shops! Listen to what the government is saying.'

18

Hajj Muhammad steered clear of the topic that was preoccupying the city. He no longer went to the Qarawiyin Mosque at noon every day to recite the Latif with everyone else, nor did he insist that his son, Abd al-Ghani, keep reciting the prayer. In fact, whenever circumstances required him to walk around the city, he made a point to avoid walking past the entryways to the Qarawiyin.

Since the Qarawiyin Mosque was right in the city centre, it was hard for anyone walking through that area to avoid finding himself in front of one of the entrances to the mosque. Even so, Hajj Muhammad went to the trouble of using back routes so as not to subject himself to the anxieties of passing close by.

Ever since he had heard that security forces had surrounded the ancient mosque and imprisoned the young men who had posed a threat to security by calling for a recitation of the Latif, he had avoided any contact with issues in which the security forces might be involved; he did not want to create difficulties of the kind that he could well do without. By now, the security forces had long since lifted their siege of the Qarawiyin, and yet Hajj Muhammad had inured himself to avoiding the mosque whenever possible – even though it was the place where his religious and intellectual development were centred. Worshippers may have been prevented from performing their prayers inside the Qarawiyin, but the Mawlay Idris shrine and the mosque close to his house were alternative resources. So, if the authorities had stopped people reciting the Latif in public, then it could be done in private. The rosary with its glistening pearl beads provided a clear path of access to God.

Hajj Muhammad felt as though he were waking up after a nap. 'As long as public recitation of the Latif displeases the "government", he thought, 'why shouldn't I show my defiance this way?' He paused for a moment's reflection, sensing that his reactions were getting away from him. 'Displeases the "government"?' he thought. 'What has recitation of the Latif to do with the government, whether in public or private?'

His mind was a confused jumble of questions. He could no longer condemn the government for opposing this kind of worship, although no one had ever dared forbid it before. At the same time, he could not condemn the crowd of believers either; they had used this form of worship as a way of expressing their opposition to an action that the government had taken. It all left his mind in a whirl, and he could not discern the true course of action in the context of this challenge which pitted the will of the people against that of the governing authorities. He concluded that he himself could not get involved in such an act of defiance, something he disapproved of. He had to maintain a distance, even if that involved not praying in the Qarawiyin Mosque or ceasing to recite the Latif along with the other worshippers.

No sooner had he reached this conclusion than his brain started swirling all over again, because Abd al-Rahman's concerns – heavily influenced by the disturbance that this storm of anger had aroused – had been relentlessly increasing. His comments at home had acquired a vengeful edge directed against those foreign usurpers governing the country who were so supercilious in their dealings with people and were now preventing everyone from expressing their anger in a peaceful, religious fashion.

Their tranquil household, which had never before involved itself in such matters, now found itself enmeshed – through Abd al-Rahman's commentary – in reckless defiance. He described the imprisoned young men as embodiments of the popular will in resistance to the attack that had been launched against the Berbers, and their imprisonment as a criminal act on the part of the government in the face of a popular uprising which was an expression of the people's desire for unity. The attack that had been launched against the Moroccan Berbers and their Islamic tradition was an imperialist act, to be resisted by mobilising the powerful will of the people.

Echoes of everything Abd al-Rahman was saying kept ringing in Hajj Muhammad's ears, though at first he paid no attention. However, after due thought and consideration, he came to realise that the young men arrested by the government were no older than Abd al-Rahman himself. In his opinion, Abd al-Rahman was still a child, and any young man was still a child until he grew a beard or married. They were all young men who had not yet reached the age of discretion. This was what the homilist in the mosque had claimed (under pressure from the government) as a way of absolving the people from the young men's behaviour.

It made him consider what he was hearing from Abd al-Rahman. 'Utter recklessness! If Abd al-Rahman says things in the street like he's been saying them in the house, he could suffer the same fate as the young men arrested by the authorities.'

Hajj Muhammad made up his mind to put a stop to Abd al-Rahman's careless talk, and he began listening more carefully to the flaming row between Abd al-Rahman and Abd al-Ghani.

'If we were real men,' Abd al-Rahman was saying, 'the government wouldn't be able to separate Arabs from Berbers.'

Abd al-Ghani was furious. He was in no mood to listen to Abd al-Rahman talk about heroism when he was already fed up with all his talk about the academy. His anger was clear enough in his bitter response.

'You're still a child,' he said, 'and you're talking about men?! Concentrate on your books and your academy, and leave politics to other people.'

'That's the way you always talk! You stay aloof from your own community, as though someone were actually authorised to push you away. Forget about what's current, you say, forget about knowledge... So, now the government can tyrannise us because there's nobody around who's not a defeatist.'

The word 'defeatist' hit Abd al-Ghani hard. 'What can children like you do to the government?' he asked. 'It has authority, power, weapons, and police. Then along come a bunch of kids to resist them all with the Latif prayer!'

Abd al-Rahman was no less angry than his brother, whose scorn had stung him like a scorpion. 'The Latif,' he replied, 'is a metaphor, one that enshrines ideas in words. The idea here is that we need to resist aggression and aggressors – not to mention defeatists, like you.'

'You, resisting me?!' Abd al-Ghani retorted with a loud guffaw. 'Now that's a rare display of courage! So, now you're going to forget about the guards who have prevented you from praying and reciting the Latif and resist me instead?!'

'You're defeat personified. In a dynamic community aspiring to freedom there's no need for people who worship money and pursue the path of submission.'

These spiteful words made Abd al-Ghani leap up. 'There's only one person,' he said, 'who can properly discipline the people who are playing with your minds, and that's Ibn al-Baghdadi. He knows how to pour water on hot heads.'

'Ibn al-Baghdadi is a living symbol of the barbaric situation that our country is enduring. A day will come when he'll be burned in the public square!'

Hajj Muhammad had been following this conversation from a distance, and it thoroughly alarmed him. 'Abd al-Rahman! Abd al-Rahman!'

Abd al-Rahman, Abd al-Ghani, and Mahmud were all shocked by their father's shouts. They had imagined that this conversation was being conducted out of earshot. Now their father's outburst brought them back to bitter reality. Abd al-Rahman shuddered. Suddenly the room had gone completely quiet. He hesitated before responding to his father, and Hajj Muhammad shouted at him again, even louder and more stridently than the first time.

As he responded to his father's orders, he was in two minds: resist or admit defeat? He was already aware that, because Hajj Muhammad had summoned him and not Abd al-Ghani, his father was about to scold him for what he had been saying.

'Yes, Father?'

'Come over here, and make it quick!'

Abd al-Rahman went over to his father, while Abd al-Ghani sat there gloating and barely suppressing a laugh. Mahmud was anxious to find out which of the two brothers was going to win.

'What's this drivel you're saying? Have you gone mad?'

Abd al-Rahman stood there looking at his father, furious but not saying a word.

'Speak!' his father yelled. 'Say something!'

Abd al-Rahman thought about his first move on this path to either resistance or defeat. 'I only spoke the truth!' he said.

'The truth?!' Hajj Muhammad yelled scathingly. 'The truth! You're telling the truth! And where did you learn this truth you're spouting? Is this what happens when you go to that school? Is that what they're teaching you?'

Abd al-Rahman felt himself spinning. He could feel defeat facing him as he confronted the extent of Hajj Muhammad's fury, which almost robbed him of his usual equanimity. Even so, he decided to continue resisting. 'I don't need the school to teach me how to love my country,' he said.

He felt that this response was the best possible way of addressing the raging storm in front of him. But Hajj Muhammad was not happy to hear this from his son. He felt that Abd al-Rahman was disregarding his opinion.

'Love of your country?' he yelled. 'I've never heard you use those words before. Does love of your country include insulting the government and defaming the pasha, our city's governor?'

As Abd al-Rahman was adopting this rebellious stance for the first time in his life, he decided to keep his nerve, and said nothing. But his silence made Hajj Muhammad even angrier. 'Haven't you heard about the people the pasha's had arrested and flogged?' he yelled at his son. 'Just for defying the government. They deserve to be flogged, exiled, and imprisoned.'

Abd al-Rahman finally ran out of patience. 'Imprisonment, flogging, and exile,' he replied, almost in a whisper, 'will eventually elevate those men to the status of national heroes.'

'Heroes, heroes! Maybe you're looking for prison too, rather than a life of ease. Maybe you're hoping that your words will make you a hero as well!' As Hajj Muhammad pronounced the word 'heroes', his tone was particularly scornful. 'More, more!' he went on. 'Nowadays even children have started talking about heroism. Is that the way it is?!'

Abd al-Rahman decided to swallow the harsh comments without admitting defeat. 'Children turn into men,' he challenged his father. 'But the path to manhood is not paved with roses.'

Hajj Muhammad glared at Abd al-Rahman with fury in his eyes. His anger finally boiled over. 'Get out of my sight,' he yelled. 'It'll be a black day for you when your meddling gets you involved in things that don't concern you.'

As Abd al-Rahman withdrew, he could hear the sound of Abd al-Ghani's barely suppressed laughter in the adjoining room.

19

There was no great opposition when the time came for Mahmud to move from the Qur'an school to the secular academy. Abd al-Rahman had already paved the way, and attendance at that school was no longer a major event in the life of the household. The transfer had become something quite normal, with no worries attached nor any criticism from Hajj Muhammad's friends or people concerned about their sons' futures. There was nothing to encourage opposition to Mahmud's transfer to the school; he had stayed at the Qur'an school until he was over thirteen years old, but he had not been able to memorise the Qur'an or master writing it. The jurist from the south had given up on the boy even more than Hajj Muhammad had, and could not understand how Hajj Muhammad and the family had such a weak spot for Mahmud. So the jurist seized every opportunity to wreak vengeance, insulting the boy's honour when he was not even angry. 'Good-for-nothing servant's brat!' he would say. 'A miracle if he's of any use at all!'

If he wanted to make an example, Mahmud's leg, head, and back would be used to teach a lesson to any lazy, slovenly, or stupid boy, or anyone who was late arriving at the school. He did not imagine there would be any opposition from Hajj Muhammad – and in fact there was none – and he exploited this freedom to use Mahmud as the sacrificial lamb whenever the children got on his nerves or life got on top of him to such an extent that he needed to relieve his pent-up anger. He would find such relief every time he made Mahmud's head bleed or whipped his legs.

Mahmud found no escape from his fate. Hajj Muhammad had

entrusted him to the jurist with the customary pledge, 'you do the killing, and I'll bury him'. So Mahmud had no opportunity of recourse to his father.

In any case, he only ever saw his father occasionally, coming or going. He avoided letting Hajj Muhammad know what the jurist was doing to him, since he was well aware what his father's response would be: 'May God grant him good health!'

His only source of consolation was his mother, Yasmine; it was she who would salve his wounds in rueful silence. She had sympathy, but all she could do was offer some painful advice: 'My son, do your best to memorise what's on your tablet!'

When Mahmud tried to explain his miserable situation, he could not. The words used by his brothers and other boys in the quarter rang in his ears: 'Nigger! Servant's child!'

Reality brought him back to his misery, and he managed to explain it to himself through the same hateful words. The jurist was the very embodiment of those words. The children no longer uttered their aggravating and malicious remarks about him with an almost innocent grin, nor did their teacher use them as a way of coping with his own anger. However, the latter did allow the idea of them to suffuse his vicious use of the cane and the knotted rope that lifted Mahmud's legs high off the ground until he was left resting on his neck or head. Mahmud convinced himself that this was the true rationale behind the cruelty that this teacher from the south showed towards him. The only solution that he could find was to escape to the secular academy, as his older brother had done before him.

He encountered no difficulties in joining the academy. The officials there had convinced the elite of the city that their sons needed to be enrolled in order to learn how to achieve mutual understanding with the authorities and serve as intermediaries between them and the populace on matters such as taxes, mail, and civil affairs. The parents duly complied, although some of them still felt a lingering doubt about removing their sons from the Qur'an school, where they would memorise the sacred text, and transferring them to the secular academy, where they would study that foreign language which had by now become at least a temporary necessity.

When Mahmud enrolled in the academy, most of his fellow pupils in the initial class were over thirteen years old. He kept hearing the phrase 'sons of the elite', and when he looked at them he could tell that they were indeed from that class, the same as in his own house, where his brothers belonged to the same group. The clothes they wore suggested luxury and care, things that by comparison he lacked. When he was at the Qur'an school or with his brothers at home, he had not noticed this lack. He had become inured to the distinctions made inside his house, and all sense of the discrimination between what his brothers were given and what he was given had been eradicated. It was only when he now found himself in a classroom with other boys from the elite that he became aware of the distinction. It was then too that he began to realise that the French teacher – just like the Qur'an-school teacher before him – regarded Mahmud through the prism of the colour of his skin and the clothes he wore. Schoolteachers were particularly attuned to their students. They had garnered information from the reports describing them in the Civil Affairs Administration. As a result, they were already aware of the distinction between boys born to wives and others born to servant-women, and made assessments of their futures based on that information.

Mahmud became aware of this when he observed the way the teacher dealt with him. It was not marked by the cruelty and vengeance he had encountered with the Qur'an-school teacher, but it was definitely a new kind of discrimination that was based on a person's birth mother. Even so, he found enough in the academy to encourage him to rid himself of the backward thinking that had characterised the Qur'an school, and he started competing with the really elite boys. He discovered that he could beat most of them and come out ahead. When this happened it had a clear effect on the teacher, who was duly surprised by Mahmud's enthusiasm for studying. That surprise was reflected in a softening of the way he treated him; sometimes it was almost as if he were dealing with an intelligent colleague.

So Mahmud remained at the academy, observing the struggle taking place in the minds of both teacher and fellow pupils between regarding him as a second-class person on the one hand, and on the other acknowledging that he was really trying hard and was earning a place at the head of the class.

He was also witnessing another kind of struggle inside his own house. Sitting among his brothers, he regarded Abd al-Ghani as his beloved hero. Contemplating his eldest brother, he searched for the secret source of that heroism. Abd al-Ghani always talked as though he were delivering sage advice, due to his firm belief in the validity of his own personality, which derived its authority solely from the fact that he was the eldest brother. He tried to impose this authority on his younger brothers, and Mahmud had always happily acknowledged it ever since he had been a child. Even today he had no plans to disavow it, since he still regarded Abd al-Ghani as a heroic figure, the only one of his brothers who could undertake any given task.

Abd al-Ghani constantly spoke about making money and the profits from the shop as though he were some kind of great plutocrat. In this way he resembled his father, Hajj Muhammad, who – in Mahmud's opinion – derived his forceful personality solely from the money, land, and properties he owned.

Every time Mahmud sat down with his brothers, he always observed Abd al-Ghani; he could not explain why he was so curious, except that he himself perhaps wanted to be Abd al-Ghani, with money (in amounts that he felt must be unbelievably enormous) ready at hand. He started watching Abd al-Ghani in order to glean something about the secret of this wealth, and his apparent gift of generating it. And he kept on watching...

When he looked over at Abd al-Rahman, whose personality was beginning to exert itself to the full, he could see another kind of hero, one like the teacher at the academy. He admired Abd al-Rahman's questioning attitude. Every time his elder brother spoke,

Mahmud would be awestruck – jaws agape, eyes popping out of his head, and ears on the alert. It was as though he were bringing all his senses to bear in order to discover the secret of where Abd al-Rahman got his strength, which was seen here and also inside the walls of the academy.

Abd al-Ghani talked about money and commerce, about his fellow merchants and neighbours at the Qaysariyya Market, about his deals and negotiations with customers and the way they could double his profits. His entire conversation revolved around a single topic: money. Abd al-Rahman on the other hand talked about numbers, men, and documented texts; about teachers, students, and debates; about books, notebooks, pencils, and geometric instruments. He had also started referring to the city gossip about the young men who had challenged the government by reciting the Latif in the Qarawiyin Mosque: they had been subjected to flogging and torture, but in the future they would be regarded as heroes. He also told stories about Ibn al-Baghdadi, who flogged young men with a good deal of mockery and not a little provocation.

The conflict between Abd al-Ghani and Abd al-Rahman had another aspect to it. Between the different arguments of the two elder brothers, Mahmud found himself playing the role of a perplexed arbiter, looking back and forth between the two of them, amazed at the way they each managed to best the other.

Mahmud had also followed the course of the argument between Abd al-Rahman and his father with a rare sensation of admiration. For the first time ever, he had watched as someone openly defied Hajj Muhammad; it was almost as though Abd al-Rahman were refusing to acknowledge the true extent of his father's supreme authority. He had stood there in utter astonishment as Abd al-Rahman had emerged from the incredible confrontation with an expression on his face that managed to combine confidence, defiance, and sheer determination.

Mahmud found himself considering these different models and the disagreements that emerged from them as he carried on his own life between academy, home, and street. At the academy he now began to attain a sense of his own self. The part of his life that involved the Qur'an school and the jurist from the south was over. Now the lessons were easy, and the path was open for him to excel. He was no longer inferior to boys born in wedlock, and his feet, head, and back were no longer a field where the jurist's cane and ropes could besport themselves to their heart's content. All the walls separating him from his fellow students, the sons of the elite, had now collapsed.

He listened as Abd al-Rahman made his preparations for the next day's class, finding it all easy to understand, because that world was no longer strange to him. He now sat there, mouth agape in sheer admiration for Abd al-Rahman as he did his homework. He had the impression that he too was following the same path as Abd al-Rahman, with very little difference.

One evening, these thoughts preoccupied his mind as he sat as usual with his brother and watched him assiduously, mouth agape as he had done when he was much younger. He carefully observed Abd al-Rahman – his face, his head, his build, his complexion, and the book he held in his hands.

'So, how is he different from me?' Mahmud asked himself. 'We have the same father and mother... No, his mother is not mine. That's right, his mother isn't mine. But how is his mother different from mine? I don't have a light complexion like his, but who's to say that that's better and more refined? The other boys keep calling me "maidservant's child", but that's just talk. Their children's logic has remained with them. Abd al-Rahman's mother, Khaduj, hates me, but my own mother, Yasmine, loves him... He used to hate me too, but I love him. Now he doesn't hate me any more; he treats me like a little brother. At least there's that: he no longer feels about me the way he feels about the Qur'an school, the teacher, and the children there. Ever since I enrolled in the academy, he's started to respect me. I ask him about the things in my book and my notepad, and he tells me... Sometimes he's angry, other times he's supercilious, but he responds like a young teacher. The book he's holding no longer scares me; I have a book to hold as well. Abd al-Rahman is my brother, no more and no less.'

Mahmud perked up, as though he were about to express an opinion or respond to an objection. But, grabbing his notepad and pencil, he buried his head deep into his book, just as Abd al-Rahman was doing. The book, pencil, and notepad allowed him to avoid staring vacantly at his brother as his beloved hero.

The only thing that disturbed him was Abd al-Ghani, who slouched into the room in his normal fashion. His vacuous expression was that of a minor figure incapable of becoming a major one. He threw himself over the table like a sack of flour falling from an aged camel, then dug his knees into the couch, again like a camel on a mound of sand where it cannot get down if it does not first sink to its knees. He let out a sigh like an old sage sitting down to rest his weary body from the burden of time. Abd al-Rahman looked up for a moment in disapproval, then quickly went back to reading his book, as though to say, 'This void in Abd al-Ghani's life, with his increasingly flabby body, is almost killing him. What is he doing to himself? Once he's closed up his shop and taken the money he's made, his day is over. That's a life destined to be both short and limited. Why doesn't he pick up a book, a piece of paper, or a pencil? If he felt like it, he could record his shop business on paper at least, in numbers.' Scissors and chit-chat were all Abd al-Ghani thought about, along with the old woman who used to buy a few metres of cloth, the poor man who used to haggle over the price, and the flirtatious girl who would visit the Qaysariyya Market to quench her thirst by staring at the men and sharing lewd conversations with them.

For a moment Mahmud was taken up with his numbers again, and he forgot about Abd al-Ghani, almost as though he were not even there. But then his thoughts turned away from the book and back to his eldest brother. As he stared once again at his brother's face, his physique, and his ever-widening bulk, he was distracted by further thoughts: 'My dear elder brother – and that's what he actually is – has become a man who can conduct himself as he pleases. Every morning he sets out for his shop. Once there, he deals with money, selling things and making more money. He counts it all and stares at the dirhams with a steady gaze; his eyes wander as he puts the money in a drawer, one coin on top of another, clinking as they come into contact. From morning till sunset the money grows. He's wealthy, rich; he can feel the money in his hands, how pure it is and how it jingles. He's free to spend it and can buy things. His shoes are brand new, and his jallaba is fresh, clean, and pristine. He even buys halva and laudanum. If he needs a notebook, a pencil, or a book, he doesn't have to send intermediaries to ask his father. He can use a key to open a box that he owns himself and feel the coins in his hands. He can take out whatever he wants, reclose the box, and spend the money as he wishes.'

When Mahmud came to himself again, Abd al-Rahman was asking him what he was supposed to be doing. Mahmud found that he was staring at Abd al-Ghani, his mouth agape, with a smile on his lips that managed to combine admiration, awe, and curiosity. He snapped out of it, reminding himself of what Abd al-Rahman would ask him from time to time: 'Why is your mouth gaping open like an idiot? Have you discovered something new about him you haven't seen before?'

He tried to concentrate on his notepad again, but that word 'new' made him look at Abd al-Ghani again. Before today he had not felt the need to think about how rich his brother was. What motivated this line of thinking was that Mahmud could only purchase the notepads, pencils, and books he needed in school if he managed to persuade Abd al-Rahman to act as his intermediary, or if Khaduj was willing to ask Hajj Muhammad for the cost of them.

Once again he made up his mind to rid himself of this infantile sense of awe with which he enveloped Abd al-Ghani, like a kind of halo whose light was reflected upon his own ambitious soul with all its naive innocence.

'So, who is Abd al-Ghani?' he asked himself. 'Isn't he Khaduj's son, not Yasmine's? Khaduj and Yasmine – two names that never stop cropping up in our family life, like some sort of fate that's pre-occupied with organising our world for us. No, no, I'm approaching manhood now. So be it: Khaduj isn't my mother, and Yasmine is. And I am Hajj Muhammad al-Tihami's son. From now on, nobody's going to ask me about my mother. In school, on the street, with students and teachers, with books, notepads, and pencils, this thing in my life about 'Yasmine or Khaduj' is over and done with – a household matter perhaps, but street- and school-life will have nothing to do with the household. Isn't it your complexion that makes you different from your brothers?'

This question lingered deep down in his consciousness. What wrenched him out of his internal monologue was the sound of Khaduj's voice yelling to Yasmine.

'Bring in the dinner! It's time for your master to come home.'

Khaduj would be sitting in her usual indolent fashion, wearing her favourite clothes and staving off the boredom which coloured her entire life by repairing some of her children's clothes as a diversion. Yasmine, meanwhile, would be buzzing like a bee in her non-stop activity, running between different rooms and the kitchen to set everything up for dinner. She would continuously clean things and wait for instructions from Khaduj, like any maid who devotes her life to service, obedience, and accepting orders from someone else.

Only when he heard one giving orders to the other did Mahmud gain a sense of the differences that separated one woman living a life of idle luxury and another living for work and service. It was his new awareness of his own self and its essence that made him sensitive to the issue. Now his eyes were open to the realities of the household, with a mistress and a servant-woman.

He went on living his usual life in the household without asking any questions – almost in spite of himself, as though some new element had entered the picture, or he had gone through a transformation that was forcing him to think in a new way, in which the words 'Khaduj' and 'Yasmine' weighed heavily, with all their import, difference, and distinction.

The entire issue continued to nag at him, and he dearly wished to respond to it by changing the situation. Instead, he found himself still unable even to get the notepad and pencil he needed, unless he won Khaduj's affectionate sympathy and she managed to convince Hajj Muhammad to give him some money to buy them. He made an effort to find something else to think about, but the only solution was to bury himself once again in the notepad he was holding.

20

Night-time, and a moderate breeze from the west wafted over the burning-hot city; the sun had set, leaving space for a quiet night replete with sweet hopes. When the summer heat was at its height, night-time in Fez was a serene moment; it descended from on high, and the people waited for it just as they did for the delights of Ramadan. They removed their jallabas and kaftans and, liberated from the constraints of walled rooms and high roofs, sat in the open-air central courtyards, where wafts of breeze from every direction came together to blow away the awful traces of daytime.

The evening group broke up, and Hajj Muhammad found himself alone with Khaduj in their wide room. He had already rid himself of the burdens and clothes of the day. A thin curtain was pulled over the doorway; it could block out shapes but still allowed wafts of breeze to pass through it and reach those who were longing for such relief.

When Hajj Muhammad was feeling relaxed and his mood was favourable, he would usually start talking amiably to his wife. This allowed her to gauge his frame of mind, and she had learned how to save up her requests and suggestions until the moment was right; that precise time occurred when there were no unpleasant circumstances and no material or psychological worries to roil his temper.

On that night, Hajj Muhammad spent a good deal of time talking about the wedding celebration at the home of the family of al-Hilw, a friend Hajj Muhammad had known for a long time. He was aware of all the little details that women's customs dictated for such events, the things they loved to relate along with plentiful observations and diverting titbits – not to mention the criticism which inevitably had to accompany such public celebrations and ceremonies.

Hajj Muhammad looked delighted as he told Khaduj that the bride had come down from the upper floor in al-Hilw's house to the lower one because she was the groom's cousin and had grown up with him in the same household. The groom's father had encountered no difficulty in selecting a bride for his son.

Khaduj seized on this information to propose something that had been preying on her mind. 'I wonder, does your brother, Sidi al-Tayyib, have a daughter about Abd al-Ghani's age?'

The impact of this idea could be read on Hajj Muhammad's face, but all he did was give a smile. 'If only...' was all he would say.

He made a point of returning to his previous comments, as though Khaduj had not interrupted him. She realised that this opportunity was slipping away and that such moments as this occurred only very occasionally. After listening until he had finished what he was saying, she decided to tackle the subject head on.

'And what about us? When are we going to celebrate Abd al-Ghani's wedding?'

Hajj Muhammad thought for a long time, staring hard at the floor, which was decorated with a colourful mosaic in blue, red, green, white, and black chips. Looking at his expression at that particular moment, one might have assumed that he was either counting the colours or seeking inspiration from one of them as to how to respond to his own self, which had been rattled by this abrupt question.

Khaduj said nothing more, as though her very silence were intended to hem him in, and she was not about to let him wriggle out of a response to her question.

Hajj Muhammad looked straight at Khaduj. 'Abd al-Ghani's still young,' he replied, feigning a sense of calm deliberation.

'Young?'

Her response showed obvious disagreement, but she said it in a gentle voice, so as not to make Hajj Muhammad lose his temper.

It was clearly not a good idea to get him annoyed at the precise moment when she was making her requests and suggestions.

'He's not young,' she continued. 'He's twenty. Did you wait till you were over twenty to get married?'

Her question triggered memories, and he was able to reminisce about some of the sweetest days in his life, taking him back to his youth. His lips formed into a smile that did not reveal its sources but nevertheless spoke of pleasurable things. He was happy, and he understood Khaduj's point. But then he recalled that Abd al-Ghani was actually not yet twenty, and countered Khaduj's argument with a more forceful one.

'Abd al-Ghani's still just eighteen. Not only that, he's still not fully settled into his job in the shop. Let's allow him to become a full man.'

Khaduj now realised that her argument was not a strong one. At the same time she understood that this was an appropriate time to get Hajj Muhammad to agree with her suggestion in principle. 'God preserve you and grant you all felicity!' she replied affectionately. 'Marriage will get him to settle down. Like you, I want our house to be full of children. Ah, how I long to have brides sitting beside me and to see their small children here. What do you think? Which do you want, boys or girls?'

Hajj Muhammad looked vaguely happy. 'Do you want to be a grandmother that soon?' he asked her, with a guarded smile. As he looked at her face and body, he felt aroused, a feeling that was only amplified by the fact that he had taken off his outer clothes. As he stretched out his hand, his eyes were devouring her curvaceous body. 'You're still a young bride yourself,' he said, 'and you're already wanting grandchildren!'

Khaduj let out a little laugh. 'Haven't you ever seen a young grandmother?' she replied. Giving him a seductive glance, she went on, 'Or a young grandfather?'

Hajj Muhammad appreciated this gesture, which he sensed was a pleasant kind of flattery. 'Even so,' he replied without objecting, 'grandchildren give people the impression that grandfathers and grandmothers have reached a great age.'

'"Grandfather dear" is an expression that suits you, Hajj.'

'The reason you want to see Abd al-Ghani married is that you want to have a bride calling you "Lalla" and a little child babbling "Lalla"! Isn't that right?'

Khaduj laughed. 'God preserve you for all of us,' she said, 'so we can hear "Lalla" and "Grandfather dear"!'

Hajj Muhammad now thought for a long time about the project that Khaduj had proposed. In such matters he consulted nobody but himself. Khaduj nagged him for several nights, to know what his response was to her suggestion, but he asked her to leave the subject until he had time to think and make a decision, and he cautioned her not to breathe a word of it to anyone, especially Abd al-Ghani.

Eventually he concluded that the time was indeed right for Abd al-Ghani to marry, but the key issue was to identify the prospective in-laws whose family background conformed with the social and financial status of the Tihami family.

He thought for a long time and considered the various families that he knew – Barrada, al-Hilw, Ibn Kiran, and al-Siqilli – but he always came to a dead end when it came to their wealth.

'When the son of a wealthy family gets married,' he told himself, 'the wife needs to be richer. Richer? The husband doesn't have to exploit his wife's wealth, but he can't live with a woman who doesn't have money at her disposal... Money's a matter of security and must protect the family as much from the mother's side as from the father's. What's really important is social standing, good reputation, and the bride's honour and reputation. But what's even more important is the land, property, and commercial interests the father owns. As yet Abd al-Ghani doesn't own anything like that. I own a lot, but Abd al-Ghani is still a child, on the threshold of his life. I'm the real guarantor of what he'll own in the future.'

This internal debate kept Hajj Muhammad preoccupied. He was already aware of families and family groups with girls who were over fourteen, but he wanted to conduct a genuine enquiry into which of them was wealthiest and which one's wealth was backed up by land and property. Commerce was significant, but provided no guarantee for the future.

He took his thoughts with him and disappeared, even from Khaduj. He had no intention of either seeking advice or listening to the opinions of anyone else. What he wanted was to make enquiries, draw up a plan, and then announce his decision.

Meanwhile, Khaduj grew tired of waiting for him to make up his mind. She tried several times to ask him how it was all going, but he gently repelled all her approaches without giving her the chance to ask or insist. She had to wait a long time for a suitable moment. On a night with hopes blooming, Khaduj managed to edge Hajj Muhammad towards the topic without making her purpose obvious. Having tempted him thus far, she was ready to hear the joyous news. But when Hajj Muhammad revealed his decision, it was a great surprise.

'I've chosen Hajj Abd al-Latif al-Tazi's daughter for Abd al-Ghani!'

Khaduj looked completely taken aback. While she had been waiting for so long, she had surveyed many families and family groupings. But her ambitions had never gone so high as to even think of the al-Tazi family, because it was so immensely wealthy and prestigious.

She burst into tears. So great was her delight that she could not keep her inner self under control. Quite unable to express her thanks, she leaned over in all modesty and fervently kissed Hajj Muhammad's hands and feet. Gratitude now blended with temptation and seduction, and Hajj Muhammad proceeded to slake his thirst. The occasion of this final answer was to keep them both secluded beneath its shroud.

21

Khaduj found it difficult to contain her joy at the news of Abd al-Ghani's engagement, although she did the best she could. Her delight made itself felt throughout the house and its household. However, she only gave small hints as to what lay behind her excitement. Everyone in the house, from the servants to Hajj Muhammad's own sister, realised that the family was about to celebrate a happy event, but no one knew exactly what it was, and nobody asked Khaduj to reveal her secret. That would have to wait for Hajj Muhammad; everyone knew that, when the day came that he allowed the news to come out, Khaduj would not be one to keep it hidden. So, the women did not pester Khaduj with questions, although they did allow themselves to express their joy by reciting prayers in which they asked God to extend His blessings on Hajj Muhammad and his happy household.

Khaduj now started thinking about the forthcoming wedding, about the string of events that would have to be held, from the engagement announcement through to the dowry presentation and the eventual ceremony itself, and about the room that the new bride would occupy in the house. As she thought about the preparations, she was delighted by the idea that, once the new bride started addressing her as 'Lalla', her own status within the household would be further enhanced.

At first Khaduj could not think what it was that was bothering her from time to time and spoiling her joy, but then she asked herself a pertinent series of questions: 'What about this bride? What does she look like? How beautiful is she? What's her name?'

She realised she had no answer to any of them, and yet she could not ask Hajj Muhammad, because she was aware that he could not answer them either. He did not know, and in any case he would certainly not let her ask him such questions because Hajj Abd al-Latif al-Tazi's daughter must of course be beautiful. And if she were not, then she was still the daughter of a man with both money and status.

Hajj Muhammad had a surprise in store for her. 'Tomorrow,' he said, 'you're going with your sister and Lalla Fatima to visit Hajj Abd al-Latif al-Tazi's house to finalise the engagement.'

'Will we see the bride?'

'That's not important. But, if you have a chance to...'

Khaduj now felt relieved; she was going to see the bride and get a look at the girl who would be calling her 'Lalla'.

Now she was even more excited. Abd al-Ghani's marriage was really going to happen, and as a mother-in-law she could look forward to becoming a grandmother too.

Khaduj's visit to Hajj Abd al-Latif's household was not a surprise to that family, but it was disguised as such: they were of course aware that the al-Tihami family members were coming to request their daughter's hand, but according to custom they were not supposed to be aware of this, and should welcome the visitors as though it were all unexpected. For Khaduj, the visit also had its more cryptic aspects. She only hinted at her objective as she arranged to catch the prospective bride unawares and with her face uncovered.

A pleasant conversation ensued between the guests and the ladies of the house, all of it based on a pretence of not knowing anything. Zaynab, Khaduj's sister, opened the conversation by introducing her sister to al-Batul, the mistress of the household.

'On this happy day,' Zaynab said, 'Khaduj was most anxious to pay you a visit.'

'You're all most welcome,' al-Batul replied in delight. 'A happy day indeed! How we've been looking forward to your visit. My husband, Hajj Abd al-Latif, has been telling us wonderful things about Hajj Muhammad, extolling his virtues and his illustrious family.'

'We in turn would like to make our relationship closer,' Khaduj said, 'and – God willing – become one family.'

'It may be destiny, for nothing is beyond God's power.'

'Mr. Abd al-Ghani,' Zaynab added, 'is both intelligent and calm, just right for your daughter – God preserve her.'

Al-Batul pretended to be shy and said nothing, busying herself with tea preparations, to avoid having to give a direct response.

The olive-skinned maid al-Anbar started to speak. 'Mr. Abd al-Ghani, of course—'

Zaynab took it up, saying, '—is in the Qaysariyya Market: his shop's the most famous one there.'

The maid gave a broad smile.

'God preserve him!' said al-Batul. 'Men who have businesses in the Qaysariyya are always fortunate.'

'Mr. Abd al-Ghani knows only the Qaysariyya, the mosque, and the house, nothing more.'

'He's his father's son,' al-Batul rejoined. 'My husband Abd al-Latif says that Hajj Muhammad knows only the mosque and the house.'

'You were all created to be relatives,' said Lalla Fatima. 'The whole thing is a wonderful blessing!'

The women of the household now all took part in the exercise of surprising the girl who was busy sewing in an isolated corner of the next room. She had never greeted female guests nor spoken to them. None of the ladies of the household made any attempt to stop their guests entering her hiding place so that she could evade them. Khaduj, her sister, and Lalla Fatima were all delighted when the mistress of the house used her hand to delicately lift the prospective bride's face from her sewing and give her a kiss on the brow, wishing her all happiness in the future.

By the time Khaduj left Hajj Abd al-Latif's house, something lay heavily on her heart. Her happiness had turned to profound sorrow: the surprise had been anything but a joyous one. She had been expecting something entirely different from the girl whose face had been delicately lifted from her sewing. She was expecting a pleasant oval face, white as snow, a tiny mouth like a ring, black eyes, level eyebrows, and a full body. Instead, she had been shocked to see a small brown-complexioned face, a wide mouth with full, almost bulging lips, vaguely blue eyes, eyebrows so thin that they might have been drawn with a sharp pencil, twin strands poking out from a head-kerchief to reveal frizzy hair, and a thin body with slender, spindly hands.

The shock of it was enough to leave Khaduj speechless, and she said nothing. Her sister and Lalla Fatima sympathised with her plight, but they decided to say nothing until Khaduj herself had spoken. They all hurried back home. Khaduj's feelings made her want to hasten the journey as much as possible, as though she needed to unload the burden of her disappointment as soon as she reached the door.

All the way home Khaduj could not stop thinking about what had just happened. The visit had been a traditional one, and there was no hope of either changing Hajj Muhammad's mind or avoiding the implementation of the decision that he had reached and the engagement he had arranged. As she hurried back to the security of her own home, she constantly reviewed the sequence of events. Once home, she took off her veil and looked around. Her sister, Lalla Fatima, was watching expectantly as though waiting for a word to be uttered against an accused.

Yasmine and the other servants around her were making a great fuss to congratulate Khaduj on the happy event, and she manufactured a false smile to hide her sorrow.

'May Mahmud share the same good fortune,' she told Yasmine in a kind voice.

'And Abd al-Rahman as well.'

'And Lalla Aisha too.'

'And Mr. Abd al-Latif.'

Ululations now broke out – it was Yasmine who could not conceal her happiness.

Amid all this ululation and shouting, Abd al-Ghani himself

appeared at the door, as though just in time for the major announcement. He had no idea what had happened, nor did he know that he was about to be married. Even if he had thought about marriage, he would not have considered it any of his particular business; even when he had the usual kind of adolescent imaginings, they were regularly buried deep inside him. After all, he was still very much at the mercy of his father's will, so how was he supposed to give any thought to things outside that context, even things connected with his own future, or a wife?

The shock for him was enormous when Yasmine came rushing over and gave him a hug and kiss. 'Here's the groom!' she shouted. 'Here's the groom!' And she proceeded to let out some magnificent ululations.

Other members of the family were there too. Abd al-Rahman looked utterly astonished, while Abd al-Latif, Mahmud, and Aisha all just stood there, as the entire household, having been looking forward to some truly joyous event, now celebrated noisily. But there was one person in the room whose heart was skewered by sadness, a feeling that had to be kept hidden as everyone else rejoiced, and that was Khaduj.

The noisy celebration came to an end, and family members went their own way, swallowed up by the realities of daily life. The children set about their normal work, and Khaduj found herself face to face with her sister, Zaynab, who gave her an affectionate look and tried to make light of things.

'God be praised,' she said in honeyed tones, 'the bride is a little beauty... but—'

'But... but... My dear sister, she's black! Am I to marry my son to a girl who's dark-skinned? Dark-skinned!' She would have burst into tears had she not been afraid it might lead to something even worse. She firmly believed it was not a good omen when there were tears on the occasion of a wedding.

Zaynab realised that her function in this instance was to assuage her sister's sadness, whatever the logic involved. 'Khaduj, my sister,' she said, 'the girl's still very young and pretty. Maybe her skin will lighten after they're married.'

'Lighten, or get even darker? That's all nonsense, Zaynab!'

'Does Hajj Muhammad realise the girl's dark-skinned?'

'Does he realise? How's he supposed to realise? But now, how is anyone supposed to broach the subject with him or oppose the decision he's made?'

Zaynab did not reply. Khaduj seemed totally distracted as she thought about the situation. There was a heavy silence between the two sisters. Zaynab made no attempt to alleviate the dismal mood. The issue was obviously much more serious than could be dealt with through some simplistic logic. Looking at her sister, Zaynab saw that Khaduj's hand was on her cheek, and she was almost sobbing. She closed her eyes, as though seeking a solution to the problem in the colours of the mosaics.

This heavy silence was suddenly broken by a horrendous sob from deep inside Khaduj's heart. Zaynab's eyes were immediately wrested from the multicoloured mosaics, and she looked fearfully at her sister.

'Did you notice that tawny-skinned servant?' Khaduj asked as she swallowed her sobs. 'The one who greeted us with a smile and spoke to us in a brazen fashion far more than the lady of the house did?'

'Certainly I did,' Zaynab replied. 'What of it?'

'She could be the bride's mother,' Khaduj went on sadly, scarcely finding the words to say what she needed to express.

'The bride's mother?'

'See if I'm not right!'

'The servant's daughter? Abd al-Ghani is to marry the servant's daughter? No, no, Khaduj. You need to talk to Hajj Muhammad!'

The words terrified Khaduj: 'servant's daughter', 'Abd al-Ghani's bride is a servant's daughter', 'talk to Hajj Muhammad'. The thoughts buried themselves deep in her mind, and yet they still resonated with horrific volume.

The time came for Zaynab to leave, but Khaduj stayed where she was, ruminating and silently enduring her misery. Eventually Hajj Muhammad returned home from the sunset prayer.

'So, how did you find the bride?' he asked.

In asking the question, he was not expecting any particular reply. Khaduj's visit to the al-Tazi household was a matter of custom, and he assumed there would be nothing significant about it. Even so, he was delighted when Khaduj responded to his question with a phrase entirely devoid of meaning, mouthed while distracted.

'A wonderful blessing.'

In the room where the children gathered, Abd al-Rahman was talking to Abd al-Ghani about his forthcoming marriage, playing along with him in a manner that was not totally without provocation. He put down the book he was holding and looked straight at Abd al-Ghani.

'You're getting married,' he said. 'Do you know who your fiancée is? Have you ever set eyes on her?'

Abd al-Ghani opened his eyes and stared at Abd al-Rahman. He was astonished at the need to address a question that had never even occurred to him.

22

The official relationship between the two families, the al-Tihamis and the al-Tazis, began with a formal session organised in the Dar al-Silaa, the large shop owned by Hajj Abd al-Latif al-Tazi. Two friends of each of the two heads of household had been invited to attend the meeting, as had Sidi Jaafar, a sharif hasani – that is, a descendant of the Prophet Muhammad through his grandson al-Hasan. It was a custom in the al-Tazi household not to take any important decision without him being present. Hajj Muhammad had also invited Sidi al-Tayyia, another sharif, whose advice he would usually seek on any matter of significance, though without necessarily following it.

The two sharifs started laying the groundwork on the subject of a matrimonial relationship. They recited prophetic accounts in a melodic colloquial dialect, and mispronounced Qur'anic verses which had no real relevance to the subject of marriage. They completely understood one other, however, and were working jointly towards the desired goal of bringing about an engagement between the two families. One of them would start reciting either the Qur'anic verse or the prophetic account, and the other one would finish it – although even then the addition might not conclude it correctly. And one of them would point to a particular argument so that the other could provide an elucidation or commentary on it.

Their task was to bless the linkage of the two families and make light of any difficulties that might stand in the way of the agreement's completion, and they both performed the task with a good deal of enthusiasm and exaggeration. They realised how much the two families wanted to finalise the relationship and appreciated, on the basis of their long experience at the task, that it was possible to surmount any difficulties, however hard it might seem at first.

Hajj al-Tazi presented his requests for the dowry. For the formal engagement ceremony he was asking for a large amount of money, jewels, trinkets, pendants, clothes, and jewels. Hajj Muhammad was not in any way surprised by the size of the demands, because he was an expert bargainer and could use his skill to bring Hajj al-Tazi's request down to a much lower level.

Now the contest between the two merchants began, both of them being adept at haggling after having spent their long lives doing so. Every time the negotiations reached a tricky point, the 'reconciliation committee' would become involved, and whenever clouds appeared on the horizon, the two sharifs would invoke citations from the Qur'an and prophetic tradition.

Finally, an agreement was reached – indeed, it had to be reached. Each of the two merchants was convinced that he was the winner, meaning that the desire that each of them had to conclude the deal was no less cogent than that of any two dealers in a situation where one was buying and the other selling. As a result of the negotiations, each thought he had won.

The engagement between Abd al-Ghani, son of Hajj Muhammad al-Tihami, and Saadiyya, daughter of Hajj Abd al-Latif al-Tazi, was duly announced in the Mawlay Idris shrine, where friends of the families, guests, sharifs, and jurists were all invited to hear a recitation of the Fatiha as a token of the sacred ties binding the two noble families together.

'Who's the bride and who's the groom?' – no one who attended the ceremony asked himself those questions. They all blessed the link that now united the heads of these two prominent families without bothering about the identities of the prospective bride and groom. Those remained secret, perhaps only to emerge with the witnesses who were to execute the actual marriage contract.

Several months went by, and all Abd al-Ghani knew was that

he was now engaged to be married to a girl about whom he knew absolutely nothing. He was engaged, like it or not. He had never thought about it before; all he knew was that he had never expressed any desire to get married and had never felt like addressing the issue – something that in any case he could only do in his own mind, and then only when his nerves could stand it. Now, those same nerves had kept on at him mercilessly for many months. He tried to suppress such feelings and keep calm whenever he started to feel his agitation increasing. He was clearly affected by the whole matter, and yet each return to reality made it clear that there was no room for such emotion. He was a bachelor about to get married, and a potential husband to an unknown entity. While he was still a bachelor in reality, he had no right to behave like one, either psychologically or socially.

He did his best to forget his situation; everything was designed to get him to do so. Ever since the Fatiha had been recited and he was engaged, there had been no indications that the family into which he had been betrothed in absentia was now thinking about anything to do with his actual marriage. It was out of the question to talk to anyone about it; he was the very last person who was supposed to talk about something that was considered no concern of his at that point. He was still living in his own private world of youth and adolescence, nerves and psyche. All he could do was to talk to his own world and hear what it had to say.

'Saadiyya al-Tazi,' he said to himself. 'That's all I know about this creature who's to become a life companion. Life companion? Will the day ever dawn when I have a companion in my life...? Saadiyya, what does she look like? What colour's her complexion? How old is she? Maybe she's like my mother, Khaduj. If so, she'll be an ideal wife in appearance and temperament.'

These dreams danced as he imagined the unknown girl. And yet, the images had no dimensions to them. And so, in spite of the dreams, he had to live in a kind of fog where the only thing he could make out was the vague form of a woman.

Time eventually rescued Abd al-Ghani from his dull, colour-less existence. After two years of waiting, the family finally started making preparations for his marriage celebration. He was still, like all his other brothers and sisters, going hither and thither to help get things ready without being asked for his opinion or advice on the story in which he was to be the principal hero.

The celebrations began. Everyone in the household was happy, even the people who had to work hard all day and every day in order to prepare for the happy times ahead. But there was one person who could not find any happiness, someone who was separated from that happy world because his dreams had yet to find a secure resting place. He could no longer maintain the dialogue with his nerves and dreams. He was now a person with no heart, a body with no spirit, moving like a machine that has started to lose its power source – list-less, active, but without any awareness.

The entire family celebrated in the best possible way. Hajj Muhammad was celebrating not only his son's wedding but also the acknowledgement of the family's status in the city and the Makhfi-yya Quarter. He was eager to show the in-laws that his position was no less prominent, wealthy, or highly regarded in the local context than theirs. With that thought in mind, he was making every effort to come out on top in the tacit struggle taking place between the two families involved in the one wedding.

Eventually, Abd al-Ghani was taken to a small canopied area at the far end of the huge room where he had been born and spent his childhood years, a space that had been witness to a vigorous marital life, the hero of which had been Hajj Muhammad, and with mul-tiple heroines – Khaduj and Yasmine.

This was a wedding chamber, the centre of which had been decorated with a lofty pyramidal structure of silk curtain material decorated with gold thread. To either side of the chamber itself were two smaller rooms: one for the groom, and the other for the bridal matron, whose job it was to make the bride feel comfortable and offer advice and encouragement to the groom.

Abd al-Ghani was the first to arrive, driven there like a condemned man about to meet his fate. He kept tripping up as the cluster of women pushed him along amid a cacophony of ululations and guffaws. He felt so shy and frightened that he almost fainted. The shouts of encouragement from all directions only served to make him even more uncomfortable and confused. He began to feel as though the path he was taking – from the door of the house to the bridal chamber – was the 'straight and narrow' path which he had heard about in his lessons at the Qur'an school. Now he was feeling scared to death as he proceeded along it. Amid the crowd of women and servant-girls the path was a long one, longer than any he had taken before. Finally he rushed to the door of the chamber, to be greeted by the bridal matron with more ululations and prayers to the Prophet – peace and blessings upon him! She grabbed him by the hand to introduce him to his bride. She then went and grabbed the bride by the hand to bring her out into the centre of the chamber, surrounded by a cluster of other women who proceeded to extol the girl's beauty and shout her praises in tones akin to singing. The whole ceremony was interspersed with a prayer to the Prophet and choral ululations intoned by voices both melodious and hoarse.

Now that the unveiling of the bride was completed, Saadiyya was led over to the chamber door. As a group of women whispered words of encouragement in her ear, her veil was removed. One of them brought her over to her husband with a series of bold phrases. She then withdrew and lowered the curtain. Now Saadiyya found herself alone with Abd al-Ghani.

Abd al-Ghani had never imagined that he would find himself in this situation. Here he was face to face with a young girl whom his eyes could not take in. With her eyes closed and her head lowered she seemed like an immobile statue. He was feeling so befuddled that he could not think of any way of introducing himself to her. He tried raising his eyes to look at her face, but he still felt completely at a loss. He tried to say something, but his tongue would not co-operate. He did not even think of stretching out a hand to her; his entire thought process was paralysed.

So, Abd al-Ghani sat there like a statue as well – one statue facing another.

It fell to the bridal matron to come back into the chamber and break this wall of silence. Her knowledge of the trade had made her aware that when she brought Abd al-Ghani and Saadiyya to meet their fates her services would be needed to get them moving. She spoke to them both in soothing terms, including references to how attractive both bride and groom were. She then started tearing down the wall of shyness between the couple. Some of the things she said were raunchy, the aim being to demolish the bashfulness of the young girl, who had never used such words before, even when talking to herself. The girl turned beetroot-red and lowered her head still further, so that her facial features completely disappeared into the cluster of jewellery and billowing clothes that covered her head and tiny body. Abd al-Ghani was no less bashful than his bride, but the words he was hearing from the bridal matron were sufficient to prepare him to break out of this cordon of silence.

The matron withdrew again, threatening to come back in if she did not hear some conversation going on behind the curtain. Abd al-Ghani now spoke a few disjointed words, but they were not enough to prompt the bride to say anything. Even so, they marked the beginning of a slippery slope, one where the matron continued her interventions, which did not end until two nights later, when she finally left.

On a wonderful, joyous morning, full of anticipation, she emerged, with ululations and prayers to the Prophet, holding in her hands the evidence of the bride's virginity.

23

During Abd al-Ghani's wedding, his sister Aisha was the happiest of girls. As far as she was concerned, weddings were festivals that filled her imagination with sweet dreams. Ever since she had matured and left her innocent childhood behind, she had been deprived of the enjoyment of such celebrations.

Young girls were normally not allowed to attend wedding ceremonies for fear that their mothers would be accused of peddling their wares on the market. No beautiful girl who was from an illustrious background and had a rich father would ever appear in public as a way of attracting the attention of prominent families, when one of the mothers might decide to come and ask for the girl's hand. The only way to get a glimpse of such girls was in the bosom of the family, inside the house; the only time the girl would leave the house was to go to the bathhouse or to visit her grandparents. However, a family celebration provided a golden opportunity for the girl to have some fun and to appear as a rosebud in a society where only fully opened flowers would be seen on such occasions.

Aisha was overjoyed by her brother's wedding. For the first time she was fully aware of what was happening as she witnessed a wedding ceremony. She was wearing beautiful clothes and was free of the restraints imposed by her mother's watchful eye, her father's worries, and her brother's strict control. She was also participating in the preparations for the occasion and was happily wearing herself out helping with the various entertainments involved. For the first time too she would be sitting with the older female guests and conversing freely with them.

Indeed, people did start looking at her. She was lively, energetic, and blooming. A child no more, she had become a young woman, lovely and enticing. People did not normally look at a girl like her just to assess her beauty and discover her talents; part of their interest involved thoughts about possible marriages and selecting a prospective bridegroom for this beautiful rose that had now fully opened and was ready to be picked.

It was not just Aisha's beauty that made people look at her. Hajj Muhammad's financial and social status had several of the women present thinking carefully about a closer connection. If he had not actually had a daughter, they would certainly have wished he had one so that a relationship, and a powerful link with another noble family, could be established. These thoughts were going through the minds of the female guests as they noticed Aisha moving among them with such grace and liveliness. A whole series of comments ensued.

'God grant that I may come to your wedding!'

'Enough. It's already time to celebrate your wedding as well.'

'I dearly hope that I can be of help at your wedding celebration.'

The young girl blushed bashfully. For the first time, she was hearing words that gave her the idea that she too would one day be a bride and people would celebrate her marriage. She did her best to hide herself from these words and the peering eyes that kept staring at her. But those same words beset her as much in secret as they did in the open. Wherever she went, all she heard was more comments.

'Well, Khaduj, when will you be celebrating Aisha's wedding?'

'God bless her beauty and youth!'

'You don't need matchmakers. The whole house is full of them!'

'Aisha, would you agree to be married to my son?'

Aisha would have much preferred not to have to avoid these comments, smiles, and stares that took in her attributes with both affection and anticipation. She liked hearing the words – they were like sweet melodies that moved from her ears to her very core, which thirsted for such tunes. However, as it was, modesty forced her to direct her stumbling footsteps away from all these ladies and servant-women as they continued to extol her beauty and wish her a happy future life. Even if modesty had not forced her to move away, she would have had to do it in any case. No young woman of marriageable age was allowed to look at such ladies and servants, or listen to chatter about her beauty and marriage prospects, without fleeing as soon as possible and hiding from these people whose sole right it was to discuss the affairs of men and women.

So, she fled – but she was unable to escape the magic of the words that now enveloped her entire being. She could feel them in her heart as though her ears were still listening.

'It's time you were married—'

'Would you agree to marry my son?'

'God grant that I may come to your wedding!'

All of the sweet and wonderful words were still ringing in her ears. But, gradually, the magic began to fade and a more rational approach took over. '"Marry my son?" Am I to be a bride one day? A wife for a husband? A woman for a man? A *man*!'

Her thoughts came to a halt at that word, 'man'. Her memory, and her conscious and unconscious imagination, contained many visions and images of such a creature. She had never met a man outside her family in her entire life, and all she knew came from conversations with the servant-women, who would talk to her and explain what the word really meant.

'Aisha,' Yasmine would whisper to her, 'men are shifty. My little one, you should never trust any of them. If one of them stares at you, make sure you look away. He's only staring out of his own lust. Men eat fruit, then they spit out the pips. Make sure you're never one of those pips.'

When Aisha had started to emerge from her childhood and become a teenager, a whole host of words had battered her ears.

'Men destroy a girl's moral compass, Aisha. If you set eyes on a man, you must realise that there's some scandal involved.'

'Scandal?' Aisha had asked.

Her young mind could not fully grasp the dimensions of the word 'scandal', but it obviously implied some major risk, something that was both hurtful and damaging.

'There was a beautiful young girl your age,' another story went, 'just as beautiful as you are. The man involved deceived her, then laughed at her. Her family disowned her, and the wretch himself did the same. She was left with no family and no one to look after her.'

Such stories made Aisha even more confused and distressed. 'What did the man do?' she wondered. 'How did he deceive her? How did he come to laugh at her? Why did her family disown her?'

She could not answer any of these questions because her young mind had yet to learn how to give meaning to such terms; she did not understand what Yasmine meant by giving her this dire warning. It was only the expression on Yasmine's face, serious and rigid, that gave her an inkling of what was intended. She looked straight into Aisha's eyes as she spoke, but hardly had she done so before she deliberately looked away. Yasmine's eyes hid a lot, but at the same time they also expressed a great deal. Aisha made sure to pay close attention to her careful warnings whenever they were alone together.

'Listen, Aisha! Men will tempt you, they'll say they love you. Young girls don't understand men. Make sure that no man ever tempts you or tries to say he loves you. You don't even realise what lies beyond the initial temptation and declaration of love.'

Aisha now lived in mortal terror. Yasmine's words had created a threatening picture of men in her mind. But now, here were all these ladies and servant-women wishing her to have a husband, a bridegroom... a man!

She may have been able to escape the talk of these women and servant-girls about her beauty and wishing her to find a husband and spouse, but the words they used stuck to her and filled her world with echoes that went deep. It was almost as though her ears could only pick up the words 'husband', 'bridegroom', and 'man'.

'This is the temptation that Dada Yasmine has been warning me about,' she told herself. 'A man falls in love with me from afar; his name evokes a persistent curiosity inside me. I need to be clever about this, so I won't suffer the same fate as that girl who was disowned by both her family and the man in question.'

As the celebrations of Abd al-Ghani's wedding proceeded, Aisha no longer listened to the compliments and aspirations. The female guests' honeyed words no longer filled her ears with notions of a bridegroom. However, she did open her eyes to a brand-new phenomenon in the house: Saadiyya, Abd al-Ghani's wife. She was about the same age as Aisha, a little older but not that much. A young, beautiful prize, but one who had a groom, a husband, a man! She was living inside their house as though no man had ever hoodwinked her, or laughed at her. Her morals were still unsullied. She looked happy with the way things were going, her feelings evident in the sparkle of her beautiful, honey-coloured eyes. Her tawny cheeks were a brilliant rosy red, and her eyes were lined with dark black kohl. Aisha wondered whether Saadiyya had looked that way before she was discovered and married to a man.

'How is it,' Aisha asked herself, 'that Saadiyya does not feel utterly disgusted' – in Aisha's case, the effects of the concept had now reached the point of nausea – 'at the mere mention of the word "bridegroom" or "man"?' It seemed to Aisha the reason was that she did not have someone like Yasmine beside her to explain what bridegrooms and men were all about. However, Saadiyya was happy; she seemed to have discovered some new world, one where she did not need to run away, or feel disgusted and nauseous.

This small idea now plunged Aisha into a terrifying vortex. The blood in her veins kept pulsing with a summons she had never known before, challenging her personal calm, putting her on edge, and making her feel a sense of revolt, or defiance – a new paradigm invading her untroubled youth, a summons that occasionally pulled at her sense of modesty and filled her with dread at the thought of this interloping idea that had transformed her into a modern girl living in a modern world.

The vortex continued to envelop Aisha and her small idea. The words that she had heard from the ladies and servant-women attending the wedding celebrations were delightful and pleasant, with dimensions and horizons that had never confronted her before: groom, husband, a world strewn with roses and blooms giving off a lovely scent from afar for a thirsty soul. When? When would that distance be shortened, overlaid with a world of roses and flowers?

Still that vortex.

Man? Groom? Husband?

Yasmine's advice still rang in Aisha's young ears, as though she were hearing it for the first time. 'If you set eyes on a man, you must realise that there's some scandal involved. If any man stares at you, avoid any eye contact.'

Then she thought, 'The world of roses involves scandal? The Devil's started washing his feet inside my heart. No, no, I'll never have any thoughts about men. They're dirty and scurrilous. They destroy your morals, they...'

And still the vortex.

'Saadiyya has a husband, a bridegroom, a man. Even so, her tiny eyes radiate happiness. She's obviously happy, happy in the arms of a man...'

Aisha spent a lengthy adolescence in this frightening perplexity, its length not measured in months or years. Instead, it was measured in frightful phrases that violently jolted her feelings, phrases that sent her into a dangerous mental state whose primary focus was men.

24

Abd al-Rahman's countenance showed all the signs of anger and aggression. His nerves had stirred themselves to adopt a course of violent revolution. No longer was he that quiet student or rebellious child who would never cause a big fuss. By now he had become a reckless and stubborn young man, aggressive and confrontational, his nerves always on edge. When he came home, he could not stand talking to his mother, his brothers, or the servants, and he continued to erect a substantial barrier between his father and himself. He no longer made any attempt to approach his father as he had often done in the past, and was no longer happy to share a meal with him as he had done whenever Hajj Muhammad softened his stance a little and invited Abd al-Ghani and Abd al-Rahman to join him at the dinner table.

By now Saadiyya had commandeered all Abd al-Ghani's attention, so he hardly ever left her bridal bower when he came home from the shop. Abd al-Rahman could now avoid those stupid, probing questions that got on his nerves whenever Abd al-Ghani came into the room that the children of the house used. He was also relieved of Abd al-Ghani's nasty, dubious glances, the stupid and annoying remarks he made, and the clicking sounds of the chewing gum against his teeth, creating a flood of juvenile drool.

Now, Abd al-Rahman would launch into a tirade against Mahmud whenever he approached and said something nice, and would scold Aisha if she came close – at which point she would discover that her brother was a type of man that Yasmine had not identified for her.

He managed to find some peace and quiet among his books, but even they occasionally annoyed him: in some of them he could detect Abd al-Ghani with all his stupidity, nosiness, and aggression; in others Mahmud with his wounded soul and his almost inevitable complexes; and in still others Aisha, Yasmine, or his mother. All of this led him to rebel against the siege wall that enveloped him, leading him to resort to complete solitude, in all its futility.

His nerves gave him no rest. They did not leave him alone to think straight; instead, they kept agitating him in a way that led him to chew on his fingers, as though according to some kind of pact between his nerves and himself.

Nevertheless, he still cogitated. 'What's the future of my country without freedom? How are we supposed to face our future, when frivolous hands keep rolling it towards an abyss in various carefully planned phases?'

From the future his thoughts turned to the present. 'My fellow countrymen are still surrounded by a circular fence. Those same frivolous hands are still clipping away at the wings of our non-existent freedom. Our country is now threatened by a terrifying explosion. What about me? A feather blowing in the wind... I can never be "me" if I don't unleash my own power to put an end to the violence that is threatening the elite of my country.'

The question posed itself again, more insistently, 'What about me?'

'You?' a voice proclaimed with a resounding laugh that refused to acknowledge his solitude. 'You, put an end to the violence? So who are you? And what is this power that you're proposing to unleash to put an end to this violence?!'

He went on thinking. This time he was a little more humble. 'Me, with my cell, my friends, the group that's thinking along with me and projecting my own fate,' he said. 'I'm my own generation, the young people of my country, my nation, my fellow citizens. I'm my country.'

At this point the small idea found what it was missing; the young soul managed to relax after some anxious moments – or, at least, it had the impression that it was relaxing.

The voice that refused to leave him alone now spoke again, this time more quietly and craftily, without the resounding laughter, and it did not talk about the turmoil to come. 'What's the cost? For the most part it'll be prison, arrests, beatings, hunger. You're not yet ready for such deprivation. You can't stand violence.'

Abd al-Rahman put his fingers to his mouth and chewed on them unconsciously. A sudden ray of light illuminated his thoughts. 'Millions of citizens,' he said, 'are already living in prisons and detention centres, whipped, tortured, and hungry. Am I so far removed from them in their sufferings? It's for my sake that they're being imprisoned, arrested, tortured, and starved. Can I not share their ordeal, to get a sense of what they're going through for my sake? No... I shall be with them. The world will never know how extensive the violent resistance actually is if it is not made much more general, if it does not involve me personally. I'm a citizen of this country.'

The voice now let out a great shout. 'What about your school?' it asked menacingly. 'Your studies? Your future? If you get involved in risky activities like this, you'll have no future.'

'What do you want? For me to be like Abd al-Ghani?'

His nerves jumped, as though he had been touched by the Devil himself. His ideas started to fade, and he thrust his hand into his pocket in search of a smoke. He had begun by experimenting with inhaling a cigarette that one of his friends had given him. Now he found smoking both relaxing and intoxicating, but only felt the need for it because this threatening voice kept reverberating in his conscience. But he found no cigarette. Even if he had one, he would not have dared to smoke in a house dominated by Hajj Muhammad. So, he returned his fingers to his mouth and chewed furiously.

'I'll plan my own future,' he told himself. 'My school is life itself. Violence can never stand against my own conscience. I shall carry out my mission, and let whatever happens happen.'

As he returned to his lonely self the voice began again, but he stood up, intent on terminating a conversation that had led him to a clear decision, and anxious to rid himself of the alien ideas he had struggled hard to reject.

When he left the house he had no particular goal in mind; no club to go to, because there was none; no one to look for – neither schoolfriend nor cellmate. He set off walking aimlessly along the streets, as though searching for something without locating it. He stared at people's faces, looking into the eyes of men, young and old, then at a woman carrying her baby and holding out a quivering hand in a request for alms. He looked unconsciously at the baby, barefoot and in rags, eyes afflicted by disease and face by hunger. He recoiled sharply as though the sight were completely unfamiliar to him. His conscience screamed, 'Haven't you ever seen a starving baby with conjunctivitis before?'

As he walked amid the rabble of life, he heard a voice behind him sharing a piece of news with his companion. 'They've arrested the leaders. This afternoon there's going to be a protest demonstration starting at the Qarawiyin.'

Abd al-Rahman turned around as though his senses had been seared by a flame. 'Who told you?' he asked. 'Who said the leaders have been arrested?'

The man gave him a suspicious look, but then his expression turned into a smile. Apparently Abd al-Rahman's youth assuaged his doubts. 'It's true. I know it for certain.'

Abd al-Rahman now set off in a hurry, as though the fact that he had turned around would not hold him back from the goal he now set himself. He carried on walking, going where his legs took him until he arrived at the Qarawiyin Mosque. On the way, prying eyes stared at him, secretly observing him as they swivelled in their sockets and kept track of anyone heading for the mosque. But Abd al-Rahman paid no attention, nor did his eyes connect with those malicious other eyes observing him so closely.

Inside the mosque the intentions of the men gathering there coalesced with all their anger, resolution, and premonitions of disaster. Grim determination was printed on their faces, and their eyes flashed. There was no need to talk; they did not engage in any conversation. Instead, they all looked at each other as though to say, 'Are you determined to fight as well, to fight until victory?'

'God is greatest,' intoned the muezzin, the crier of the mosque. 'God is greatest.'

In an orchestral whisper, thousands of voices responded, 'God is greatest, God is greatest.'

Abd al-Rahman's body shivered, as though he had never heard a muezzin intone the call to prayer before. His eyes almost overflowed with hot tears, but they soon dried as he took in the stolid, firm looks on people's faces that told him this was no time for such emotion.

The worshippers performed the prayers, their hearts bowing in submission to God, with the request that he grant them resolve, patience, and an increase of faith. As the final 'Peace be with you!' sounded, a modest voice proclaimed, 'O gentle God, help us!'

Thousands of voices now echoed the call. 'O gentle God, help us!'

The demonstration emerged from the mosque, loud, powerful, and angry, urged on by young voices chanting, 'Down with colonialism! Release our leaders!'

In Najjarin Square a young man suddenly appeared from nowhere like a beam of light; he was in the prime of life, was tall and thin, and had veined cheeks and a riveting stare. In a weak but forceful voice imbued with deep faith, he began preaching. His enthusiasm, initiative, and courage were astonishing; he feared nothing, held nothing back, and did not falter. His few words were a fire that filled the hearts of everyone gathered there with faith and enthusiasm, but it was his youth that had the greatest effect on the assembly. It was Abd al-Rahman.

'Down with colonialism,' everyone yelled behind him. 'Glory to our homeland!'

But when the demonstrators looked around, they found that

a cordon had been placed around the small square. They were led away to detention camps and prison cells.

News of Abd al-Rahman's arrest reached the house faster than the news about the demonstration itself. Hajj Muhammad was jolted by a thunderbolt. 'Abd al-Rahman's in prison!'

25

Hajj Muhammad leapt up from his seat at this dire news. 'My son in prison? No, no! Impossible... my son... Abd al-Rahman in prison? What a disaster, what an insult...! O Lord!' he implored, raising his eyes to heaven, 'You have imprinted this disaster on my forehead. You have given me an impious offspring. Night and day my prayer to You has been that You provide me with pious children. I ask Your forgiveness, O Lord. I acknowledge the fate You have determined and I surrender to Your tribulations. My son in prison!?'

He now wept hot tears; he had fought them back for a while when the news had first shattered his fortitude and patience. But now his chin glistened with tears, and his voice cracked. He could no longer suppress his sense of total defeat or keep his misery under wraps.

'My son in prison? What are people going to say from now on? If only I could have died before this happened. Where can I bury my face so people won't see it? Where can I hide from malicious glances, bright shining faces, and nosy stares, fingers pointing at me, whispers all around me, government officials with whom my name has been blackened thanks to Abd al-Rahman's behaviour, friends and enemies?'

He could not control his tears any longer. He felt short of breath. His hoarse voice gradually gave out and finally disappeared between the folds of his utter dejection. Then he looked up between two wetted hands and breathed deeply, life returning to his voice.

'This is the academy's doing! My heart told me nothing good

would come from it. Ever since he went there, his behaviour has become worse and his mind has gone so off course that he's landed in prison.'

'It's all your own fault!' said a voice deep within his conscience. 'You gave way to his demands, accepted the idea of this academy, and acceded to the freedom he was enjoying.'

'Yes, it's my fault!' Hajj Muhammad admitted, his voice choking, as though he were arguing with someone right in front of him. 'I had the idea that the academy would lead him down the path to respectability; in my delusion I told myself it would lead to a position as a government official. But it turns out it was the path to prison!'

Since hearing the news, Khaduj had been unable to console her husband, and had retired to her room to weep a mother's tears. She could not face Hajj Muhammad; she was as frightened of him when he was angry as she was when he was suffering. When both emotions were combined at the news of Abd al-Rahman's imprisonment, the notion of confronting him scared her to death. Staying in her own room, nursing her tears and sorrows, she avoided such worries.

Everyone in the household accepted the news of the disaster with a patience that was in short supply. Yasmine wept in the kitchen, being no less fond of Abd al-Rahman than Khaduj; she loved and admired him so much that she dearly hoped her own son Mahmud would eventually possess the same kind of intelligence, shrewdness, and devotion to his books and lessons. She liked him too because he managed to get his father worked up; she was pleased that Hajj Muhammad reacted to Abd al-Rahman in a way he did not with Mahmud. For Yasmine, then, Abd al-Rahman was her son, in the hope that he would achieve what Mahmud could not. Her tears were mingled with a vague hope that, if Mahmud were to be the victim of a similar situation, then for once in his life he might be able to get his father to shed some tears of pain and affection. Even so, she now thought of Abd al-Rahman as no more a prisoner than he had been when he was 'free'.

Abd al-Ghani was suffering as well. Deep down he was profoundly sad at the course that Abd al-Rahman's life had taken. Even so, he began to gloat, and his inner self started to talk to him spitefully. 'He was always stubborn and quarrelsome. He never took my advice. I could see all this coming. My heart told me, but he was just too stubborn to do what I said. Who knows? Maybe prison will be a good way to teach him!'

Aisha, Mahmud, and Abd al-Latif were all in tears, but they did not know how to explain what had happened. Abd al-Rahman had never done anything that deserved to be punished. They had never even heard of imprisonment: the family had never even encountered the idea of prison before.

But, in fact, the one person who did know was Mahmud. He realised that the nationalists had gone to prison, and that Abd al-Rahman was among them. His elder brother had talked to him about something called colonialism and something else called nationalism. He had given Mahmud some ideas about the fierce struggle that was starting to intensify between the two sides. But, Mahmud wondered, was this struggle now at a crisis point, and had that crisis expanded to include Abd al-Rahman in its clutches?

At this point he stopped thinking about it. He could not answer these questions, so he retreated into his sorrow. From now on, he would be on his own, with Abd al-Rahman no longer around. He had formed the habit of keeping his own ideas under wraps and confiding in his brothers, in a household characterised by a huge gulf between father and sons, between affection and love, between shadows and tranquillity. Mahmud bitterly regretted the world he had now lost due to Abd al-Rahman's absence.

Even now, Hajj Muhammad could not weep his tears inside the house. He did his best to stay away from people because his honour would not allow him to let them see in his face the father of a prisoner and criminal. But people's curiosity allowed him no peace; people in Fez liked to give congratulations, to convey condolences, to express sympathy – but they had never before been in the kind of situation into which the fates had now thrust them. Were they supposed to congratulate the father of a young man who had decided to challenge their political situation by delivering a speech in Najjarin Square in which he had fired up the crowd and yelled 'Down with the usurpers! Set our leaders free!' or should they express their sympathies for a father whose unsullied ear was now assaulted by the word 'prison' with such brutal force?

Hajj Muhammad's isolation was interrupted by one caller after another. They took their cue on what to say from his frowning expression and tear-filled eyes. If they had simply left him to his sorrows it would have given him more consolation than the hurtful words that only made him feel even more miserable, rather than lessening his suffering: 'God give him guidance! He's still young. He'll learn. He has no right to plunge you into this agonising grief. If you'd been stricter with him, he would never have dared... God grant him release! Only grown men go to prison. You don't deserve such a trial as this; no one in your family has ever been to prison. Don't worry. He's got other young men and sons of well-known families in there with him...'

However hard Hajj Muhammad's visitors tried to sympathise and console him with kind words, the impact on his heart was like deadly poison. The only way he could respond was to knock the beads of his rosary against each other, palpably upset. Each bead seemed to crash violently against its neighbour.

But a whole group of Hajj Muhammad's friends did not come to visit. He expected them to offer at the very least some words of consolation and he waited for them to come, but his expectations were not to be met. He could certainly have talked with them about the great problem Abd al-Rahman had created, and could have opened his soul to them without feeling ashamed. What he really wanted was to muster the courage to talk over with one of them something that had been worrying him for some time.

He spent many hours thinking. 'Ask Hajj Ahmad,' he thought. 'But no, he might refuse... or he might not. But he would never agree to do what I want. Better to have a quiet word with Mawlay

Fadul... I wonder if our relationship is still as strong as it was... It would be best for me to stay well out of this entire arena... But then there's Abd al-Rahman and what he's done to my reputation. Even so, I should not hesitate. I'll talk to Mawlay Ali, he can do it. If he did, the way forward would be entirely in his hands. But Mawlay Ali? He has a loose tongue and the whole of Fez would learn the secret I am anxious to keep between the two of us. No, Mawlay Ali's not right for this task. Aha, there's Hajj Ibn Allal; he's an honourable man, and he's proud of our acquaintance. He won't refuse.'

Hajj Muhammad went on chewing over these thoughts as he waited for the arrival of his friends, people who had been proud of his friendship, people he would ask to do their utmost to get Abd al-Rahman released from prison. But he was left with his thoughts and no end in sight. His name was now enough to scare away the people who grovelled to the authorities. The government no longer condoned their friendships with Hajj Muhammad or their visits to his home, and the streets were full of spies. How could they risk coming to the house where Hajj Muhammad had welcomed them on so many occasions and accorded them all honour and hospitality?

Bitter days went slowly by, laden with fervent emotions. The whole city of Fez smelled of the stench of prison and expulsions. Its streets and alleys were subjected to a siege, and its people to maltreatment, infringements of honour, and the loss of freedom.

In Najjarin Square the resident general proclaimed, 'I'm going to crush the nationalists under my feet.' The stares and gloomy expressions all reflected fear; smiles vanished from lips that had long been used to breaking out into peals of laughter. But the words had a more bitter impact on Hajj Muhammad – the news he heard filled his heart with utter despair over Abd al-Rahman's fate.

26

The worlds of Hajj Muhammad and Abd al-Rahman were now completely separate. Both were suffering through this trial in misery and languishing in the deepest dungeon – but each lived in a world completely different from that of the other.

For the first time in his life, Abd al-Rahman found himself witnessing a trial in court. Several trucks had been loaded with nationalists and guarded by black soldiers who pointed their guns directly at the prisoners. Each group got out of the truck, but the captives had barely made their way through the huge gateway to the court when they re-emerged with a two-year prison sentence hanging around the neck of each man.

Abd al-Rahman entered the court chamber in one of these groups. He was particularly curious, a feeling hardly diminished by the news of the harsh sentences being handed down to his colleagues, clear enough from their expressions as they emerged from the court gateway, even before they could make any kind of gesture. Court, judge, accused, lawyer, deputy prosecutor, legal proceedings... Abd al-Rahman had read about the way courts operated and how they were organised, and this was what he had in mind as he was driven to the court after a dark night spent cramped on the flat ground under the sky. Spurred on by the urge for knowledge, he wanted to see the judge applying legal logic in all his judicial splendour, to witness the arguments, and to listen to the deputy prosecutor – even though he himself was now the accused.

His group climbed down from the truck and were shoved roughly towards the gateway to the court. Each man was contemplating the fate that awaited him – but not Abd al-Rahman, who was thinking about the court before worrying about his own fate. Inside the court, the group was ordered to squat on the dirty ground like dogs. The court guards surrounded the prisoners, spewing a torrent of abuse and foul language, though none of this had any effect on them.

Abd al-Rahman waited to be ushered into the court, and started thinking about what he was going to say to the judge when he was asked to explain the things of which he was being accused. A wave of conviction came over him.

'I'll confess,' he told himself. 'I'll tell the judge that no foreign interloper has the right to pass judgement on us. The people who've been arrested must go back where they came from.'

There was a commotion by the gate at the entrance to the court, which wrenched him out of his thoughts. 'May God pour blessings on the life of our dear master!' intoned a powerful voice that echoed around the space. The court officials all repeated the phrase, as they bowed their heads. Abd al-Rahman looked left and right. A hubbub permeated the great court chamber, but then a gruff voice rapidly calmed everything down. Abd al-Rahman focused on its source: a red-faced man with a handsome appearance, honey-coloured eyes holding a severe gaze, a face enveloped in a thick blond beard, a body that was hefty but short in stature, and a head crowned with a huge white turban carefully arranged on top of a red head-cap. There he stood, proud of his authority, his arrogance and vanity only increased by the fact that he was positioned amid a group of accused prisoners whose fate he was about to decide in the flash of an eye. Beside him stood another man, tall and pale faced, clean shaven, bare headed, wearing foreign clothes, and staring at the prisoners in sheer hatred and disgust, his vicious glances shooting out from behind his thick spectacles.

A deathly silence now pervaded the court. Abd al-Rahman stopped thinking. Anxious faces kept glancing at the pasha-judge. His eyes gleamed as though he were hunting for prey, and his face twitched anxiously as though he were eager for revenge; his tense body gave the impression that he wanted to leap on his quarry. The accused looked from the pasha to the governor; anyone who had been in court before was aware that the real judge was the French governor who lurked in the pasha's shadow. Abd al-Rahman was not one of those people, so he continued to focus his attention on the portly body that filled his field of vision. He stared at the man's mouth, expecting a verdict, not a political harangue.

For a strained moment the pasha turned to the governor; from the way his lips moved Abd al-Rahman gathered that he was asking a question. In reply the governor whispered a few words in his ear, but to the curious observer they were clearly focused and specific.

The pasha made ready to speak again. 'May God pour blessings on the life of our dear master, the governor!' he intoned again in the same terrifying tone. The aides and guards now realised something important was about to happen that required their total attention.

Having pronounced his obeisance in ringing tones, the pasha's thick lips exhibited a slight smile, which was soon replaced by an expression intended to show that he was the authority: it seemed he felt the need to give people a true sense of his importance. He was eager for his assistants to present him as such to the prisoners, as the person who was about to announce his verdict on all of them – all the more since they had been accused of sedition, and so they must be given the clear impression that they were standing before an authority that would brook no such rebellion. It also seemed that the pasha felt the need to make them appreciate his position as someone enjoying the confidence of the governor. The fact that he could converse secretly with the governor pointed to the significance of his position, particularly in front of these rebels.

Thus, the ringing shout of 'May God pour blessings on the life of our dear master!' repeated by the court aides made the pasha feel his own importance. His dreams of authority, power, and force toyed with his mind as he found himself caught between his own feelings and the specific instructions he had received in his office from the governor, who had repeated those instructions in no uncertain terms in front of the accused in order to make it completely clear that, while the pasha was the law's representative, the authority, power, and force did not reside in that corpulent body with its thick blond beard and huge white turban, but rather lurked inside the governor's own bald head and his eyes hidden behind thick spectacles.

The pasha now cleared his throat, anxious for the prisoners to register his presence. This noise, which might normally result from something stuck in the gullet, was a way of confirming his presence before this group of people who might well disdain his status.

He proceeded to speak, mangling the 'r' sound to such an extent that he strained his vocal cords and his voice turned hoarse. The fat red face flushed, the blond beard quivered, and the gleaming eyes intensified. 'Reprobates!' he roared. 'You've no shame! You incite rebellion and defy the government. Like idiots you go out into the streets stirring up trouble. Who do you think you are, raising your voices against the government? Obedience is an obligation for all. I will not forgive a single person who rebels. I'm... I'm the pasha who rules this land.'

There he paused for a moment, as though he had just said something wrong. He looked over at the governor, who appeared quite unconcerned but was actually paying close attention to every word the pasha uttered; he did not even bother to look over at the pasha, as though no one were looking in that direction.

'You're all rebels,' the pasha went on, 'and you must all be punished.' At the mention of the word 'punished' his nostrils expanded, as though the very idea excited him. He went on. 'And I know exactly what your punishment will be.'

He shook his hand to indicate a caning motion, as though somehow the words themselves were not enough to convey his meaning. As he uttered the word 'punishment' again his whole body shook, until his legs could barely support him. Abd al-Rahman had the impression that what the pasha really wanted to do was to pounce on them all like a hunting falcon; he was concerned the pasha might have a seizure as he availed himself of the authority represented by the governor who was standing calmly by his side.

'If this man would just let me talk to him for a minute or two,' Abd al-Rahman thought, 'I'd be able to demolish his sense of power and authority and calm him down.' But the pasha's frenzy only increased, and Abd al-Rahman's thoughts were disrupted as he heard his next statements.

'If His Excellency the Governor had not interceded with me, I would have had you whipped right here and now, before the punishment you will receive in the prisons and detention centres. But I have no intention of showing you any mercy. I know from previous experience that the best way to put your perverted and errant minds back on to the straight path is to...'

Abd al-Rahman's nerves were on edge, and his blood boiled. His ears could not tolerate the verbiage they were now hearing. He stood up and raised his index finger in the air, the way he used to do at the academy when responding to an opinion expressed by the teacher with which he disagreed. 'Your Excellency, Pasha!' he said in a muted but firm voice.

A pair of coarse and violent hands reached to his neck, grabbed him by the collar, and put him in a choke-hold using his jallaba, in an attempt to stop him opening his mouth again. They tightened their grip until he was almost throttled. A third hand came down on his neck with a mighty cuff that knocked him down. The rough hands clung to him as though he had just been arrested in the act of committing a crime. The pasha stopped speaking and looked daggers at him, like a victim who was trying to escape his clutches. All his aides now stared viciously at Abd al-Rahman, waiting to be told what to do with him. The pasha stared long and hard, knitting his thick eyebrows and examining him with eyes bursting with hatred. The room was as silent as a grave, as though some terrible event had rocked the havens of justice. The prisoners watched the pasha's mouth, as if anticipating the fate that would soon emerge from it. He did not remain silent for long. Turning to Abd al-Rahman, the pasha addressed him in a tone dripping with contempt. It was almost as if he could not see the young man's youthful form before his eyes. His voice was now much lower, as though he considered himself above the need to address a child whom he could only despise.

'Who is your father?' he enquired, rather than asking about Abd al-Rahman himself. He was too proud to talk to a child, but it would be appropriate to talk to his father and pass judgement on a man rather than on a child.

'I am Abd al-Rahman—'

The pasha raised his voice. 'I asked you who your father was.'

The rough hands came crashing down again. 'Tell him your father's name!'

Abd al-Rahman now raised his head proudly. 'I am Abd al-Rahman, son of Hajj Muhammad al-Tihami.'

'Abd al-Rahman, son of Hajj Muhammad al-Tihami,' the pasha repeated. His eyebrows twitched as he recalled a name that resounded in his ears for some considerable time. 'Your father's a good man,' he went on. 'How is it he's abandoned you to these' – and here he used an ugly word – 'to addle your brain?'

Abd al-Rahman's face turned crimson as he heard the abhorrent term the pasha used to describe his fellow prisoners. It seemed to him that it was all his fault. 'If only he didn't know your father,' his conscience told him. 'If only you hadn't raised your finger, if only—'

'You must be punished,' the pasha said, interrupting his thoughts. 'The same fate now awaits you as all these others. That will put a stop to your bad behaviour.'

Abd al-Rahman felt somewhat relieved. He had been worried that, in addition to insulting his fellow prisoners, the pasha might also insult him personally by releasing him because of his age and out of respect for his father.

'The government knows no mercy,' the pasha now declared, reverting to his previous stentorian tone. 'Your punishment... your punishment...' He looked at the governor as though to check on something, and the governor nodded in agreement. 'The punishment decreed for all of you,' he announced, 'is two years in prison. Now get out of here!'

With that, the pasha, the governor, and their aides turned and disappeared en masse through the door of the ancient office. Guards now surrounded the prisoners like a pair of handcuffs. Coarse hands grabbed them by the scruffs of their necks and pushed them out. At the court gateway they were loaded onto the trucks.

'Court, judge, deputy prosecutor, lawyer,' Abd al-Rahman thought to himself, 'and now two years' imprisonment.'

27

As the prison gateway enveloped Abd al-Rahman in its clutches, that sequence of words – court, judge, deputy prosecutor, lawyer – still rang in his ears, as he relived the few moments he had spent inside the pasha's domain. His neck still ached from the stranglehold that those coarse hands had used to twist his jallaba until his eyes almost popped out. The image of the pasha – with his thick beard, puffy face, and thick neck – still occupied his vision, as though he had never before seen such a sight.

Abd al-Rahman was the first to enter through the gateway. Suddenly a gleam appeared in his eyes, one that blew away the confusion in his thinking. Between the twin doors of the gateway he felt his head reeling, but did his best to stay on his feet, hunching his head between his shoulders to stop it from falling. Then he received a brutal and powerful left-handed blow, aimed at his right cheek. It reverberated in his ears like the crack of a whip. He tried to recover, but the hand that had slapped his cheek now shoved him back to leave space for his colleagues to receive their fair share of the traditional 'welcome of honour' imposed on nationalists as they entered the prison. It was customary for the guards to give the newly arrived prisoners a clear idea of what prison meant; rough hands administered two powerful slaps to each new guest when the huge gateway was opened to admit them. Abd al-Rahman realised that this was merely the first insult in a world of insults. It set his nerves on edge, but an experienced fellow prisoner calmed him down with a tacit gesture. Abd al-Rahman now watched as the vicious blows rained down on all his colleagues, and he heard the kind of filthy language that he could never imagine emerging from the mouths of people who had any self-respect. He was filled with anger that was expressed only in his thoughts.

'My entire country's a prison, with guards standing on its neck. A slap on the cheek, foul words ringing in my ears, vicious stares hounding me everywhere... I'm a citizen, one among millions living in a country with slaps, insults, and foul language, their honour impugned, turned into sheep. People... "natives"... My sense of honour finally exploded into action on the day I decided to lead the demonstration, all so that my fate would be to receive yet more slaps and foul language.'

When Abd al-Rahman received the vicious slap by the gateway and banged his head against the edge of the iron structure, making it bleed, he let out a groan of pain and lost all contact with his thoughts. His colleagues, bunched together between the twin doors, turned around to see where the groan was coming from. One of them tried to help him, but a guard grabbed him as though he were about to commit a crime. With tears in his eyes Abd al-Rahman gave Abd al-Aziz an affectionate look, and the pain vanished from his expression, to be replaced by a severe, determined look that presaged an impressive challenge. From within the folds of Abd al-Rahman's pain there emerged a beaming smile that lit up the faces of those on whom pain had inflicted such a gruesome wrong. This smile of victory now provided inspiration to all the prisoners.

'What we need,' he thought, 'is experience, more insults to reinforce our spirit of resistance. The blow inflicted on my head is better than a thousand books that I might read about nationalism or memorise about history.' The smile shone like a flood of light that revealed his complete understanding of the realities of the world – realities that now gleamed in souls darkened by humiliation. Lips that had previously curled in fury, eyes that had festered in pain, now turned into smiles and gleeful looks.

The huge iron gate of the prison hid away the group that included Abd al-Rahman and Abd al-Aziz, but was this not the last time the great gateway would give them its welcome as it enclosed them within its world of misery, deprivation, and suffering. As they came and went each day, it would open to grasp them, overwhelmed, their naked bodies staggering from disease, hunger, exhaustion, and deprivation. It would open again to spit them out at sunrise so they could go out to the fields, where they would plough, sow, or reap; pull up palm-roots, grass, and dry weeds; or wander round the rugged heights smashing boulders and breaking rocks.

They could not object or resist. The whip was always behind them to check any idea of resistance they might have. The effort left them exhausted; hunger, thirst, heat, and cold all destroyed their very being. Intimidation – whips, cuffs, and foul language – pursued them everywhere. But they were above all ongoing victims of the notion that was deeply ingrained in the minds of the prison guards: 'Shut up! Prisoners have no rights.'

On steaming hot days, when the burning sun set the entire firmament on fire, the impact of hunger and thirst on the prisoners was much worse. On one such day, a squad was in the stark mountains, where they were breaking up rocks and carrying them a long way to the place where they had to break them down still further into smaller stones and tiny chips. The mountain stubbornly resisted the efforts of muscles that were exhausted by labour and wracked by hardship and deprivation. Their endurance was sapped by the sweat that poured off them and the intolerable strain they were under. In a moment of sheer despair Muhammad, the work gang's leader – the prison authorities would choose such a leader for each group – raised a finger to ask the guards to hear what he had to say. He was middle aged and could not tolerate this level of labour in such conditions. He was a bulky man, but sheer exhaustion had diminished that bulk until he looked like a pining lover laid low by illness. He was known for his endurance and patience – but hard work had finished off his endurance, and thirst had put an end to his patience.

He raised his finger and, since he did not expect to be allowed to say anything, yelled his protest like a wounded lion. 'Sirs,' he shouted, 'we're thirsty and completely exhausted. Give us a rest and let us have some water.'

The simple words were like an arrow directed at the guards' authority, something that always alarmed them. The chief guard, who was vicious and poisoned by hatred, leapt up in fury, his eyes almost popping out of his head.

'Shut up, or else I'll smash your head in!'

Despair forced Muhammad to raise his finger again. The cruel whip cracked in the air, and the chief guard came over to him, looking as though he had been personally insulted. Once again the whip cracked, but this time on Muhammad's head. The bloody lash came down on his head and his cheek, but it did not stop there: it kept cracking the air and coming down hard on the man who had simply asked for a drink of water.

The men stopped digging. They all stood up and leaned on their pickaxe handles. Anger was boiling inside them, but they were surrounded by a troop of guards, each with his whip at the ready, and armed guards with their rifles aimed. In the distance another whip came down on someone's back, but the fury of the savage hands began to subside and the flaming eyes of both prisoners and guards now turned to look at the central scene: Muhammad had collapsed under the rain of torturous blows he had received, and now a dark flow of blood was coming from his mouth, nostrils, and ears. The guard simply stood there with his mouth agape. The prisoners threw down their pickaxes and rushed to hold Muhammad, but it was not long before a voice rang out.

'There is no god but God! God was in the past, and He will continue...'

During the two years that Abd al-Rahman spent in prison he witnessed nothing but life's cruelty and violence. But even with all the suffering, his thoughts were pulled in two contrary directions. He was in despair, and the world appeared dark before his eyes. The path was long, arduous, and rough. The guards were armed to the hilt with power and authority, and a wave of aggression was rampant. The prisoners were just a small, modest collection of dreamers, their dream being to bury their current situation – while having no means of doing so beyond the pickaxes with which they pulverised rocks. Unrelieved despair was the rule of the day.

'We embarked on a reckless adventure without weighing the consequences,' Abd al-Rahman told himself. 'A gruesome fate awaited us. What kind of idiocy possessed us to end up in suffering, revenge, and even death? If I had followed Abd al-Ghani's advice, I would be at school today, studying quietly with my schoolmates and living like other students who had not been so stupid and arrogant as to let themselves be exposed to prison, suffering, revenge, and death. If only I had done what Abd al-Ghani told me to do.'

But his thoughts came to a halt with Abd al-Ghani's name. An image came to him of the other kind of world in which Abd al-Ghani lived, with all its trivial and random aspects. The idea of living like Abd al-Ghani was something he could not conceive, and a sudden shift in his thinking made itself known.

'If the people of this country lived the kind of lives that my father's generation would like to impose on them, along with Abd al-Ghani's attitudes,' he told himself, 'I wouldn't have been able to go to the academy. Abd al-Ghani represents the middle generation; he is its personification, and his ideas are dominated by the profit motive. He's fearful and cowardly. It was that cowardice that led him to advise me not to take risks.' The question came back to him once again, 'Suffering, cruelty, death – is that it?'

Then came the response, without the slightest hesitation, 'Yes, everything has its cost, and the cost of our desires is suffering, cruelty, torture, death, and... two years in prison.'

28

No sooner did Hajj Muhammad set eyes on Abd al-Rahman, still alive two years later, than his eyes flooded with tears. For the first time in his life, he found himself in a position of weakness. He never dreamed he would be standing like this, facing his son, who had never veered from his stubborn and steadfast behaviour towards his father. During the two agony-filled years, Abd al-Rahman's features had changed; no longer a fresh-faced boy, he was now a man whose face showed all the marks of exposure to the unrelenting sun. The crushing hard labour he had endured had robbed his body of its softness; now he looked taller, thinner, and more serious. His expression was stolid, powerful, and determined, and he seemed pained; his eyes lacked any sign of affection or gentleness. He looked around aggressively; his expression demanded respect, and brooked no intrusion.

Hajj Muhammad could find no outlet for the suppressed anger he had nursed for two years. He now found himself faced with an entirely new person, someone with no connection whatever to the Abd al-Rahman of earlier times. He was expecting Abd al-Rahman to proclaim his innocence of the crime whose stain had become attached to the family, which could not recall any of its previous members being imprisoned or defying the authorities – or for him to acknowledge that he could not tolerate the pain he had endured or the stain he had caused to the family's reputation.

However, once he looked at his son's expression, he realised that he was confronting a different person, someone he did not dare challenge. Hajj Muhammad simply stood there, not knowing what to do and wrestling with an internal struggle that involved on the one hand his own posture towards his son and on the other the diffidence he felt as he realised that this Abd al-Rahman was a different person, someone who was challenging him without uttering a word. It was his face that presented the challenge, along with his forced, barely perceptible smiles and his powerful and composed way of speaking, decisive and determined, that brooked no argument or opposition.

At first Hajj Muhammad was surprised by his own reaction. His mind was full of ideas and opinions that he had waited until this moment to be able to explain to Abd al-Rahman. He had long been practising the discussion of such matters in his own mind while sitting with other people, so why was it that he could not do the same thing now, in privacy with his son, with no barriers between them?

Hajj Muhammad made no attempt to explain this new factor, which had robbed him of his authority inside the house and made him – the absolute master decision maker – feel incapable of putting his ideas into words. In the past he had had no problem taking action, but now he was starting to cede some of his authority to Abd al-Rahman without even asking himself why or how. Without quite being aware of it, Hajj Muhammad found that a new authority was impinging on his own. The authority that had come down to him from his forefathers and ancestors, and his absolute control over the household's opinions, actions, and behaviour were both concepts that now began to agitate his mind.

Abd al-Rahman went back to the academy, where he faced the complications raised by the administration because of his prison term. Eventually he managed to rejoin his class without even needing to consult his father; from now on, his conduct would be completely independent of Hajj Muhammad.

He also faced fresh burdens in his nationalist struggle. Day or night he would leave the house with no opposition or anger from Hajj Muhammad. He argued with Khaduj, but Hajj Muhammad made no effort to either speak out or defend his household authority.

He told Aisha that on no account should she marry a man she did not know and did not agree to marry. A person should not be deprived of the right to choose, he told her. In any case, he would support her if she chose to object, but if she gave in there would be no way he could help her. When Khaduj heard of this provocative talk, she immediately told Hajj Muhammad, but neither of them felt able to stand in the way of the forward march of ideas.

Abd al-Rahman also spoke to Mahmud. 'Don't be weak hearted,' he told him. 'In school, you're no different from the other students, and at home you're no different from your brothers. Khaduj may not be your mother, but Yasmine is just like Khaduj. Their fathers are both of one type, from a single male species. Don't let the fairy tale about the mistress and the servant-woman affect you in any way. You're a man and the son of a lady, even if, to my father and mother, Yasmine is a servant purchased in the slave market. Raise your head high, my brother! This is not the time for slaves and masters.'

This too reached Hajj Muhammad's ears. Abd al-Rahman was keen that nothing he said should be a secret, and he declared himself to those people he knew for sure would pass it all on. Hajj Muhammad pondered the whole thing, but he kept his thoughts to himself; by now he had learned to restrict the considerations and internal debates to himself, within his own mind. He even managed to create an imagined clone of Abd al-Rahman for himself, and could rant and rave at it for all he was worth – though the reaction of the replica was compliance, obedience, apology, and a pledge not to do the same thing ever again. This provided a degree of security and satisfaction, and allowed him to return to the reality of the situation: namely, that Abd al-Rahman had emerged from prison with a flame blazing inside him, vowing to use it to set fire to chaff.

When Abd al-Rahman spoke to his elder brother, Abd al-Ghani was both nervous and perplexed. Abd al-Rahman had bothered him even when he was still an immature child, and when he had gone to the academy and started showing his contempt for his elders and betters, Abd al-Ghani had grown fed up with his arrogance. Now that Abd al-Rahman had come out of prison, Abd al-Ghani found himself dealing with someone he could no longer boss around and whose taunts he found intolerable. Even so, they were both sons of the same father and mother, and shared a house and dining table. The vestige of brotherly feelings that he still had demanded that he try to remain close to his younger brother and make an effort to be friendly and offer advice. But he found he could not face this new personality that had emerged from prison and invaded the family atmosphere.

Abd al-Rahman did not leave his brother alone in his nervous perplexity. Instead, he launched a bold attack, almost violent in its fury. 'You... What's the point of your life?' he said. 'You eat your food and walk around the markets. What mission do you think you're performing for your country? You're getting ready to put your arms around your little nest like a chicken with rotten eggs. You've started a family now. Are you planning to bring up your children to be just like you? Open your eyes. Times are changing, and they're going to leave you behind. You need to understand some of the consequences of the mistakes you've made. You haven't learned anything. In fact, you've always resisted learning anything. Maybe that won't be possible with your children.'

This kind of talk demolished Abd al-Ghani's self-esteem. The only way he could find of ridding himself of the siege wall that Abd al-Rahman kept erecting around him was by keeping his anger buried, chewing his gum as hard as possible, making it click so loudly that it echoed in his ears. It was almost as though he were trying to use the clicking noise to drown out what Abd al-Rahman was saying.

However, Abd al-Rahman was not entirely content with himself, nor was he sure about his own role in life. He had certainly borne his share of responsibilities and acquired a rebellious spirit. Now he found himself radiating that same spirit outside the house, where it was both expansive and effective. However, when he tried to do the same thing inside the house, he came right up against the family fortress with its lofty walls and closed windows through which the only light or air that penetrated came from whatever minuscule amounts filtered through the aperture in the roof to the courtyard below.

The convulsions going on inside Abd al-Rahman took the form of a demon-jinni that had been kept inside its bottle for centuries and generations. It stomped around and let off steam, but the world was not big enough. Instead, it clashed with a nightmare that kept its eye on the world so as to limit its revolutionary energy.

Now that the majority of Fez's sons had returned from exile and prisons, the city was full of newly invigorated hopes. Life ticked along at its usual deliberate pace – unassuming, and content to be so; comfortable, but not to an excessive degree; industrious enough to earn a loaf of bread, but not greedy or competitive. The city lived a life of self-satisfaction, with all its own little ideas, hopes, and aspirations. If the idea of nationalism were mentioned, it would almost never leave the city limits. As a result, the struggles in the outside world rarely reached the city itself. Even when the kind of ideas that can usually slip in along with daylight, sun, and air were involved, that very same property of self-satisfaction had already converted the city into an impregnable fortress. It was content with this posture; no one felt any kind of lack, and in fact people appreciated it because it brought with it a sense of felicity, liberty, and contentment.

This was how it affected its inhabitants, and this was how its young folk were, and this was what strangers would sense when they came to visit. The welcoming expressions, laughing eyes, and words brimming with hope and confidence in the future all conveyed the same impression.

But then something happened to change this way of life, an event that imposed a thick, dark curtain on the welcoming expressions, the laughing eyes, and the words brimming with hope. Fez's inhabitants were not ready to assess the true extent of the danger that this curtain brought with it, nor were they prepared to change their ways. But the curtain came down suddenly, changing bright light into darkness and joy into unhappiness and hardship.

Abd al-Rahman was the first person to sense the thick, dark curtain as it descended on the city, because it had a direct impact on the revolutionary spirit churning inside him. And Fez and Abd al-Rahman were by no means the only ones to be overwhelmed by a world war whose savagery spread from the capitals of Europe.

29

War... war... war!

The words rang in the ears of the citizens of Fez, like any other words that are habitually weighed for their seriousness and variety. If the words had been 'peace... peace... peace', the effect would have been no different. Young people in Fez had never heard anything about the Great War; they had heard about the Rif War and were scared of it, but even that war had not showed them its nasty side. They were aware of conflicts between the children of one quarter and another, but those only involved single children here and there, and simple wounds that could be staunched with spiders' webs so the blood would not stain the victim's clothing – for, if it did, the fathers would find out and punish the boys who had the wounds rather than their assailants.

But this new war did not spare the young folk of Fez. On the contrary, it insistently infiltrated their inner lives and weighed on each person's consciousness. Abd al-Rahman realised that this war was not one of those local Moroccan conflicts – artificial bubbles bursting in the tranquil atmosphere, to be followed soon afterwards by the announcement of peace, like children welcoming the new moon at the beginning of Ramadan. This time the entire world was enveloped in destruction, misery, and suffering that might well result in the loss of complete generations – and could lead to the weakening of the authority that powerful countries had exerted over weak peoples. It might also impose a limit on the activities of the freedom movement in which the youth of Morocco were engaged. The foreign administration would find it an ideal opportunity to finish off its foes, in the name of regulations and precautions dictated by war.

Such thoughts haunted Abd al-Rahman as the first explosions started to go off, deafening the world's hearing, but he did not have the heart to let people know what he was thinking. Instead, he told himself he should be giving people some sense of hope, and war was certainly a way to achieve that goal. Any talk about its malign effects would only make already-despondent hearts even weaker and more despondent still. But, in spite of his best efforts, talk of war invaded his personal domain. Abd al-Samad, a smart young man who was known for offering information to console people, blocked his path every time they ran into each other, and told him things with an authoritative air.

'Don't you know what's going to happen in a few days?'

'No, what?'

'Hitler's going to invade Morocco from the inside... He'll chuck the French out.'

Abd al-Rahman took this in with a smile and a generous grain of salt, but Abd al-Samad hurried to eliminate the doubt that was obvious in his expression.

'Believe me. The era of the French occupation is over. Hitler will grab them like you grab a chicken in a cage.'

Abd al-Rahman gave a smile of almost desperate hope, and Abd al-Samad, who was never going to be duped as much by his innate perspicacity as he was by his sources of information, took that as encouragement. 'Hitler's very close,' he went on. 'In just a few days you'll see him strutting his way around the Najjarin district!'

Abd al-Rahman managed to extricate himself from the impasse by convincing Abd al-Samad that he believed he was right and his information was correct, and Abd al-Samad then launched into a declaration for anyone to hear, whether they were in the know or not.

'Hitler will be infiltrating Fez!'

But the same impasse plagued Abd al-Rahman inside the house as well as in the street. The elder folk felt a need for the younger ones, because they were the ones who read newspapers and knew what was going on in their land of war and conflict. Hajj Muhammad relented in his attitude towards Abd al-Rahman, and refused to sit down to dinner unless he was there as well. Abd al-Rahman was well aware of what was going on in Hajj Muhammad's mind, so he steered the conversation away from talk of war, Hitler, and Mussolini. But Hajj Muhammad still launched an assault.

'People said today that Hitler's closing in on China.'

Abd al-Rahman had a hard time suppressing an explosion of laughter that almost paralysed him. 'Dear Father,' he said, 'don't believe everything people are saying on the streets. Hitler's in western and central Europe. China's in east Asia. How can news like that possibly be getting around?'

Hajj Muhammad felt a cold sweat oozing out of his sleeves; it was as though the stain of ignorance was showing on him for the first time. His sense of pride was wounded by Abd al-Rahman's hurtful words. 'I realise that,' he said by way of retort. 'I'm not telling you what I think; just what people keep saying.'

This made the conversation between the two of them easier.

'I don't understand,' Hajj Muhammad went on, 'why everyone's so concerned about this war. It's far away from us.'

'The war's far from us, but it's also near. There's no more near and far in the world now.'

This statement blanketed Hajj Muhammad's mind in a cloud. He clearly did not understand what Abd al-Rahman was saying.

'France obviously looks on Morocco as being a wide imperialist gateway to Africa. On the day that Hitler impinges on that imperial territory, France will leap to its defence.'

'We pray to God that Hitler won't do that!'

Abd al-Rahman's blood boiled. 'The war's our big chance,' he said. 'If France's imperial territory is demolished by whoever it may be, then it'll be hard for them to rebuild it.'

'But that will bring the war to us,' Hajj Muhammad replied, thinking of himself.

'War's ensconced in our country's very heart, even if the fighting's in the heart of Europe at the moment.'

Hajj Muhammad did not understand, and his expression framed a large question mark.

'Our sons are crossing over to Europe,' Abd al-Rahman said, 'to die under the French flag.' He forestalled the curious look in Hajj Muhammad's eyes and the furrows of his forehead by adding, 'Yes, our sons! They're grabbing them from the mountains, plains, valleys, and small towns and villages, and enlisting them to defend France.'

Now Hajj Muhammad seemed to understand.

'Not only that,' Abd al-Rahman went on, 'but our agricultural production is being stolen from us in order to feed the army and our children over there.'

Hajj Muhammad widened his eyes in amazement, as though a lightning bolt had dazzled him. He stared off into the gloom. Abd al-Rahman realised what his father was thinking. What had suddenly wrested the tranquil look from his father's eyes was the terrifying thought that the government would be seizing the harvest from his land: the wheat, the barley, and the fruit.

'We're going to starve,' Abd al-Rahman went on, to underline the idea that had now possessed Hajj Muhammad's thinking, 'and all so that our own sons in the army and the French military can eat. We'll be deprived of cover, clothing, and protection as well because the people who normally supply us with such things will convert their businesses into making bombs, guns, tanks, and aeroplanes.'

Hajj Muhammad pricked up his ears as though there was some kind of blockage preventing him from hearing properly. But there was no blockage; it was just that the shock of it all was affecting his hearing, and he now leaned forward to take in what his son was saying.

'There'll be even more tightening of restrictions on our freedoms,' Abd al-Rahman continued, taking full advantage of his father's close attention. 'Because war always takes away people's liberties. And war renders slaves even more enslaved than before.'

Hajj Muhammad did not seem disturbed by what he heard, and Abd al-Rahman realised that freedom was not something his father was much concerned about. He had no sense of his own liberty being forcibly taken away. All he knew was that the wealthy white lords and the masters like himself who owned large mansions, lands, and properties were free – and that slaves were the servants you bought, as many as you needed. But he did not offer any objections. He attributed all this talk to the onset of passionate ideas that had afflicted Abd al-Rahman's life and made his young mind think of strange things like freedom, slavery, nationalism, and independence.

War careered its way forwards in a variety of vicious and intense currents. People now opened their eyes to an entirely new world, one in which they forgot the stories about Hitler and faced a reality that deprived them of bread to eat, warm clothing to wear, and protection against disease. The windows of their minds were opened to vast new horizons. Fez was no longer everything to them. Personal contentment was no longer enough to satisfy their aspirations and desire for knowledge. They heard about world capitals, theatres of war, army commanders, political leaders, victory and defeat, occupation and liberation, and new military weaponry.

The city of Fez dwindled in the minds of its inhabitants. They began to feel that the life they were living inside its narrow walls was the limit of their natural aspirations, and the misery that the war imposed on them only made them even more unhappy. Typhus, resulting from filthy conditions, infected the city and was spread further by people coming in from elsewhere. Disease, misery, and deprivation all had their effects on people's sense of pride; they started to feel a need for some kind of revenge to restore their self-esteem.

None of this impinged on Abd al-Rahman, who lived through the war and its various stories carrying his thoughts to infinite levels: leaving the city's concealed alleys and narrow squares behind, they would soar out to battles in the Pacific, thousand-bomber raids on cities, the wholesale destruction of continents, and the pulverisation of millions of lives. He did not anticipate any kind of peace for Fez in the shadow of its tribulations, just war with its ongoing news of terror, killing, and homelessness.

His nerves were not affected by the general atmosphere in the city. He was more bothered by the loss of freedom than upset by the misery of his countrymen. After all, misery could turn into plenty, and darkness could become light once again. All wars had their limits, but the forward march of freedom had no connection to the course of war. One or other side might emerge victorious, and yet that would be of no benefit to the many people of the world, the domination of whom was the principal cause of the conflict.

'If we give in to the tragedy of pride,' he thought to himself, 'the pride that has been crushed by misery and weakened by disease, we will emerge from this war still miserable and diseased – nothing more. Instead, we must emerge victorious. Misery and disease are simply obstacles standing in the way of progress. We have to move beyond it all so we can achieve true freedom.'

As he indulged in these ideas, he did not forget that thoughts of freedom in a world of war were a crime unforgiveable under war's own rules. But he found a refuge for himself in the new openness that had enveloped the city, transforming its character from one of self-satisfaction to a kernel based in a world with wider boundaries. This war had opened people's eyes to a new world and their minds to fresh horizons that even war could not delimit.

Freedom's forward path involved a sense of need – the need for an open world in which the free could have their share.

30

It was the logic of Abd al-Rahman's thought that made its way to his heart. When it spoke to him, it was as though it were singing, its attractive sound ringing in his soul like a melody played on a stringed instrument made by a master craftsman. He smiled, a winged smile that floated on his young, laughing face, his eyes glistening with a gentle, attractive gleam from which flowed a spirit of youth, delight, energy, and beauty.

Madeleine was an employee at a city bank. Her young mind had not yet been polluted by racist thoughts, and she enjoyed chatting with Abd al-Rahman, who represented for her the aspect of the country that demanded she find out more about it. She was a young Frenchwoman, born into a French family, educated in French schools, and with French friends. And yet she liked to observe Moroccans and hear stories about Moroccan families, households, and culture, learning what she managed to pick up from random conversations and passing comments.

When she came to know Abd al-Rahman, her curiosity found a way to penetrate a world about which she was anxious to learn more. In him she discovered a young man who spoke good French, coloured with the attractive accent of people from Fez – an accent which was smooth and had about it the delicacy of the speech of young girls. She also found in him a young man who had managed to demolish the wall separating her world from the one beyond the city wall – the worlds of old Fez and modern Fez. She was eager to learn about the old city, which to her was veiled like a virgin girl keeping her face hidden out of modesty and shyness, so that prying eyes would not see how beautiful she was.

Madeleine noticed furtive glances in Abd al-Rahman's bashful, handsome expression that revealed what was hidden behind. Her response to him was no less fervent than his was to her, and he now discovered a face different from the faces of those foreign invaders who managed to infuriate him with the domineering way they exerted control over his country. His teacher at the academy may have revealed to him the cultural and scientific side of the colonising nation, but now Madeleine showed him the more aesthetic and spiritual side, where people spoke about beauty, subtlety, and softness.

As a young man Abd al-Rahman was open to the future, his interest in revolution being no less than in his own biology. His soul was now open to the idea of love, and his heart had begun a search for somewhere to settle, after having previously declined any offer of open arms to embrace him.

When Madeleine spoke to him, it was with a lively mind, a sharp tongue, sparkling eyes, and a cheerful expression; she was opening her own heart to be an abode for his. He did not deliberately long for her, nor was he in quest of a place to settle with her; rather he was inevitably attracted by the element of novelty that Madeleine provided for him whenever she spoke frankly and argued freely with him. Between them developed a being that was neither just man nor just woman, but instead a woman and man using mind, emotion, and life to engage with each other.

Abd al-Rahman began to experience something like the feelings he had read about in books at the Qur'an school and in collections of poetry. He now felt what he had only theoretically known as 'love', though he did not dare admit it to himself. He was still labouring under the weight of tradition that recognised only the physical aspect of love, and he had no wish to think about that 'dirty' subject – although there were many occasions when he had asked himself exactly what that dirty aspect was that everyone linked to love. He was also weighed down by his negative feelings towards the outsiders: was Madeleine herself not the daughter of those very people who turned a racist eye on Moroccans? This would explain why he had no desire to be frank with himself about his growing feelings towards Madeleine – but he found he could not stop himself seeing her, meeting her whenever possible, far away from the prying eyes of other people.

Once when they were talking, she surprised him by inviting him to visit her parents and have dinner with her family. She had told them about her friendship with Abd al-Rahman, and they wanted her to introduce them to her Moroccan friend – 'One who moves beyond the walls,' she laughed, 'to form a friendship with a girl outside.'

Abd al-Rahman was stunned. What could she have been thinking to dare tell her parents about her passing friendship with a young Moroccan man? 'What will they think of me?' he wondered. 'A foreigner invading their daughter's life? Are they suspicious of my intentions? Why do they want to get to know me? Could this imply some kind of scandal, or crime? Should I accept? It would be risky... Or should I decline? That would certainly be impolite, and would put in question the intentions of a young man who accepts a girl's friendship and then refuses to meet her parents. What does meeting her father and mother imply? Are they going to suggest I marry her?'

The word 'marry' set bells ringing in his mind; the sound was neither unpleasant nor entirely desirable either. Even so, it was an accurate reflection of his own self, in that his heart tended towards Madeleine to the extent that he could by no means rule out marrying her. His mind was in a whirl. He did not like the idea that his life companion would be a non-Muslim, a foreign girl, so liberated that she could tell her parents about her relationship with a young Moroccan man; nor did he like the idea that his life companion should be linked with the French nation that had placed itself in a position inimical to Morocco and installed its own sons in enemy headquarters. However, his heart could not give up on the idea.

Madeleine realised he was being slow to accept her invitation. She noticed the distracted expression in his eyes, and it surprised her that her invitation could provoke so much hesitation and thought. She sensed that if she pushed him for an answer, he would be upset. Even so, she wanted him to accept.

'My parents really like the idea of getting to know you,' she said. 'You might enjoy meeting them too.'

This opened a door for Abd al-Rahman and, his mind now fully alert, he accepted with a smile. 'Indeed, I shall be very happy to meet them.'

She was glad, and smiled in return.

Abd al-Rahman entered Madeleine's house. He met her father, who lived a life full of activity and liked to fill his mind with new ideas about life and people. He was a teacher who spent most of his time with children and their world of learning. Beyond that he devoted himself to books, painting, music, and sports. He was close to fifty years old, and yet his face was that of a much younger man in the prime of life. He talked to his guest about a variety of subjects and recalled a number of fond memories. He had many questions about aspects of life in the city about which he knew nothing. How did the men and women there live, not to mention the girls? Abd al-Rahman was a little bashful as he concealed half the truth, but he discovered he could divert the conversation to the more pleasant aesthetic aspects of family and household life.

He was introduced to Madeleine's mother and saw in her the kind of woman that Madeleine would become in twenty years. She was still beautiful and elegant, and smiled at life. She too had retained her love of enquiry and knowledge; her feelings were uncluttered by idle fancies and fairy tales. She never mentioned arguments among women or silly resentments and hatreds.

He also met Madeleine's brothers, and discovered that they were all children of the same father and mother. None of them felt their lives to be affected by issues of either race or gender; all they talked about was schoolwork and the competition to succeed.

The evening showed Abd al-Rahman another side of the life of the foreigners he regarded from behind the city walls, seeing only what the army, the administration, and the military regime chose to show him.

He had no regrets about accepting Madeleine's invitation; indeed, he felt she deserved his thanks. She had already shown him a new world, but now she had rid him of the tension he had felt in becoming her friend. Now he had an even greater love and respect for her. She made no attempt to conceal their friendship because she saw nothing dishonourable about it, nor did she intend it to lead to anything inappropriate. Meanwhile, he felt guilty when he recalled the thoughts he had had when she first suggested he pay a visit to her family.

He now busied himself with Madeleine even more than before. The friendship developed into a strong love, dignified by both respect and admiration. He had the impression that she was drawing closer to him, feeling an even greater affection for him, and disclosing her secret love, although – despite her youth and broad experience – she was too chaste to embark upon a frivolous adventure. Her honesty and self-respect were factors that increased his love and his conviction that he too could remain chaste in spite of his own youth and experience, so as not to dishonour her or ruin their friendship.

They embarked on an exciting discussion of the depictions of love, both happy and sad, to be found in stories and novels. He was not particularly fond of this type of writing, but Madeleine managed to make it more enjoyable for him by telling him about the heroes and heroines of the romances. He began borrowing stories from her and lending her stories and novels as well. In all of them he read his own love story and imagined his own experiences.

One day she surprised him by talking about a novel she had just read. 'You're always choosing sad novels for me!' Her tender look seemed to be asking him a question.

He had not given the subject any thought, so her comment came as a shock. He gave her a cheerful but unconvincing response, trying as he did so to brush off the implied accusation with an affectionate smile. He then extended his hands and drew her face towards him.

A veil of despair held him in its clutches as his thirsty eyes drank their fill of her lovely features. 'I'm in love with Madeleine,' he told himself, a thought that sent his mind into a spin. 'But what future does this love have? Shall I marry her? Should I remain loyal to this love in spite of everything that is happening? In spite of all the years I've spent opposing the French? What will happen to my reputation if people find out about this secret love? What will my father think?'

Then an idea ripened in his mind, and he grabbed it from the maelstrom of other thoughts which had been swirling around for some time. 'Madeleine's a friend; she'll be my friend for life. I'll never imprison her in a marriage. She and I are a couple separated by as much as we are joined. I shall never rob her of her life, nor will she rob me of mine. What there is between us will remain what her family understood it to be that evening when I went to her house for dinner.'

He was brought back from his lost dream by a pair of green eyes enveloped in a halo formed by bushy black eyebrows and a veil, as though to prevent their shining light from beaming at random. He stared curiously at these green eyes that had forcefully blocked his path. All he could tell of their owner was her soft, white skin, her somewhat plump body, the obvious elegance of her flowing jallaba, and her silken veil.

He told himself she must be the substitute for Madeleine. At least, she would never make him live a life of contradictions like those that Madeleine had plunged him into when he asked himself whether she might one day be his wife.

He did not spend much time thinking. He had come quickly to the conclusion that he must rid himself of the magic of those green eyes, just as he had done with the overwhelming power of sweet logic. But now he found himself unconsciously making the decision. 'My world belongs to the past. It will never allow me to take a wife from outside the walls of the city, or indeed from inside. So I need to get away from both Madeleine and the girl with the green eyes.'

31

'If a man's eyes cross your path, make sure to avoid looking at them.' These words had preoccupied Aisha's conscious and unconscious thoughts ever since Yasmine had first spoken them to her, when Aisha had been swept up in the celebration of Abd al-Ghani's wedding. She kept ruminating on the ideas that the words aroused. She was used to listening to advice from her mother – although there were things her mother did not talk about – and to pieces of advice offered by the servant-women. The veil of modesty, upright-ness, and respect drawn between mother and daughter, as between father and son, must remain both strong and thick, unassailed by any counsel that might prove embarrassing, or diminished by words that might breach the barrier of reticence that marked the relationship between parents and children. This was why Khaduj did not talk to Aisha about the future that awaited her. By now she had grown old and did not tell her daughter what to do if her quiet life was disturbed by something that might stir things up and ruffle its calm surface. It was Yasmine who took on the task, introducing her to the idea of men in the way she had imagined such things herself as a young girl before her own virginity was assaulted – in her advice to Aisha, Yasmine was presenting an image of the girl's own father, Hajj Muhammad.

'If you see a man,' Yasmine told her, 'you should realise that there's always some scandal involved... Men are tricky. Never trust them, my little girl!'

The ideas kept whirling inside Aisha's mind; her veins pulsed with disturbing thoughts that excited her and made her feel a longing, a revolt, a sense of recalcitrance... a whole new world invading her youth. When that new world collided with Yasmine's cautionary advice, the revolt inside her reached its peak and placed her in a world where men were the problem.

Even as the ideas whirled, Aisha was no less sensitive to things than Yasmine. Whispered conversations kept her awake at night, and probing glances aroused her curiosity. When Hajj Muhammad whispered to his wife Khaduj that Hajj Abd al-Qadir had requested Aisha's hand for his son, Aisha was the first to sense that something was happening, even though she had no idea what it was. It was just that, one morning, as she bent over to kiss her father's hand and looked into his eyes, she could detect a kind of probing: his eyes were searching for something in her bosom and her face. 'Maybe he's rethinking what he knows about me,' she thought. 'Have I grown up? Am I now ready to become a woman?' When she looked over at her mother, she noticed a smile in her eyes and on her lips. That smile, she felt, had to mean something... something about herself. 'Perhaps she's thinking about some happy news my father's confided in her,' she thought. 'If only I knew what it was, if only she could tell me.'

The whirlwind enveloped her once again when the whispered conversation in Hajj Muhammad's room turned into news that spread from the mistress of the household to its servant-women. Yasmine learned about it and started spending more time with Aisha, treating her kindly, showing her a beaming smile, and astonishing her when she took a careful look at her bosom.

'How happy I am for my little lady!' she said with a delighted laugh. 'Now the husband has started looking down from his window!'

Aisha looked up to make sure she had heard correctly and discovered that Yasmine's face let on even more than her words. The whirlwind started up again. 'Husband', that person whose gaze you were not supposed to return. Why was Yasmine, the one who had always given her warnings, now behaving like this? Behind every man there's a scandal, she had said. But now she was saying how happy she was that a man would be able to look down on Aisha from above.

Aisha was anxious to learn more, so her instincts led her to push back. 'You're the one with the man,' she said. 'I don't need one.'

Yasmine wanted to respond to Aisha's resistance without slaking her thirst by providing too much detail. 'Fairly soon you'll see,' she replied with a smile. 'He's going to snatch you away from us. What luck for me! I'll be able to visit our bride in her boudoir.'

Aisha did not react, not even to blush in embarrassment. Yasmine was just a servant after all and, even for Aisha, her status was not that of a lady who could make young girls feel embarrassed.

However, Yasmine did not provide any further details, and Aisha was anxious for a clear explanation of the contradiction between the ideas that Yasmine had emphasised so insistently when giving her warnings about men and the happiness now evident in her expression as she proclaimed glad tidings. But she found no clarification in Yasmine's eyes, nor any information about this person who was making the whirlwind spin even faster.

She went to spend some time alone with Saadiyya, Abd al-Ghani's wife, something she always liked to do. The impenetrable curtain that separated Saadiyya from Khaduj and the other ladies and servants of the household did not work on Aisha. They belonged to the same generation and had the same feelings. Even so, Aisha had begun to feel that they were growing apart as Saadiyya's married life continued. The happy smile that had shown on her olive-skinned face every morning had started to disappear; the care she took of her physical appearance, making her a beautiful bride refreshed as the days rolled by, had now been replaced by a certain indolence and neglect; and the youthful spirit that had always been part of her expression had vanished since she had given birth to her son, al-Tayyib.

But Aisha still found Saadiyya to be a girl with whom she could find some stability whenever the whirlwind spun out of control. As they talked about nothing in particular, they sat on either side of the sewing machine. Aisha really wanted Saadiyya to tell her the secret, which was public knowledge throughout the household but about which she knew only that it concerned a husband who had started looking out of a window. But Saadiyya only smiled, burying her head in the sewing while she counted threads, almost as though she did not care about what was bothering Aisha.

By now Aisha was fed up with this conspiracy of silence. 'You're thinking about something, aren't you?' she asked. 'Why are you staring at me with that mysterious smile?'

'I'm thinking about the same thing as you. Tell me, are you happy to be engaged?'

Aisha pretended to be surprised, but her rapid response cancelled it out. 'I don't know anything yet about an engagement. Do you know anything about it?'

Saadiyya smiled again and gave a quizzical look. 'You know full well, you little devil!' she said, tickling Aisha's chin. 'But you're hiding it.'

'I don't want a husband, or a fiancé, or any man,' Aisha replied. 'I'm perfectly happy as I am.'

The whirlwind started again, a voice within it shouting, 'If a man's eyes cross your path, make sure to avoid looking at him... If you see a man, you should realise there's always something scandalous about him.' The smile left Aisha's eyes, and she started swimming in a world far removed from that of her companion.

Saadiyya looked at her sympathetically and thought, 'Maybe Hajj Abd al-Qadir's family doesn't satisfy her... Perhaps she knows something about her fiancé that makes her feel she won't be happy with him.'

She made an effort to bring Aisha back to reality. 'We all used to say things like that,' she said. 'But marriage is a house that all girls enter. You'll see that it's a warmer and nicer situation than the lonely world you're living in at the moment.'

Aisha was not convinced. She objected, as though asking Saadiyya to clarify things that Yasmine had not been able to. 'But men... are tricky,' she said. 'There's something scandalous behind every one of them.' Her eyes filled with tears. If Saadiyya had not stretched out her hand, grabbed her by the chin, and raised her head, she would have burst into sobs.

'Don't be a child, Aisha,' she said. 'You're a girl who's about to achieve your proper station in life and embark on your future. Men are like women: some of them are tricky and cruel, others are nice and kind. Your father would never choose a husband for you who is unsuitable.'

This made her feel a little better, but the whirlwind did not stop.

As soon as she learned that the Hajj Abd al-Qadir family was about to visit their house, she disappeared from view. Marriage arrangers were always fully aware of this particular game, having all gone through the same phase themselves. They would usually manage to discover the girl, who was actually keen on being near them – but not too near. However, in this case they could not find Aisha in the nooks and crannies of the big mansion, in spite of the mighty efforts that Khaduj put into locating the missing girl. The visit came to an end without the visitors getting to meet the girl Hajj Abd al-Qadir had requested from Hajj Muhammad as a fiancée for his son.

Abd al-Rahman was one of the first to learn about the engagement that the two families were proposing between a young man and a girl who knew nothing about each other. He wished he could ask the young man whether he knew anything at all about the girl that they had convinced him was the best possible wife for him and mother of his children. He also wished he could ask the boy's father whether he had initiated the process deliberately and on the basis of previous knowledge of the families involved. He admitted he would not be able to ask such questions – but why should he not talk to his own sister, who was so close to him?

Aisha was self-conscious as she resorted to Abd al-Rahman for advice; she wanted him to help her resolve the contradictions that

Yasmine had created. So far neither Yasmine, nor her mother, nor Saadiyya had shown her a way out of her dilemma. She found herself confronting a wall of modesty that kept her and her brother apart, yet at the same time she felt her brother was giving her enquiring looks – but about what? She did not have to wait very long to find out.

'Listen, Aisha,' he told her, much to her surprise, 'do you realise they're going to marry you off?'

The shock of it tied her tongue, and she had nothing to say.

'Why don't you say anything?' he asked. 'The whole thing concerns you more than anyone else. I realise you don't know a thing about the man whose father has come to ask for your hand. Are you willing to marry a man you don't even know?'

The word 'man' rang in her ears as it had when Yasmine had first spoken it. She was anxious to flee from the mention of it, and wanted to resort to her brother as protection against the danger that the idea of this 'man', this 'fiancé', posed for her. She really wanted to burst into tears, but instead she simply stood in front of him with tears welling up, fighting off the whirlwind and giving her brother a pleading look.

He could read the pleas in her eyes. 'I'm going to check on this man for myself,' he told her. 'If he doesn't satisfy both you and me, then he won't be a suitable husband for you.'

His words provided Aisha with the peace of mind she had been craving as a means of rescue from the wilderness.

She gathered all her senses together as she watched the vigorous discussion between Abd al-Rahman and his father. It may have all been conducted in whispers, but it was also clearly angry, involving gestures and stubborn expressions. Not a word was audible, as if they were arguing about something secret.

Khaduj was present for part of the argument, sitting beside her husband. 'The man's wealthy and from a rich family,' she told herself as she left the room. 'Isn't he educated, and hasn't he attended the mosque school?' She had the impression that Aisha could hear what she was thinking, so she stifled her thoughts. Even so, she went on walking to and fro, obviously upset; it was as though the whirlwind had engulfed her too.

For a few days, life continued on its usual course, and Aisha heard nothing more about the engagement. She was distinctly unsettled by the apparent calm that prevailed once the furious argument she had witnessed was over; it was almost as though she had been watching a theatrical performance from behind a pane of glass.

It was Abd al-Rahman who eventually broke the mood. 'Good news, Aisha!' he said, much to her surprise. 'I've convinced my father.'

'You've convinced him about what?' she asked anxiously.

'To turn down your engagement to Muhammad, Hajj Abd al-Qadir's son.'

He did not expect her to reply. The lovely, grateful smile visible in her eyes spoke clearly enough.

32

Hajj Muhammad was not entirely happy about turning down Aisha's engagement to Hajj Abd al-Qadir's son, but neither was he too upset. He had no knowledge of the son, Muhammad, who was supposed to marry Aisha. Since he was acquainted with the boy's father and would have been content to have him as an in-law, he had not even given any thought to whether he knew the boy. Likewise, Hajj Abd al-Qadir did not know Aisha, the girl he wanted to be married to his son. He too had given no thought to whether he knew her or anything about her, since he was acquainted with her father and would have been content to have him as an in-law. Hajj Muhammad's motivation for approving the marriage was thus not inspired by any particular desire on his part or by some unassailable logic, but rather by Hajj Abd al-Qadir's wealth. Such wealth was not the exclusive preserve of Hajj Abd al-Qadir, though; Fez had many such people.

However, Khaduj could not tolerate the blow. She had looked forward to celebrating Aisha's wedding and could not even conceive of turning down a rich Fez family who had come to ask for her daughter's hand. She regarded the rejection as a bad omen for her daughter. Chance never likes to be frustrated, otherwise it can go on forever.

She felt pessimistic. She worried that all the families in Fez who might be inclined to link themselves to her family through marriage would now know about this particular affair – the rejection of a marriage proposal without good reason. They could all talk about how beautiful Aisha was and how unsullied her reputation, but what if she reached the age of eighteen without another family of the same calibre coming to ask for her hand? Her life would be ruined.

No such worries were going through Aisha's mind; she was simply delighted by the removal of the shadow that had been causing her so much distress. It was not Muhammad, Hajj Abd al-Qadir's son, in particular who was that shadow, but rather any Muhammad, any prospective husband. She could only look into the future through Saadiyya's eyes.

'Poor Saadiyya!' she thought to herself. 'Happy in her own universe... She's achieved her own identity and dreams, tranquil dreams undisturbed by a man, a husband, glances that might cause scandal, dreams unflustered by knowledge.'

Even so, Aisha could not avoid listening to the siren call that came to her every time she was on her own. It would hail her from afar and grow in volume as it drew closer and closer, until the point came when it overwhelmed her senses and shattered her nerves. The spell of it would take over her entire self, presenting her with a picture of a wonderful life as open as a spring rose in bloom. But then it would shout again, pulsing and throbbing through her veins, raging, shaking all her senses, and robbing her of sleep.

As she lay awake in the black robe of all-enveloping darkness, she thought about men and husbands. 'I was stupid to object and refuse to get married,' she told herself. 'Will I ever get another chance?' she asked herself in despair.

There was no immediate response to that question, but every time Aisha found herself shrouded in darkness, the issue hounded her. That siren call in all its magic and softness kept haunting her, pulsing noisily through her veins.

And the whispering started again, all eyes staring silently in her direction. No one dared spread the rumours or talk openly. This time, Yasmine did not dare share what she knew with Aisha. She could still feel the pain that had wracked her conscience whenever she recalled how she had let Aisha know about the event that she had assumed would be a happy one. She had managed to arouse Aisha's dearest hopes. But then the whole thing had gone up in smoke. No doubt it had left a residue of pain in Aisha's heart. Yasmine felt a sense of responsibility for it all.

There was still one person who did not resort to whispering. He felt obliged to make the person most concerned by it aware of what was happening, so that she could be the one to make her own decision about her future. Abd al-Rahman confronted Hajj Muhammad on the subject.

'Before you consult anyone else,' he told his father, 'you must find out what Aisha thinks.'

Hajj Muhammad was astonished. He had never imagined that any discussion of the subject with Abd al-Rahman would involve finding out what Aisha wanted. He had been the one to decide that Abd al-Ghani would be married; he had chosen the family and bridegroom himself without Abd al-Ghani, his mother, or the bride knowing anything about it. No one in the family had objected, or asked to be consulted. But this time he had agreed to ask Abd al-Rahman's opinion, and now his son was forcing him to make yet another concession, asking Aisha what she felt about the matter. So, was Aisha now going to decide her own future? Was she going to choose the husband she wanted?

A wave of pain, despair, and humiliation came over him as he turned things over in his mind before responding to Abd al-Rahman. He could not bring himself to speak, but simply stared wide-eyed at his son and frowned; the pain he felt robbed him of all grace and dignity. As he stared at Abd al-Rahman, his expression was a mix of anger, despair, bewilderment, and resignation. He stood up, unable to bear talking any more with his son, whose rebellion had now reached the stage of demanding that his father renounce the status he had proudly maintained all his life.

Abd al-Rahman sensed that he had won, and allowed himself a cryptic smile as he walked out behind his father – a figure with bowed head and bent back.

'Come here, Aisha! Have you heard the news?' he said.

When Aisha looked up in response to her brother's call, her expression was more open and confident than before. She made no attempt to hide anything or put on a display of fake surprise. 'I've been hearing whispers,' she told him, 'but nothing's clear and no one's told me anything.'

'A young man named Ahmad from a middle-class family has asked for your hand. He's a teacher at a primary school.' At this point Abd al-Rahman paused to assess his sister's reaction, as though interpreting impressions other than those caused by the mere shock.

When Aisha heard the news, the confidence she had been feeling totally deserted her. All she took from Abd al-Rahman's statement was the surface of the words. She did not take in 'young man', 'Ahmad', 'a teacher who's asked for your hand in marriage'; instead, it was 'a man', 'a husband' – someone with whom you did not exchange glances and behind whom there had to be some scandal.

She looked unhappy, but this time she did not blush in embarrassment. Instead, she turned as pale as death, and her eyes looked down as though searching for something on the ground. It seemed she could not face the reality of what Abd al-Rahman had told her. Her lips quivered, as though searching involuntarily for words to reflect the distress she was feeling. 'This time they're going to marry me off, whether I want it or not,' her thoughts kept telling her. 'They'll thrust me at a man... It's so difficult! If only, if only Yasmine would explain to me precisely what the scandal actually is. I don't want it, I don't want it!'

Abd al-Rahman was aware that the news was upsetting Aisha. He was anxious to give her the opportunity to be on her own and think about things without him there to influence her. As he was about to leave, the situation felt as though a gust of wind were blowing on someone struggling for breath.

'Think about it, Aisha,' he told his sister. 'Now you have the chance to think seriously about things and make a conscious decision about your own future.' He did not wait for a response, but as he left the room he asked himself, 'Why did she blanch when I told her someone had asked for her hand?'

It turned out that Aisha did not raise any objections, and Abd al-Rahman convinced her that Ahmad was a nice young man. He himself would have no objections to her marrying him.

Hajj Muhammad was not entirely happy when Khaduj told him that Aisha had accepted the proposal. He had always had the feeling that Aisha, as the youngest of his children after Abd al-Latif, had inherited his own ideas and decisions. Even so, he was still delighted that her response was positive: he could not bear to think of yet another proposal being rejected because Aisha had refused.

Hajj Muhammad put on a huge celebration for his daughter's wedding, the very best possible. He was anxious to show the family of Hajj Abd al-Qadir every detail concerning the parties, the trousseau, and the gifts that accompanied Aisha as she moved to her husband's house. He was equally keen for the streets of Fez to be witnesses throughout the seven days of celebration to the gifts and spreads of food amid all the ululations of bridesmaids and the traditional chants. But beyond that, and above all, he was anxious to hear the news that was on the minds of the bride's mother and father, as Aisha was to become the lady of a household where her husband would be expected to acknowledge his new wife's purity, chastity, and virtue.

The first few days rolled slowly by, spoiled by the emergence of discouraging news from the bridal bower. Shouts of encouragement began to batter Aisha's shyness, and confronted Ahmad, her husband, with an almost scandalous candour. The lively smiles that the bridal couple kept exchanging with each other could not lessen the tension felt by both their families. In both households, whispers began to spread among the female celebrants.

'A problem with penetration?'

'No... She just doesn't want it.'

No one had any real idea of what was actually happening – or not happening – inside the bridal bower. The bridal facilitator tried to intervene to break down the wall of silence between the couple, but Ahmad politely sent her away and paid her the amount usually anticipated for announcing the glad tidings. He had to handle Aisha's resistance patiently, treating her frowns as smiles and her silence as speech. But every time he approached her as a newly-wed husband would his bride, she surprised him by blanching, turning cold, and forcefully rejecting his advances.

Ahmad did not give up; he attributed her behaviour to her innocence and youth. Even so, he started feeling the burden of this relationship which had yet to take its natural course, not to mention his own responsibility to society, the two families, and his friends.

For her part, Aisha felt no such responsibility towards her family and friends. She gave no response to the messages being sent by Khaduj through her messengers, who would visit the bride every morning for one reason or another. Aisha simply resorted to silence and to the world of her own thoughts.

'Men! So here I am, now faced with one, trying to impose his evil on me. He's the kind of person Yasmine warned me about, still doing his best to rape me. He keeps on being violent, forceful, and difficult. Where can I escape to now to avoid his stares, and indeed his clutches, when I'm actually right in front of him?'

'But he's nice and polite,' an alert consciousness kept shouting at her. 'He's treating you kindly and showing you his affection and love. He's *not* showing any signs of violence or anger.'

Then the image of Yasmine appeared in front of her dreamy eyes. 'Don't trust men, my little one!' she had told her. 'Treachery and scandal, that's what they involve.' Once again she found herself in a whirlwind, making her even more confused and lost.

Ahmad went on living with Aisha, showing her love, affection, and sympathy, looking after her as though she were still a spoiled little child. She in turn gave him her heart, her love, and her loyalty. And yet, every time he tried to approach her, he became the cruel man, the would-be rapist behind whom some scandal or other was lurking.

33

Mahmud was totally absorbed in writing on sheets of paper; all around him were drafts where he had erased some lines and rewritten them. In front of him was another pile that he had torn up. As he wrote, he looked both committed and emotional. His hand trembled as though it had never held a pen before. Once in a while he looked towards the door to make sure no one would surprise him and try to find out what he was writing. His mind was at sixes and sevens, uncertain whether to go on writing or give up: this was why he had already torn up so much and rewritten it.

Abd al-Rahman came in, and was obviously interested. Mahmud tried to hide what he had been writing, but Abd al-Rahman strode confidently towards him.

'So, what's that you're scribbling?' he joshed. 'Are you writing a book or composing a poem?'

Mahmud heard the affectionate tone, and his anxiety vanished. Abd al-Rahman was not someone to make him worry if he learned what he had been writing, although he still preferred him not to find out.

'Nothing in particular...' Mahmud replied, somewhat casually.

Abd al-Rahman persisted. 'Is it a creative piece that's flummoxed you, so you've covered the floor with discarded bits of paper?'

'No, it's not.'

'Well, then, are you writing a personal letter to someone?'

'No, I'm not.'

Abd al-Rahman laughed. He wanted Mahmud to tell him, so he had resorted to the kind of interrogation used by teachers at school when they catch a student in some infraction. But he had failed.

'Okay, I get it!' he said with a laugh. 'You're composing a talisman to protect yourself from the evil eye!'

These ironic words were enough to make Mahmud relax more, and he could not help laughing out loud. But he stopped suddenly, as though struck by a new thought. He stared at Abd al-Rahman, anxious to check on something, in the way he used to do when he was a child. But his brother's expression revealed nothing about his concerns, nor was he able to rid himself of his feelings of confusion. Abd al-Rahman now looked away, as though their conversation had left no impression on him.

Mahmud then spoke in a tone of determination. 'I've decided to quit,' he said confidently.

Abd al-Rahman looked up, surprised not by the suddenness of it all but by the word 'quit'.

'Quit? What do you mean, quit?'

'Quit school and studying,' Mahmud replied casually, reflecting both his own resolve and the frequency with which he had mouthed the words to himself.

'Quit school?' As Abd al-Rahman pronounced the same words in amazement, his tone shifted from surprise to reproach. 'Why? Does the teacher hit you? Did they throw you out because you don't do your homework? What are you going to do? Sit in Abd al-Ghani's shop and help him do the measurements and cutting?'

Mahmud was well aware of the derisive tone Abd al-Rahman was using and realised that his brother was deliberately not giving him the chance to think and respond to the hail of questions he was throwing at him. So he decided to endure it and retain the self-assurance that he always felt when talking with Abd al-Rahman. His eventual response was terse.

'No, Abd al-Rahman,' he said firmly. 'I've decided to quit school so I can join the civil service. I was writing a job application.'

'The civil service?'

'Yes. Is that so peculiar?'

Abd al-Rahman was surprised; he had not expected Mahmud to confront him with such a question.

'Peculiar?' he replied, somewhat perturbed. 'No, there's nothing peculiar about it. But who gave you the idea in the first place?'

Mahmud paused for a moment. 'It was nothing but the realities of my life that gave me the idea.'

'But what is it about your life that would lead you to quit school and join the civil service?'

A whole cluster of complaints did a dance in Mahmud's mind. He was on the point of saying, 'My mother... the colour of my skin... the way my father chooses to ignore me...' but he decided not to follow this path. He had resolved that whenever this distressing reality imposed itself on him he would bury it deep inside himself. It was enough for him simply to be aware of its existence. But he had to say something in response to Abd al-Rahman.

'Actually,' he said, banishing all such thoughts from his mind, 'my life is one of poverty, and now that I'm grown up I can no longer send intermediaries to my father to ask for money to buy pencils for school or to pay bathhouse costs.'

Abd al-Rahman stared at Mahmud. He could envisage his brother's miserable life, since it was similar to his own, but while he could always get Khaduj to provide a path to his father's pocket, what about Mahmud? Abd al-Rahman repeated to himself the sad words that Mahmud had used: 'My life is one of poverty.'

'But poverty's not a good enough excuse,' he replied, for the sake of argument. 'I'm poor as well, but I'm certainly not going to ask for a job with those people.'

A whole series of replies now sprang into Mahmud's mind. He dearly wanted to say, 'You're not poor! You have a mother to defend you and a father to look after you. But what about me? I'm not a full son, only half of one, with only half a father.' But he swallowed these words, anxious to keep them buried deep in his consciousness, even if his secret feelings might be apparent to others. As he tried to come up with a response, reality came to his rescue.

'Our teacher LaFouret told us we should apply for a job in the administration. He was addressing the best students, and singled me out in particular.'

'And was it really just because you're the best student in the class?' Abd al-Rahman asked sarcastically.

'No,' Mahmud replied, fully aware of the derision in his brother's tone, 'but also because I'm Hajj Muhammad's son, and he's one of the notables of Fez.'

'So, they're choosing the very best students,' Abd al-Rahman guffawed, 'so that they won't finish their studies. But why are they choosing the children of notables?'

This question left both brothers in a quandary for a moment or two. Mahmud ventured a dubious response. 'Perhaps it's because the children of notables are the ones who most deserve to sit behind government desks?'

However, that response was not enough to stop Abd al-Rahman pondering the subject in depth. Silence now prevailed for a while, only to be broken when al-Tayyib, Abd al-Ghani's son, came into the room.

'Uncle, uncle!' the little boy shouted. 'Give me some money to buy sweets!' Neither uncle paid any attention to the little boy, and he left disappointed.

Abd al-Rahman looked up, having finally come up with an answer to the question. 'They're choosing the children of notables because they don't trust the rest of the populace. The concept of "notables" is a fairy tale invented by those idiots to create a compliant social class.'

Mahmud thought about what Abd al-Rahman was saying. It was a line of thinking that was new to him. 'But that's the way things are,' he replied, somewhat diffidently. 'The notables of Fez are merchants, proprietors, and landowners. Everyone else is a craftsman or tradesman.'

'True enough, but class distinctions are a new factor for both groups. What separates them is wealth and poverty, and yet they work with each other in daily life as though nothing distinguishes them from each other. But then the foreigners arrived and started categorising people like cattle: good and bad, notables and everyone else.'

This philosophical approach aggravated Mahmud. 'Whenever we talk about anything,' he replied acerbically, 'you use the occasion to deliver a lecture. We were talking about looking for a job, and now we're discussing class organisation in society.'

The word 'job' brought Abd al-Rahman back to reality. But rather than saying anything he indulged in some deep thinking, prompted by the bewildering difference between Mahmud's logic and his own. 'Mahmud is living in poverty,' he thought, 'and has no means of escaping it; he's now become a young man with life's demands laid out before him. This job would certainly lift him from poverty and isolation within the family. But he will be rid of one kind of enslavement only to fall into another. Employment, after all, is another level of slavery imposed by the powerful without justification, even if a wage is paid at the end of each month.'

Abd al-Rahman now felt he had put a distance between himself and his brother. When he looked at Mahmud, he realised he was still waiting for an answer. 'Don't you feel you're jeopardising your future?' he asked.

'What kind of future do I have,' Mahmud sighed, 'that I am jeopardising?'

Abd al-Rahman was stumped once again. Mahmud's realistic logic brooked no argument. He decided to try again. 'Your future is to learn more, and get a diploma.'

'Then what?'

'You'll become a doctor, a lawyer, or an architect.'

'And then what?'

Abd al-Rahman now realised that Mahmud did not believe in any kind of future. He would get a government job with minimal education, but he might never become a doctor, lawyer, or architect. 'Here's a young man at the threshold of life,' he told himself, 'who's lost all faith in the future. He's thinking only about how he's been wronged, being the son of Yasmine.'

'Don't you realise,' he asked Mahmud, 'that by accepting a job now, you'll be offering up your youth and experience to give credibility to the colonial power?'

'Does it even need me to do that?' Mahmud chuckled. 'What gives it credibility, sir, is the army, the police, and the real administrators. We'll just be the assistants, serving as intermediaries between the populace and the power. A few dirhams will suffice as a reward for our work.'

Abd al-Rahman leapt up as though he had been stung by a scorpion. 'My disappointment in you,' he said, 'will only be equalled by the disappointment of future generations in their predecessors. You, your name, your qualities, your Moroccan identity, your youth, your knowledge... You're going to put all these at the service of a structure that you should be fighting against and bringing to an end. Quite simply, you're placing yourself in a situation that you should be challenging, but...'

The words stuck in his mouth, yet the fury in his face expressed his thoughts. 'Is this a generation of young people living with the mentality of old men, with only cold blood creeping sluggishly through their veins?' Then another thought occurred to him, one that had often impinged on his mind: 'He's a maidservant's son. What can he do but grovel in the dirt?' But he immediately opposed this idea: 'His mother isn't defined by being a maidservant. She's a woman who happens to be from the south.' He remembered the story Yasmine had told him when the children were all clustered around the stove on a bitterly cold evening, the story about the man who had kidnapped her when she was young.

Returning from these thoughtful meanderings, Abd al-Rahman found himself still staring at Mahmud. 'So,' he managed to ask, 'what have you decided? Are you going to become part of the structure that is swallowing your homeland, or will you steel yourself to avoid becoming one of their slaves?'

By now Mahmud had given up on this bitter discussion. Standing up and leaving the room, he muttered, 'I've decided not to be a slave to poverty.'

34

Fez had never experienced the kind of anxiety and restlessness it was witnessing now, nor had it known the quiet worry that people were feeling in their hearts and discussing silently through the expressions in their eyes. All faces showed it as clear as day, reflecting how everyone had been drastically affected by poverty, hunger, and disease.

After its glorious past, Fez now felt despised. It withdrew into itself, as though blight had blunted all feeling, the inhabitants shrinking from any idea that might make them turn against their city and want to leave it. This blight afflicted everyone, men and women alike, and they all felt weak, impaired, and paralysed. As the feeling intensified, people no longer feared death. With the departure of a friend, relative, or loved one, there was no longer any sense of pain, anguish, or sorrow. The degree of people's sensitivity rose so high that basic instincts about death no longer robbed them of their minds or took over their feelings.

Anxiety took over the entire city, and no one knew why. Perhaps it was a comfort, serving as a substitute for the ongoing misery to which they were by now all inured, and which no longer caused them any pain or grief.

Echoes of this feeling began to make themselves felt throughout the long-suffering city. Talk replaced mere whispering, and echoes of that talk became louder and louder, though people could not always find the right words. War was a savage reality, and the government in Morocco was being run by a defeated nation. People were keen to push the disaster as far away as possible, unwilling to accept the idea that anyone might try to diminish authority from the fringes or to even think of rebellion, for which the least penalty would be death.

This was why people found it difficult to speak openly. But, in spite of it all – the disease, the misery, the government tyranny – they still tried to glimpse what might lie beyond the curtain, a new order for the various forces in the world, a post-war vision peering from behind the clouds, lights, and storms. If they could sit it out for a little longer, enduring the misery, deprivation, and tyranny, they might live to inherit a world very different from the one before it.

They could now define the kind of anxiety they were feeling, understand why they were feeling this way, and appreciate the unease for which the only explanation they could give was the city's current state of misery and humiliation after an era of glorious efflorescence.

Now feelings of anxiety were no longer a secret to be communicated by downcast looks or wan expressions. Tongues started mouthing opinions and hopes, at times cautiously but at others openly, throwing caution to the wind. Whispered comments abounded.

'The war's going to be over...'

'The winners will be dividing up the spoils of victory...'

'Freedom will prevail...'

'No, freedom will be lost...'

'Nazism will be defeated...'

'Imperialism will win...'

'The Atlantic Treaty will be implemented...'

'It'll be annulled...'

'But what about us? Where do we stand? What's our future?'

Amid all the comments and questions, this last one hung in the air unanswered. Now the level of worry intensified, preventing people from thinking about what was behind the illness, the families that had been affected, the young men who had been lost, the misery impacting the entire city, and the distress that continued to threaten its inhabitants.

Abd al-Rahman was one of those young people whose expressions did not reflect what they were thinking; or rather, they did not spend a lot of time talking, but left that to other people. Previously he had always been quite frank, scoffing at the very idea of being afraid and poking fun at his colleagues who acted scared. For a long time he had practised living by his ideas, but he had always been very careful to keep those ideas hidden, without giving them the freedom to discover an outlet for exchanges with other attentive minds and alert consciences.

'In every war,' he told people, 'there are spoils and prizes. We must make sure we're not going to be part of the spoils of the victorious nations again. Our people must be liberated – otherwise this will be just another page in the history of imperialism... The war is our opportunity. If we let it go, it'll be a long wait for another one.'

The only responses came from people with anxious expressions and aspirations for something new – and he encountered some fierce opposition to his ideas.

'You're still out to destroy yourself.'

'In wartime no state will ever tolerate extremist views.'

A guffaw emerged through a set of teeth worn down by old age.

'I think they're fighting for our freedom.'

A powerful, alert voice added, 'At least we'll get the reward for all the young men we've sent over, and we still—'

This man was interrupted by a thunderous voice yelling, 'What about our generation? What will be written about its history that deserves to be recorded? We don't want any rewards or costs. What we want is our rights!'

These comments echoed in Abd al-Rahman's mind, and he thought for a while. 'Their young hearts are pulsing with initiative,' he told himself, 'but are their eyes still capable of seeing what lies beyond the horizon?'

He looked to the distant horizon himself, in case he could spot something that might rid him of his uncertainties. His gaze combined piercing eyes and focused thought with a conscious mind.

His expression now changed; he looked as though he had

received inspiration from the heavens above; a light from afar shone brightly in his conscience, a single word: 'independence'.

Suddenly, people's expressions no longer seemed so worried, their complexions so pale. Now they had guidance, and they knew where they were going. That single profound, conscious, and motivational word 'independence' was being spread from mouth to ear. There was neither discord nor fear, no further cause for thought or opposition. People accepted it, as though the idea had been ringing in their ears for the past three decades, a dark period in their history that was now being overtaken by a gleaming light coming from the distant horizon, enveloped in an inspired notion sent down from the heavens.

'Independence!' the entire nation yelled behind him.

The word itself did not proclaim independence, but what it did was create a record of a new phase in the nation's history, when all thought of the inevitable continuity of the previous era came to an end.

Abd al-Rahman had not been happy with the way people used this word. They spoke it even while wandering aimlessly in a desperate state with troubled expressions and thoughts, and above all with no sense of direction. But now he felt happier, because the word had emerged from its captivity; it was on everyone's lips and bandied about from mouth to mouth. From this point on, there was no holding it back or preventing its forward momentum.

'Independence' was one of those words that make history. It provided the principle, and launched itself into spheres where every ear took it in, and it entered everyone's consciousness. All other ideas absorbed it, as though a jinni had finally been released from a bottle and it would be impossible for any magician to put it back inside, however powerful and effective his magic might be.

With the word 'independence' buzzing in his ears, Hajj Muhammad looked over at his son, his expression a mixture of doubt and confusion. Abd al-Rahman in turn gave an affectionate smile, eager to hear his opinion. 'I really need to know what he's thinking,' he told himself, 'so I can explain to him clearly where I stand on the issue.'

'My dear son,' Hajj Muhammad allowed himself to say, 'I lived through the first independence. It brought us nothing good.'

Abd al-Rahman shivered, eager to refute his father's statement, but instead his expression took the form of a great question mark. Hajj Muhammad continued. 'Cities were prey to Bedouin attack. It was total chaos, and there was hardly any security.'

'Wasn't that because of the foreigners?'

'This was before they arrived.'

Abd al-Rahman realised that Hajj Muhammad did not fully understand the events he had lived through. He decided not to pursue the historical dimension any further. 'Things change with time,' he said. 'Independence now will bring security, freedom, justice, and order to our country.'

Hajj Muhammad shook his head, unwilling to believe what he was hearing. 'All of you are all young and immature,' he said. 'You've no real experience.'

'Experience is what we get from living.' Abd al-Rahman felt like telling his father, 'If we relied on your experience, we'd remain in imperialism's clutches forever.' But he said nothing and let Hajj Muhammad continue.

'So far,' his father said, 'life has not taught you how to make a needle, so how are you supposed to administer an independent country?'

'It's freedom that's will teach us how to experiment and make needles.'

'Freedom? Who's ever stopped you enjoying it, or taken it away?'

Abd al-Rahman now understood that Hajj Muhammad was far from dazzled by the gleam of the word 'independence', and he tried to bring the conversation to an end. 'Well, we've demanded independence, and that's the end of it.'

'It's up to all of you. You'll have to deal with the consequences.'

Nothing alarmed the protectorate authorities so much as this word that was now echoing its way through valleys, plains, and mountains. They knew they would never respond to the demands, but were nevertheless troubled by the fact that the word had now turned into a principle, emerging from the hearts of people who had long remained hesitant. Now they had opened up a space within which the potential impact of the term in both near and distant perspective could be explored in greater detail. As they moved ahead, their pent-up fury was being buried in the idea of retribution, the people's primary goal.

Fez entered a state of siege, threatened by hunger, thirst, and dark shadows. Gunshots and bombs resounded through the streets and alleys. The army and the *garde* caused havoc, and spies did their utmost to destroy the core unity of the city. Young men were taken away to detention camps and prisons.

But 'independence' still resounded in the heart of every citizen, like a light to satisfy the city's longing, bread to feed the hungry, water to quench people's thirst. Independence, independence, independence – the word still echoed in everyone's ears.

Finally, the crisis ended and the city recovered its pride. Once humbled by disease, its spirit once crushed, Fez could now once again raise its head high.

The city had only been able to feel life in the light of glory. With 'independence' now resounding throughout its quarters, glory had been restored.

35

'So, you've brought independence in by the tail, have you?!' This was how Hajj Muhammad had greeted his son when he came home for a second time after another lengthy prison term, but Abd al-Rahman refused to get angry in front of his father. Instead, he accepted the joshing gracefully, knowing that his father was not gloating or showing his scorn so much as resorting to the kind of mild irony that he always liked to use in the face of Abd al-Rahman's logic and his burning enthusiasms. Hajj Muhammad's remark did not upset Abd al-Rahman or make him lose his temper. Instead, he accepted his father's comment with an open heart. It provided him with a new logical tack that he could use to try to best his father, in the particular context that he had chosen. 'On the contrary,' he replied immediately, 'we've opened the road wide in front us. Independence will know how to establish itself.'

Hajj Muhammad gave a dubious smile, which revealed his profound unease about the dreams that Abd al-Rahman and his coterie projected and believed in. They were all young, something their fathers could not claim to be. But the smile also reflected his obvious delight that his son had now come home. He had suffered terribly when Abd al-Rahman had gone to prison for a second time for the sake of his principles. But this time he did not feel humiliated, nor did he have the impression he had been banished from society. Instead, he had a genuine affection for his son and felt both sympathy and sorrow for the experience he had gone through. This time, his smile was an expression of the pleasure he felt at the end of a trauma he had been living with for the past two years.

He looked at Abd al-Rahman again and noticed that his son's eyes were fixed on him, as though the younger man longed to pursue the discussion which his father had started.

'My dear boy,' Hajj Muhammad said, with a serious expression, 'we all want independence, but—'

Abd al-Rahman thought he had won. 'I'm thrilled!' he interjected. 'So, you're a nationalist like me...'

The brash interruption annoyed Hajj Muhammad, but he ignored it, as though he had not even heard it. Instead, he finished his previous sentence. 'But you're all dreaming.'

Abd al-Rahman frowned. This was a disappointment he was not expecting. He gave his father a pleading look, as Hajj Muhammad went on.

'You're all dreaming because you believe the occupying powers are going to grant you independence.'

Abd al-Rahman now summoned the courage to contradict his father. 'We've never believed they'll grant us independence. What we do believe is that we're going to take it.'

Hajj Muhammad gaped in amazement. It was clear he had never imagined that these young people would be so deluded as to claim that they could simply take what was not being offered and defy an authority that was stronger and more stubborn than they could ever be. He now realised that he could not argue with such aspirations. But he could not admit defeat, either. 'So, you're going to use your fingernails to grab it, are you?!'

Abd al-Rahman understood the ironic tone once again, but he still did not react. He wanted to gauge how far the old views had changed; Hajj Muhammad was a mirror on whose surface a large number of opinions were reflected, a mirror with both intellectual and material interests. His comments, his reactions, the expressions on his face, his sarcasm, and his sincere tone of voice – they all continued to reflect the widespread views that he represented. Abd al-Rahman's goal in provoking his father like this was not to push him to change but rather to get him to understand the way that his views mirrored the past. However worked up he might feel, Abd al-Rahman was anxious to maintain a calm appearance, and to carefully use language that was provocative but not hurtful. This was a lesson he had learned during his lengthy terms in prison. 'The armour that the people can bring to bear,' he replied, summoning all his resources, 'is much more powerful than any military might.'

Hajj Muhammad's eyes darkened. He had no idea what these popular armaments might be, nor could he imagine there could be a force stronger than the army. He was perplexed by the delusion that was driving Abd al-Rahman, who seemed to believe in something called 'the people's armour'. He was confused by Abd al-Rahman's strange logic and new terminology, and was on the point of telling him to leave his room – as he used to do when his son was a boy, and as he still did with others who had not previously invaded his inner sanctum. But he found he could not face down Abd al-Rahman in that way, nor could he keep a handle on his own emotions. Looking at his son, he saw that tears had appeared in Abd al-Rahman's eyes, as though to challenge the thick cloud that had enveloped his own eyes. Hajj Muhammad now felt yet more unsettled and was about to leave the room himself, but his love for Abd al-Rahman demanded that he remain patient in the face of his son's delusions and continue this conversation, which had been suspended for two whole years.

It was not just love for his son that made him linger; there was something else as well, something he could not even admit to himself. He actually wanted to know more about this delusion that so preoccupied the attention of Abd al-Rahman's coterie. What was this conviction that kept pushing them all to such levels of self-sacrifice, whose dignity and risk no one could any longer deny? And yet, in spite of that, he was anxious to rescue Abd al-Rahman from the course of action he had set for himself. Even though he knew that was not possible, he was still keen to continue the discussion.

'Listen! I'm your father, and I understand the power wielded by the people you're demanding should leave the country and grant us independence. But they're more powerful than you think. You think you can defeat them because they've been defeated by Germany, do you?'

Abd al-Rahman was on the point of rejecting the idea, but Hajj Muhammad put his fingers to his lips to indicate that he should remain silent.

'They've recovered their lost power now,' he went on, 'and they have the British and Americans behind them. So, where is the force needed for us to confront such a collection of powers and win our independence?'

Abd al-Rahman laughed out loud.

Hajj Muhammad was certainly not expecting such a reaction from his son. He gave him a quizzical look, surprised that his son should be challenging this information, which he assumed to be sound and accurate.

'Do you really believe that the forces of the independent nations are actually more powerful than those of the colonised ones?'

Hajj Muhammad gaped in amazement. He had not been anticipating such a question and had no idea how to respond, or how to think about it, so he went on staring distractedly at his son.

Abd al-Rahman realised what was going through his father's mind. 'We're not going to launch a war to get our independence,' he said. 'We're going to build pressure, in order to persuade people that we're right.'

'Enough, enough, enough!' Hajj Muhammad shouted. 'You're all dimwits. You're still thinking in terms of persuasion and adopting the logic of truth and falsehood. Truth and rights are linked to power. People without power have no hold on the truth.'

Abd al-Rahman was amazed to hear this sound logic emerging in proverbial form from his father's mouth. It was a point of view that had often impeded progress, but it still nested in the minds of many people. 'Power isn't truth any more,' he replied. 'When the war's over, oppressed peoples with no real power will become important. Our world is a new one, and we'll need to use fresh ideas and different actions to deal with it.'

'What's new is that the authorities will crush you, like chickens in a cage – detention camps and prisons. That's the punishment that awaits anyone who chooses to defy people more powerful than himself.' Before Abd al-Rahman could respond, Hajj Muhammad stood up. 'Spare me all of that,' he said with a gesture. 'I've almost missed the afternoon prayer-time.'

Abd al-Rahman left feeling disappointed. Now that he was out of prison, he had been hoping he would detect a significant change in his father's attitude. 'Change?' he asked himself, as he huddled in a corner of his room. 'Years in prison have kept my mind in the dark about reality. If I had really aspired to create some new mode of thinking, I'd have some grain of hope left. But my thinking is not a mirror that reflects the real situation in my country. Instead, the rust of multiple previous generations has accumulated, blocking all reflection from its shiny surface.'

Just then he became aware of Mahmud's voice, affectionately congratulating him on his release. Mahmud told him he was no longer a minor bureaucrat occupying some remote corner in the provincial office but had now been transferred to the court. His excellent work, his serious demeanour, and the testimony of his superiors all meant that he was a candidate to become a judge.

'A judge?' Abd al-Rahman shouted in amazement. 'You're going to be enforcing the law on Moroccans?' he went on. 'Using the law to throw them in jail?'

'I'll be finding them innocent as well,' Mahmud replied, as though he felt the need to defend himself.

'Using the law codes?!' Abd al-Rahman asked with a grimace.

Mahmud understood what his brother was implying. 'The law?' he replied. 'Who in this country governs by law? Did you go to prison because of the law? I will be the law.'

'You?! You mean... you?!'

Again Mahmud understood his brother's point. 'I'm a minor token authority,' he said. 'I represent a higher cognisant authority.'

'Imperious, you mean!'

'Imperious or discriminating, whichever you like. I'm a government employee.'

For a moment, Abd al-Rahman thought to himself, 'Government employee, efficient machine! Judge with no law. From the front ranks at school to the court bench. So, Mahmud, Yasmine's son, is going to be a judge.' When he came to himself again, his mental horizon was murky. 'Well, good luck!' he said. 'I hope to have better luck next time if I find myself standing before you!'

Mahmud laughed. He was stunned by the realisation of a possibility he could not avoid, one that he was nevertheless anxious not to acknowledge. Laughter was his only resort. 'Well then,' he told his brother, 'I'll be glad to declare you innocent!'

'But what about that higher cognisant authority you mentioned?'

'A minor authority can keep a higher authority content.'

'In that case, you've become a dangerous man!' Abd al-Rahman stood up. It seemed to him now that he had emerged from one prison only to enter another in which he was hemmed in between his father and his younger brother. What he needed was a waft of fresh air with more freedom, more purity, and more realism. Heading for the great doorway leading out of the house, he rushed into the street and slammed the door hard behind him, reassuring himself that he had firmly closed it on Hajj Muhammad and Mahmud.

36

When Abd al-Rahman slammed the door to his father's house, he had the same feeling as when he had finally turned his back on the prison gates: the need to fill his lungs with a fresh breeze, one filled with hope and life. Indeed, he felt a refreshing current of air blowing through the city's narrow streets and long twisting alleys. He had no doubts that Fez, now released by shouts of freedom and independence from the misery of disease, fear of war, and humiliation of poverty, had flourished and become yet more liberated during the two years he had spent in prison, when a veritable downpour of ideas, emotions, and feelings must have slaked its thirst.

He wandered around the city streets with no particular goal or direction in mind. He opened his eyes in a totally new way to the narrow horizons defined by the city walls and the twisting thoroughfares; he kept his ears open as though longing to hear a melody or birdsong. He surveyed the streets and alleys in a way that was different from how he had looked at them before. They all seemed bright, open, and prosperous, as though they had never known misfortune, angst, or darkness. As he walked, Abd al-Rahman felt as though he could actually touch the light with his hands. He stared at the ancient walls, imagining they had been made new again and had forever cast off the accumulated rust of ages past. The narrow squares seemed to have expanded more and more until they were even wider than his own welcoming heart. When he gazed up at the sky, it no longer looked as though it were clamping the lofty walls in its grip, as before; instead, infinite blue horizons were opening up to him, radiant and full of light.

Looking at people's faces, he searched for the misery that had marked them for years. In his own eyes there was the glint of a smile, like a flood of sweet, pure water, a smile that reflected his sense of the contentment of Fez's population, which he could see in their expressions. At first he sought the source of that contentment in signs of luxury and wealth, but found nothing new or different from that point of view. Rather it was an internal feeling, a happiness that had opened its windows to faces that had for so long been eager for it. He stared wide eyed at the people passing by, almost stopping in his tracks out of a desire to ask them... what? As he pondered, he had no idea what it was that brought him back to this thing in people's expressions that he had never seen before. But then the answer came in a rush.

'A belief in the future, that's what it is,' he thought. 'They've all been reborn, and the call for independence is their new birthright. Ever since they raised the cry, the whole population of the city has seen the light... They've liberated themselves from the darkness, from the misery and gloom that had been imprinted on their faces for so long. Now the gleaming light of a fresh morning is reflected in their expressions, newly born and bursting with hope and glad tidings.'

This explanation came to him as he continued to stare curiously at his fellow countrymen; it felt as if he had discovered a new world. He did not approach anyone, but preferred instead to assess the novel element in their expressions from a distance.

Suddenly Abd al-Rahman stopped in front of the entryway to the Qarawiyin Mosque, and his wandering gaze focused on a face he knew very well. The man immediately gave him a great hug of welcome, his eyes watering with tears. 'Praise God for your safe return!' he shouted. 'Praise be to God!'

Two powerful hands now pushed Abd al-Rahman away a little so that the man's weak eyes could take an affectionate look at his face, as though they were trying to discern what two years of imprisonment, suffering, and hardship had wrought.

'Well, Abd al-Rahman,' the man said, 'things haven't changed you much!'

Thus spoke Abd al-Aziz as he stared with sympathetic affection at his old friend's face. His mind was filled with a tissue of memories: of al-Adir prison, seven long years, the impact of which was now triggered again by seeing Abd al-Rahman's face – every detail, every line clearly visible, with all their accompanying sorrows and agonies, as though from only yesterday.

Abd al-Aziz took another look at Abd al-Rahman through teary eyes that obscured the features of his friend's face, making him seem again the young man of gentle visage before his appearance had been ravaged by sun, hunger, and thirst. Abd al-Aziz's tongue failed him, his voice choked up, and his tears flowed. But he soon recovered, and Abd al-Rahman's face once again came into focus before him, smiling and full of courage and virility.

'How did you manage to live through all those months and years?' Abd al-Aziz managed to ask. 'Were you in al-Adir again?'

'That's all past and over,' Abd al-Rahman told him. 'Those days and months are long gone, like all the others. We don't have time to live in past memories; now what we need to do is live our lives in hope, in the future – through what we're going to do, not what we have done.'

Abd al-Aziz stared at him, surprised by Abd al-Rahman's serious and steadfast tone. In Abd al-Aziz's eyes, Abd al-Rahman grew to become a kind of giant looking down at his friend from above.

All Abd al-Aziz could do was bless the words he had spoken, and go on contemplating this new entity in front of him. 'You're right,' he said. 'We must think about the future... The past is dead and buried.'

Abd al-Rahman was delighted at the enthusiasm with which Abd al-Aziz greeted his ideas, but it was no longer the time for just ideas. He grabbed his former cellmate by the hand in order for them both to move forward. But now he realised that he was moving ahead along with the entire populace, with all its naivety, enthusiasm, inflamed emotions, tolerance, and simple discussions. The persistent question that Abd al-Aziz had almost shouted out loud once again popped into his mind: 'So, how did you spend those two years in prison?'

'That's all over now,' Abd al-Rahman responded insistently in reaction to the question. 'We don't have time to live on memories. We've cancelled the past, buried it.' Abd al-Rahman smiled happily.

In convincing Abd al-Aziz, he had managed to convince himself too; he got the impression that some other person was yelling at them both, 'We've buried the past!' The source of this message was actually the two more years he had spent in al-Adir prison, years that had taught him not to think about the present. His own present had then consisted of hurts, sorrows, captivity, and suppression of the natural pulses coursing through his veins. He had learned to treat the present as the past – something he only sensed as he moved forward; he had also learned to bury the past – something discarded as he moved forward. Yes, he had learned to bury the past, and now he had no sense even of its existence. His thoughts were focused on the future, and from now on that was all he could feel.

'While we've been away,' he asked, as he turned away from the past, 'have you been preparing for independence?'

The door of hope opened before Abd al-Aziz, finally allowing him to speak. Since his own question had bounced back upon him, he had begun to feel wary of Abd al-Rahman. He had the impression that the last two years that had kept them apart had turned Abd al-Rahman into a different person, difficult to approach. But Abd al-Rahman's question now restored his self-confidence and freed him of the worry that had beset him as his friend philosophised about past and future.

'We're not ourselves any more,' Abd al-Aziz said. 'And yet the past which is dead and gone has prepared us for the future, putting its trust in the idea of independence until everyone is convinced that they really are independent, and all that's needed is the official announcement.'

It seemed to Abd al-Rahman as if someone behind him were posing a series of questions: 'Which is the more powerful foe – the standing army or the range of imperialism?' This led him to use his father's logic in addressing his friend. 'But we're facing a powerful force, equipped with weapons, money, army, and air force...'

Abd al-Aziz smiled as he paused before responding. He was not sure what Abd al-Rahman was getting at, but even so he eventually came up with a reply that was not hard for him to expound. By now Abd al-Rahman had reopened the gate to his soul; it was no longer firmly shut in Abd al-Aziz's face.

'No one's scared of power any longer,' Abd al-Aziz said. 'No one believes in the efficacy of arms alone. We've moved beyond that testing period.'

'And did we pass the test?'

'With distinction.'

Abd al-Rahman's quizzical look was not an expression of doubt but rather a plea to his friend to keep talking and explain his thinking.

Abd al-Aziz took the cue. 'We passed it with distinction,' he went on, 'because we still believed in our right for independence. We had to cross the conceptual threshold first for it to become a conviction. That constitutes a kind of victory over ourselves.'

'A victory we needed.'

'The hardest kind of victory there is.'

'Our enemy uses murder, expulsion, imprisonment, and exile against us.'

'We've stormed all their strongholds. Even our cloistered women have been killed or thrown in prison, and they've become accustomed to seeing the army spread debauchery in their homes and to saying farewell to their sons at their doors, never to welcome them home again. That's how we have learned conviction. Can there be any more powerful force?'

As Abd al-Rahman looked at his companion, he saw a countenance pulsing with determination, conviction, and enthusiasm.

Even so, he launched another assault on that conviction by asking, 'Don't you think we're a backward people? Independence has its consequences.'

'You've reminded me,' Abd al-Aziz replied with a laugh, 'of the kind of thing I used to hear my uncle Mahjub say. "If you all got together to manufacture a needle," he'd scoff, "you couldn't do it. So how is it you're demanding independence?!"'

'And what did you say to that?'

'I told him that even if we remained under imperialist control for thousands of years we'd never be able to manufacture a needle.'

Abd al-Rahman smiled. Since he had gone to prison he had neither raised his voice nor laughed; over two whole years he had learned to whisper rather than talk openly, and not to laugh out loud. He banished the thought that had made him smile, and asked, 'But how are we supposed to manufacture that needle once we're rid of imperialism?'

'So, you've buried the past, and I'm not thinking about the future!' Abd al-Aziz said firmly, albeit with a laugh. 'We'll make the future with our own hands. We won't be able to do that if we're not free to do it ourselves.'

Once again, Abd al-Rahman smiled. 'It seems to me that you've turned into a philosopher, stripping time of its interventionist role and robbing the present of any share in the future.'

'You're the one who's taught me philosophy,' Abd al-Aziz scoffed, 'with your burying of the past!'

'What's important now,' said Abd al-Rahman, suppressing a laugh, 'is how we achieve independence. The path ahead is far from clear.'

Abd al-Aziz looked eagerly at his friend's face, hoping to find in his determined expression the encouragement he needed to respond. In turn, Abd al-Rahman gave him a quizzical glance, as though his friend were taking too long to reply.

'Okay, so tell me!' Abd al-Rahman said. 'Don't you have an opinion on the subject?'

'My opinion?' said Abd al-Aziz. 'Maybe it's the same as yours.'

'What makes you think it's my opinion?'

Abd al-Aziz now plucked up his courage. 'Maybe it's not. Even so, to be frank, the path ahead is quite clear. We may already know it, but now we have to follow it.' Looking again at Abd al-Rahman, he detected a large question mark imprinted on his stolid face. 'The path ahead,' he went on, 'involves seizing our independence by engaging in the struggle to get it and keep it. They snatched it from us through their own sacrifices, and now we must do the same to get it back. We can do that – but it involves shedding our own children's blood.' He choked on these last words, and stopped talking, as though to recover his breath.

Abd al-Rahman's entire being was stirred, as though some inspired message were echoing in his ears. He stared at Abd al-Aziz with warm tears in his eyes. Profoundly moved, he embraced his friend and planted a grateful kiss on his brow.

37

Since Abd al-Rahman had come home from his long spell in prison he had been observing Hajj Muhammad's expressions closely. Whenever he bent over to give his father's veined hands a son's obedient kiss, he noticed them shaking with affection. For the first time he discovered something new, something he had refused to acknowledge throughout the many years past. His eyes missed that former intimate feeling between father and son, and he found himself confronting a new feature in that familiar face that had previously filled both his eyes and heart. There was something new as well about his father's voice, one that had filled the whole house and its many rooms in days past with echoes of his power and authority. As his lips brushed his father's hands, formerly agents of violence and instigators of both good and evil, there too he sensed that something was new and different.

Abd al-Rahman now discovered a wrinkled face, as long as it was broad, with deep creases extending across his pale cheeks and a beard in which white hair now overwhelmed black. The lips looked pale as well, time having sucked out of them all rays of hope, subtle sensitivities, and profound longings. Light had gone out of the eyes, and they had lost their gleam, almost as though they could not bother to focus. Veins now appeared prominently on his neck, which had previously looked full and well nourished. The hands were now thin, and dark veins showed through the skin. And the posture was stooped, as though in preparation for full prostration in prayer.

Abd al-Rahman also noticed changes in the way his father neglected his dress; his clothing had faded and no longer appeared neat and elegant. In fact, his garments suggested poverty and gave an impression of adversity rather than respect and admiration.

Hajj Muhammad's personality had changed too. Old age seemed to have caught him unawares. Abd al-Rahman had the feeling that his father had deteriorated rapidly, robbed of his pride and self-esteem, not to mention his energy and his habit of hard work. He stayed in the house and no longer visited the country farm to check on the peasants' productivity. He no longer supervised the business to see how things were developing, nor did he visit Abd al-Ghani's shop to make sure the work was being done properly and profits were being made. He even stopped regularly attending homily sessions at the mosque, something he had done throughout his life; now he would go only occasionally. When the nights turned cold, he now preferred to perform the evening and sunset prayers at home.

Abd al-Rahman and his mother were the only ones to notice these changes. In fact, Khaduj was even more aware of the impact of old age because it was she who spent hours with Hajj Muhammad when no one else was around. She could sense the great difference between the powerful young man he had once been, who could make full use of his youth and prowess, and the man whose energy now dwindled at night like a flower that opens only in daylight. Now she lived with her memories of Hajj Muhammad, the man who had filled her life with his manhood, her hearing with his powerful voice, and her feelings with his noisy breathing that reverberated as she slept beside him. Inside her, she sensed the melodies of youth that made her feel comfortable and warm. She had lived her life with those regular grunts, which had become weaker over time, accompanied by coughing fits that seemed to come from a dark cave.

Khaduj's mind was beset by grim thoughts as she spent long hours sitting and nursing her concerns. In spite of her anxieties, she did not feel able to share them with anyone, including her own sons. Her only consolation came in the form of a prayer that she repeated whenever needed: 'God bring us a safe release!'

One morning, when Hajj Muhammad woke alone, he could not

get up out of the bed; he had spent a sleepless night awake. He had a splitting headache, his temperature was up, and a burning sensation was making him feel as though his stomach were on fire. It all felt as if a powerful force were tying him to his bed.

Abd al-Ghani did not dare visit his father; he simply asked about him and his mother before taking off for the shop. Mahmud did not dare ask either, but simply questioned his mother, Yasmine; she too made do with asking Khaduj in a whisper about her husband. All she heard in reply was the usual prayer: 'God bring us a safe release!'

But Abd al-Rahman did dare. When he learned from his mother that Hajj Muhammad had spent a restless night, he entered his father's room, took hold of his hand to feel his pulse, and felt his temperature. He realised that his father had a fever, and his condition warranted care and attention. Hajj Muhammad was not fully conscious, so he could not talk to him. He told Khaduj that they had to call in a doctor.

But his mother was totally against the idea. She had never been able to comprehend the issues which she considered the province of men, but even so she was not prepared to decide whether Abd al-Rahman had the right to call in a doctor.

'A doctor?' she asked herself. 'What's the point of calling in a Christian doctor? If Hajj Muhammad could, he'd visit the shrines of Mawlay Idris or Sidi Ali Bu-Ghalib and be cured on the spot. His devout belief in the saints always makes a cure that much easier. Ah me, if only Lalla Shama would visit us, she could take his handkerchief to Mawlay Idris's shrine and dip it in the pure water at Sidi Ali Bu-Ghalib's sanctuary.'

When she returned from her reverie, Abd al-Rahman was still staring anxiously at her, waiting for an answer. 'We need to call a doctor,' he pressed. 'He has a high temperature.'

'A doctor?'

'Yes, a doctor.'

Khaduj felt uneasy in the face of her son's insistence. She still said nothing, but the word 'doctor' went on ringing in her ears.

'I'm going to call a doctor now,' Abd al-Rahman decided.

Khaduj felt that she had to say something. 'That's not a good idea,' she told him. 'He's just feeling a bit weak, so we'll give him something hot to drink and send some of his clothes to the shrines of Mawlay Idris and Sidi Ali Bu-Ghalib.'

This sent Abd al-Rahman into a rage. He raised his voice so loud that it roused his father.

'What's all this fuss about?' Hajj Muhammad asked in his semi-conscious, feverish state. 'Don't you realise I'm here...? Have a little shame!' It cost him so much effort that he collapsed into a faint again, his voice petering away to nothing, but still echoing inside his feverish mind.

Khaduj could not take any more and left the room, her heart pained. Tears ran from her eyes, which she dabbed with the edge of her scarf. Abd al-Rahman followed her out, disturbed by her distress. He would have cried too, had he not realised that he was the man here, the one who was supposed to remain firm in adversity. He looked pleadingly at his mother, as though to tell her without words, 'Dear mother, the doctor will know how to cure him and can give him some medicine.'

But she was stern. 'Please, Abd al-Rahman, leave me alone, and your father as well. God alone will cure him. If he knew you were going to call a doctor, he'd certainly stop you.'

Abd al-Rahman could not think of a way of arguing with his own mother, but, as he gave way to her, he felt a bitter sorrow. And as he left the house, he could not rid himself of the strong sense of something wrong that had overwhelmed him as he argued with his mother both silently and out loud. He began wandering aimlessly, letting the force of habit guide his steps.

'We're still a long way from being able to distinguish between modern medicine and hot drinks,' he thought, 'even though those drinks have done away with thousands of souls. They're a generation with "the past" inscribed on their foreheads. But it's a past that's over, dead; we've buried it.'

As he came to himself again, another voice inside him said, 'He's my father... It's my responsibility to save him. It may be the past with regard to the realities of life today, but I still have to devote my entire being, my whole existence, to my own present, using the seed of revolution that is growing inside my soul.'

'But your responsibility's over,' the present came back to counter him. 'You can't transform the past into the future. You can't bring a statue to life – unless you're either a clown or an artist.'

'But my father—'

'What have fathers and sons to do with the law of life?'

'It's my task to change history.'

'Your task is to stand facing the stream to make sure it doesn't go straight from past to future.'

'So, then, am I a nihilist...? Totally negative?'

'No, you're an existentialist, and positive. Your will is not conditioned by the past that is over, but rather by the future to come. So, respond to your will, and stop burning your energy trying to resurrect the past.'

This inner conversation was suddenly interrupted by a loud bray from a donkey that had collided with a Bedouin, earning a strong rap on its muzzle.

Hours later Abd al-Rahman went home again, feeling no need or desire to know how his father was. Nevertheless, he gave his mother an enquiring look, but failed to find any sign of the tragedy he had seen earlier in the day. Now her expression looked hopeful.

'Is my father feeling better?' he asked eagerly.

'God be praised,' she said, 'he woke up and had something to eat.'

'He ate something?'

'Yes, eggs and yogurt.'

Abd al-Rahman looked surprised.

'Yes, he was hungry, thank God!' Khaduj went on. 'I told you. Doctors, what do they know? God is the only doctor. How many times have we been sick, and God alone has cured us?'

'No doctor, no medicines?'

'We dealt with it ourselves. Lalla Fatima, the Prophet's descendant, gave us a medicine she made from her own supply of herbs. Her hands are indeed blessed. God and her good fortune can cure us of any disease.'

Abd al-Rahman said nothing, but simply gave his mother a languid stare, as though a heavy weight prevented his eyelids from lifting. In his ears he heard a loud voice saying, 'The past, the past, the past...'

By next morning, Hajj Muhammad was no longer feverish, but the illness had left its mark on his frail body and injured soul. When he greeted Abd al-Rahman that morning, he was eager to see his son. He felt the fever had put a distance between himself and his children, and that he had spent years and years away from his world, his home, and his family. He was especially keen to talk to Abd al-Rahman, being still fond of him in spite of their disagreements and the fundamental differences between them. He could not help admiring and respecting his son and harbouring a belief in the rightness of his son's ideas, which he was incapable of shutting out.

He looked fit and well as he gave Abd al-Rahman a welcoming smile, as if he had never had a fever. Abd al-Rahman was filled with hope, a warm feeling he put into a fervent kiss that he planted on the feeble hand that the fever had left looking like a piece of torn cloth, devoid of life.

His father's appearance spurred Abd al-Rahman to open his heart. 'I was determined to call a doctor to treat you,' he said.

Hajj Muhammad shuddered, as though the fever had returned. 'Doctor?' he said. 'No doctor's hand has ever touched me. How could you think of bringing in a Christian doctor to treat me? No, no, never think of such a thing again.'

Abd al-Rahman was crushed, and all hope vanished from his expression. Staring at the floor, he felt giddy. The colours of the mosaic on the walls seemed to dance before his eyes, the greens, blues, reds, and whites all blending with each other. Defeated, all he could think to do was utter some words of encouragement.

'God be praised for your recovery,' he said with a broad smile. 'You're fine now, and won't need a doctor.' Planting a cold kiss on the feeble hand, he left the room, as that same terrible voice echoed in his ears: 'The past, the past, the past...'

38

When Abd al-Rahman entered the house, he was panting, his face ashen in the searing heat of the Fez summer. Sweat was dripping off him as though he had just emerged from a swimming pool. He was escaping from the air of the city streets, which the sky above had imprinted with its opaque colour, scorching the ground with its hellish heat and spreading it over the city's lofty walls, which seemed to be hewn from hell's own rocks.

Abd al-Rahman was sensitive to extreme heat, and it affected him badly. His nerves were on edge, and the process of outrunning the heat left him short of breath. Everything closed in around him, and the house was the only place he could find relief. Inside, the temperature was more moderate, and there was cool water and shade to protect him from the rays of the sun that went straight from his eyes to his nerves, upsetting him and making him lose patience.

As he entered the room, Abd al-Rahman heard Mahmud talking to Abd al-Ghani in a crowing tone.

'He told them, "Everyone can sweep his own doorstep..."'

Abd al-Ghani was on the point of responding, but Abd al-Rahman's abrupt entry surprised him, and he went back to chewing and making his popping noises as though he had not had the chewing gum in his mouth for some time.

Abd al-Rahman gave Mahmud an angry look, creasing his forehead into a frown. No one spoke, but the walls reflected the dagger looks exchanged between Abd al-Rahman and Mahmud.

Mahmud said nothing, but Abd al-Rahman could not let things go. 'We'll get *him* to sweep our doorstep for us,' he said, throwing his jallaba angrily to one side. He stared at Mahmud. 'Do you understand me?'

'If he doesn't sweep you off all the streets first,' Mahmud replied with a smirk.

Abd al-Ghani stopped chewing, his eyes open wide. Mahmud's answer was more forceful than he had expected. Abd al-Rahman's eyes were aflame with fury, as though he had been slapped on the cheek. But then they too opened wide, as though to confront the challenge by enveloping the widest possible field of vision.

'He may be able to wipe us off the streets for a while,' he said, 'but we're going to wipe them out of Morocco forever.'

Mahmud's laugh was loaded with all the scorn he could muster. 'A midsummer night's dream!' he said. 'One night seven years ago you dreamed that the world of the great powers was at an end. But, my dear brother, that same world has stood on its feet again. It's the same France that was on its knees back then that now has its general issuing orders that everyone's to sweep their own doorstep.'

'And does that same logic apply to the courts and the judiciary?'

Mahmud was busy clipping his fingernails, but he looked up at Abd al-Rahman. 'Being a judge demands the logic of reality,' he replied. 'Imagination is the realm of literary types.'

'Using the same logic, Morocco is destined to follow the same path as it has for the last half-century.'

'Hold it a minute – I wasn't even born half a century ago,' Mahmud replied with a laugh, as though sensing an unexpected victory.

'But you were there,' Abd al-Rahman said, 'in the minds of your forefathers and ancestors. They all regarded the world of those great dominating powers with the utmost admiration and respect, just as they did their own overlords. You're still using the logic of slavery.'

The word 'slavery' escaped his lips without him even being aware of its implications. As Mahmud leapt to his feet, Abd al-Rahman suddenly realised what he had unwittingly implied. The image of Mahmud's mother, Yasmine, floated in front of his eyes. Mahmud was about to respond in fury, but Abd al-Rahman tried to repair the damage caused by his unguarded comment.

'You're all free, the sons of free people, whether brown skinned or white,' he explained. 'But the logic you're using is that of the people of olden times who used to cringe and look up to the people who were dominating them.'

'So now you've turned into an orator,' Mahmud commented. 'Or is it a schoolteacher?'

'It's not an issue of orators or schoolteachers. It's a basic question of understanding. When people can't understand things for themselves, they need an orator or a teacher.' Abd al-Rahman was well aware that he had insulted Mahmud by using the word 'slavery' in a fit of anger. 'Young people are not lacking in understanding,' he said, using a much softer tone, 'but they don't have to act like a mirror that reflects the mentality of the past.'

'But, in the same way,' Mahmud replied, 'they shouldn't ignore the present either by burying their heads in the sand so that they can't see things as they really are.'

'Both reality and the present confirm that we're moving towards a future totally different from the one planned by those who order us to sweep our own doorsteps.'

'But they're the ones doing the planning. It's their job to make people follow the plan they've devised.'

'Firstly, don't you believe that the era of outdated fantasies has passed?'

'Firstly, don't you believe that the era of dreams has passed?'

'Dreams,' Abd al-Rahman countered, 'are a substitute in the unconscious world for failures in the conscious one. But we haven't failed yet, so there's no space for dreaming in our society. The reason is that our reality is too powerful to leave our internal mentality to fulfil itself in the world of the unconscious.'

Such philosophising annoyed Mahmud, and he needed to confront Abd al-Rahman to avenge his own sense of dignity. 'Forget about the world of dreams and wakefulness,' he replied. 'Let's go back to reality. Or is it that you feel able to face down the general when he threatens to fill your mouths with straw if he hears any outcry from now on?'

This made Abd al-Ghani laugh out loud, so that he almost lost the chewing gum in his mouth. He pushed the wad back in, like a runaway ball to its goal.

'The marshals and the general have all started talking like shepherds,' Abd al-Rahman retorted angrily. 'Maybe we're in an age in which classes don't exist any more. Isn't that so?!'

Mahmud gaped in amazement. 'I can assure you you're dreaming,' he replied with a gulp. 'You'd better bring that fairy tale to an end. If only you'd recognise the truth: France is stronger than you.'

'Stronger or weaker, it doesn't matter,' said Abd al-Rahman. 'We have no desire to engage in some kind of boxing match with France.'

'So do you believe your quest for independence is actually a midget provoking a powerful boxer?'

'Or, rather, do *you* believe that such a quest is my right, your right, and that of the entire Moroccan people?'

'No, that's not my right. I'm in no way bound to the quest for independence when it involves a country that's not ready for it.'

Abd al-Rahman's face darkened, as though Mahmud had impugned his honour. But, yet again, he managed to keep his anger under control. 'Ready, you say?' he replied. 'What's your gauge for readiness?'

'Good sense. When people can't manage their property themselves, a judge is appointed to take care of things.'

'And who's the judge who decided to put France in charge of things? Is it you, my dear honourable judge, sir?'

Mahmud blanched, but he was not prepared to admit defeat. 'The judge is the people themselves. If the people weren't incompetent, they wouldn't need to leave things to the trustee in the first place.'

'And what happens if the trustee is asked to give up his trusteeship?'

'Merely asking for something,' Mahmud replied with a shrug of his shoulders, 'doesn't imply that you're ready to take it over.'

'But I intend to do just that.'

'I don't believe it will happen.'

'Your belief won't stand in the way of the people who are marching forward.'

'So, deluded youngsters are now claiming they're marching forward!'

'Yes, they're marching forward, even if weary eyes can't see them!'

'Are you sure of what you're saying?' Mahmud asked, with another smirk.

'You'll see for yourself,' Abd al-Rahman replied defiantly. 'That is, if your eyes are not so tired that they can't see.'

'Whatever the case,' Mahmud went on in the same caustic tone, 'maybe you'll stop the forward march from engulfing me. I'm your brother, after all.'

'Noah didn't save his own son from the flood.'

'Is the age of the flood coming back then?'

'A new kind of flood, one unknown to history.'

'Ha, ha, ha! So, now you're crafting a new world unknown to history!'

'Those who crafted the world before us had minds no different from ours.'

'And will your new world be as beautiful and prosperous as ours?'

'Why should you worry about its beauty if you're not part of it?'

'Even for a simple judge like me?'

'The judges in this new world will not be simple. They will be shepherds of justice.'

'Justice that you will define.'

'No, justice as defined by the law.'

'So, there'll be idealist judges in a world—'

'Idealist?' Abd al-Rahman interrupted.

This angered Mahmud. 'Listen, Abd al-Rahman,' he yelled, 'we used to be nationalists who loved our homeland.'

Abd al-Rahman gave a hearty laugh, which did not stop Mahmud.

'But we're not fanciful dreamers,' Mahmud went on. 'Nationalists should not be making such outrageous demands that they're asking for something inconceivable.'

'Love is an emotion that may be perfectly sound,' Abd al-Rahman responded, as though giving a class at school. 'And yet the love you have for your son means nothing if you can't protect him from evil and help him in his need.'

'Provided you're capable of doing that.'

'Being incapable is a sign of a lack of love. If you truly loved your country, you would keep on trying, and you wouldn't be incapable.'

'I will never attempt the impossible.'

'The impossible is a mere invention of people who are ignorant and impotent.'

'No,' Mahmud scoffed, not a little amazed, 'The impossible is something that doesn't exist.'

'It doesn't exist, you mean, for those who have no backbone. When their minds, their consciences, their feelings render them incapable of action, that's what they rely on.'

The word 'conscience' reverberated in Mahmud's mind, even more than in his ears. 'My brain won't allow me to ask for the impossible,' he replied.

'That's because it's not enlightened.'

'No, but it's realistic.'

'I'm afraid it has no reality to it.'

Mahmud stared at his brother in alarm, his nerves on edge. 'If it's a matter of conscience that I should be a nationalist like you,' he replied, 'then indeed it has no reality to it.'

'Maybe you've finally discovered your own true self.'

'No, it's you who's made that discovery.'

'Both at once.'

'What's important is that I know what I have to do.' And with that, Mahmud stood up, grabbing the edges of his jallaba with his fingers. Abd al-Ghani stood up as well, still chewing his gum and not saying a word. They both headed for the door, pursued by Abd al-Rahman's angry gaze.

'You're going to follow your path to the very end,' he said.

39

Abd al-Rahman was sitting in front of the radio, listening carefully. A soft voice was reading the breaking news in a monotonous tone, as though reciting a memorised text. The regular intonation made the information lose both its import and significance. The voice had none of the emotion that was affecting Abd al-Rahman's nerves as he listened to the words loaded with anger and hatred.

When he switched off the radio, he just stood there, looking pale. His gaze wandered aimlessly, his nerves were shot, and his mind was at sixes and sevens. He roamed around the house, trying to sort out his thoughts – but about what? His eyes were opened wide, but precisely what were they looking for?

The lofty walls of the house got on his nerves, and he felt that something heavy was weighing on his chest. Putting his jallaba over his shoulder and grabbing his fez, he rushed out of the front door, as though out of prison.

In the wide space of Makhfiyya Square, he took deep breaths as though filling his congested lungs with the fresh air of life. He was still wandering aimlessly about when he bumped into Abd al-Aziz, who was walking fast as though he had a message to deliver.

After extending his hand to greet his friend, Abd al-Aziz paused for a moment. Both of them wanted to say something and were searching for the right words, but they failed. Finally it was Abd al-Aziz who withdrew his hand. 'I told you the storm was close,' he said. 'Now the maelstrom is enveloping us once again. Didn't I tell you?'

'You're always thinking in the past,' Abd al-Rahman replied, out of patience. 'You say "didn't I tell you?" and "I told you so". Well, here we are now in the centre of the storm. So, what are your expectations for the future?'

'They said they were going to feed us chaff and make us sweep our doorsteps. Now they've carried out their threat.'

'Dear friend, throw off the curse of the past. For example, tell me instead: what are we going to make *them* eat and drink?'

'Our bodies, blood, and spirits; that's all we have. So, let's offer those as food and drink for the tree of freedom.'

Tears welled in Abd al-Rahman's eyes, blurring the image of Abd al-Aziz as he stared at him long and hard. His friend seemed to represent the conscience of past, present, and future, of the generations that had inherited the nation. Now he was standing tall, speaking with total clarity, the only mode of expression he knew.

Abd al-Rahman was aware he was appearing weak. He shook his head and used a handkerchief to wipe away the warm tears. He did his best to shake his thinking out of its lethargy, so he could listen to what Abd al-Aziz was saying. He tilted his head to one side, as though preparing to receive wisdom from a philosopher, and looked down the narrow alley they were walking along. Suddenly, as they turned a corner, there was Hajj Muhammad wearing his jallaba and wrapped up in his burnous, walking slowly as though afraid the surface beneath his feet might crack. The wan sunlight in the alley shone on his wrinkled face, which appeared pale but eloquent in its silence, as though narrating recent history.

Abd al-Rahman left Abd al-Aziz and went over to his father. He grasped his hand and kissed it gently without saying a word.

Hajj Muhammad's expression opened up, but there was no smile. 'Where are you going?' he asked his son.

'I'm walking around for a bit with my friend,' Abd al-Rahman replied, pointing out Abd al-Aziz. 'I'll be back.'

'Fine, but don't be late.' Hajj Muhammad continued walking at his slow pace, while Abd al-Rahman and Abd al-Aziz went on their way, each thinking, without telling the other, 'There goes Hajj Muhammad, content and untroubled.'

'At the moment the fight's happening in Casablanca,' said Abd al-Rahman, resuming their conversation. 'But it's going to spread.'

Abd al-Aziz thought for a while before commenting, 'I'm not as happy about the fighting as I am about something else.'

Abd al-Rahman's expression became a question mark, but he remained silent, thinking and questioning himself.

Abd al-Aziz looked up, hoping to see in Abd al-Rahman's eyes what he was not hearing with his ears. 'I'm happy that the fire has now spread to the straw. Casablanca's seized the ball in order to score the goal.'

Abd al-Rahman seemed to be thinking again, his gaze wandering. But his expression soon returned to normal. 'Casablanca's the right place to take the first positive steps. Fez is a cage with limited horizons. For our determined foe, Casablanca is the most sensitive spot.'

'Yes,' Abd al-Aziz replied with a gleam in his eye. 'Their money, companies, and personnel are all there. It will be the gateway to the defeat they've brought on themselves.'

'Do you believe the volcano they've allowed to erupt will eventually sweep them all away?'

'It's more than just a belief. In a highly organised life that depends on hard work and suffering just to get our daily bread, allowing the volcano to erupt is a guarantee of our success.'

Abd al-Rahman gave him an admiring look. 'But is it right,' he asked, smiling as though to provoke his friend, 'for the enemy to give all the glory to a city other than Fez?'

Abd al-Aziz gave a start, gesturing with his hands as if to block Abd al-Rahman's words from reaching his ears. 'Fez will never play the same role as Casablanca,' he said. He paused for a moment, apparently feeling a need to explain himself. 'We're a group of actors,' he went on, 'putting on a play called "freedom" for the world. Every one of us has a role he's good at—'

'The role that will make the play a success,' Abd al-Rahman interrupted.

'What's important is to know how to distribute those roles and arrange them properly.'

'That's the party's function.' Abd al-Rahman seemed to have forgotten what he had just heard on the news bulletin, and Abd al-Aziz cut him short. 'Party?' he objected. 'Didn't you just hear the news? All the party leaders and organisers have been put in prison. Now they're busy rounding up the second tier.'

Abd al-Rahman let out a deep sigh, as though a cloud of despair had settled on his heart. He said nothing for a while, quickening his pace and chewing his nails mercilessly.

Abd al-Aziz found the silence unbearable. 'Common sense,' he continued, 'haven't we learned that yet?'

Abd al-Rahman returned from his mental excursion, apparently not understanding what Abd al-Aziz meant. Once again, he had a quizzical look on his face.

'What I mean,' Abd al-Aziz added, 'is that we're the ones the party has charged with offering guidance and instruction. Aren't we ready yet to assume that responsibility?'

'For sure we are! Our generation is now at the forefront of nationalist aspirations.'

'Then we both need to be figuring out what to do.'

'So, General Guillaume has announced the dissolution of the party!' Abd al-Rahman commented with a laugh, as though emerging from his own crisis.

'No,' Abd al-Aziz replied, retaining his serious tone. 'He's solved the party problem for us. We party members are now absolved from the obligation to observe any law imposed on an officially recognised party.'

'So, you're still dreaming of freedom,' Abd al-Rahman laughed joyfully, 'even if it involves throwing off chains to get there.'

'Freedom's not given,' Abd al-Aziz went on. 'It's taken. If you can't grab it while you're still in chains, then it's not freedom.'

'And when did you learn philosophy?' Abd al-Rahman asked with delight.

'When I started thinking,' Abd al-Aziz stated firmly with a smile. 'And when did you start thinking?'

'When I realised my country couldn't think for itself.'

This made Abd al-Rahman laugh again, the realistic logic in Abd al-Aziz's ideas helping him forget how bad things actually were. But it did not stop him looking anxiously at people's faces. He continued to listen to his friend, but at the same time he was reading the chronic suffering, suppressed anger, and spirit of violent revolt in the expressions of passers-by, who communicated more through their faces than with their tongues. A number of people they knew walked past them, but everyone was using their eyes as if to signal a secret rendezvous. They both took in the message, yet neither of them said anything or made any sign.

The whole city of Fez was afflicted with a profound sense of grief; it was as if its ancient walls, its limited area, and its pure sky had all been cloaked in black garb. The streets no longer pulsed with activity; markets and shops lost their prosperous smiles, and the buzz of citizens in their various activities no longer reverberated like a beehive. Instead, everything was as quiet as during a festival day, with all the sorrow of a funeral and the misery of a catastrophe.

Abd al-Rahman could sense the scale of the tragedy, but could not convey his feelings to Abd al-Aziz, worried they might have a negative effect on someone like his friend, who had never known any sense of defeat. But as it turned out, Abd al-Aziz had also detected the new garb Fez had acquired for itself.

'The news has shaken the city up,' he said, making an effort to show how happy he was. 'Everyone looks as though they've just lost their most beloved son.'

'I feel like I'm in a Fez as it was before the events of 1944.'

'With the basic difference that it was too happy then and it's too distressed now.'

'How can you be so upset that it's distressed, when our intellectual elite is in prison?'

'You seem to be reverting to the past...' As Abd al-Aziz said this, he looked straight at Abd al-Rahman to see what impact it had. He saw a happy smile, as though Abd al-Rahman approved of his logic.

'What's the past got to do with it?' Abd al-Rahman asked.

'It imposed its authority, but that was yesterday. Now it's over. The city should not be grieving about the past, but rather finding ways of preparing for the future.'

'What about the recent past?'

'What about the present?!'

Abd al-Rahman laughed, as though to say, 'I like your radical stance', but he cut short his laughter when they unexpectedly ran into Mahmud as they walked towards Qattanin Street. Mahmud came over and greeted them.

'Have you heard the news?' he asked.

'Yes,' Abd al-Rahman replied dryly, 'we've heard it. But you'd better hurry,' he went on, as though he did not want to give Mahmud a chance to engage in conversation. 'Father and Abd al-Ghani are looking for you.'

Mahmud was well aware that Abd al-Rahman did not want to give him an opportunity to gloat. He shook Abd al-Aziz's hand. 'The radio said that all your leaders have been arrested,' he said pointedly, deliberately avoiding Abd al-Rahman.

Abd al-Rahman grabbed Abd al-Aziz's hand to pull him away. 'I told you to hurry,' he chided Mahmud. 'They're waiting for you.'

'Goodbye, au revoir!' was Mahmud's retort as he went on his way.

Abd al-Aziz looked at Abd al-Rahman to gauge what impact Mahmud's words had had on his brother. But Abd al-Rahman anticipated any comment he might make. 'It seems to me,' Abd al-Rahman said, 'that the city's current distress is merely a cloud before a violent storm.'

'But when's that going to happen? When? It's been a long wait.'

'There's no hurry. As the saying goes, for every time there's an appropriate text.'

'The text we're going to write with our own right hand,' replied Abd al-Aziz, out of patience. 'I've decided—'

'What have you decided?'
'That I'm going to write it.'

40

Once again Abd al-Rahman passed through the prison gateway. By now it had become difficult for any programme to be implemented, given that all the people who were thinking about their country or working with its populace were either buried or locked up in prisons and internment camps. Abd al-Rahman's mental preparedness for going to prison was now stronger than it had ever been in the past. He felt that a heavy atmosphere was weighing down the city and its inhabitants so oppressively that they could hardly breathe. He sensed that the pressure had now become a genuine nightmare that had transformed people's lives into a living hell. Only those who were in their graves or the cells could escape.

He therefore found a kind of peace and psychological calm inside prison. He now felt he could no longer stand the nightmare that had been imposed on Morocco, nor tolerate the life that Moroccans were living now that all nationalist plans to overcome the imperialist forces had been exhausted. Prison was a refuge from the kind of pressure that had become so severe that it had begun to make his life hell.

This time, his incarceration was not a trial or hardship. It was in an internment camp which seemed to be reserved exclusively for nationalists from every part of the region; by now the actual prisons were too small to accommodate all the prisoners. He did not feel he had lost his freedom here or that he was a prisoner, but felt instead that he had been given an opportunity he had only occasionally encountered outside of prison, to mix closely with the freedom fighters he had previously known only from a distance. Any contact between them before would have led to a detailed police investigation, but this time the French authorities had gathered them all together in a single cage, and they all felt they were enjoying a kind of freedom they had never savoured before: the freedom to think together, exchange views, and plan for the future.

Abd al-Rahman was the leader of this group. He organised their life in prison and set up the discussion sessions. They all consulted him when arguments became fierce or an issue was so complex that they could not decide which point of view should prevail. Supervising a group of nationalists from various regions and different social and intellectual levels made him especially happy.

But he found himself missing one particular person. He had expected that at some point the gates would open to admit Abd al-Aziz, as they had already done for many of his colleagues and friends. Like every prisoner who feels the boon of freedom while still shut in prison's dark shadow, he wished his friend were with him; he could then enjoy conversations, discussions, and arguments based on his friend's realism and courage. But Abd al-Aziz did not arrive, and his name kept coming to Abd al-Rahman's mind for a long time, though he could not say why.

He thought about the factors that made him feel so relaxed here, and his colleagues so free.

'This feeling we all have,' he asked himself, 'is it freedom from chains, or freedom in the shadow of chains?' In his mind the question was shrouded in cloud; he could not see how to make it clearer for himself. But he went on posing it every time he searched for signs of sadness or pain in the prisoners' expressions and failed to find any.

He then pursued the line of thought further. 'What we've done is to compensate for the miserable situation outside by keeping ourselves happy inside.'

But his conscience protested. 'The reason,' it clamoured, 'is that we couldn't bear the responsibility to its conclusion.'

'That's not true!' he responded vigorously. 'We did bear the responsibility, and that forced the colonial authorities to put us all in prison.'

'No,' his conscience said. 'We gave up. We didn't have to let the authorities grab us like one grabs a chicken.'

'But we did take the initiative,' he replied, warming to his defence. 'We enlisted all our fellow countrymen against government violence and abuse of authority.'

'And now we're happy,' his conscience insisted loudly, 'because we're rid of all responsibility.'

'But we've landed up in prison!'

'No, we've landed up in that banal state of happiness people reach when they have no responsibilities.'

'But we did our duty.'

'And now we can relax, like all failures.'

Abd al-Rahman did his best to object. 'But what about all those people,' he asked himself, 'who sacrificed everything – family, children, wealth, and honour, only to find themselves locked up behind seven hellish gates and immured behind high walls, guarded by brutal men who deprive them of freedom, rights, and choice? Are they really failures?'

'They all deserved something better,' his conscience retorted, 'after sacrificing freedom, family, children, and wealth.'

'It was a noble sacrifice on their part.'

'No, simply hubris.'

Abd al-Rahman continued at odds with his own conscience, until the national sense of tragedy finally culminated in the forced exile of the Moroccan king, which for Abd al-Rahman was the clearest possible manifestation of the enemy's real intentions.

His conscience was now harsher than ever. 'Do you see what's happening beyond these prison walls? So, what use are you to your country, luxuriating in freedom inside these walls? People who know how to stay out of the way of the authorities now realise they must do their duty at a time when the country really needs people to do that.'

This thought made Abd al-Rahman more miserable than ever. He surrendered to profound grief, and despaired completely. Then he heard the news.

'There's a puppet on the throne... Hordes of prominent figures, religious scholars, local notables, and members of the cultural elite are flocking to pledge their fealty... France is now opening up a whole new page of absolute dependency.'

Abd al-Rahman surrendered to his misery. He avoided the crowds of prisoners, and his nerves went to pieces; he was in shock. His fellow prisoners were sad to see how miserable he was. All signs of the sense of freedom they had been enjoying inside the prison now vanished, and they felt as if the responsibility they had disposed of had now been placed on their shoulders again – responsibility in its fiercest form. Now the crisis of conscience hit them, as though they were all Abd al-Rahman.

Abd al-Rahman was sitting on his own in the prison store. 'Everything we've built has been destroyed,' he told himself. 'The current was simply too strong for our bridges made of sand. Even though we broadened our group, we didn't include the populace in it. And they needed to be motivated again.'

'The perfidy of the elite,' a voice within him pointed out, 'is what neutralised the impact of the people. The so-called government, the jurists, the lawyers, they've all lowered their heads and kissed the hands...'

'But the elite has never been the gauge of the public conscience,' Abd al-Rahman thought in response.

'We've regressed by dozens of years,' the same voice said. 'Now the foreign occupation is complete.'

'Don't we bear some responsibility for that?' Abd al-Rahman asked himself. 'Weren't we moving too fast?' Now he rounded on the voice of his own conscience as though he had been stung. 'The snake of betrayal is raising its nasty head,' he thought. 'It's hissing and exuding poisons that are fouling your very soul.'

He now started pacing around the store as though trying to rid himself of these disturbing thoughts. But instead they became yet more insistent: 'How can we take all those years that have thrown us backwards and use them to move ahead?'

The question kept coming back, but there was no glimmer of light to illuminate the darkness in front of his eyes. The questions went on. 'Generations have been lost, and life's gone back to the way it was. Is it even possible for us to begin afresh yet again…? The entire cognisant class in Morocco is either in prisons and internment camps or in exile. Now the foreigners will be able to demolish all the essential elements of our country.'

'And Mahmud's mentality will win,' the voice inside him interjected.

'No, no!' he responded angrily, 'That's impossible! People who loathe society and take revenge on people, impugning their honour?'

At this point the image of Hajj Muhammad loomed in front of him with a wry smile on his face, and around it a huge question mark. Abd al-Rahman stopped pacing for a moment, as though waiting for the image to speak, but its silence and the look on its face only made its impact yet more powerful and mocking.

'Going back to the past,' the voice intruded, 'implies that Hajj Muhammad's way of thinking will be coming back as well.'

'History always moves forwards,' Abd al-Rahman responded, as though addressing a stubborn opponent. 'It never goes backwards.'

The image of his father came back, this time with an even broader smile.

'And what about the people?' the voice asked. 'What have they done? Don't those millions feel this blow was aimed at them rather than the king and the nationalists?'

Abd al-Rahman was stumped when faced with such forceful logic. He stopped pacing, as though a barrier had been placed in his path, and, putting his fingers in his mouth, he started to bite his nails mercilessly. 'The people?' he thought, in answer to the voice. 'They still don't realise history is changing. They're relying on a group of nationalists who are fighting on their behalf as though the country were theirs alone. All the years that the nationalists have spent setting things up have been useless. The populace is weak and timid... The blood in its children's veins has congealed.'

Now his emotions got the better of him and he started to shout. 'No, no! Despair... no present, no future. All I can see is the gloom of the past. Thick clouds approaching from the past to cover our world in darkness and despair.'

His strength gave out; it was as if his nerves had never encountered defeat before. He burst into tears, and only came to himself again when a fellow internee, breathing fast and looking distracted, called to him.

'Did you hear the news? They've attacked the puppet and killed him. Allal ibn Abdallah stabbed him!'

41

'O God, be all around us but not against us!' This was Hajj Muhammad's response to the news of the incidents that had taken place in Casablanca, incidents that had carried the torch lit by the young martyr Allal ibn Abdallah. He had launched an assault on the puppet monarch, but contrary to the news that had reached the prison he had failed in his attempt and instead had surrendered his young life as a victim to his unprecedented initiative.

The events were narrated to Hajj Muhammad like legends from the past: a young man of fifteen stopped a policeman and, before anyone knew what was happening, the policeman dropped to the ground dead, while the young man vanished as though swallowed by the earth... A man carrying a bomb in a basket left it in the central market, and the explosion engulfed the whole area and everyone in it... Another young man put a bomb on a train, then disappeared while the explosion scattered chunks from the train all over the place... A woman attacked an army detachment, but it was later discovered that it had been a man in disguise.

These pieces of news alarmed Hajj Muhammad. They provoked his interest in the broadcasts on the radio and drew him closer to people who read the newspapers and could give him reliable information.

He was motivated by a nagging desire to hear about this new element in Moroccan life that was leading people to challenge the powers that, until now, had always brutally confronted any opposition.

In addition, he was eager to hear about the events in Casablanca, because they reminded him of similar events in Fez when he was young and foreigners had attacked the city. A group of young men, known for their courage, defiance, and bravado, had banded together and resisted the first units of the foreign army. They had put the heads of the defeated army officers on their spears and paraded them around the city streets to announce that this would be the fate of all invaders.

Recalling what he had heard as a young man about the way that people in the countryside had rebelled against the occupying forces, Hajj Muhammad thought of the panic-stricken days the city had lived through when the war approached its gates, and when the city authorities warned that their very souls, their wealth, and their safety were all under threat.

The bullets fired in Casablanca brought back all these memories, which led him to take up his rosary and rapidly finger the beads as he intoned, 'O gentle God!' The clacking beads created their own rhythm, and the sound echoed in his frigid soul as though demanding more. The only things that could pull him away from his rosary were the news broadcasts giving him fresh information, and his conversations with Mawlay Zaki, who visited him now and then to discuss the events and share rumours.

Once, he heard the resident-general speaking on the radio in his broken Arabic, stating how dangerous this enemy was who could ambush the security forces and then disappear, unseen by human eyes, leaving behind nothing but demolition and murder. Hajj Muhammad listened, expecting the general to claim that his forces would be able to crush these destructive elements, but instead he admitted they were incapable of dealing with this enemy that operated in the dark.

This made Hajj Muhammad even more anxious. It sent him back to his rosary, and he went on playing distractedly with the beads until he was torn away from his thoughts by Mawlay Zaki's pounding on the door. He had come to share the news that he too had heard from the general on the radio.

The two men stared at each other, each wishing the other would start the conversation. What they had heard was difficult to believe, and it felt as though whoever spoke first would be accused of not speaking the truth. Almost without thinking, Hajj Muhammad began fiddling with the beads on his rosary again, all the while engaging Mawlay Zaki in small talk, but eventually Mawlay Zaki grew tired of the evasion.

'Did you hear today's news?' he asked. 'Things are getting serious now. The French are finally admitting it's serious.'

Hajj Muhammad stopped clicking his rosary. 'That's right,' he replied with a deep sigh. 'God help us all!'

Mawlay Zaki was eager to gauge what effect the announcement had had on Hajj Muhammad. 'It seems to me,' he said provocatively, 'that the general's admission is a ploy to scare the nationalists.'

'That's what I think too. Surely France can't be scared of a bunch of young men who strike and then escape on bicycles!'

'They're not scared of them, but they still can't finish them off.'

Hajj Muhammad found this logic irrefutable, but he was not ready to accept it. 'Is there anything the French can't do?' he asked. 'They can do anything.'

'So, why are they letting them get away with it, then?'

'I don't know... I just don't know. But I think...' He stopped and thought for a while. 'Because it's in our best interest,' he eventually replied.

Mawlay Zaki took a noisy sip of his tea, but said nothing. His wide-open eyes suggested serious thought. 'I think it's as you say. It's in our best interest.' Then he frowned as though struck by something profound. 'But what benefit can there be,' he went on, 'in leaving bombs to explode in markets, men dropping dead one after the other, and fires spreading across farmlands?'

The question bothered Hajj Muhammad. 'How should I know?' he replied sharply. 'There must be some discernible benefit in it.'

Mawlay Zaki was dubious. Pursing his lips and raising his eyebrows, he looked distractedly up to the heavens without saying a word. Then he shifted in his seat, put his teacup on the floor, and slowly inserted a hand in his pocket to bring out a dark red handkerchief with black decoration, in which was wrapped a snuff-pipe. Putting the pipe to his nostrils, he inhaled until his eyes watered. He then wiped his hand over them and rubbed it on his jallaba. Lifting his cup to his mouth, he sipped some tea with relish; he seemed to have needed all these elements in order to continue with his thinking.

'God be praised!' he sighed with evident relish, making it clear how much he had enjoyed the snuff and the tea. Now he turned and looked at Hajj Muhammad. 'Perhaps you believe the interest is that it permits those young men to disrupt security in our country?'

'God alone knows,' said Hajj Muhammad, admitting defeat. 'Even so...' He stopped, not even knowing himself how his retort might continue.

Mawlay Zaki did not wait for his companion to complete his answer. 'I feel there's no interest in that,' he went on. 'But...' He too stopped, not daring to speak openly about what was on his mind.

'But what?' Hajj Muhammad challenged him. 'Is it all over for France, then?' Mawlay Zaki hesitated, and Hajj Muhammad went on with a laugh. 'Don't hand your mind over to other people. The Germans and the English did not defeat the French, so how do you expect these young men to do it?'

Mawlay Zaki looked back at him, ready to defend himself. 'I didn't say it was all over,' he said. 'But France can't... kill them.'

'You'll see! The same thing happened in Fez in the early days of the occupation, and the overwhelming force of the occupiers soon put an end to it.' Hajj Muhammad paused for a moment. 'Do you think that the power of the French army, with its rifles and guns – not to mention aircraft – can be matched by these young men who strike and run away?'

It was Mawlay Zaki's turn to laugh. 'Do you expect them to strike,' he joked, 'and *not* run away?'

'That simply shows that they're not a real force,' Hajj Muhammad replied.

'At any rate,' Mawlay Zaki replied, realising that there was not much more to add now, 'may God grant us a safe outcome! The times are not good.'

'So far we're safe,' Hajj Muhammad said. 'These problems are all in Casablanca, and we're far away. Praise be to God, our own city is quiet.'

'Quiet? Yes, you're right, it's quiet. But these days things cannot be all that far away.'

'No...' Hajj Muhammad replied after a moment's thought, 'Fez can't possibly witness events like those in Casablanca.'

'Why not?' Mawlay Zaki asked doubtfully.

Hajj Muhammad could not come up with a response, and only repeated, 'Because Fez can't possibly witness events like the ones in Casablanca.'

'Anything's possible. What happened in Marrakesh – wasn't that even more serious than what happened in Casablanca? Have you forgotten that a bomb was thrown at the new sultan?'

'But God has always protected Fez from disaster.'

For a while, Mawlay Zaki said nothing. Frowning, he searched in his pocket again for the handkerchief with the snuff, and once more inhaled deeply until his voice cracked. 'Didn't the city go through something like this in the early years of the occupation?' he asked.

'That was then, and this is now,' was Hajj Muhammad's defence. 'They didn't realise yet how strong France was.'

Mawlay Zaki was not convinced. 'Every era has its own men,' he replied. 'The men now...' But he did not dare continue. On the point of getting up, he leaned on his hand. 'By the blessings of Mawlay Tihami!' he said, invoking the name of one of God's saints.

'O God, be all around us but not against us!' Hajj Muhammad whispered, as he bade his friend farewell.

It was not long afterwards that the first bomb went off in Fez's streets, eliminating a major collaborator whose evil machinations were such that no one had felt safe; nobody had dared stand up to him. But this was no isolated bomb attack that killed just one person, as others had killed dozens every day in Casablanca. This was a huge bomb that shook Fez to its foundations, causing an enormous shock, as though debris from the Hiroshima atom bomb had hit the city. No one panicked, and nor did the men, youths, and children flee from the markets to hide behind the high walls of the houses, as they had done earlier when a frightening rumour had been put about by some meddling shaykh, or a lunatic on his behalf, craving a blessing from him. Instead, the city's inhabitants rushed to the markets, in an emotional response to show that commercial and social activities would carry on as normal. No one was looking for business or profit; rather, they wanted to hear the latest news and to demonstrate their happiness that the city was continuing its tradition of resistance.

The nationalists did not miss the opportunity of the bomb blasts (which now went off at frequent intervals and took out collaborators) to mock the authorities and scoff at the French general, who, far from making them eat chaff as he had threatened, was now tasting his own humiliation and defeat. His collaborators and other Moroccan supporters were now having their taste of bombs and explosions. People talked of the army of God terrifying the army of Satan. The older and middle-aged men now thought back to assert that today's resistance fighters were the children of the earlier ones. It was no surprise to meet someone who would swear that the young man who had assassinated Colonel Hammu was the son of Sidi Faddul, who had put Capitaine Jean's head on his spear at the beginning of the occupation and paraded it around the streets. Someone else might equally assure you that he knew everyone, all the people responsible for igniting the candle of resistance in Fez – though, of course, he could not name any of them for fear of putting their lives in danger.

The bombs in Fez struck a note of fear in the two men's discussions of past and present. Their explosions had a counterpart inside Hajj

Muhammad's mind as well, and his anxieties could no longer be hidden. He stayed inside his house as though anticipating a disaster; in the morning he would expect it that same evening, and in the evening he would anticipate its arrival next morning. He was left alone with his prayers and his rosary, but he did not forget to offer praises to God for the fact that Abd al-Rahman was not in the city. Imprisonment protected his son from being one of this satanic group of people who had destroyed Hajj Muhammad's personal sense of security. Part of him wanted to listen to the radio, but for his own sake he did not, to avoid having to hear news of an explosion somewhere in the city.

Friends no longer came. Their number had dwindled; Mawlay Zaki was at the head of the few who remained. But even he was delighted by the mood in Fez, and stopped thinking about Hajj Muhammad or paying him regular visits. Instead, he divided his time between listening to the radio and meeting up with other people, both of which provided him with information and catered to his need for explanations and commentary on what was happening.

Hajj Muhammad's health deteriorated, as did his morale. No longer caring about anything, his only concern was the potions that Khaduj mixed for him and which everyone with an opinion assured him would cure the illnesses conspiring against him. He never complained about any specific illness, nor did he know exactly what was wrong with him, but symptoms of a general deterioration in his health were evident in every aspect of his bodily and mental condition. Now Hajj Muhammad was living isolated from the city of Fez. It too was isolated from him, and ever since he had locked himself away it had started to forget him. He no longer reminded the city of his existence, as had always been his habit when he made his way to and fro between the Makhfiyya Quarter, the Qarawiyin Mosque, and the Mawlay Idris shrine.

Fez was shocked again when the prison gates were opened to receive a whole new batch of young men who had never been locked up before but were nonetheless happy to be entering prison, their bodies showing obvious signs of the torture to which they had been subjected during the few days they had spent in police detention cells.

Abd al-Rahman came to know all of them, as well as Abd al-Aziz, who was locked up at the same time, having been accused of forming a terrorist group.

42

When Abd al-Rahman met Abd al-Aziz in the prison store, he was in a terrible state, as though he had just come off a battlefield. His features were unrecognisable, his posture was bent, and he could not stand up straight because some of his ribs were fractured; his legs could barely hold him up, and his breathing was laboured and shallow. There was a look of terror in his bloodshot eyes, as though he had spent time with the Devil incarnate.

Abd al-Rahman's quiescent feelings were suddenly aroused as he welcomed his friend. His conscience pained him as he looked at the face that had once brimmed with conviction but was now transformed into a misshapen mass, barely clinging to life. Abd al-Rahman tried to gather his emotional resources, but it was as though an electric shock had shattered his nerves. Tears poured down his face, his voice choked, and he could neither offer comfort nor ask for details.

But then a voice – familiar for its confidence, though now broken and short of breath – spoke up. 'No, no, don't cry,' it gasped. 'I wanted this... and so did God.'

Abd al-Aziz's words gave Abd al-Rahman new determination and wiped away his tears. 'I always knew you to be steadfast and brave,' he replied. 'Things are still...'

Abd al-Aziz nodded as if to say, 'You'll find out. You're going to find out a lot about our courage and determination.'

All was at an end. Abd al-Aziz and his companions had arrived at the prison only after the police had extracted confessions, found out all the information they needed, arrested the whole cell, and put an end to everything. The general in Fez boasted to his counterpart in Casablanca that the city of Fez had once again surrendered.

When Abd al-Aziz heard the news in prison, he wept. Abd al-Rahman wept not for the same reason but because he was seriously worried about Abd al-Aziz's condition. He had previously had complete confidence in him and knew he would be able to lead one cell after another if he could stay in the field. But now all hope had vanished. The man who had once said, 'Our bodies, blood, and spirits; that's all we have. So, let's offer those as food and drink for the tree of freedom,' was now finished.

But Fez did not surrender. Instead, it hid its embers, the way fire can be concealed under a pile of black coal. The city's young folk were anxious for fear the city might indeed give up. For them it was out of the question for history to be altered and a new, unprecedented page written. So they lived with the French general's declarations as though engaged in a contest with his dreams – dreams that he aimed to achieve, while they aimed to prove them false.

The nationalist cells now emerged from their zone of silence, and their members explained the goal to the young conscripts. Groups now started confirming the inevitability of history and proving the general's dreams to be false. Fez was reinvigorated as never before. Now that Abd al-Aziz's group had watered the city with a rain shower of self-sacrifice, it felt a flourish of springtime. Fez only ever blossoms with the fresh green of spring, and now spring was arriving amid a winter so gloomy that everything was dark and night seemed to last forever. And people's hearts pounded with intimations of victory to be achieved by the young men in cells and resistance groups.

It was all up to the general. Even with his huge body, red face, twisted moustache, and uniform full of medals celebrating honour and victory, he still could not achieve the victory in Fez that he dreamed about. His pride was hurt, and the glory that he had won in other theatres of war would now be destroyed by a group of young men with their secret plans unknown to the army, police, and guards.

The general inevitably had to take revenge for his injured pride and honour. An army's glory lies on the field of battle, and the imperialist general was not about to let that glory be impaired by a small city. The ensuing struggle was brutal and harsh. Every window, every street in the city was occupied by soldiers. Guards watched over houses and buildings, as well as cobblers, weavers, and tanners; police lurked inside mosques and by the doors of shrines and tombs; squads of secret police brought over from France to look for members of the resistance took to the roofs of buildings – in Fez, the roofs had always had their own history of resistance. The general took charge of the whole operation from his headquarters.

He knew that the leaders of the resistance were young men with training, but the traces they left made it clear that they were using only the most basic methods; their primary resources consisted of sheer courage and confidence rather than good organisation and clear goals. Faced with these realities, the general found himself in a dilemma: for someone of his military rank, the field of conflict did not involve a closed city that, even when occupied and in a state of submission, nevertheless continued to resist. He was an army general who was now bringing all his basic principles and his military career to bear in order to fight a group of young Moroccans whose only strategy involved an engaged conscience, a narrowly defined nationalism, and a truly reckless bravery.

'Conscience,' he said to himself. 'That has nothing to do with military life, so how is it now so clearly intervening between myself and my duty? I've learned military ways very well; they require me to take command of this city, which is currently rebelling against my soldiers. Indeed, the army is always prepared. But today I'm fighting a war with no battlefield. I'm supposed to be a governor, but I'm fighting as a general... and against whom? A group of youngsters with no experience or training. They can vanish behind doors and down turnoffs and narrow alleys; they can strike, then run away. So, here I am, a great general leading a campaign against a group of youths whose only weapon is the recklessness that leads them to try their luck with ancient revolvers. Is this to be the summation of my career, standing here in all my past glory, chasing groups of youths? It would be better if the police did the chasing.'

He was jolted out of these thoughts by the sound of more gunshots somewhere in the city. More victims – collaborators, authority figures. More than ever before, he now had the feeling that his military and administrative honour were being weighed in the balance. Too bad for his military honour if the government decided to relieve him of his post because he could not stop a few ancient revolvers being fired. 'No, no,' he told himself. 'I have to succeed. The city has to surrender. It's not just my honour that's at stake, but France's as well, and I'm one of its generals.'

He convened a meeting of his advisors, and they all decided that the citizens of Fez had to be humiliated.

Now everyone with an illustrious or noble name was seized, and the gates of the internment camps were opened to admit the leading citizens of Fez, as though being arrested were still regarded as humiliating. The city went into a rage, and full fury prevailed. But it was not the general's aim to win sympathy or lift the burden of tyranny and rage. By now his only goal was to put an end to the shots being fired from antique, rusty revolvers. Even so, he endured many sleepless nights, and his nerves were on edge.

Then came good news. A soldier on guard duty came rushing into the general's office, stamped his feet as he came to attention, extended his quivering right hand in a salute, and tilted his head to the side by way of announcing that the lieutenant-colonel was at hand requesting an urgent meeting.

'Good news, General,' the colonel reported. 'We've captured the terrorist group.'

'Is that true?' the general cried, his face bursting into a smile. 'So, Fez has finally surrendered.'

The word 'surrender' held a particular magic for the general, both when he mouthed it himself and even more so when he heard it from others. The surrender of Fez was directly tied to the glory earned by those marshals and generals who had preceded him in the conflict. How eager he was to inherit that same glory, even if it only involved a bunch of youths who had managed to rattle his nerves.

He rose to his feet, hand in his pocket, unlit cigarette between his lips, and began pacing around his office, as though he could not bear to sit in his seat. His pacing carried him away to a place where he imagined himself young again – a junior officer, strong and sturdy, issuing commands to soldiers and subordinates. He was bursting with excitement. When he came back from this private journey to past glory, a smile of victory played on his face.

'Tell me again,' he said, still staring off into the distance as though not addressing the officer standing in front of him, 'how the surrender came about.'

The lieutenant-colonel paused for a while over the word 'surrender', and took his time responding – it implied something much bigger and more extensive than merely arresting a group of youths. But he was a soldier who followed orders and had no wish to argue with the general, of whose status he was well aware.

'It was all very simple, General,' he said, but then backtracked, worried the general might not be satisfied or might belittle the operation he had just supervised. 'What I mean,' he went on, 'is that the operation was successful. We carried out your orders, General. We surrounded the city, closed off the entrances to the streets, and kept watch from the rooftops. Then we initiated a great search operation fully worthy of your great legion. My own troop launched a flanking search of the Talia Quarter.'

'Yes,' the general interrupted. 'I've repeatedly pointed out to the security director that he needs to tighten security there. I was sure that a terrorist group was lurking in there somewhere—'

'But, General,' the colonel continued, 'we didn't find anything. The houses were perfectly normal, and the residents were quiet. It was only when the troop launched its search that people started to panic—'

The general laughed gleefully; his nostrils expanded and he

turned red. His whole body shook as he laughed and coughed. 'I know,' he interrupted. 'I'm sure they started yelling and screaming as though they'd been touched by demons. But we're never going to beat them if we don't scare with them our raids, even at night. Fine, carry on.'

'The troop continued its searches, moving from one quarter to the next until it reached the Udwa Quarter—'

'No, no!' the general interrupted. 'Udwa's peaceful. You'll never find anything there.'

'Our search was meticulous; we searched from house to house. Eventually in one house we stumbled across eight young men sleeping in a single room in a remote part of the house. They were all from different families, but similar in age. They looked upset and nervous. The raid took them by surprise, and they paled in fright. The discovery that they had weapons with them was a clear victory for our troop: they were caught red handed, and there was no way they could deny anything—'

'Deny anything?' the general interrupted once again, blowing smoke from the cigarette he had now lit. 'They've been arrested, that's what matters,' he continued. 'It's no concern of ours whether or not they deny anything.'

'As we arrested them, the women kept yelling and screaming.'

'Enough!' the general cried. 'I don't need any more details. They're in your hands now, aren't they?'

'Yes, General.'

'So get back to your job, and take good care of them!' he said, laughing. 'I'll arrange for a military tribunal.'

And so, once again Abd al-Rahman in prison welcomed a new batch of young men who looked like ghosts, their bodies battered and their spirits crushed by the torture they had suffered. As they entered, their eyes radiated fear: they were terrified of anyone and everyone. Abd al-Rahman knew them; they were members of a nationalist cell. But they appeared not to recognise him, since terror had erased their memories. They were looking for someone who was not a soldier or a policeman, but saw no one to trust. They resorted to silence, saying not a word. Abd al-Rahman did his best to restore their sense of security, but they simply stared at him in fear and said nothing; it was as though they saw hatred in the eyes of every person, and felt that every hand would land blows, every mouth utter obscenities.

When Abd al-Aziz came back from the prison clinic, where he had been treated for his wounds, he entered the prison store and felt new sets of eyes staring at him, while his own eyes registered faces marred by violence and disfigured by terrible assaults. He knew all the faces, and he wept. He now realised that the single cell he was relying on to kindle the flame of resistance had been arrested and imprisoned.

Ali, the head of the group, confirmed in a whisper that they had all confessed to creating a resistance cell.

43

They were all now in prison. In the times when they were allowed to gather, they debated the country's future path now that the resistance cells were rounded up and the colonial authorities were once again enjoying a period of relative quiet, no longer clashing with people saying 'No!' The prisoners surveyed the disaster with total gloom. The vengeance wreaked by the French upon the nationalists would be as brutal as such revenge demanded.

Ali's conscience plagued him. 'We're going to be responsible for the extra suffering for our countrymen. We've fallen into the trap without even thinking about it. Why did we embark on such a risky venture without being sure we would come out on top?' His colleagues listened carefully to him, the head of their cell.

Until this point, Abd al-Aziz had been willing to compromise with these young men; after all, this was their first experience of prison. But now he had had enough. 'You all need to do your duty, like everyone else,' he told them bluntly. 'None of us is responsible for the outcome. We're a mere drop in the ocean; it needs us for it to be filled, and yet we're not responsible for filling it.'

While he was speaking, Abd al-Rahman watched him closely. He wanted to make sure his friend could manage to relieve his colleagues of their crisis of conscience. To alleviate the impact of Abd al-Aziz's straightforward remarks, Abd al-Rahman told them, 'Although you've been put in prison, you're still involved in the struggle. The spirit you've evoked still courses through cities and villages, plains, valleys and mountains.'

'Even though we haven't completed our task?' asked Abd al-Rauf, a young member of the cell.

'But you have completed your task,' Abd al-Rahman responded calmly. 'I completed mine too, before you. Now the situation has to develop so that people more capable than us can carry the banner forwards and confront the situation as it is.'

'Couldn't we have done that?' Ali asked angrily.

'Of course you could,' Abd al-Rahman replied, 'but the situation has to keep developing. Our arrest will impel other people to take up the standard. They wouldn't do that if we hadn't been imprisoned first.'

'We're more capable than others,' Abd al-Rauf said impatiently. 'If we were still there, we would be moving things forwards.'

Abd al-Aziz gave Abd al-Rahman a pleading look as though asking him to intervene, but he remained silent because he was convinced that Abd al-Aziz could rescue the situation. Eventually he said, 'If only they had let us be, if only we had stayed where we were... if only we hadn't... But that's all over, finished. We can't bring back the past for the simple reason that we're now part of that past. There's no point chasing after something that we can no longer accomplish.'

The young men's jaws dropped, as though they were hearing a bitter truth for the first time.

'Can we somehow resist our imprisonment?' Abd al-Aziz continued. 'Can we escape from the cages that cramp our will and prevent our spirits aspiring to attract other nationalist spirits to us? Can we achieve genuine revolution from behind closed prison gates and in spite of all the guards and weapons? As we proceed from past to future, from oblivion to existence, and from nothingness to presence, this is what we must bear in mind.' These words stirred the young men to thoughts of revolt, while at the same time lodging in their young minds the powerful concepts of 'nothingness', 'oblivion', all the way to infinity.

Ali wanted to erase the ideas that plagued him. 'True enough!' he said enthusiastically, as though to wipe away the traces of 'oblivion' and 'nothingness'. 'Why are we still stuck in these prison cells waiting to be sentenced, as though we're not due to appear before the military tribunal? Let's get out of here!'

The words 'get out' had a galvanising effect, but Abd al-Rahman, who knew the prison well and could predict how the guards would behave, realised that the whole idea was reckless and dangerous. But since he had no desire to douse young minds longing for freedom, he did not respond to what Ali had said, instead trying to turn the conversation to something more hopeful. 'Prison is certainly a crisis for all of us,' he said, 'but then it's over. You'll learn from experience that, however long the prison term turns out to be, each little bird will eventually be set free.'

Abd al-Aziz gave Abd al-Rahman a dubious look. Ignoring him, Abd al-Rahman was happy to see the positive effect his words had had on the young men.

'Once we're free again,' Abd al-Rauf commented, 'we'll go back to work and liberate our country.'

Abd al-Aziz clapped. 'Bravo, now I'm happy!' he said. 'Your country deserves you!'

The young men were wrenched from their conversation by the gruff voice of one of the guards, who entered the cell following the sound of the door bolt being pulled back. 'On your feet!'

Everyone stood up, removing their head-caps as they did so.

'Abd al-Aziz ibn Ahmad,' the same voice read out from official documents, 'Ali ibn al-Tahir, Abd al-Rauf ibn Abd al-Wahid, and Salim ibn Muhammad, your date to appear before the tribunal of the French Armed Forces is scheduled for 4 p.m. next Monday.'

The guard turned around and left, fate having spoken through his tongue. The bolt was thrust back into place, and the sound echoed inside their hearts as 'Imprisonment!' and 'Tribunal!'

The young men stood before the French military tribunal. They were confident, courageous, and bold; their expressions were defiant and committed; they felt relaxed and content. They knew what their path was to be, and had followed it to its conclusion. They also realised what their fate would be and did not flinch. Their defiance was clear as they stood, one after the other, before a white-haired judge with a determined and resolute look in his eyes. To his right and left sat a group of young officers representing the authorities, there to ensure that the ruling handed down by the white head and intelligent eyes was the right one.

The tribunal issued its verdict: death by firing squad for all the members of the terrorist gangs who had posed such a threat to the internal and external security of the state.

Everyone listened with a heavy heart as the judge pronounced the verdict. Women seated behind the accused burst into tears; each one of them had a brother or son among the condemned men, who themselves turned pale as they heard the verdict, though their inner faith could be seen in their eyes: there was no sorrow, and no tears.

The same courage loosened Abd al-Aziz's tongue as the court was about to end its session. 'Long live Morocco!' he shouted from the depths of his soul.

'Long live Morocco!' the young men repeated, as guards tied their hands behind their backs. 'Long live independence!'

Abd al-Rahman was waiting tensely for his companions to come back, to hear what was to be their fate. With every delay, his fears intensified. He was well aware of the circumstances in which they had been arrested and how serious were the charges against them, so he kept his hand on his heart, waiting to hear what he already knew but his heart did not dare to admit.

The halls and blocks of the prison were all quiet; lights in the stores and cells had been put out – but this was the calm before the storm. The prison gates were abruptly opened, and the sound of bolts being pulled back mingled with the click of weapons as the guards put their rifles to their shoulders.

'Open up Cell 13!' came the call.

The hearts of the imprisoned nationalists leapt when they heard this. Abject misery led Abd al-Rahman to chew on his hand, and without warning his tears began to flow. He put his ear close to the cell door to hear more. Steady, powerful steps could be heard, interspersed with the sound of chains, as though to create a particular rhythm. He heard Abd al-Aziz cry, 'Guardians of the homeland!' followed by Ali shouting, 'Long live Morocco, long live independence!'

The footsteps receded, and the voices disappeared behind the huge door of Cell 13. Now a world of darkness, isolation, and chains kept the young men apart from their nationalist colleagues, and from any world at all apart from that of execution, death, and oblivion. Abd al-Aziz resorted to the Qur'an and recitation of its verses, while the other young men turned to prayer, prostrating themselves as they called 'God is great!' and then standing up again as they repeated the same phrase in their hearts, all this in the quiet of the pitch-black night – though, for them, day and night were the same. The words 'God is great' opened the gates of the future to them, and their hearts aspired to it with both confidence and humility. Their spirits were suffused with the kind of faith they had never experienced before, and they stopped thinking about past, present, or future, in favour of contemplating one thing: God. They went about their functions in life as best they could. Their existence was no longer connected to a dimension in which the yardsticks for beneficence and misdeeds, good and evil, had been established.

In the same pitch-black quiet, Ali stood praying in the dark. Hearing a keening deep inside himself, he realised he was weeping.

The next morning, Abd al-Aziz took him to a far corner of the cell. 'Why were you crying?' he asked. 'Hasn't God promised you paradise?'

'I wasn't crying for my bride, nor for the embryo bumping inside her womb, nor for my father and brothers. I was crying for our country and its freedom.'

This brought Abd al-Aziz himself to tears. 'Our blood will water the tree of freedom in our country,' he said, looking humbly at Ali's face. 'I can foretell that it will sprout leaves and spread its fragrance all over our homeland.'

'So, our blood won't have been spilt in vain!' Ali replied gratefully. 'Speed your way here, death! My life's task is at an end.'

On the eve of the Eid festival the young men were allowed to receive a visit from their families. At dawn on the festival day itself the prisoners were snoring through pleasant dreams: the festival day would dawn, and its beloved sun full of sweet hopes would shine on them all. Their families would knock on the prison gates to bring Eid greetings to a beloved husband, a devoted son, a loving father, or a dear brother. There would be festival gifts brought by mothers, fathers, or wives, each one pulsing with love and conveying smiling hopes. But these dreams were interrupted by agonised shouts from Cell 13, which jolted all the other prisoners and internees awake. They listened as voices came from afar through windows or cracks in doorways. Then the voices suddenly became powerful, clear, and strident: 'Dear friends, we'll meet in paradise. Farewell, and long live Morocco! It is time to part. Hear the glad tidings, beloved friends. The country will be independent!'

An anthem rang out as the regular stamp of military boots was heard: 'Guardians of the homeland, O guardians of the homeland!'

As Abd al-Rahman listened to the sounds outside his cell door, his heart ached. He easily picked out one dear voice from the many.

'Till we meet in paradise, Abd al-Rahman!' called Abd al-Aziz. 'Be glad. Our country will be free!'

Abd al-Rahman's eyes flooded with tears of agony. He held his breath and buried his teeth in his fingertips to conquer the pain he felt. The voice began to recede, and Abd al-Rahman was afraid he would not be able to bid farewell to the dear friend whose self-sacrifice and devotion had so inspired him.

'Farewell, dear Abd al-Aziz!' he shouted. 'Till we meet in paradise!'

Then his brave demeanour failed him, and he surrendered to tears as he heard the prison gates slam shut once again, a final farewell to the young men who had fulfilled God's destiny.

The quietude of death now enveloped the prison, with images of the young men imprinted on the thoughts of thousands of prisoners and internees.

On the morning of Eid, the city of Fez resounded to the echoes of volleys aimed at the hearts of its young men.

44

The echoes of the shots struck at the heart of every Moroccan. The young men felled by the bullets of the French army had had the heart and soul of every citizen with them as they ran their operations, and in prison they had become the sons of every parent, the brothers of every sibling; even to those who had no experience of fatherhood or brotherhood, they were innocent freedom fighters.

Fez was shaken by this ill-omened news which, according to the computation of days and months, came on a festival day. But when measured in bitter reality it was an occasion for public mourning. Following this catastrophe the city underwent a wave of pessimism, to be seen in frowning faces, defiant looks, and a general sense of melancholy. It was a festival day on which the whole of Fez displayed its melancholy collectively; it was indeed a day of public mourning.

Following the execution of the young freedom fighters, the general in charge of Fez was not concerned with echoes. Indeed, his aides and informers, doing the rounds of the grieving city and touring all the quarters, alleys, streets, and squares, heard none – though they could gauge people's feelings from their expressions, their gestures, and their clothes. They could see it all in the city's earth and sky, its walls, its springs, and the ripple of its waters.

The general now knew that the city had suffered a terrible catastrophe, and his vengeful face broadened into a smile of victory. '*Now* Fez has surrendered,' he gloated.

Hajj Muhammad was dozing in a far corner of the large room. Weakened by illness, he had gone into seclusion. As feelings of weakness and incapacity weighed him down, he had retired to his bed, enduring a life of illness and pain. He stayed away from other people, as they did from him. He no longer involved himself in their affairs, nor did he react when they discussed politics and events in Morocco, because he no longer listened to the radio or what people were saying. He was focused only on listening to his own illnesses and on the pain afflicting him between his long or short siestas, intervals that provided his senses with a modicum of relief. The constant pain left him feeling exhausted, so whenever he was transported on his own magic carpet to a world without sensation, he looked relaxed and content.

One friend who visited him regularly, and particularly on festival days, was Mawlay Zaki. He remained loyal to Hajj Muhammad, whom he had known in the mosque, the shrine, and the street. More than that, he remained loyal to the man with whom he could share news and whose curiosity he could satisfy through conversation, like a writer whose pen insists he consign his own self to paper. What fascinated him about Hajj Muhammad was that he presented a genuine and receptive environment, someone who had always been up to date on the latest news and whose explanations brooked no argument.

When Mawlay Zaki entered Hajj Muhammad's room, a delighted smile crossed the latter's face as though wrenching itself from the depths of history, and he overcame his pain enough to raise his head from the pillow. With quivering hands he looked for his rosary and, in a kind of daydream, listened to Mawlay Zaki's gentle taps on his snuffbox and watched him lift his fingers to his nostrils to inhale some of the pure, warming powder. It made his eyes water, and his voice was choked as he asked Hajj Muhammad how he was feeling. Swearing by his ancestor, the chosen Prophet, Mawlay Zaki assured him that he looked fine, and Hajj Muhammad smiled even more broadly, happy that Mawlay Zaki had taken the trouble to pay him a visit and doing his best to forget about his pain. He was thrilled to have a friend visit him at a time when other friends found it hard to bear watching him live with the constant ailments that dogged him.

Mawlay Zaki looked at Hajj Muhammad and came to the point. 'What news do you have?' he asked, and then continued without allowing him time to respond. 'But then, it's you who needs news now. God grant you respite, there's nothing good to report.'

'All this illness allows me is to take care of my own health,' Hajj Muhammad replied, overcoming his feeble state. 'Even so, I'm always eager to have you come and tell me what's going on outside this enforced prison I have to live in.'

The word 'prison' made Hajj Muhammad sad. It brought to mind an image of his incarcerated son, and made an ill-starred future loom before him. Because of his ill health, weakness, and lassitude, he constantly anticipated that something terrible might happen, something that his private thoughts would not allow him to name. As it was, the son of whom he was so proud and for whom he felt deep down the greatest admiration was absent, kept away by huge gates and lofty walls.

'Will those gateways ever be opened before fate comes to pass?' he wondered feebly. He ignored his own question and went back to Mawlay Zaki, only to find him struggling with his snuff, brushing the rest of the powder off his clothes with his fingers.

'What news, you ask?' Mawlay Zaki said in his nasal twang. 'My dear Hajj Muhammad, there's nothing to report except sorrow, grief, and pain. You're sick already, so don't bother about other painful things.' As he said this, he looked carefully at Hajj Muhammad, hoping to find an opportunity to say what was on his mind – and his friend did not disappoint him.

'God willing, everything's fine?' Hajj Muhammad said, anticipating his wishes. 'What is it? Are things still unsettled?'

Mawlay Zaki now realised that Hajj Muhammad had no idea what had happened. 'Haven't you heard?' he asked. 'They killed them... They condemned them all to death.'

Hajj Muhammad moved with a jolt. 'Killed who? Condemned who? Who was killed? Who was condemned to death?'

Mawlay Zaki realised it was not a good idea to shock Hajj

Muhammad, so he tried to slow things down. 'Take it easy,' he said. 'Don't alarm yourself. Things are not as bad as you think.'

'But you said "killed" and "condemned to death". Explain – tell me what happened.'

Mawlay Zaki now decided to give him the details so that he would not leap to the ultimate conclusion – he did not want his friend to link those terrible words to his imprisoned son. 'You've already heard,' he said, 'about the group of young men who've been terrorising the city, killing informers, policemen, and suppliers.'

'Yes, I've heard about them.'

'The tribunal took its revenge and condemned them to death.'

'Condemned them to death?'

'Yes. It's what God decreed.'

'Help me remember their names. My memory's letting me down.'

'Who among us knows them?' Mawlay Zaki asked, feeling the need to lighten the blow. 'Young men from oppressed families. But I did hear that one of them was called Ali, another Muhammad, and a third Abd al-Aziz.'

'Abd al-Aziz?' Hajj Muhammad exclaimed, horrified. 'That must be Abd al-Rahman's friend.'

'God offer you guidance, Hajj Muhammad. This group is made of a different clay from Abd al-Rahman.'

'But Abd al-Rahman definitely knew a young man by that name.'

'There are plenty of men called Abd al-Aziz. I'm sure there's no link between this group and Abd al-Rahman.'

'Is there any news about my son's companions?'

'No, there's no news, but they're all fine.'

This helped Hajj Muhammad feel calmer, and he nursed a faint glimmer of hope, although it came out in angry tones. 'They condemned all those young men to death? But they'll surely eventually release the others.' As he said it, he looked over at Mawlay Zaki to see what effect his words had, but encountered a blank stare. He was not happy to think that Mawlay Zaki had his doubts about the possibility of release. 'You don't agree?' he asked. 'You'll see. They can't possibly condemn young children to death when their only crime is not having a proper education.'

Mawlay Zaki lost his patience. 'But they did it,' he replied tersely. 'Did what?'

'Condemned them to death, God have mercy on them! It's over.'

Hajj Muhammad's face clouded over with sorrow. For a long time he said nothing, but his thoughts raced through a rapid series of images which kept changing like a screen in front of his eyes, with Abd al-Rahman's face front and centre in all of them. He came to a halt when confronted with an image which kept inserting itself: Abd al-Aziz walking beside Abd al-Rahman on the day he had passed them in one of the neighbourhood's alleyways. This was the same Abd al-Aziz who always came to see Abd al-Rahman when dark clouds covered the sky. They used to wander the streets together in intense conversation. Friends and enemies alike would stare at them, and, whether they whispered or talked out loud, their conversations were always serious and determined.

When Hajj Muhammad returned from his private thoughts, it was to find Mawlay Zaki tapping on his snuffbox, obviously eager to get back to their previous discussion.

'Take a bit,' he said, holding out the silver box. 'It's good, and not too strong.'

Hajj Muhammad gestured that he did not want any. Mawlay Zaki guessed what was on his mind.

'The son of my uncle Mawlay al-Tahir visited the prison,' he told Hajj Muhammad. 'He talked to him about the other prisoners. They're all fine.'

Hajj Muhammad took a deep breath, and the information filled his lungs with a fresh breeze. 'Praise be to God!' he said, allowing himself a wan smile. 'May God release him!'

At this moment Mahmud came into the room to visit his father. Since taking up his post as a civil servant, he had made a habit of paying a visit to his father morning and evening. And since Abd al-Rahman's imprisonment, he had sat with his father for a while to compensate for his loneliness or to tell him some of the news about people that he had either heard or read. In this way, he had managed to break down the thick wall that previously kept him apart from his father, who was now more cordial, showed him a modicum of respect, and trusted the information he provided.

Mawlay Zaki looked at Mahmud as he came in. From his point of view, Mahmud's arrival was a welcome interruption, to counter the heavy atmosphere he could feel as he sat alongside Hajj Muhammad. He sensed Mahmud could provide the forward-looking ideas that were needed at this point.

'Greetings, Sidi Mahmud!' he said as the young man leaned over to kiss his father's hand. 'What news have you brought us?'

Mahmud paid no attention to Mawlay Zaki's question, but simply extended a flabby hand in greeting. 'How have you spent your day?' he asked his father, and then went on without waiting for a reply. 'You look better than you did yesterday. I'm sure of it. Your face has a slight blush to it, a sign of good health.'

Hajj Muhammad gave a nod by way of reply but said nothing, as though to express his doubts about what Mahmud had said.

Mawlay Zaki hesitated for a moment, wanting to stop Mahmud asking his father more about his health and making pronouncements that he well knew were not true. 'So, Sidi Mahmud,' he eventually asked, 'what's the news?'

Mahmud paused for a while before answering. 'You already know more about it than I do,' he said. 'They've condemned a group of terrorists to death.'

'Yes, indeed,' Mawlay Zaki replied, showing intense interest in the topic. 'It makes me terribly sad. Executing young men like that is hard to bear.'

'We all feel that way,' Mahmud replied angrily. 'But they're the ones who hurled themselves to perdition. Who told them to aim their revolvers and kill innocent people?'

The word 'innocent' jolted Mawlay Zaki, and his gaze wandered, as though he were using his eyes to think. He looked at Hajj

Muhammad and saw that he was nodding in agreement, placing full confidence in what Mahmud was saying. But after a short while he returned to look fixedly at Mahmud. 'Whatever the case,' he said, 'they were just young men whose future is now lost.'

'The law makes no distinction between young and old,' Mahmud responded in legal terms.

Hajj Muhammad nodded his agreement again. For Mawlay Zaki the invocation of the law in this context was inappropriate. Stretching his hand to his snuffbox yet again, he inhaled until he almost choked. He looked anxiously for his dark red handkerchief, which took him a while to find, and used it to wipe away some dark drops pouring out of his nose. For just a moment he considered responding to Mahmud's remark, but then remembered that he was employed in the pasha's courts. Putting a hand on the cushion by his side, he used it to stand up, whispering, 'O Mawlay Tihami' as he did so.

He ended his visit abruptly. 'My dear Hajj, excuse me,' he said as he bade his friend farewell, 'but we all hope to see you soon at the Mawlay Idris shrine and the Qarawiyin.' He smiled at Hajj Muhammad, who shook his head as though to dismiss the idea.

'God willing,' he whispered in reply. 'God willing.'

45

As Mahmud talked with Mawlay Zaki, he had been thinking about the cases that had been brought before him. A group of young men had been brought before his court on the charge of conspiring with the group led by Ali. They were all young, their hearts bursting with enthusiasm. When Ali and his group were arrested, they spoke with a great deal of pride about their acquaintance with Ali, their friendship with Abd al-Rauf, and their acquaintance with Salim during their schooldays. They all spoke fervently of what had happened: police and prison lay behind everything they talked about. Their case had been forwarded to the court where Mahmud was the judge.

As Mahmud looked into the files of the case he was about to adjudicate, he could envisage in Muhammad, Izz al-Din, Ahmad, and al-Tahir a mirror image of his own brother Abd al-Rahman, and his friend Abd al-Aziz. They all talked about the same ideas that had circulated in the small room where Abd al-Rahman used to sit and the cramped rooms where Abd al-Aziz would sometimes join them. Abd al-Rahman regularly tried to keep Mahmud away from these gatherings, but he was still able to pick up some of the things they were discussing, ideas that still echoed in his ears. As he read in the investigation files about the kinds of things that this particular group had been discussing, he heard the echoes of his brother's conversations again.

'So, who are these young men in these files,' he asked himself, 'on whom I'm supposed to pass judgement? They're deluded youths, but they're carbon copies of my own brother; they mouth his thoughts and talk about things that he would sometimes whisper but more often than not discuss out loud. Who am I judging? Am I judging my brother? Abd al-Aziz? How close he now seems to my own heart, God have mercy on his soul! He could be Abd al-Rahman himself... No, no, it's their ideas I'm judging. They were never going to be successful in foisting those ideas on young people... on children.'

The voice of an aide interrupted his thoughts. 'Sidi Mahmud,' the man called, 'the supervisor's asking for you.'

As Mahmud gathered his papers, his hands shook. 'How does the supervisor seem to you today?' he asked the aide. 'Happy or annoyed?'

The aide gestured with his hands and eyebrows. 'His nerves are totally on edge today,' he said. 'It seems she set his back on fire before sending him off to work, that Christian woman!'

Mahmud allowed himself a grin through quivering lips as he hurried to the supervisor's office. He entered and bowed in greeting.

'Have you prepared the file on the terrorists?' the supervisor asked, before Mahmud had a chance to say a word.

'I've looked over the file and still have to investigate certain aspects of the case.'

'Investigate what?' the supervisor thundered. 'Isn't the case clear enough? A group of killers conspire with another pack of murderers who have been condemned by the military tribunal and executed. The whole thing's obvious.' The supervisor searched irritably for a piece of paper and read it. 'For Muhammad, death sentence – and the rest, life sentences with hard labour. That's the verdict you'll give tomorrow.'

Mahmud wrote down what the supervisor had dictated to him. He waited for permission to leave, but the man was bent over his papers. Eventually he gave him a contemptuous look. 'We've finished,' the supervisor told him. 'You can leave.'

As Mahmud stood up, he felt he had been too slow in dealing with the case. Leaving the office, he stumbled under the weight of hatred and vengeance he felt towards this group of terrorists. 'They're murderous killers,' said a voice inside him as he entered his own office. 'It's a just sentence I'm going to announce in court.'

Sitting at his desk, he closed the file. Work on the case was now over, and there was no need to investigate anything further. Leaning back in his chair, he lit a cigarette and inhaled deeply. 'Are they seriously trying to expel the French,' he asked himself, 'as though they had as much strength as the French army, not to mention powerful ideas and tight-enough organisation? They're just a bunch of crazy kids with wild notions picked up here and there. They actually believe they can achieve the impossible. All they're adding to this crumbling society is more of the same.' He paused for a while at the notion of 'crumbling society' and sucked again on his cigarette. A question that had been nagging at him for some time now posed itself clearly: 'Who are you to judge that society is crumbling? Whose son do you think you are, to make yourself an enemy of this society?'

Stubbing out his cigarette in the ashtray, he felt ashamed. He was Yasmine's son, the child of a servant who lived in the kitchen.

'And what about Hajj Muhammad?' an argumentative voice insisted on asking. 'Your father!'

'He's just a rapist,' came the stern and unhesitating response.

'So, Yasmine was simply a victim... and you're...'

As Mahmud stood up to leave his office, the words still rang in his ears: 'You're the product of rape.'

Leaving his office, he walked slowly, not knowing where his feet were taking him. The thoughts buzzing inside his head were pulling apart his whole essence. 'You're a judge,' the voice whispered to upset him. 'Now you have the opportunity to pass judgement on this society, to announce your verdict, to take revenge, for you to—'

'Watch out!' a loud voice yelled at him, abruptly interrupting his thoughts. 'Clear the street!'

Turning round, he saw a huge mule with strong flanks and powerful muscles. It had a splendid saddle and decorated bridle and was being ridden by a bulky old man, well dressed and with a thick beard and luxurious appearance. The mule was pounding the ground as though in a race, and behind it an olive-skinned young boy was running as fast as he could and yelling.

'Watch out! Clear the street, make way!'

Mahmud backed up hard against the wall to make way for the mule and its rider, leaving as much space as possible. The mule disappeared from view, leaving behind the echoing sounds of its iron hooves on the stone pavement of the street and the regular shout, 'Make way, make way!'

Now another question occurred to Mahmud, out of the shouts of the servant-boy: 'So, is he another, I wonder? Serving his master and running as fast as he can behind the mule – is he the product of rape too?' As he left that question hanging in the air, another voice inside him hissed, 'Revenge... vengeance... your opportunity...'

When Mahmud left the courtroom after pronouncing the sentences, he felt relieved, as though he had just rid himself of a heavy burden and had managed to deal with a problem that had weighed heavily on him. He felt more relaxed, but then he came across a group of weeping women and men with tears in their eyes: they had heard the verdicts passed on their sons and brothers. He overheard their whispered comments.

'A very harsh verdict... death sentence, hard labour? They're innocent. What did they do? A very harsh verdict. They've been wronged!'

The comments impinged on his thoughts as though intending to rip apart his recent feeling of relief in announcing the verdict. Turning the comments around in his own mind, he came up with a response that was both frank and bold: 'A harsh verdict, they say? Who hasn't been the victim of a harsh verdict? I myself was such a victim before I was even an embryo in my mother's womb!'

In his mind he now pictured a fast-moving film of his mother's life: from a little girl, whose eyes with their bushy brows had been full of hope in life, she had turned into a mere lump of flesh, spending her days in front of a stove to prepare lunch for other people to eat. As he left the court, he was feeling better, although there were hot tears in his eyes and his ears still rang with the agonised cries of the condemned men's families.

It was a Saturday, a day when work finished at noon, and when Mahmud had a regular appointment in Meknes, which would allow him to avoid the meddling enquiries from people in Fez who knew him, and who were merciless towards people they knew, never allowing anyone to escape their inquisitive pursuit. So, he was happy to escape, along with his caprices, to a city where hardly anyone knew him. Once in Meknes, he could enjoy a freedom which was impossible to achieve on the narrow streets of Fez, which had nurtured him as a baby, a child, and an adolescent without giving him space to do anything but walk in a straight line towards a specific goal.

So, Mahmud climbed into the car he had owned since he first knew he was going to be a court judge. As he headed for Meknes, he was anxious to put behind him a week of work that had been difficult and had rattled his nerves. He had hardly left the city and its narrow streets before distant vistas loomed in front of him. His gaze wandered off to limitless horizons so remote it was as if he had never witnessed the like before. For someone who spends the whole week behind imposing walls and narrow alleys, streets, and bends, the horizon will always stretch out like a distant, boundless world. That expansive horizon now released Mahmoud from the prison in which he had enclosed himself.

But now he was not thinking about Meknes any longer, nor the freedom it offered. Instead, he began thinking again about the court where he had sat in judgement. The echoes of those anguished voices came back to haunt him again.

'They've been wronged... a harsh judgement... they're innocent...'

The agony in those voices hurt his ears like a burst of thunder. Looming before him was the hateful stare of those desolate eyes that welled up with hot tears.

Again that voice screamed in his ears. 'They've been wronged... a harsh judgement... they're innocent...'

His entire body shook as it might do if rubbing against a piece of rusty tin. Opening his eyes wide, he discovered the open road in front of him. The noonday sun shone brightly, and a mirage drew his attention as it hovered over the black asphalt surface. His whole being trembled, as though eager to express its objections to the idea of countermanding the images he had tried to put behind him as he left the court. Now he was on his way to Meknes. He put his foot down on the accelerator, and the car took off at speed on the road with tall trees on either side, which seemed to be rushing towards him in their attempt to come together in front of his car. As he raced on his way, he kept staring at the trunks of the huge trees, and suddenly he felt scared, for behind the trunk of every tree was a face, laughing in challenge, which would appear, then vanish, only to reappear behind the next tree.

The steering wheel veered in Mahmud's hands, and the car swung over to the left, but he brought it back quickly to the right. His gaze focused on the middle of the road, as though he were trying to escape from the trees and their defiant faces. The car continued on the open road for some time, but then suddenly the freedom fighters he had dispatched to their fates from his judgement seat that morning burst out from behind the trees. There was Muhammad, the innocent expression and gentle smile of the morning now replaced by a hateful look, apparently defying the machine gun pointed at his heart. And there was Izz al-Din rolling up his sleeves, ready for action. Ahmad and al-Tahir bared their chests as though trying to stop the car. Behind them stood a large crowd, and although Mahmud could not make out their faces, they blocked the horizon of the road.

He slowed down and tried closing his eyes in the hope that the frowning, defiant faces would disappear. When he looked again, it was to discover that that the whole road ahead was filled with them, and when he looked more closely he could make out the figure of

Muhammad, who had raised his fists in the air, anger written all over his face and brow. He seemed to be approaching the car in fury with the intention of destroying it. Mahmud tried to call out, to beg for mercy, and pressed the car horn hard. The noise reverberated like thunder, and yet it did not seem to reach as far as the people filling the road in front of him. Muhammad raised his voice to chant, 'Guardians of the homeland, O guardians of the homeland!'

The world resounded with the anthem sung by thousands of people. Mahmud's ears were ringing as his entire universe was filled with angry faces. Powerful echoes filled his hearing. He completely lost his nerves and pressed a shaking foot down on the accelerator pedal as far as it would go. The world in front of him went dark, and all he could see was the trunk of a huge tree coming towards the car with a great crash.

People gathered round the fireball that was gradually burning itself out. The ambulance men were looking for anything they could find, but there was nothing. The police made a search too, but all they discovered was a brass plate still fixed to what was left of the car. On it was carved the name Mahmud ibn Hajj Muhammad al-Tihami.

46

Abd al-Rahman came out of prison. His two years spent behind the great gates and high walls under the gaze of brutal armed guards were finally over, and with them the violent events that had so affected his nerves. During those two years he had lost his dearest friend, Abd al-Aziz, along with the group of young men that his friend had led. The echo of Abd al-Aziz's last farewell still resounded in his ears like some repeated call from the world of the beyond.

'Till we meet in paradise, Abd al-Rahman!'

When he returned from prison, the whole family was in mourning. Hajj Muhammad still lay in a corner of the large room. The world now passed him by, as it does anyone whom illness keeps hidden away for more than a few weeks – and Hajj Muhammad's illness had gone on for months now. The family had lost one of its sons, Mahmud, in a dreadful accident that had wrecked his car on the road to Meknes. All that remained of him was a skeleton burned in the fires of hell. The family was already in distress over Abd al-Rahman, who had been in prison for two whole years, throughout which Khaduj and Hajj Muhammad would both place their hands over their hearts whenever they heard the sound of revolvers being fired on the streets of Fez or learned about an assassination or a death sentence.

The tragedy cast its long shadow over a household that for many long years had only been known to flourish. But now everyone had the impression that an era was over; the household had moved beyond old age to something akin to termination.

Abd al-Rahman went to visit Yasmine, who was mourning the loss of her son and had chosen to seclude herself. As he approached to offer his condolences, her old age got the better of her and she collapsed in tears of loss. She talked about Mahmud. He had not really experienced life yet, being blessed neither with a wife nor offspring. He had not been able to remove the humiliation she had suffered all her life. In spite of the disgrace surrounding his birth, he had made her feel she was a woman with her own identity, the mother of a son. Now he was dead, what did she have left? If only... If only death could have waited a little longer so that he could bury her before he surrendered his own cheek to the grave.

Abd al-Rahman felt sorry for Yasmine and was saddened by her tragedy. And yet, he remembered at the same time that fate had its own system of justice, and he was content with that. To be sure, Yasmine was grieving, but so were other mothers in various parts of the city; their sons' tragic ends were causing them grief as well. When they had heard the sentences imposed on their sons, those flowers whose buds had not yet opened, a tragic loss had implanted itself deep in their hearts.

Abd al-Rahman now lived on a street which hardly knew Fez in its current form. Its sons from his own generation were now dead and buried, shot by firing squads, or else still incarcerated behind prison gates and imposing walls. People's faces were shadowed with grief; smiles and joy were no longer to be seen. They had all dispensed with the gentle contexts that had given their lives a loving texture and provided their conversation with a brightly coloured, delicately shaded, and sweet-smelling fragrance. Nowadays they all frowned, and their conversations were as dry as dust; there were no more jokes, and speech was curt. All that remained was a slim vestige of hope whose flame still burned in Casablanca. There was resistance in Aknoul to the north, and in the holy march from the Atlas Mountains to Ouad Zem, which turned a feeble hope into a firm conviction that victory was at hand, and a profound belief in imminent salvation.

Faced with the battle in Ouad Zem, Abd al-Rahman contemplated the inevitability of history. 'Our struggle involves not just cities and plains. The only path to salvation involves the mountain peoples coming to support those in the plains. The mountains of the Rif, the Middle Atlas, the Great Atlas are fearsome barriers, locations at whose thresholds the forces of imperialism have been crushed even during its heyday. Today our imperialist foe is trying to deal with just the cities and plains because that way they can keep the young people under control. But raise the cry loud enough, and the Rif will explode again, and so will the Atlas. We need help! How indebted we are to this noble country of ours,' he thought, his eyes welling with tears, 'a country that is always ready to rise up in order to repel the humiliation that other nations try to impose on us!'

At the large cafe on France Square, Abd al-Rahman had an appointment with a cup of coffee, as well as with fresh breezes, since the summer heat in Fez was oppressive and people were coming out of the narrow alleys to more open spaces as the sun began to set. Holding his coffee cup in one hand, Abd al-Rahman shook hands with Abdallah with the other. They embraced affectionately. They had been separated even before going to prison. Since his arrest Abdallah had been moved around and had been imprisoned in Rabat, Casablanca, and Kenaitra, while Abd al-Rahman had been incarcerated only in Fez. The two friends had not met since release.

'Things seem to be moving in our favour,' Abd al-Rahman began.

Abdallah's quizzical expression was fuelled by sheer despair. He did not respond.

'The rebellion in Ouad Zem was really violent,' Abd al-Rahman went on. 'The nationalists paid a heavy price.'

'Very heavy!' Abdallah's response was terse, and his expression was still sorrowful,

'It was a price that had to be paid,' Abd al-Rahman insisted with a smile. 'Any candle which can rid us of darkness has to make use of all its power!'

'But what about this French *ratissage* – their sweep-and-search operation?' Abdallah commented, abandoning his cautious silence. 'An unbelievably violent and cruel process that's pulverising everything in sight. They used their tanks to pound every inch of territory and everything living on it. But it was our fault. The only kind of fighting that the mountain people know involves violence. They too have always known how to crush everything, even without tanks.'

'It's revolution,' Abd al-Rahman responded calmly.

'Revolution has its limits. Ouad Zem has severed all hope of reaching an understanding with the French.'

'Was there ever a possibility of such an understanding?'

'Many possibilities.'

'What about now…?'

'Ouad Zem has destroyed that bridge.'

For a while Abd al-Rahman said nothing. He stared at Abdallah as though studying the features of someone he had not known before. 'On the contrary,' he then said angrily, 'Ouad Zem has opened up a clear path.'

Abdallah glanced over at Abd al-Rahman, without looking him in the eye. In his friend's expression he could see a clear challenge. 'You don't know our enemies,' he replied, 'because you've never had to live in their midst. They never give way to obstacles.'

'But *you* don't know people. There are obstacles that can humiliate even tyrants.'

'But Ouad Zem was so violent. You won't find a single French official who will submit to such violence. On the contrary, they've now suspended all communications with us. Every time we knock on the door, they simply reply with "Ouad Zem".'

'They'll be the ones knocking on our door,' Abd al-Rahman said after a moment's thought, 'praying that we'll open it.'

'God willing!' Abdallah replied in despair, tossing his cigarette butt to the ground as he stood up to say farewell.

Events passed Abd al-Rahman by, some quickly, some slowly. As he continued to live in the open city, he felt he was reading a chapter in a history book recording a period of dangerous change in which events proceeded apace, one chasing the other. He observed them, but tried to delay the ending of the chapter, as he himself longed to catch up.

His ears and his heart listened attentively. Violence and cruelty took hold of Morocco in the cities, villages, plains, and mountains. Freedom fighters burst into view everywhere, their proclamations echoing the whispered calls of their colleagues in the city, responding with rifle fire while their urban counterparts sought cover behind revolvers.

Abd al-Rahman's ears and his heart combined to make him consult his conscience again. As he did so, he allowed himself a smile, which bore silent witness to his sense of self-satisfaction.

Meanwhile, news kept arriving from afar. There were people who were contemplating a compromise involving the king's return from exile in the near future – a medial position between imperialism and independence. All this guaranteed was that the sword would be returned to its scabbard, and that a certain lifestyle would be assured for all collaborators and people loyal to the government.

'I wonder,' he asked himself with a smile, 'what if Abdallah were here with me? Would he change his mind and support Ouad Zem? Or would he still be convinced that the bridge for negotiations has been destroyed?' Then his heart burst with joy as marvellous news reached him: 'Nationalism's worst enemy has surrendered!'

One day and two months later Abd al-Rahman returned to his home at noon. Inside, he bumped into his elder brother Abd al-Ghani, who now walked with a stoop, as though old age had started coursing through his veins too. Abd al-Rahman's ears were assaulted by the loud chomping sound as Abd al-Ghani chewed on his gum. The noise set his nerves on edge, as though he were hearing it for the first time. As he looked back at Abd al-Ghani he saw that his brother's massive frame was still bent over as he continued chewing his gum.

Abd al-Rahman entered his father's room and pulled back the

curtain that had hung across the door since that evening when Hajj Muhammad had come back to the house holding his head because the pain was so bad; he had gone to his room and had not left it since. Abd al-Rahman looked at his mother, who was squatting in the middle of the room as though on the point of standing up. He leaned over to kiss her hand, but her face was wrinkled, and its lines were wet with tears.

The kiss stayed in Abd al-Rahman's mouth, and he gave her a sympathetic look. 'Anything new, Mother?' he asked, pretending not to be aware.

His grieving mother said nothing. Sitting down beside her, he asked the same question.

'Your father,' she replied, her choking voice only speaking in short phrases. 'Your father, Abd al-Rahman. You all go out and leave me here. Since this morning all I've heard is his breathing. I keep trying to rouse him, but he barely opens his eyes.'

Abd al-Rahman took his mother's hand and led her out of the darkened room. 'He's no worse,' he told her by way of consolation. 'If he would let me bring a doctor to look at him, his pains would be less.'

'I know what his problems are and I'm well aware of my own misfortune,' she said, ignoring Abd al-Rahman's suggestion about the doctor.

Leaving her where she was, he went back inside the dark room to check on his father. Taking hold of Hajj Muhammad's cold hands, he called to him, but the only echo was the old man's weak, intermittent breathing.

By now Abd al-Rahman was aware of how serious the situation was, and went to fetch a doctor.

'The only thing we can do,' the doctor said as he left Hajj Muhammad's room, 'is give him some stimulants to deal with his general weakness.'

When Abd al-Rahman looked at the doctor's face, all he saw was a serious expression with little sign of hope.

47

Abd al-Rahman was well acquainted with the physical features of Fez. He had spent his childhood, youth, and teenage years there, reading its personality in every nook and cranny – its decaying stones, lofty walls, narrow alleys, broad squares, dark and bright areas, its sunshine and glimpses of moonlight, its market excitement and the tedium of routine activities, the energy in its locations and the anxieties of its commerce, its mosques and shrines, the faces of its men and the eyes of its women... He could read everything in Fez like an open book whose every line was placed before his eyes with conscious spontaneity.

Whenever he felt the urge to open his horizons to matters of politics and economics, he would lose himself in the city, meandering through the markets, shops, quarters, and narrow alleys, widening his eyes to gaze at everyone and priming his ears to pick up any sound, whisper, smile, laugh, shout, or conversation.

The people of Fez never kept their ideas hidden; they would always reveal their innermost thoughts to anyone they met. For them, conversation was business. All that was needed was for someone to encounter a friend, companion, colleague, or former neighbour, and the conversation would start. Politics was now a regular feature of such conversation; friends no longer talked about how much money other people had, or how much they had either won or lost. Now their exchanges concerned the foreign entity in their country, and the fact that it was high time for it to leave. They talked about the blows being struck by national heroes against the French in Casablanca, the Rif, Ouad Zem, and anywhere else the occupation forces were established. Such chatter loosened the tongues of Fez's inhabitants; they burst into smiles and appeared relaxed and happy. Their expressions clearly echoed their feelings.

From the faces of his countrymen Abd al-Rahman could tell that the days of foreign occupation were now at an end. The French were clearly ready to relinquish their authority; they were actively contemplating the idea of independence and the king's return to France... or, rather, to Morocco. They were thinking about internal independence, synchronised independence.

Hearing the word 'independence' almost made Abd al-Rahman lose his mind; it was as if he had never heard the word before, had not spent eleven years repeating it to himself, and had not been forced because of it to spend four of those years in prison. It had been a dream, an idea continually uttered in his own mind, one he aspired to see achieved. And now it had become a reality that gave light to horizons that for fifty years had been shrouded in darkness. When reality gives a dreaming soul a jolt it comes as a shock, leading to a denial of self, ideas, and dreams.

'Independence' went on banging in his ears, and its impact had a profound effect on his soul. It stayed with him as he pondered things and meandered aimlessly through the streets, examining people's expressions, conversations, behaviour, reactions, all in his quest of the true significance of the word.

On his way home from his tour of the vibrant and alert city streets, he felt he must find the real essence of life in Makhfiyya Square itself. Since he had been a young child he had regarded the Makhfiyya Quarter as the source of life; its square was the centre of the entire world. He had known other worlds, of course, but had come to realise that, for all their size and scope, they were no broader than the narrowest alley in the most ancient of cities. He thus felt the strongest affection for this particular square and considered its life to be the most fulfilling he had witnessed.

Pausing for a moment in the square, he looked at people's radiant faces and joy-filled eyes. He was happy to see the tailor chattering loudly with the flour seller; in fact, all the shopkeepers were happily talking about the revolutionary atmosphere. His ears pricked up when he heard a conversation about the neighbourhood's police presence.

'Our friend over there is about to leave.'

'You mean our enemy...'

'Friends or enemies, it's all the same. What's important is that he's going.'

'Poor devil. He's going to leave us orphans!'

'We'll send him off with ululations, drums, and flutes.'

It was Amm Muhammad, a butcher, who was talking. He was sitting beside a crumbling wall, as he often did after finishing his morning's work: he found he could not escape the tiny square, whether at work or leisure.

'Don't believe in anything good until it happens.'

Amm al-Tabbaa, a tailor, responded through his toothless gums. 'The men beat him up. After today he won't be able to lift his head.'

Amm Muhammad looked over at the small police post, where the officer sat with his back against the door. 'We're in a slaughter-house,' he said, 'but we can't be sure that the ox is finally dead until we've skinned it!'

Amm Raji, a grocer, entered the conversation. 'The men have certainly killed it. And now it's our job to skin it!'

'Bring it to me,' the tailor laughed, 'and I'll start weaving its shroud!'

Abd al-Rahman smiled silently as he listened to this chatter between the grocer, the butcher, and the tailor. It may have been simple, but it was an accurate reflection of the simple souls who were talking, full of confidence and courage. The officer had also been listening to them, but he did not seem to share their conviction that liberty was on the point of casting its protective wing over their homeland.

When Abd al-Rahman left, he felt inspired by the hope in the faces of his countrymen. As he made his way home, his mind was filled with glimmers of the certainty that people were expressing as they moved confidently towards victory.

Going into the house, Abd al-Rahman felt he was entering a graveyard. The family insisted on providing absolute peace and quiet for the old man, whose nerves were badly affected by his illness. He could no longer move or tolerate loud noises. The family took to whispering, and the entire household tiptoed around, closing doors quietly and consigning any arguments to oblivion. Thus the mansion that had been a gathering point for the living had been converted into a silent abode, akin to a city of the dead.

Abd al-Rahman was therefore surprised to find himself in a chaotic scene, whose noise reverberated throughout the house; it was like a beehive, full of the buzz of activity. Coming in through the main door he was astonished to run into Khaduj weeping like a young child that has, indeed, been stung by a bee. The blood froze in his veins, and he stopped for a moment before coming in any farther. He looked from Khaduj to Yasmine, who had emerged with heavy steps from her own quarters.

In her agony of grief she banged her head against the wall, wailing, 'O my master! O my son, Mahmud!'

When he went into his father's room, he found the family gathered around the bed: Abd al-Ghani was pacing around the middle of the room, using a handkerchief to control his breathing; Aisha had her children clustered around her and was trying to keep her weeping as quiet as possible. The doors to the dark room had been closed and the blinds drawn, and they were all crying in the dark. Abd al-Rahman approached his father and seized his cold hand to feel his weak pulse. 'Father,' he whispered loudly. 'Father!'

The only response was his father's faint breathing. And then his breathing stopped, replaced by a horrible snort.

'Father,' he said again. 'Father!'

Hajj Muhammad did not open his eyes or show any sign of having heard his son's plea. Abd al-Rahman turned pale as he faced a reality he had never anticipated. He let go of his father's hand and stood up, deep in thought.

Abd al-Ghani's voice intruded into his frenzied thinking. 'Mawlay Zaki was here,' he told his brother. 'He's gone to fetch some Qur'an readers and chanters.'

This served to rescue Abd al-Rahman from his deadly despair. He nodded as if to bless what Mawlay Zaki had done. Then he thought about his mother, Khaduj, and left the dark room, taking Aisha by the hand and leading her out along with her children.

He did his best to comfort his mother and make the tragedy easier to bear, but she shrieked at him, 'Leave me alone! Let me rue my fate. What kind of life will be left to me now our glory days are over?'

There was a loud rap on the door, and Abd al-Rahman heard Mawlay Zaki asking permission to enter. The women left and went into a room close by. The reciters and chanters came in, followed by a group of Hajj Muhammad's friends. The reciters now raised their voices and read two complete suras from the Qur'an. They were followed by the chanters, with Mawlay Zaki and the shaykh of the chanters standing on either side of Hajj Muhammad. They did not have time to finish before one of them looked over at the other. Mawlay Zaki burst into tears and leaned over Hajj Muhammad's dead body.

'There is no deity but God,' the shaykh of the chanters intoned at the top of his voice. 'God is what was and what remains.'

When Abd al-Rahman stood by the gate of the Sidi Mayyara cemetery welcoming the mourners, his voice was choked with grief. His friend Abdallah came, and as Abd al-Rahman embraced his dear friend, Abdallah leaned to whisper in his ear.

'Good news! Today the king has returned. Independence has been declared!'

Abd al-Rahman lifted his hand from the soil of Hajj Muhammad's grave and walked back to the house with a group of family members and friends.

'We've buried the past,' a voice echoed in his ear.

As he walked, his reddened eyes gleaming, the image of Abd al-Aziz appeared in front of him.

'No,' his old friend told him. 'We haven't buried it yet!'

Afterword

'Abd al-karim Ghallab's novel *We Have Buried the Past* (*Dafanna al-madi*) is set in the city of Fez, for centuries the capital city and traditional seat of successive dynasties of Muslim rulers, the sultans of Morocco. It was a deliberate act of the French colonial authorities – beginning with their occupation of the country in 1912 – to move the country's capital from its traditional location in Fez to the Atlantic coastal town of Rabat, then a relatively small settlement (originally named for its Sufi connections, in that *ribat* is the Arabic word for the house of a mystical community) and at that time much less historically significant than the port city of Salé directly opposite it at the mouth of the River Abu Riqraq. By contrast, this novel continues to stress the centrality of the city of Fez in the Moroccan national consciousness, and as the primary locus of its sense of history and tradition. Both of the latter were to stand in opposition to and in defiance of the modernising tendencies and oppressive policies of the French occupation, which was to last until 1956, the year in which Morocco finally gained its independence.

That the city of Fez as place should be depicted in this novel with such attention to detail may be seen, of course, as a predictable feature of novels penned during a particular phase in the development of that fictional genre within different cultural traditions. As is the case with the Egyptian novelist and Nobel laureate Naguib Mahfouz and his fictional portraits of Cairo, 'Abd al-karim Ghallab (1919–2017) is a son of the city of Fez; he was born there and educated at the city's University of Qarawiyin – associated with the mosque complex that is still the city's major Islamic monument (founded in the ninth century CE), much mentioned in this novel – before he travelled to Egypt in order to continue his education at Cairo University, from which he obtained a Master's degree in Arabic literature.

Throughout his lengthy career, Ghallab was a major figure in Moroccan cultural and political life, not least as editor of the newspaper of the Istiqlal Party, *al-Alam* (*The Standard*), where he initially published his novels in serial form before their eventual appearance as books. He also wrote works about Moroccan literature and the country's struggle for independence, including, most notably, *The History of the Nationalist Struggle in Morocco: From the End of the Rif War until the Declaration of Independence* (1971). There is thus a direct link between his personal and political life and career and at least three of his novels – *Sab'at abwab* (*Seven Gates*, 1965), *Dafanna al-madi* (1966), and *al-Mu'allim 'Ali* (1971), all of which are concerned with the precedents, actualities, and consequences of the French occupation of his homeland and its aftermath in the achievement of national independence for Morocco.

Like so many of its analogues from different cultural traditions, *We Have Buried the Past* (originally serialised in 1963) is a vivid portrait of the process of change and, in the effective words of the American critic Lionel Trilling, 'an especially useful agent of the moral imagination' (*The Liberal Imagination*, 1940, vii). Bearing in mind both the author's background and his profound interest in and concern for his city and country in a particularly challenging era in its centuries-long history, it comes as no surprise that both place and time are to play significant roles in this novel, being described frequently and in obviously affectionate detail. We are presented with numerous vivid accounts of the city's people and its life, all in accordance with the changing seasons of the year – the chill of winter and the unbearable heat of summer, the customs and traditions of the city's inhabitants, and the often abrupt and disruptive interventions of the French authorities (usually depicted as 'foreigners' or 'interlopers' – in Arabic, *dukhala'*). The very word 'French' is scarcely ever invoked, although in this translation I have occasionally added it when the allusive nature of the original Arabic text might not suggest such a reference to the reader of English.

The initial chapters of the novel introduce us to the oldest part of the city (known as Fas al-Bali, or Ancient Fez, in order to distinguish it from Fas al-Jadid, or New Fez, which originates from the twelfth to thirteenth centuries[!]) and the French-built modern city beyond it, the Ville Nouvelle (Modern Town). The oldest part of the city sits in a valley, with two principal conduits from top to bottom, the Talaa Kabira (Great Rise) and the Talaa Saghira (Small Rise), coming together towards the bottom end of the valley. Branching from these two relatively wide walkways (there is no vehicular traffic) are a number of much smaller alleyways, creating a veritably labyrinthine network of narrow streets, where, as happens to one of the characters in this novel, you may still hear the cry *'Baalak!'* ('Watch out!'), warning you to pin your back against the nearest wall while a heavily laden mule or donkey passes by at speed, occupying most of the space between the two sides of the walkway. Lying within this network of alleyways is the Makhfiyya Quarter, the location of the traditional residence of Hajj Muhammad's household. Typical of the often elaborately decorated residences in the old city, the house of this family consists of several floors located around a central courtyard, high-ceilinged rooms for the several generations of the family, and servants' quarters. The house and the family living there are to serve as the locus within which all the tensions involved in the confrontation of the traditional indigenous and the modern imported within this narrative are to take place.

The time period involved is that of the French so-called 'protectorate' in Morocco, one of a series of colonial manoeuvres whereby France (and, in the case of Northern Morocco, Spain) added the territories of Morocco to their Maghribi dominions. Neighbouring Algeria had been annexed to France itself from 1830 onwards, until the bloodiest and longest of wars of liberation – the so-called War of a Million Martyrs – between 1954 and 1962, by which Algeria gained its independence, an event notably captured in Gillo Pontecorvo's famous film, *The Battle of Algiers* (1966). Morocco may never have become a province of France as Algeria did, but the colonial administration of the country set out to Gallicise as many aspects of the country as possible. It is here that Ghallab's own experiences come to the fore, in that this novel provides its readers with detailed insights into the total domination by the French of the government, the legal system (seen at its most stark in chapter 43, with the imposition of the death sentence on young freedom fighters – where French authorities' invocation of the term 'terrorists' to describe the same group of young Moroccans may recall for readers of this novel so many contemporary uses of the same terminology to describe those who would dare oppose the prevailing system), the prisons and internment camps, and, of paramount significance, the education system. The contrast between the traditional *kuttab* (a Qur'an school where the sacred text is learned by rote) and the *madrasa* (which I translate here as 'secular academy'), the modes of instruction and chastisement, and the subjects taught and learned – all of them the focus of chapters 14 and 15 in the novel – are reflected in the fierce arguments between the male members of Hajj Muhammad's family.

While the protectorate period (1912–56) is the general historical background against which the events of this novel take place, the more specific time frame is the decades immediately prior to the return of the exiled Sultan (King) Muhammad V and the achievement of independence in 1956. As the nationalist movement gathered momentum and spread from cities to the countryside and mountains, the confrontation between the indigenous population and the non-indigenous colonial authorities became more tense and violent.* As Ghallab's novel moves towards its conclusion – with

---

* For interested readers, an excellent survey of this period can be found in C. R. Pennell, *Morocco from Empire to Independence*, Oxford: Oneworld, 2003, esp. Ch. 8.

ever-increasing levels of civil unrest and a growing number of explosions and co-ordinated attacks on members of the government and their collaborators – characters almost inevitably refer back to conflicts and incidents in the past that have marked the protectorate period as one of continuous political, social, and cultural confrontation. One such conflict is the uprising between 1921 and 1926 in the Rif Mountains in the northern part of the country, then under Spanish control – the so-called Rif War (mentioned in chapter 46) in which the Rifis, led by Muhammad ibn Abd al-Karim (who became an important nationalist icon, better known as simply Abd el-Krim) initially routed the Spanish army and then turned south to confront French forces, but were eventually defeated. The Second World War was also to have a significant impact in that, following the fall of France in Europe, Moroccans – like other inhabitants of the North African littoral – began to ask themselves, with good reason, about the impact of events in Europe on France's role in Morocco, not to mention German intentions. One young man in chapter 29 (which opens with the repetition of the word 'war') even envisages Adolf Hitler soon strutting his way through the streets of Fez. As the nationalist movement gained in strength through the country, the increasingly vicious and desperate policies of the French colonial regime, duly reflected in *We Have Buried the Past*, reached a kind of climax in 1953 with the deposition and exile of Sultan Muhammad V and his replacement by Mawlay Ben Arafa, the 'puppet' alluded to in chapters 40 and 41. And, as negotiations toward independence between the two opposing parties were under way in 1955, the battle at Ouad Zem in August of that year – in which Amazigh mountain dwellers attacked and killed a large number of French nationals – caused many people to fear that the savagery of the attack had, in the words of one of the characters in the novel, 'destroyed the bridge' connecting the two sides. As it turned out, however, agreement was finally reached, and Morocco became an independent state on 11 February 1956.

It is into this spatial and chronological context that Ghallab places the family of Hajj Muhammad al-Tihami. Indeed, the Hajj marks the beginning and end of this novel. Introduced as an influential figure through several chapters at the novel's outset, it is his death and burial in the final scene that coincide exactly with the announcement of the sultan's return and the declaration of independence. In fact, there are many ways in which *We Have Buried the Past* may be considered a family saga, not unlike many other narratives that make use of the complex relationships within a single family as a means of illustrating social and political realities and the tensions involved in the processes of change – all described against the backdrop of outside factors of the kind that have been identified above. As the novel opens, Hajj Muhammad is portrayed as a powerful figure both inside his own household and in the larger community of Fez. Extremely conservative in his social and cultural values, he commands absolute authority within his own family. Favourably married to his wife, Khaduj, he is the father of four children: three sons and one daughter. His house and household is large, with numerous servants, and he is also the owner of a large acreage of lands, which he has been able to extend through his astute manipulation of agricultural commerce and the vulnerability of his peasant workers (traits that are the focus of discussion in chapters 11–13). Hajj Muhammad (whose designation as 'Hajj' connotes that he has performed the pilgrimage to Mecca) regularly attends prayers and sermons at the Qarawiyin Mosque, and all his children have names closely associated with Islam: the three sons, Abd al-Ghani, Abd al-Rahman, and Abd al-Latif, are all named as 'servants' ('*Abd*) followed by one of the ninety-nine 'beautiful names of God' (*al-asma' al-husna*) cited in the Qur'an. The youngest, Abd al-Latif, plays almost no role in the events of the narrative, but the ongoing antipathy between the two eldest brothers, Abd al-Ghani and Abd al-Rahman, is a major feature of the narrative, involving both their relationships with their father and their very different functions in the world outside the household. The family's daughter, Aisha, is given the name of the Prophet Muhammad's favourite wife. Having observed with naive innocence the elaborate procedures and preparations for her brother Abd al-Ghani's marriage (chapters 20–22), she finds herself totally perplexed when she has to confront the wide variety of impressions and advice to which she is subjected as a young upper-class Moroccan woman facing the prospect of marriage herself – whether by her own choice or not (the existence of the very possibility of such a radically new decision for Moroccan women having been drawn to her attention by her brother Abd al-Rahman).

These, then, are the members of Hajj Muhammad's family – or, at least, the ones resulting from his marriage to Khaduj. However, he has also fathered another child. On a visit to the slave dealer Ibn Kiran (the existence of such a role in twentieth-century Morocco being perhaps something of a surprise), Hajj Muhammad spots a beautiful young dark-skinned girl from the south of Morocco named Yasmine, who has been kidnapped and sold into slavery. Smitten by her beauty, he purchases her as a 'servant-girl' and brings her back to the house. Taking advantage of his wife's absence on a visit to her relatives and also exploiting an interpretation of a phrase in the Qur'an (4:24), namely the legitimacy of using 'what your right hand possesses' as a concubine, he summons her to his room and rapes her. Following his wife Khaduj's return to the household, it is not long before she discovers the new situation that faces her: the presence in her own household of her husband's concubine, a reality about which she can effectively do nothing. When Yasmine gives birth to a son, Mahmud, Hajj Muhammad acquires an additional family member, although the boy's darker skin colour and the fact that his mother is a servant work to his continuing disadvantage.

It is among the male children of the family that the broader tensions of this era are exposed and illustrated within the narrative, initially between Abd al-Ghani and Abd al-Rahman but at a later stage also between Abd al-Rahman and Mahmud. The eldest son, Abd al-Ghani, models his behaviour entirely on that of his father, endeavouring to exert his authority as the eldest son on all the other children of the household. His father, however, seems well aware of his son's limitations and sets him up with a clothing shop in a nearby market, where he can both learn the trade and acquire the necessary commercial and negotiating skills of a business owner. Abd al-Rahman, the second son, is another matter entirely. Intelligent and defiant, he resists his elder brother's attempts at dominating his life, provoking furious rows that require their father's equally furious intervention. Both boys have initially attended the local Qur'an school, but, while that has proved to be sufficient education for Abd al-Ghani, his younger brother has different and higher aspirations. Much to his father's initial annoyance, Abd al-Rahman asks to be transferred to the *madrasa*, the secular academy based on French models of education. When Abd al-Rahman attends the academy and learns how to think, to interpret, and to challenge received opinion – and, probably worst of all, brings his schoolbooks home to study – he immediately arouses the ire of his elder brother, the gum-chewing and thoroughly bored Abd al-Ghani. This is a classic non-meeting of minds and attitudes, a scenario that is only amplified by the intervention of their father, who is equally challenged and outraged by Abd al-Rahman's seemingly acquired negative posture towards everything that his father (and elder brother) represent. It is, of course, not a little ironic that the French system of education from which Abd al-Rahman acquires these modes of thought is precisely the motivating force that leads to his radical questioning of those conservative values and his increasing involvement in nationalist activities. Abd al-Rahman's younger half-brother, Mahmud, Yasmine's son, becomes a youthful admirer of these new opportunities in education, and Abd al-Rahman persuades the family to allow Mahmud also to attend the academy. However, whereas Abd al-Rahman is increasingly drawn into oppositional movements against the French occupation, leading to a pair of two-year prison terms, Mahmud comes to the conclusion that his social status as the dark-skinned child of a servant-concubine will always be different. Leaving the academy, he joins the civil service and eventually rises to the position of judge in the court system. In a telling chapter (45) Ghallab portrays Mahmud, now a Moroccan court judge, being instructed by his French supervisor as to what sentences he is to impose on a group of young men from Fez who have been arrested for planning attacks on French forces. Hoping in vain to escape the consequences of the judgement that he has announced in court, Mahmud leaves the city and drives towards Meknes. In an episode that is clearly intended to be maximally symbolic, the mirage floating in front of his car as he drives along the road turns into a nightmarish vision filled with the yelling faces of young Moroccan victims of rampant injustice. Unable to erase the images that loom in front of him, he raises his hands to his eyes, and his car crashes into a tree, killing him instantly.

The servants of Hajj Muhammad's household are a tangential presence in the narrative – apart, that is, from Yasmine, who is both servant and concubine. And yet, in one exceptional chapter (7) Ghallab provides his readers with a lengthy glimpse into a unique aspect of Moroccan popular culture, a Gnawa night in a neighbouring residence, in the rituals of which the women-servants of the household joyfully participate. The drumbeats and clashing cymbals of the Gnawa performers (which can still be heard in Fez's restaurants and at the city's annual festival of popular culture) rouse the women attendees into a frenzy of dancing and merriment, allowing them to forget, if only for a few night-time hours, the drudgeries of their daily existence. At dawn on the following day they creep back to the house, where a disapproving Hajj Muhammad has preferred to look the other way rather than prevent his servant-women from attending this thoroughly traditional occasion for joy and relief.

Within the long-recognised structure of a family saga novel, Ghallab makes use of this pioneering contribution to Moroccan Arabic fiction to provide his readers with a lovingly accurate portrait of his native city as it lives through the challenging processes involved in the long march towards independence. As a European nation, France, colonises an African one, Morocco, beliefs and values collide, misunderstandings abound, tensions mount, and each side resorts to violence as a means of asserting its own agenda. Into such a fraught situation and period Ghallab skilfully inserts a Moroccan family from Fez. The lives of Hajj Muhammad's family, its personal crises, its relationships with itself and others, are all placed into a realistic context which reflects the author's own experiences and aspirations. With the eventual, hard-won achievement of independence, Morocco will face a future with new realities and challenges – the topics to be taken up by other writers, all of whom have been inspired by the example set by Ghallab, one of the Moroccan novel genre's foundational figures.

Roger Allen
Philadelphia, August 2017